EARTHDANCE

A Romance of Reincarnation

Other Newcastle Books by Eileen Connolly:

Tarot, A New Handbook for the Apprentice

EILEEN CONNOLLY

EARTH DANCE

A Romance of Reincarnation

NEWCASTLE PUBLISHING COMPANY, INC.
NORTH HOLLYWOOD, CALIFORNIA
1984

EARTHDANCE

Edited by Douglas Menville.
Cover design by Riley K. Smith.

Published by Newcastle Publishing Co., Inc., P.O. Box 7589, Van Nuys, CA 91409, USA. Printed in the United States of America by Delta Lithograph Co., Van Nuys, CA. Typesetting and production by The Borgo Press.

ISBN 0-87877-076-3

A NEWCASTLE BOOK
First Edition——October, 1984
1 2 3 4 5 6 7 8 9 10

Contents

To my husband,
To my sons,
To my daughters,
With all my love.

Acknowledgments

During a picnic luncheon on the bluffs high above Santa Barbara, looking out over the ocean, my dear friend, Anne Francis, spoke two words: "Earth Dance! That's what your book is—an Earth Dance." It was exactly right, and I offer her my sincere gratitude for her inspiration.

To Lorraine Wood, my friend, I give my loving appreciation for her support and persistence.

And a special "thank you" goes to my publisher, Al Saunders, whose faith in my books has resulted in a rewarding and successful relationship for many years.

Prologue

The boy was the last image in her dreams. As Catherine Holmes
began to waken from her afternoon nap, she tried hard to hang
onto the strange feeling. It was a peculiar, yet familiar sensation.
Keeping her eyes closed, she tried to reach back into a world that
had already rejected her presence. Yet she felt the belonging, the
magnetic pull of the boy and his sorrowful eyes. They were
beautiful eyes and they had looked into Catherine's soul time and
again ever since her experience in Sak's Fifth Avenue elevator last
June.

Once more she lay there, going over in her mind that strange day
and the pattern of events; trying to discover and understand the
silent message she felt from the depth of the boy's grey eyes.
Nothing, absolutely nothing; it was too late. It seemed to Catherine
that when she tried to focus and reach for understanding, her mind
stopped still and all she felt was a high wall. She could almost hear
voices from the other side! She couldn't make any sense of it.

Chapter One

It was chilly that day in June. Catherine had a whole day off work and wasn't quite sure what to do with it. After riding around in her car for some time, she realized she was in Beverly Hills. Parking was expensive and she didn't have much money, but she remembered she had about two hundred dollars she could spend on her Sak's charge. Telling herself that she deserved a treat, she found a garage, parked her car and started to walk down Rodeo Drive, wondering if she would see somebody famous. Turning the corner, she saw a coffee shop and thought that this would be the ideal place to accidentally meet somebody.

After a weak cup of coffee and a shuffling of chairs to let people by, she decided to make her way to Sak's. She wandered through the store, taking her time and browsing through all the departments until after a couple of hours and some cosmetic purchases, she began to feel hungry. She decided to find somewhere to eat, and then she would go home for a quiet evening. Pressing the elevator button impatiently, she began to feel agitated for no reason at all. The doors opened and she was the only passenger to enter. Then it all began....

She looked into the boy's eyes and he cried deep into her soul...she screamed down through the centuries. Her hand slipped and her body started to fall; she heard her own voice—a strange voice—calling for help...But already she was re-entering this world, with the sickening, soulful cry of "Gareth" severing her love for yet another lifetime....

Later, thinking about it at home, the whole weird thing made her feel sick. Reaching out for a cigarette and drinking the cold coffee left in her mug, Catherine struggled to understand. The phone rang and the familiar voice of Nickie, her friend from college days, cheerfully requested that she try to answer the damn phone before it rang thirty times. Catherine, still in a strange trance-like state from the deep grey eyes, wearily asked, "What the hell do you want?"

Nickie's voice had a monotonous effect which allowed Catherine to inhale deeply and stare at the wall. Her trance ended abruptly as Nickie was saying, "...I actually heard you calling something like 'Gareth,' but it didn't sound like you." Catherine felt everything inside her go tight.

"Say that again!" she yelled. "For God's sake, what are you talking about?"

"This dream I had, and although I knew it was you, it wasn't, if you know what I mean."

"Come over right away," said Catherine. Nickie started to explain why she couldn't do that, but Catherine had already put down the phone. It was cold—so damned cold. Pulling the blanket off the bed, she went to the bathroom and turned on the hot water. Thinking aloud, she said to the mirror, "I've never heard of the name Gareth. Who the hell are you, Gareth?" The apartment felt empty; she turned on the radio and heard her favorite singer finishing "The Green, Green Grass of Home." Like a neon light in her head, she suddenly saw Wales...and knew it was Gareth's home.

"You've got to be out of your mind, Catherine," Nickie said. You can't just give up your job and go to some godforsaken place called Wales."

But already Catherine was on the phone, talking to the silky voice of the airlines girl. Feeling stupid because the atlas was in her bookshelf across the room but too excited to move, Catherine asked the girl, "Isn't Wales somewhere near England?"

The smartass airtripper answered, "Wales is part of the United Kingdom, ma'am."

Catherine put her hand over the phone and said to Nickie, "This Brooklyn broad is now trying to put on a Jacqueline Bisset voice and all I want to know is where the hell is Wales."

Nickie had invaded the fridge and emptied Catherine's dirty coffee cup full of Chenin Blanc. She was about to give Catherine some advice about sleeping on it first, when she heard Catherine book the first available flight....

"Help me pack, Nick. I'm going and that's it. So you may as well save your breath. Here's a list—promise you'll do everything I've written down."

Nickie grabbed the list, feeling irritable that her friend would just go off like this.

"I think you're crazy! Yes, I can read it! 'Feed Bartholomew every two days...empty his litter every four days...call the boss and tell him my aunt died.' Now wait a minute! Remember, I work for this bad-tempered bastard as well as you. I don't want to get fired for your crazy lies."

Catherine, now busy packing, looked at Nickie like a schoolgirl and said, "Look, Nickie, whatever you say, I'm going, and the least you can do is help me out and make it sound convincing."

"When are you coming back?" asked Nickie reluctantly, resigning herself to the fact that Catherine was really serious.

"I don't kow," answered Catherine. "All I can say is, I have to go."

Nickie sat in the middle of the bed, throwing bras to Catherine as she packed. She asked her friend if she needed any money.

"I'll get a job when I get there or something. I've enough for the fare and to put me up for a couple of weeks. Maybe I'll be ready to come home then."

"Two weeks! Oh, come on, Catherine, you can't stay for two weeks in a strange country looking for something you don't know what. What are you going to do—go to Scotland Yard and ask if they know a Gareth? 'Oh, yes, I can describe him. He has big grey eyes and I saw him first in an elevator in Sak's Fifth Avenue—but he really wasn't there.'"

"Coming to the airport with me, Nickie? I need a ride."

Nickie was a real friend, but Catherine was glad to be on her own now. She could feel the plane's engine warming up as she watched people come aboard: the fat man with his fat wife and fat boy carrying blankets and luggage; the thin man with an immaculate London Fog raincoat and thin briefcase brushing his seat with the *Time* magazine; a honeymoon couple looking for a private seat in the crowded third class, arms wrapped around each other like Siamese twins. Catherine noticed that the stewardess looked kind of ordinary. She had always thought that stewardesses had to be something straight out of a fashion magazine or *Penthouse*; this one had bumps on her face and her legs were too heavy for her thin waist. With her eyes closed, Catherine tried to get back to where she had been this afternoon, but as the plane started to climb, she could not recapture that terrible falling sensation.

Now I've got to get it all together and try to decide what I'm going to do, thought Catherine. How the hell do I get to Wales from London Heathrow, and then where do I go in Wales?

Waiting for her cocktail, she closed her eyes again and began to smell cologne—a man's cologne. Opening her eyes, she felt him staring. As soon as he saw that she wasn't asleep, he asked if she would like a drink. There was something really strange about him. Good looking—beautiful teeth—but something odd.

"Wine, please," she said.

He leaned over and brushed her cheek with a kiss. She held onto her wine glass and closed her eyes.

Gently touching her shoulder, the stewardess said, "Here's your scotch."

Catherine opened her eyes and looked for her new companion. He was gone.

Dinner over...movie finished...lights dimmed...and no handsome stranger. She was alone and on her way into the unknown....

It was quiet—no one was moving. Everyone was asleep and the lights were dim. Catherine reached out for her purse and was startled for a moment, thinking that she had touched *his* hand. Grabbing her cigarettes and fumbling for her lighter, she started to shiver and tears began to flow as she stared into a black nothing. The music was soothing and sounded far away. A deep, rich voice was singing about the green, green grass of home....Feeling more comfortable now and telling herself that you just don't meet ghosts on modern jumbo jets, she listened to the voice, which asked if she would like more wine....

People were stirring now. Looking toward the restroom, Catherine could see a small group waiting. Breakfast was being served in the first-class cabin and voices seemed excited, for London was not too far away. Feeling stiff and wanting to be back in her seat for breakfast, Catherine decided to join the passengers and wait for the bathroom. It didn't take too long, and when her turn came, she was annoyed to see soiled paper towels strewn around the tiny bathroom. The toilet and washbasin reminded her of train trips she had taken when she was a little girl. Someone was knocking on the door.

"Will you be long?" the voice said. It was her mystery man from last night! Catherine felt embarrassed and hurriedly rinsing her hands, threw her paper towel with the others. When she opened the door, *he* was standing there, waiting.

"Good morning," Catherine said hesitantly. "Where did you go last night?" He smiled and seemed to drift right past her without saying a word. Feeling a little ridiculous, Catherine went back to her seat, occasionally looking around for the man to come out of the bathroom. Then the thin man walked right past her, opened the bathroom door and locked it behind him. Puzzled, Catherine began to think about her handsome stranger. Did he exist or didn't he? She couldn't decide....

Now that they were ready to land, Catherine began to feel nervous. No delay in customs, but as she was passing through, she noticed that the thin man was looking uncomfortable as the Customs Officer opened his thin briefcase. Hurrying along, she suddenly realized she had no idea where she was going and decided that the best thing to do was to call a hotel, stay the night in London, and return home tomorrow.

The phone booth was empty. Looking through her purse for coins, she found a dime, which had not the slightest effect on an English telephone. Holding the phone in her hand, biting her lip and trying to think what to do next, she heard a distant voice, very faint, almost a whisper. Thinking she had somehow cut into someone's conversation, she tried to listen, for the voice was saying her name over and over again.

"Catherine, Catherine...."

Frowning, she started to tremble. Then the voice said, *"Catherine, please answer me. I am trying to find you."*

Terrified now, standing in the busy airport, she shouted into the phone, "Who are you? What the hell am I doing here? Is this Gareth?"

The only answer was, *"Cardiff, Cardiff, my love...remember?"*

"Remember *what*?" yelled Catherine. *"Who are you?"*

Crying now and terribly afraid, still listening, she heard the voice say, *"Catherine, think of Megan and Gareth...."*

She dropped the phone as a vivid picture flashed across her mind. She could see tiny houses, a dark street, loud voices coming from a brightly lit window. She knew where she had to go, but didn't know why....

After exchanging her money for sterling, she got a taxi to the railway station. Though still frightened, she looked around her and saw people busily going and coming. Somehow she thought she would get her answers when she arrived in Cardiff. After buying her rail ticket, she went into the station refreshment room and sat down next to an older woman, who immediately began to stare at her in amazement.

"Is there something wrong?" asked Catherine.

The woman hesitated and then asked, "Do you mind if I ask your name and where you might be going?"

Feeling angry, Catherine quickly answered, "My name is Megan and I'm going to the Blue Feathers Inn in Cardiff...."

The woman smiled kindly. She could see that Catherine was distressed. Almost apologetically, she pulled out her handkerchief and gave it to Catherine, who immediately rolled it into a ball.

Not understanding why she had called herself Megan, Catherine asked, "Why did you ask me my name and where I was going?"

The woman looked embarrassed. "Well, my dear, I'm what they call a psychic, and when you sat beside me, I felt strong vibrations and was compelled to speak to you."

"Why did you feel this way?"

"I really don't know, but I happen to be going to Cardiff, and if you don't mind, perhaps we can travel together and talk some more."

Catherine didn't answer. She felt comfortable with the woman, yet she was taken aback by her first question.

"Do you know the Blue Feathers in Cardiff?"

Smiling gently, the woman said, "Yes, I do, my dear. I'm a librarian and I'm going home for my holiday. Would you like to travel with me?"

Catherine felt a kind of friendliness toward the woman now and asked, "What's your name?"

"Frances O'Hara. Am I to call you Megan?"

"I don't really know," said Catherine. Analyzing Frances' face, she ventured more information, as though she were in confession.

When Catherine had related all the strange happenings, Frances O'Hara took hold of Catherine's hands and looking her straight in the eye, said, "Whoever you are, Catherine or Megan, you have found a true friend in me. And, as I happen to be doing nothing but enjoying my holiday for the next three weeks, I will help you find what you're looking for."

Catherine was happy to have this friendly woman mother her and kind of take over, so she readily agreed by nodding, and the two strangers who had become friends so quickly finished sipping their hot tea waiting for the Cardiff train.

Frances O'Hara had indeed felt a strange and compelling attraction to Catherine. Working in the library, over the past few years she had sifted through every good psychic book on the shelves, always looking, always trying to understand unusual abilities. Her own sensitivity had always been there, but lately she was aware of herself as never before. For quite some time now, she had been having peculiar dreams in which she would see herself vividly. Each dream was like a capsule shooting off into the unknown. She had always recognized her own individuality, but the person she became in these dreams was someone else. She had been looking forward to this holiday for a long time and had promised herself that she would get as much rest as possible and try to understand all that had been happening.

As the train rumbled toward Cardiff, Catherine had fallen asleep—a deep sleep. Frances sat opposite Catherine and looked thoughtfully at her. This poor young girl was obviously upset, and Frances was determined that she would keep her company as long as there was a need. Perhaps Catherine (or Megan) would enjoy going to all the places she had on her list, or maybe there wasn't time....

Consciously trying not to fall asleep, Frances leaned over to put her coat over Catherine. Catherine was mumbling. Trying to soothe her but not wake her, Frances touched Catherine's hand gently. Immmediately Catherine began to talk in her sleep. Catching one or two phrases here and there, Frances recognized the language as Welsh. Maybe her parents spoke Welsh, she thought, and perhaps this lonely girl was reliving a childhood memory in this deep sleep. Leaning back, Frances decided to try and catch forty winks herself before they arrived at Cardiff. Closing her eyes and just beginning to drift away, she suddenly heard a spine-chilling scream.

"Gareth, Gareth, wait for me!"

Catherine was obviously having a nightmare, so Frances tried gently to awaken her. Touching her arm, she murmured, "Everything's going to be all right."

These words, though softly spoken, woke Catherine immediately. Looking anxiously at Frances, she asked, "Is something wrong?"

Frances smiled reassuringly. "Well, I believe we'll be in Cardiff in just a few minutes. I thought you might like to freshen up."

"Good idea," said Catherine, opening her bag. She took out an ornate mirror and grimaced as she saw her reflection. For no reason at all she said, "You know, I think I prefer my hair red."

"Why, did you use to be red?"

Catherine quickly put away her mirror, saying nothing.

"I like your hair just as it is," said Frances. "I've always admired beautiful long blonde hair."

Both women were now excited, feeling the atmosphere of people going here and there. The huge engine was belting out steam. Catherine was enchanted by the rosy-cheeked children running and laughing; people greeting each other; the ticket collector in his fine uniform.

"Now what?" asked Catherine. "Where do I go from here?"

Frances put her arm around this seemingly lost American girl and said, "How about a nice friendly inn with a good hot bath and then dinner? We can unwind and get to know each other."

"That sounds fine to me," said Catherine. "Blue Feathers, here I come."

The taxi driver had a wonderful sing-song voice and informed the women that the Blue Feathers was quite a drive away, just outside Cardiff in a small village called Manningstile Henlock. He went on to tell them that he could drop them off at the bus station and they could catch the 4:45 P.M. bus, if they liked.

"How much would it be if you took us?" asked Frances.

The driver smiled and said, "Well, I'd be givin' yer a real cheap fare if I charged thirty bob."

"How much is thirty bob?" asked Catherine, laughing.

Frances smiled and said, "It's a bargain. How about a beer when we arrive?"

"The bargain's sealed," said the driver as he helped load the suitcases. "Better hurry along, looks like rain."

Both women glanced up at the sky, which now looked dark and threatening. They were only too glad to get into the old car and settle back on the worn leather seats. It soon started to rain; the win-

dshield wipers were working very hard. The city looked cold and
drab, and Catherine began to wonder what in the world she was
doing.

Frances seemed to sense her dilemma and started to chat with the
driver, who responded readily, pointing out all the highlights of
Cardiff. Soon the scenery changed. They were driving along
narrow roads and the landscape was beautiful: old cottages and
farmhouses on deep green hillsides. They were now approaching
the village of Manningstile Henlock. It was a lovely setting: tiny
cottages with brightly-colored flowers, children still playing in the
early evening.

The taxi driver informed his passengers that the Blue Feathers
was just the other side of High Street, and Catherine started to get
her things together, anxious now to end the enjoyable ride.

"Won't you come in and have a beer and a bite to eat before you
start back?" asked Frances.

"Don't mind if I do, miss. Why don't you ladies check in, and
I'll be right after you with the luggage."

Catherine loved the inn and wanted to be alone. She liked Frances and the taxi driver but felt that she had to get away and think.
She asked to be excused for a little while, complaining of a
headache.

"Probably jet lag," said the driver.

"Perhaps so," answered Catherine, relieved that she had made a
good escape.

They went into the inn, and Catherine seemed to know exactly
where she was going. Frances stepped back, fascinated, as
Catherine asked the pleasant landlord if the Gable Room was
available.

"Certainly is, lady, but it's a bit more expensive because it has
views right over the valley."

"I know," said Catherine. "Will you please let me have the
key?" Then she turned toward the stairs without looking back and
went up to the Gable Room. Immediately, as she opened the door,
she knew that somewhere, somehow, she had known this room
well. Feeling herself panic a little, she went to the window seat and
looked out over the beautiful green valley. She could hardly stand
the strange feeling and closed her eyes. Stumbling to the old-
fashioned phone by the bed, she nervously asked the desk clerk to
connect her to Miss O'Hara in the bar.

Frances answered the phone quickly. "Anything wrong,
Catherine?"

"I'm having a strange feeling again and I'm scared. Frances,
please come upstairs quickly." She put down the phone, almost
afraid to open her eyes. The room was full of memories—memories
of another lifetime, perhaps. Catherine was shaking, still sitting
beside the phone, when Frances arrived. Poor Catherine looked

terrified. Frances put her arms around this new friend whom she felt she had known all her life and told her to lie down on the bed.

"Now tell me all about it while I take off your shoes and order you a sandwich or something. How about some hot chocolate?"

Catherine was trying to remember. It was difficult because she didn't know where to start. She lay down, holding Frances' hand.

Frances was aware that something was strange in this room. It was pleasant enough, but so cold. Catherine seemed to have gone to sleep, still gripping Frances' fingers. Slowly, Frances extricated her hand and sat quite still. The room seemed to change; not the furniture, yet it was *different*. She wanted to cry. Listening now to Catherine's deep breathing, she felt the need to leave the room and talk to the landlord.

Chapter Two

Creeping out and closing the door behind her, Frances went
down to the friendly bar. The driver had left by now, and the young
barmaid cheerfully passed on a message from him.

"You know the man who brought you here? Well, he hopes
everything's all right."

"Thank you," said Frances. "Tell me, please, where can I find
the landlord?"

"Oh, Mr. Thornleigh's reading the paper in the lounge; reads it
every night about this time."

Turning to leave the room, Frances thanked the girl again and
went to find the landlord. Hating to disturb what appeared to be
his nightly ritual, she touched him on the shoulder, asking gently if
he had a few moments to spare. "My friend asked for the Gable
Room when she came in tonight. Has she been here many times
before?"

"No, I've never seen the lady before," said Mr. Thornleigh.
"American, isn't she?"

"Yes," answered Frances. "But how would she know about that
particular room, I wonder?"

Mr. Thornleigh rubbed his chin thoughtfully and suggested that
perhaps someone who had been there before had told her about it.

"I don't think so. In fact, I'm sure of it. How old is this inn, do
you know?"

"It was built fourteen hundred and something. It was a fine
house then; didn't change into a pub till the 1700s. It was like a
manor house; some lord or lady had it."

"Can you tell me any more?"

"No, not really, but Miss Sheridan, who lives in Penrithy Cottage, could. She used to be a school teacher and writes bits of history in the church bulletin and things. Why don't you go and ask her in the morning?"

Frances wanted to go immediately, but was afraid to leave her new friend. She thanked Mr. Thornleigh and went back upstairs, wondering what to do next.

Catherine was still asleep, so Frances grabbed her coat and rushed downstairs, asking the desk clerk if she knew where Miss Sheridan lived.

The girl answered in a sing-song voice, "Penrithy Cottage, down by the green." Seeing that Frances didn't understand, she added, "Out the front door, turn right and it's about seven houses down to the green. Turn again and it's the fourth house on the left, next door to the Thomases."

Frances rushed out of the warm inn into the cold evening and following the directions, soon reached Penrithy Cottage.

Miss Sheridan was just pulling her drapes closed. Frances smiled, as Miss Sheridan seemed puzzled to see this well-dressed woman coming down her path.

Before Frances reached the door, Miss Sheridan had opened it and with a questioning look on her face, asked, "Can I help you?"

Frances murmured something about it being important, and Miss Sheridan had her settled in her cozy parlor with hot chocolate in no time at all.

"Now, what's it all about, my dear?" asked Miss Sheridan.

Frances asked her about the Blue Feathers Inn.

"The Manor House was built originally by a Welsh lord, Lord David Strong William, in 1493 for his bride, Megan of Manningstile Henlock. As a child, she had been chosen by Lord David to be his future wife. Her parents were poor villagers who promised their daughter to this mighty Welsh lord in return for deeds to their cottage and her father's service as a blacksmith all his living days.

"Megan the child was afraid of the dark-bearded lord who had always been attracted to the little red-headed maid. As she grew, she began to learn of her future, and played within the Manor grounds, knowing that one day she would be Lady of the Manor. Lord David would ride by on his black horse sometimes, impatient for the child to grow. Her constant playmate was Gareth of Abergavennie. His family was bought also by Lord David, and his parents were bakers of fine Welsh bread, having a tiny shop in the village and supplying all the needs of the Manor."

Frances could not contain herself any longer. She had to interrupt, although spellbound. "Can this be possible?"

Miss Sheridan, taken by surprise, didn't understand and began to relate her credentials as a local historian.

"Sorry I stopped you," said Frances. "Please continue."

With a look of concern, Miss Sheridan told Frances that she had to be away on the Cardiff train first thing in the morning and had lots to do before then. Perhaps she and Frances could get together sometime next week?

"Sometime next week?" exclaimed Frances. "Oh no, it's terribly important that I talk to you now! You see, I have this American—"

"Sorry, Miss O'Hara," interrupted Miss Sheridan. "But I really must go."

"Will you please give me a telephone number or an address where I might reach you?" asked Frances desperately.

Miss Sheridan could not understand the urgency of all this. She looked questioningly at Frances, who blurted out, "Do you believe in reincarnation?"

"Well, I don't know about that, but I do believe that I must excuse myself right away or I'm going to miss my sleep. I have an important appointment in Cardiff tomorrow."

"Where will you be staying?"

"At the Imperial Hotel." With this last comment, Miss Sheridan firmly dismissed Frances by walking to the cottage door and smiling coldly while she waited for Frances to leave.

As Frances walked through the dark village, one or two people passed by, acknowledging her with a sing-song "Good night." She fastened the top button on her coat and hoped that the cold night air would clear her mind before she reached the Blue Feathers. Feeling a deep attachment to this strange American girl helped her to forget her swollen foot. Too much running today, thought Frances. Must soak it in warm water soon as I get back.

Frances was born with a slight foot deformity which caused her to limp a little. It never bothered her except when she overdid her walking or standing. From her earliest years, she had always wanted to be a ballerina, and the grown-ups used to tell her that one day she would. Unfortunately, she believed this and became very bitter during her teen years when she realized that nothing could be done for her foot.

Her mind was full of all the day's events. She was sorry she had interrrupted Miss Sheridan's story. Thinking of Catherine, she started to hurry, but her foot was now quite painful. She could see the lights of the Blue Feathers and thought how quickly she had seemed to get to Miss Sheridan's and how long it seemed to get back to the inn.

Opening Catherine's door quietly, she saw that Catherine was still asleep. Thankfully, she went to her room and decided to study her Tarot cards while she soaked her foot. She rang down for a hot cocoa, which she was told would be brought up in a few minutes, and during this time she undressed for bed, put on her gown and turned on the gas fire. Holding her Tarot cards and shuffling them, she tried to make her mind blank, so that she would not make any mental impression on her Tarot reading. Thoughts are living things, thought Frances. And heaven knows where mine are right now.

The maid tapped on the door gently and brought in the warm cocoa. Seeing the colorful pictures of the Tarot pack laid out by this guest didn't make any sense to her. She had always associated such cards with gypsies and whatnot.

Frances caught her look and smiling, asked the girl whether she had ever seen Tarot cards before.

"Well, not really," answered the maid. "I don't know much about them, that I must say. Can you really tell fortunes and things?"

"It's just like having a wise friend. I can get another point of view on any situation I might find myself in. Then I can choose to take it or ignore it."

"Oh," said the girl. "Will you read my cards for me?"

Not wanting to disappoint the girl, Frances asked her her name.

"Mildred, Miss."

"Well, Mildred, I'm going to be here for some time. Tonight I'm feeling rather tired, so how about later in the week?"

Mildred tried not to look too disappointed and suggested that next Thursday evening, anytime after six P.M. would be perfect. With that, she left the room and closed the doore deliberately behind her.

Frances put on her transistor radio quietly and began to spread the cards.

Catherine woke up suddenly. The moon was full and shone directly into the Gable Room. Needing a cigarette and wondering what time it was, she got off the bed and tried to remember where she had left her purse. Fumbling for the light switch, she felt sure someone was in the room with her.

"Is that you, Frances?" she asked in a deep whisper. All she could hear was the Welsh wind through the open window. Moving toward the window, she could see the lace curtain rising upward like a ghost from the past.

Hell, where are my damn cigarettes? thought Catherine. Reaching the door, she ran her hand up and down the wall by the door jamb to find the light switch. She sighed with relief as the room flooded with light from the low-voltage bulb.

Standing erect now with her back to the door, she began to explore the room with her eyes. She saw the faded rose wallpaper with a partial gas fitting still sticking out of the wall, the heavy brown doors, one to the closet, the other to the bathroom. As she walked past the bed, she saw her purse and hurriedly rescued her cigarettes from the jumbled contents. Wondering what had happened to Frances, she sat by the window and looked down into the moonlit garden below.

Inhaling deeply, she saw a group of people below in the garden and heard voices. Opening the window wider to see what was going on, she saw a young man sitting on a large horse. The horse seemed agitated and although not moving, was continually clicking its hooves as though ready to gallop.

"Easy, girl," she heard the man say. Lifting up his face as though toward her window, she heard him call quietly but urgently, "Megan, Megan, make haste, dear heart."

Her blood seemed to freeze. She moved back and felt a tugging at her dress. Looking down, she saw the most beautiful child she had ever beheld. He was smiling and looking straight into her eyes with his large grey ones.

"Mama, Mama, I'm tired."

Realizing that this child was her son and that his little hand on her dark blue gown was urging her to pick him up, she put her arms around him. She could feel the texture of his green velvet suit.

"Come to Mama," she heard herself say, as she walked over to the window. Opening the window wide now, she called out to the shadowy figure below, "Pray, who art thou, sir?"

"Gareth of Abergavennie. 'Tis thy love, sweet lady Megan. I pray thee make haste or Lord David's men will be upon us."

"But what of the child?" she called back in the night.

"We are three and will carry him to safety. Let him down, Megan."

"I can't," cried Megan. "He will be hurt."

A deep Welsh voice from the shadows shouted gruffly, "Trust us, dear lady, and give us the boy."

Megan smoothed the child's soft curls from his forehead and whispered that she would be going with him for a fine ride, but he must go down into the garden first. The child's eyes were full of trust as she asked the men below to tell her when to let the child down. It looked a long way down. Gareth's voice made another anxious plea.

"Let him go, or it will be too late. Already Lord David has left the tavern."

In the next few seconds, she felt a terrible fear, not only for her own life, but for the lives of everyone here tonight. She closed her eyes as she took a deep breath, gave a soft kiss to her cherub and let him fall to safety below.

He screamed loudly, his sorrowful grey eyes boring into hers as he disappeared below, screaming, "Mama, Mama!" into the velvet blackness.

With the child's screams still ringing in her ears, Megan was startled as her bedroom door was flung open. Lord David Strong William was standing there, his face dark with anger. He grabbed Megan, shaking her fiercely. She was terrified as she felt his strong grip on her shoulders.

"Thou art naught but a fisher's wife! And this will be the last thou shalt see of thy bastard!'' With that, he left the room.

As she ran to the window, she could see the shadows of the three men on horseback riding away. She waited for awhile and saw Lord David mount his black horse.

Yelling curses, he and his soldiers thundered off after Gareth of Abergavennie and his faithful men. Afraid for the child, afraid for Gareth, Megan ran to the door, wanting to follow them, determined to become a part of their fate.

Reaching the bottom of the stairs, she was roughly held back by one of Lord David's soldiers, who had been left there to prevent her from following. He ordered her back into her room. She felt her heart breaking as she climbed the stairs.

Lying on her bed, all she could see were the sorrowful grey eyes of her son as he fell to the garden below. The agonizing stillness was shattered by her heartbreaking sobs. Never had she known so much pain. Praying for their safety and wondering where they would find shelter and protection, Megan vowed to all that was sacred that her soul would never rest until she found her loved ones, lost in the black of the night....

Catherine stirred as the morning sun caressed her face; her blonde hair was damp and formed tiny ringlets on her forehead. Trying to capture the escaping memories of her dream, she lay quite still, but the veil of reality was quickly locking out her gentle probe.

A tap on the door and Frances' voice brought Catherine's thoughts back to the present. ''Just a minute, Frances,'' she called as she slipped out of bed and put on her robe. Opening the door, she saw that her new friend was carrying a breakfast tray. ''Oh, that's wonderful,'' said Catherine. ''Just what I needed.''

''Good. And how are you on this lovely Welsh morning?''

''Not sure yet. I had a terrible dream, but I can't remember what it was about. And I think I've got a headache, too. Mmm, that toast does look good. Want a piece, Frances?''

Catherine seemed to be in a pleasant mood, so Frances was trying to think how she could approach Catherine without upsetting her. Catherine saw the serious look on her face and flopped down in the big comfortable green chair.

''OK,'' she said. ''I know you're wondering what the hell is wrong with me, and as I don't want to spoil your holiday, I'll get it over with quickly just by telling you I don't know.'' Waiting for some kind of response from Frances, she looked at her new friend with curiosity and kindness.

Frances responded with a hesitant smile and rubbing her chin, asked, ''Can you speak Welsh?''

''Hell, no,'' answered Catherine, laughing. ''Why do you ask that?''

Deciding it was now or never, Frances told Catherine how she had spoken excellent Welsh while asleep on the train. She reached for a pen. Ignoring the puzzled look on Catherine's face, she asked if there was some hotel stationery in the dresser drawer.

Catherine went to the window first, closing it carefully, sensing a cobweb memory but more than that, an overwhelming sadness. Turning to look at her friend, she half smiled and reached into the dresser drawer for the sheets of writing paper. as she walked back to the chair, she felt better again. Handing the stationery to Frances, she asked, "What the hell are you up to?"

"Please bear with me for a few moments, I have an idea. All right?"

Catherine nodded, leaned back and inhaled deeply on her cigarette, waiting.

Biting her pen and wrinkling her brow, Frances asked Catherine to concentrate and see if she had any answers.

"Answers to *what*, for God's sake?"

Excited now, Frances told her that she was going to make a list. "Number One," she began. "How did you know about the Gable Room when we registered? Don't answer yet. Number Two: What did you mean when you said you preferred your hair red? And Number Three: The name of the inn, Blue Feathers—what does it mean to you?"

Catherine frowned and shaking her head, said quietly, "I don't know, Frances, I really don't."

Seeing that Catherine was beginning to feel depressed, Frances changed the mood of things. Folding up the paper, she suggested that they both go out and explore the village of Manningstile Henlock. "Come on now, looks like a lovely day. Let's find a nice pub, have some lunch, and then we can talk more later." As Frances was leaving, she asked, "By the way...who is Gareth?"

Catherine felt that somehow she knew, yet she had no idea. Looking helplessly at Frances, she shrugged her shoulders. Frances smiled and told her that she would meet her downstairs in ten minutes.

"Make it twenty," yelled Catherine as Frances closed the door.

Deciding that first she must call Nickie in the States, Catherine gave the operator the information and lit a cigarette while she was waiting for the connection. A faint, distant voice was calling that name again on the humming wires.

"Megan, Megan...."

She slammed down the phone; she felt frightened. Staring through the windows, she felt a definite chill. Then the phone rang. Before she could speak, the voice of the operator advised her that her overseas party was on the line.

"Hi, Nickie. Is that you?"

She could hear Nickie's laugh. "Who do you think it is Gareth?"

"Now that's not funny," said Catherine. "I've only been here since last night and every weird thing in the book has happened to me."

"Gee, I'm sorry, Catherine. You really sound freaked out. Are you OK?"

Catherine couldn't help smiling. Nickie was a good friend and always seemed to be there when she needed her.

"Sorry I barked," said Catherine. "It's just that I miss you like hell already." Trying to cheer her up, she asked Nickie what she was doing now.

Suddenly Nickie interrupted the conversation. "Who's that? Is there someone else on the line?"

"I don't hear anything."

"Listen," said Nickie. "It's someone asking for Megan."

Absolutely terrified, Catherine gripped the telephone receiver hard, bit her lip and without thinking, cried, "For God's sake, leave me alone, Gareth!"

Nickie froze. She felt afraid for Catherine. Not knowing what to say next, she asked Catherine for her phone number. The only response she could get was "Blue Feathers."

"Where is the Blue Feathers, Catherine?" yelled Nickie. "For God's sake, answer me! Pull yourself together and tell me where's the Blue Feathers!"

Her voice weak, Catherine whispered, "At Manningstile Henlock."

"Say that again, please."

A big intake of breath and then, "Manningstile Henlock." But it was a man's voice—and then the phone was dead.

Chapter Three

It took Nickie nearly an hour to find the telephone number of the inn. She heard the number ringing, then a light, friendly English voice said, "Good morning. Blue Feathers Inn."

Nickie sighed with relief and asked if Catherine Holmes was in her room.

The woman on the other end did not seem to realize that this was an overseas call until Nickie announced, "Please, can you hurry? I'm calling from the States."

Mildred, the housemaid, desk clerk, or whatever was needed, asked if she was calling from anywhere near Hollywood. Nickie, the friendly-natured girl whom everyone loved, nearly exploded.

"Jesus Christ, are you stupid or something? Please—do you understand? I'm calling from the United States! Now, *will you get Catherine Holmes on the phone*?"

Mildred felt quite taken aback. Who did this silly twerp think she was? All I asked was a simple question, she thought. "I'm trying to put you through."

Nickie tried to hang onto her patience. Looking at the kitchen calendar, she muttered, "I don't believe it." And then, to the cat, "I honest to God don't *believe* it! *Jeesus!*"

"Hi. Is that you, Nickie?"

Relieved to hear Catherine back on the line, Nickie said, "Are you all right?" Then, as if to reassure herself, she asked if Catherine had heard the man's voice. But before she could reply, Nickie went on, asking who had the weirdo Laurence Olivier voice. Catherine felt some kind of order coming into her mind and heard herself telling Nickie that she would be home next Saturday, which was just four days away. Nickie was overjoyed and told Catherine she would meet her at the airport.

There was a pause in the conversation, then Nickie asked, "What will you be doing at that godforsaken place till then?"

"I suppose I'll do what I can here to find out where in the States I have to go next."

With that strange remark, Nickie told Catherine that she had better wait till they talked before she started to book any more strange air flights. "Home is where you're going. Take a few days off work, so will I, and I'll mother you, listen to you, and help you sort this whole thing out. OK? By the way, Bartholomew is pregnant. Bye now, see you Saturday."

"Bye," said Catherine. "Take care."

"You, too," said Nickie as she put the phone down thoughtfully.

The coffee smelled wonderful. Stroking her legs, Nickie made a mental note that she had better shave them tonight. She decided to run down to the mailbox so she could read her mail while she enjoyed her coffee. A strange guy was walking out of the garage, giving her a funny "I'm-gonna-get-you" look. Spotting an interesting envelope, she forgot him instantly as she ran back up the stairs to her apartment, promising herself she wouldn't open the letter till she had poured her coffee, cut her cake, and was sitting in her favorite chair. Pregnant Bartholomew was making a horrible feed-me noise. Shaking the Kelloggs box into the cat dish and pouring on some hot water remaining in the kettle, she created a steaming brown mush which Bartholomew began to stalk.

Examining the envelope, she saw that the letter was addressed to Catherine Holmes. On the neatly typed envelope were scrawled instructions to Nicola Foster: *Please open immediately.* Wow, this was really Hollywood stuff! Loving every minute of this intrigue and yelling at Bartholomew to shut up, she opened the letter.

Dear Miss Holmes:

I have instructed your friend, Miss Nicola Foster, to open this letter. It is my duty to inform you that your uncle, Alfred Holmes, your father's brother, passed away February 2nd of this year and left you a considerable amount of money and a small estate.

There are certain conditions that must be understood and accomplished before the inheritance can be claimed. It was the desire of your uncle that you and I meet specifically on August 8th in the year following his death. As you are presently in the United Kingdom, I am enclosing an airline ticket and expenses for Miss Foster to enable her to leave immediately, so that she can deliver this letter personally. I was your uncle's friend and colleague for many years and also his legal advisor. I trust that Miss Foster will contact you personally in Manningstile Henlock at her earliest. I look forward to meeting you on Sunday, August 8th, at 12:45 P.M. I have made a luncheon reservation for three at the Santa Barbara Biltmore Hotel.

Yours truly,

Jonathan Whiteside

Nickie stared at the letter, reading aloud over and over again, *"considerable amount of money and a small estate; considerable amount of money and a small estate—."* "I don't believe it. I really don't believe it." Her mind told her a thousand and one things to do. She shrieked and laughed hysterically. Seeing Bartholomew, she looked him in the eye and said, "If you, young man, can have kittens, I suppose Catherine can be rich. What the hell am I going to do with you? Because *I'm* going to Manningstile Disneyland!"

Fresh, crisp one-hundred-dollar bills—ten of them—with a paper attached for expenses, plus a first-class airline ticket, fell out of the envelope.

"Welshy Wales, here I come," sang Nickie. Already she had decided to spend her savings and announce this fantastic news personally. Tomorrow she would go, but first she had to call the monster boss! She knew that her position was the most insecure one in all of West Los Angeles because the son-of-a-bitch Chief Draftsman was convinced that only the superior male sex were capable of designing.

I'm going to enjoy this, thought Nickie, really enjoy it. She could imagine the look on his face when he was deprived of the pleasure of firing her. But wait...How does this Whiteside guy know me? And how does he know where Catherine is? Picking up the letter again, she saw a phone number. It was in Oregon somewhere.

Hands shaking, she dialed the number direct and heard the answering machine click on; she was ready to put the receiver down when she heard her name.

"Miss Foster, this is Jonathan Whiteside on recording. Thank you for calling. There is no need to be concerned. Please follow the instructions in my letter. I can assure you that Miss Holmes' inheritance is quite genuine. Do enjoy your flight. I look forward to meeting you when Miss Holmes returns home. Bon voyage, Miss Foster."

Feeling absolutely stunned, Nickie poured herself a stiff drink. Going over the last half-hour, she wondered how she could possibly think of giving up her job, even though it was hanging by a very fine thread. Everything seemed so unreal. Reaching out to the coffee table, she picked up the crisp one-hundred-dollar bills and examined the airline ticket. There was her name on a first-class flight! Somehow she felt that giving up her job at this time would be opportune. With this extra money, she could manage for a while and catch that plane to see Catherine.

Wishing she could understand all that was happening and shrug off her fears about this strange sequence of events, Nickie decided to worry about it all later and began to pack for her trip.

Chapter Four

Frances was waiting downstairs. Looking pensive, she was trying to think how she could help Catherine with her dilemma. Hearing her name, she turned and saw Catherine, who had changed into a good-looking pair of slacks and a big white Irish sweater. They began to stroll through the village, looking in tiny shop windows and admiring the local scenery.

"Hungry yet?" asked Frances.

Catherine hesitated awhile and suggested they walk a little farther. On the narrow, winding lane out of the village, they both jumped to the side as a man on horseback galloped by.

"Gee, he was going at a hell of a pace," said Catherine. "Just look what the idiot did to my sweater!"

Frances tried to brush the wet mud off, which made it look worse. Feeling angry, Catherine said she would have to go back to the inn and change before they had lunch.

When they arrived back at the inn, Catherine suggested that Frances get a table in the dining room while she went upstairs to change.

Looking around, trying to find the dining room, Frances met the landlord, who kindly escorted her to a table by the window.

Mildred arrived at the table, wiping her hands vigorously on her apron. "What can I get yer, Miss?"

Explaining that she was waiting for someone, Frances asked if she would bring her some coffee.

The man at the next table grinned. His hair was curly and tousled and he looked the picture of health. He was also the mud splasher.

"Would you like a drink before lunch?" he called over.

"No, thank you," said Frances, thinking to herself that he had a lot of nerve.

Seeing that he was being ignored, the man stood up and walked over. "Is there something wrong with me?" he asked.

Not knowing how to deal with this man, Frances looked up and informed him that she was waiting for her friend.

"Is that the girl I saw you walking with in the lane?"

"It certainly is, and she's not going to be too pleased to see you here."

"Why not? Look, my name is Jason Griffiths. Let's shake hands and be friends."

Reaching out her hand and smiling, Frances saw Catherine come into the dining room. Walking over to the table, Catherine gave Jason a big smile and asked him if he intended to throw any more mud around today.

Jason was apologetic and surprised when he found out why the girls were somewhat cold to him. Realizing that he had not deliberately thrown mud all over her, Catherine began to enjoy Jason's friendliness.

Jason was a writer and had come to this Welsh village to finish his next book. Asked how he liked Manningstile Henlock, he screwed up his face and paused before expressing his feelings about the village and surrounding areas. He was really here for two reasons: to write and to relax, in order to cure what seemed to be a permanent headache. For the past month or so, he had been experiencing strange dreams, and in each of the dreams he always met the same woman. He knew everything about her, the way she walked, the way she talked.

Frances was glued to the chair, waiting for something like a miracle. Not being able to contain herself anymore, she asked, "Have you seen this woman yet?"

"Unfortunately, no. But somehow, I don't think it will be too long before I do."

"Why do you feel destined to meet this girl, Jason?" asked Catherine.

"I don't know," answered Jason. "All I know is that she's very special, and we shall both recognize each other."

Catherine smiled wearily and said, "It may be harder than you think...like finding a needle in a haystack."

"How long are you here for?" asked Frances.

"Well, I have a couple of weeks' vacation and I thought I would just tour around."

"What a great idea," said Catherine. "Is it working out?"

Jason gave a glimmer of a smile and quietly told the two women that he felt it wouldn't be too long before he met his dream girl and that when he did, they would both know, for it was karmic.

"What do you mean, karmic?" asked Catherine.

"Well, karma is the law of cause and effect—you reap what you sow kind of thing—and this is done through several lifetimes."

"Wait a minute," said Catherine. "You mean you believe this?"

Jason looked troubled, not knowing quite how to answer. "I think I do. It's the only thing that makes sense."

"How exactly does karma work?" asked Catherine.

Jason, wondering how he could explain the theory, simply asked, "Do you know what reincarnation means?"

"I've heard about it," said Catherine. "I find it scares me."

Frances, enjoying this conversation tremendously, told Jason that she had read many books on the subject and was deeply intrigued. "Do you fully understand all the complications of the reincarnation theory?"

"I think so," said Jason. "In fact, it's the only theory that seems to make any sense out of life."

"Why is that?" asked Catherine, feeling excited and curious.

"Well, it explains the whole balance of human existence. Why, for example, some people are well off and some are povertystricken. Why some get rotten breaks in life and others seem to hit everything just right. Then there's a sensible theory for children who, for example, can take to music or math or whatever without prior apparent knowledge. Now who was the composer who was writing music and playing the piano without any formal training at the age of five?"

The waitress came to the table, yawning, and mumbled something.

Jason looked at the girl and said, "Excuse me?"

"I said, I have to be clearing the table, sir, 'cause we have to set up again for dinner."

Apologizing for having kept her waiting, the three got up and went to the front desk to pay their bill.

"May I?" asked Jason.

The girls refused but promised that they would have dinner with him at eight o'clock that evening.

"Great," said Jason. "I'll pick you up at seven-fifteen and we'll drive into Cardiff. I know a fabulous place to eat, and I know someone I think you'd both like to meet."

Jason left the women in the hotel lobby. Frances wanted to go back to the village to do some shopping and asked Catherine if she wanted to join her. Catherine was feeling tired and decided she would rather go to her room for a nap. They were both looking forward to going out to dinner with Jason. Before going their different ways, they arranged to meet for afternoon tea at 4:15.

Catherine locked her door and closed the curtains. Taking off her shoes, she lay on the bed, looking at the ceiling. When she closed her eyes, she felt transported to another century. Her mind drifted and found peace in the strong arms of Gareth.

Lying together, gently touching each other, they made soft promises in a room bright with moonlight. Leaning over to see his face and looking into his eyes, she asked, "Art thou truly my beloved husband?"

His answer was to hold her close and whisper endearing words into her ear. "I love thee, little one. Thou art a part of me and I of thee."

"How much dost thou love me?" she asked.

"Beyond the moon and into forever, where there's no ending, my love."

She clung tightly to him as though their nearness could prove the truth of every word he said. Always, she felt a little insecure—she didn't understand why, because he often told her how much he loved her, and yet she needed him to reassure her constantly.

"Never leave me, Gareth, please, never leave me."

Leaning over now, he looked into her face, stroking back her red hair and smiling at this sweet, sweet girl who was child and woman at the same time. Kissing her eyelids and whispering enduring love, he held her close. She loved his nearness and tried to capture the expression on the handsome face of this wonderful man who was her husband. She never wanted to forget the way he looked right now. The night was forgotten and, as he murmured her name again and again, they held each other, afraid but secure in each other's love.

"Wake, little one," she heard him say. Not stirring and keeping her eyes closed, she felt his lips on her face.

"Megan, Megan, we must go now."

She dreaded this moment and wanted to savor every available minute left. This man, her husband, was ready to leave. His mind was on what he must do. Hers was still nestling in the warmth of the bed. Lifting her arms, she beckoned him to come close.

His mood changed. He bent down and avoiding the bed, said, "I love thee," but the words did not sound like those spoken in the night. His eyes were no longer attracted to her beauty.

She felt all this with hurt. How could she tell him how she felt? He was almost too casual now, as though last night had never happened.

"Tell me thou lovest me, Gareth."

"I love thee, Megan, but now I must go."

Her eyes pleaded for understanding. She wanted so much to be able to keep him this day. But it was always the same—always he had to go. He would never know the anguish she felt. Whenever she tried to tell him, he smiled and said he understood, but she was certain he did not.

"When wilt thou return, Gareth?"

He was already pulling his cloak about him. She lay in the warm bed which no longer excited him. It was done, it was over, he loved her but he was satisfied. Holding her and trying to reassure her, he told her that all being well, he would return soon. Throwing her a kiss, he smiled as he left.

Megan turned over in the still-warm bed and wept, for she needed a softness and an understanding that her husband did not have the time to give.

"Must it always end like this?" sobbed Megan. "One day, dear Lord, give me a morning after. He loves me, I know, but I need to walk and talk with my husband. It is cruel to be left; I need his arms about me."

Running to the window, she looked down with the kind of smile she thought he expected and waved goodbye. His rearing horse and his face in the early morning light made her heart ache. Would they ever be together as man and wife? Or would their life continue this way? Angry with herself, she stopped crying, and tried to decide what she would wear on his next visit....

The first thing on Catherine's mind after her nap was what she was going to wear for dinner. It seemed to have a lot of importance. Thinking of Jason excited her, but only because of his interesting theories. Whenever she thought of being in love, the same overwhelming feeling came over her. It was strange and distant. When she was a little girl, she had had the same feeling, but then it felt stronger, for although she couldn't remember her childhood impressions, she did remember that she enjoyed thinking about someone who was never there! Catherine wondered if Gareth was a person she had known when she was a child. Certainly he wasn't a figment of her imagination.

"Gareth." She said his name quietly and felt an overwhelming sadness. At the thought of his name, a vivid picture flashed into her mind—she could see him, really see him! Not understanding what was happening, she blinked her eyes. He was still there.

Standing by the window was a young woman in a long green silk dress. Her hair was radiantly red with the sunlight shining through it. She turned to Gareth after he said, "Megan, thou must try to understand. I will get the child, but I must leave now or it will be too late."

Megan ran to the door where he was standing, pleading, "Let me go with thee! I know that the little one cries for me."

Gareth held her firmly and wiped the tears from her cheeks. "Please, my love, let me bring Patrick; it is a dangerous mission and every minute is precious."

"Will they hurt him?" asked Megan.

Gareth smiled as he assured her that it was hardly possible that soldiers would harm such a young babe. Pulling her away from him, Gareth lifted her gently and carried her to the bed. He kissed her forehead and left hastily.

Catherine stared at the bed and looked at the carved scroll. It was the same bed. What she had seen and heard was incredible. Realizing now that she was Megan, she wondered where Gareth might be. The phone rang. It was Frances.

"Are you ready for tea, Catherine? Must show you what I got from the little dress shop."

Catherine said she would be down right away, but she was loath to leave the room that had held her past throughout the centuries.

Frances was excited about their dinner date. This holiday really was different. She led a rather quiet life, with a small circle of friends, and went to the ballet whenever possible. She felt protective towards Catherine and a closeness she had not known with her other friends.

Frances was thirty-six and had never married. Looking at her, no one would think that she had had an affair which lasted for six years. It was not the usual affair—it was comfortable, and when Frances looked back, she found it to have been a rewarding experience. Martin had been considerably older than she, and it seemed that she had come into his life at exactly the right time. Martin was a retired doctor and often came into the library where she worked. It all began with a smile and sadly, ended that way when he died. They never married because he felt that although he didn't love his wife, at least he owed her loyalty for the many years they had been together. They lived more like brother and sister, and meeting Frances had given him much happiness. He seemed to sense when the end was near and knew that if he left Frances anything in his will, he would create sadness in his wife and also in Frances. Three years before his death, he and Frances escaped for a day to Stratford-upon-Avon. It was a beautiful day. They strolled through the town, browsing in shop windows. Martin was very happy and suggested they walk toward the river. Just off the main street he turned, and as they reached a certain tiny thatched-roof cottage, he stopped at the garden gate and asked Frances what she thought of it.

"It's like a dream house," she said. "Wouldn't it be lovely to live here?"

"That's exactly what I have in mind for you, sweetheart."

Her eyes questioned him unbelievingly. "What are you saying, Martin?"

"Let me explain. But first, let's find a cafe and have lunch."

Frances remembered his face as he touched her arm. As they walked to the cafe, she was speechless. He walked quietly at her side, and not until they had ordered lunch did he venture to say anything. Looking seriously at her, he reached across the table to touch her hand. He began slowly, trying to explain how much he loved her and appreciated her love and that one day he would not be here. Not wanting to hurt her or his wife, he had decided to buy a small cottage in her name, and with that he gave her an old-fashioned key. Frances could not have been more moved if she had been handed the key to heaven. Since that day, she had never had a need for anyone else, for she kept alive the love that she and Martin had shared within their tiny cottage.

Sitting in the leather armchair in the hotel lobby, Frances reached into her purse for the book she had bought that afternoon. It was about reincarnation. As far as she knew, there weren't any books that really told the reader much. They dealt mostly with people who had experienced past lives, and then there was the popular story about the little Indian girl who recognized her family from a past life. Browsing through the book, she saw a Tarot card in rich full color. It was from the Major Arcana and one of her favorites. It was called the World and portrayed a beautiful woman surrounded by a large garland or wreath. Frances found it to be quite inspirational when meditating and wondered why it was here in this book on reincarnation. Well, the card could be associated with reincarnation, she thought. Then, remembering her Tarot Handbook that portrayed the card, she thought of the verse:

> *Free to choose your path at last,*
> *You've learned your lessons in the past.*

Pondering the association, she heard Catherine apologize for keeping her waiting. Frances smiled and began to pour the tea.

"What are you reading?" asked Catherine.

"Well, you know my interest in the unknown? When we were talking with Jason about reincarnation, I decided to see if I could find a book on the subject."

"Is it any good?" asked Catherine a little too casually.

"I really don't know yet, but one thing caught my eye. I happen to be very interested in the Tarot and I use the cards quite often. When I opened this book, I saw a Tarot card and I'm just wondering how it might be connected to the theory of reincarnation."

Catherine stirred her tea, wondering whether to tell Frances about her experience that afternoon, but then Mildred came and appeared to attack the table as she fell over the chair leg.

Looking sorry for herself and glowering at the chair, she asked, "What will it be, then?"

"What will what be?" called Mr. Thornleigh, the landlord, from behind her.

The girl seemed to shift gears; and for a moment she sounded halfway efficient. "Would you like afternoon Devon tea, ladies?"

"Not for me," answered Frances, smiling. "How about you,

Catherine?"

"Yes, thank you."

Mildred murmured something and slouched back into the kitchen.

"What are you going to wear tonight?" asked Frances.

Catherine had decided to buy an evening skirt to wear with her white blouse. When she told Frances of her intention, Frances suggested that she first look in her wardrobe, for she had brought everything but the kitchen sink! Catherine was relieved that she wouldn't have to spend unnecessarily, so after tea, they went up to Frances' room and spent the next half-hour finding something for Catherine to wear. Her final choice was a black velvet skirt which she thought would look great with her blouse.

"How about these earrings?" Frances asked.

"Mmm, thanks. I'll try them on when I'm dressed and see what they look like." Catherine excused herself, saying that she liked plenty of time to get ready.

Frances was glad to have a little time to herself, as she wanted to spend a few minutes with her Tarot cards.

Strange how my leg keeps paining me on and off, she thought. Pulling her red wool skirt out of the wardrobe, she held it against her and thought how good she looked when you couldn't see the leg.

Jason arrived promptly, looking quite handsome, his blond hair well groomed. Both women had met earlier and were enjoying a cocktail in the bar downstairs. After having a drink with them, Jason brought the car around to the front of the hotel. Everyone was in a happy mood, ready for a good evening. Opening the car doors, Jason told the women that his plans to take them to Cardiff had been changed, for his other guest had been delayed and would not be able to make Cardiff in time for dinner.

Not in the least perturbed by the news, both Catherine and Frances sat in the back seat, feeling perfectly relaxed for the first time since they had met. Catherine sat back and looked at the bright Welsh moon as the car sped through the countryside. Sometimes the moon seemed to light up a whole field and the scenery became a haunting Celtic landscape of nocturnal beauty.

"Where are we going, Jason?" asked Frances.

Jason inhaled deeply on his cigarette and glanced over his shoulder. He told them that he wanted them to come to his house for dinner and meet his mother and elder brother.

"What a wonderful idea," said Frances. "How very nice of you."

But Catherine couldn't help wondering why he would want to do this. In the nicest possible way, she asked, "I don't want to sound ungrateful, Jason, but isn't it rather unusual, even for a Welsh man, to take two ladies home for dinner when he doesn't even know them?''

Jason laughed. "I suppose it does seem rather peculiar, but I wanted to make up for the mud bath, and who better to help me than my mother?'' He tuned on the car radio. It began to play softly "The Green, Green Grass of Home.''

Soon the green Jaguar turned off the road into a winding drive with tall trees. Catherine almost gasped in surprise when she saw the house, or was it a castle? Both women looked at each other, not saying a word. Frances pulled out her compact and patted her nose with make-up. Catherine smoothed her hair and checked the button on her blouse. Better fasten one more, she thought, not knowing what to expect.

The car stopped in front of an impressive double door, a light went on, and the butler opened the door grandly. Jason leapt out of the car and helped them both out. As they entered the grand hallway, they were impressed by the beautiful interior.

Coming down the stairs was a small, plump lady who greeted them with a warm smile. The butler quietly asked for Catherine's coat and then Frances'. Jason introduced the pleasant lady, who was his mother. She appeared to be very happy to meet her guests.

"Where is Alan?'' she asked Jason.

"Not sure, Mother.''

The butler then addressed Jason. "Sir, your brother is waiting in the library.''

"Thank you, Albert,'' replied Jason. "Will you inform Lord Alan that our guests have arrived?''

"Yes, sir.'' Albert disappeared through one of the many doors off the hallway.

Catherine was really excited at the prospect of dining with a lord. Drawing Jason to her, she whispered, "What do I call your mom?''

"Lady Margaret,'' he whispered back.

Frances was enjoying every minute of this whole venture. They followed Lady Margaret down three steps into a magnificent dining room.

Hollywood couldn't have done better, thought Catherine.

Standing by the fireplace was a huge man as dark as Jason was light. Smoking an intriguing pipe shaped like a mermaid, he came forward and introduced himself. "I'm Alan, the brother of this young pup. Happy to have you dining with us.''

Jason, smiling at his brother's remark, introduced the women.

Alan seemed to be about forty. He had dark, curly hair and beard and a smile that showed beautiful white teeth.

Frances was really enchanted with everyone and everything and found it easy to make small talk. Catherine on the other hand felt strange and found herself staring at Alan as though she could remember him from somewhere. Suddenly it came to her: Alan had been the mysterious "man who wasn't there" on the plane! But that was impossible! She dismissed it as just another of the strange hallucinations afflicting her ever since the incident in the elevator....

The evening went beautifully. The dinner was superb and the wine excellent. Catherine looked around the room as though searching for something. Jason realized that she was looking at the paintings and offered to show them to her.

"Shouldn't there be a tapestry over the fireplace?" asked Catherine.

Everyone stopped talking, for this was a strange remark from someone who had just arrived at Cardiff House.

Lady Margaret spoke first. "As a matter of fact, there was a tapestry over the fireplace many years ago—a very fine one indeed."

"What happened to it, Lady Margaret?" asked Frances.

"My late husband, Lord Robert, donated it to the museum, along with some other artifacts."

"Shall we retire into the drawing room?" asked Alan, walking over and offering his arm to Catherine.

"Yes, that's a lovely idea," said Lady Margaret. "Are we all finished with dinner?" Everyone agreed.

Jason offered both arms, one to his mother and the other to Frances. As Frances started to walk, her leg gave her severe pain and accentuated her limp. She was relieved to sit down in the drawing room.

Alan asked Catherine if she would like to look at some of the family paintings. Nodding her head and feeling rather overpowered by this dark man, she accompanied him to the great hall. Jason decided to go with them, for already his mother and Frances were deep in conversation. The great hall was absolutely splendid: all the walls were covered with family portraits, each one having a small brass plate identifying the subject.

As Catherine mounted the grand sweeping staircase, she thought she heard music. It was faint, but she could recognize the melody: Chopin, without a doubt. This music seemed to disturb her; Alan looked at her and asked if she was all right. They continued to look at the majestic portraits, and either Alan or Jason described each painter and the year in which the portrait was completed. When they were little boys, their father, Lord Robert, had insisted they learn the history of the family and understand the value of their rich inheritance.

Reaching the top of the stairs, they walked along the balcony which overlooked the great hall and part of the library. Both men, perfect hosts, continued to talk about the paintings, now and then mentioning a piece of furniture or laughing at a childhood memory that occurred to them.

Catherine realized she knew Cardiff House—knew it well. Although she could feel fear and apprehension building inside her, she had to go on.

"Where's the nursery?" she asked Jason. He smiled and told her that it was on the next floor. She looked directly ahead, where the east wing divided the balcony. There were many bedroom doors, yet she knew exactly where the door was that led into the nursery. The door was locked and although the balcony was brightly lit with a splendid chandelier, Catherine felt eerie.

"I'll get the key," volunteered Jason. "Won't take a minute." He leapt down the stairs, while Catherine waited with Alan.

"I'm curious," he said. "You seem to have been here before." "Why do you say that?"

Looking thoughtful and stroking his dark beard, he answered, "I don't know, but I also feel that I've known you before."

Catherine could feel her hands perspiring. Her body felt like lead. She wanted to go back downstairs, yet she couldn't move.

"Listen," he said urgently. "Did you hear that?"

From behind the nursery staircase, they could hear a small child calling. *"Mama, Mama!"*

Catherine swayed as though she were going to faint. Alan had to hold her to prevent her from falling.

In that second, she saw that the nursery staircase door was wide open and a child was trying to come down the stairs, crying. Catherine turned to look at Alan but she could not move. Lord David would not let her go to Patrick, her son.

The child was sobbing painfully, still calling, *"Mama, Mama!"*

Lord David slapped Megan hard across the face. The child screamed in fear and fell down the dark steep stairs.

Frances was calling, "Catherine, where are you?"

Alan answered, "We're up on the balcony waiting for Jason to bring a key. Why don't you come up?"

Looking up at the balcony, Frances smiled and started up the main stairway to join them. She could feel the pain getting worse and decided not to go any further.

"Sorry," she called. "My leg is causing me a lot of trouble today." Laughing nervously, she retired back to the drawing room.

Catherine pulled herself away from Alan, meeting Jason on his way up as she ran down the stairs. Jason looked at Catherine as she ran into the drawing room and glanced back up at his brother.

"Is anything wrong?"

Looking bewildered, Alan shook his head and started to walk down the stairs.

"But aren't we going to look at the nursery?" asked Jason.

"Not tonight. The lady has changed her mind."

Shrugging his shoulders, Jason went to join the women, and Alan pulled out his pipe and started to puff. Deep in thought, he went to the library. Albert was pouring after-dinner drinks and asked if he could be of assistance to Lord Alan. "No thank you, Albert. Tell Lady Margaret and our guests I'll join them shortly."

"Yes, m'lord," said Albert as he took the silver tray away.

Pulling a large book from the shelf, Alan sat down in the desk chair directly underneath a portrait of Lord David Strong William and began to read.

Chapter Five

Frances had been chatting pleasantly with Lady Margaret for some time, when she suddenly had an overwhelming desire to find Catherine. Excusing herself, she left the drawing room and met Catherine as she was coming in.

"Are you all right, Catherine?"

Her friend still looked pale; as she reached out to put her arms around her, Frances felt an excruciating pain in her leg. Alan was coming down the stairway. Frances asked if he could bring some water. Catherine was terribly shaken and wished she was back home in North Hollywood. Then Alan was handing her a glass; but as she sipped, *she tasted a rich, sweet red wine!*

Jason appeared then and asked everyone to settle down in the drawing room. The fireplace had a warm fire going and they sat around making friendly conversation.

"I wanted Catherine and Frances to meet George this evening, but unfortunately, he couldn't make it," said Jason.

Before the conversation got any more involved, Catherine asked if they would mind if she went home now, as she thought she might still be suffering from jet lag. Both men got to their feet and apologized for not being aware of her tiredness. Alan offered to take the women back to Manningstile Henlock, and Jason said, "Only if I come along, too," giving a wink to the girls.

Saying goodnight to Lady Margaret, they both felt a sense of relief as they stepped out into the chilly evening. Jason's Jaguar was still outside the front door. Alan sat in the back with Catherine, offering Frances the front seat so that she could stretch her leg. Alan was fascinated with the evening's events and asked Catherine how she knew about the nursery staircase.

"I don't really know," answered Catherine. "But believe me, so many curious things have happened since I arrived in Wales that I don't believe anything could surprise me now.''

The conversation entered a lighter mood. Everyone was talking and laughing, yet Catherine could not erase the vision of Patrick falling down the stairs. She was very conscious of Alan sitting beside her. In her mind, she could still hear what he had said when Jason went to find the nursery key: "*I also feel that I've known you before.*" What could he mean? What was he trying to say? He was a powerful-looking man but apparently gentle. Catherine felt an overwhelming desire to console him, which didn't make sense.

Jason was feeling pleased with himself; it had been a successful evening and his mother had enjoyed the company of his new friends. The conversation had slowed down now, and as he took the turnoff to Manningstile Henlock, he tried to inject some life back into the dark car.

"Won't be long now before we're back at the Blue Feathers. Any chance of getting a nightcap before we go back to Cardiff House?" Having directed this question to no one in particular, he was hoping that everyone would react.

Frances was the first to speak. "That sounds like a good idea. How about it, everyone?"

Alan leaned over toward Catherine. "You're not feeling too tired?"

Catherine, a little startled at feeling his hand on hers, said, "Oh no, that would be a good way to finish the evening."

"Good," said Jason. "Then we're all agreed?"

Catherine and Alan were the first to get out of the car. Jason helped Frances, who was having difficulty with her leg. As Catherine and Alan approached the door of the inn, Alan held it closed, preventing Catherine from entering.

"I must talk to you," he said. Still holding the door, he looked her directly in the eye and added firmly, "Tonight."

Not knowing what to say, Catherine pretended that she was looking for something in her purse. Again he spoke, urgently this time, for the others were joining them. "Will you see me tonight, Catherine?"

Answering him quickly, she said, "Yes."

"Good. Now we'd better get inside. The evening air is chilly."

"I'll have a Bloody Mary," said Catherine to Jason when they were inside the warmth of the inn.

The landlord was very friendly and seemed to enjoy serving his guests. "What will you have, Miss O'Hara?"

"Oh, make mine a gin and tonic, please."

"I'll take scotch," said Alan.

"Me, too," said Jason to the landlord.

The fire was burning brightly; there were still a few other guests about. The inn was comforting, and these four strangers seemed to be content with their destiny for the moment.

Lighting his pipe and sucking the stem in a slow rhythm, Alan raised one eyebrow and said, "Catherine and I have decided we're going to take a walk in the village. Don't worry about the car, Jason. I'll stay at the cottage." Catherine was taken by surprise but managed to smile as Alan said, "Ready, Catherine?"

"I—I think I'm going to need my coat," she said. "Please excuse me for a moment."

Frances saw the look on her face and was curious, so she thought it an opportune time to excuse herself also in order to have the chance to speak to Catherine.

When both girls had gone, Jason laughed and asked, "Alan, where on earth are you going to walk?"

"None of your damn business," said Alan good-humoredly. "But I'll tell you one thing: There's something bloody odd about everything tonight." He sucked on his pipe and gazed thoughtfully into the fire.

Jason looked puzzled. "Don't you like the girls?"

"Of course I do, but something isn't right. I've got to talk to Catherine."

Jason ordered two more drinks and they sat in silence, waiting for Catherine and Frances.

Frances followed Catherine to her room and closing the door, asked if something was wrong.

"I don't know, Frances, I really don't." She told Frances about her feelings in Cardiff House and how she knew about the nursery staircase and Baby Patrick and what Alan had said.

Frances tried to digest all this and encouraged Catherine to have a good talk with Alan to see if any of the jigsaw pieces would fit together.

"What are you going to do?"

"Oh, don't worry about me. Jason is a nice enough chap; I'm sure we can find plenty to talk about. Please call in tonight and be sure and tell me everything that happens."

Catherine laughed. "That's a strange remark. What do you mean, 'everything that happens'?"

Frances just smiled, and they decided to go downstairs to join the men.

As they entered the foyer, Alan took Catherine's coat and helped her put it on. Jason and Frances stood near the fireplace staring at the fire, both wondering at the reason for Catherine and Alan being together.

Stepping into the night air, Catherine turned up her collar. Alan touched her elbow and directed her to the taxi waiting at the curb. Smiling, Catherine turned to ask Alan where they were going. He smiled back, nodding his head to reassure her. The taxi driver already knew their destination, for they were heading out of the village in no time at all.

"Feeling warmer now?" Alan asked.

Catherine nodded and began to think how stupidly she was behaving. Here she was with someone she didn't know, going to God knew where. She glanced at Alan, who smiled and leaning over to the taxi driver, said, "Turn left here." The taxi slowed down, stopped in front of a cottage.

Alan paid the driver, and they went up three stone steps. He rang the doorbell. A friendly woman opened the door and greeted them. Catherine was helped off with her coat as they went into a comfortable living room with a bright fire. The room was full of brass and interesting pictures. The woman came back into the room with a tray and two steaming cups of cocoa.

"Will that be all, m'lord?" she asked.

"Thank you, Gwyneth, I'll call you when I need you."

With that, Gwyneth closed the door behind her and Catherine was alone with Alan.

"Look, do you mind telling me what this is all about?" asked Catherine.

"I suppose I do owe you an explanation," said Alan. "Our meeting has had a strange influence over me, and I just had to be alone with you and try to talk it over. I don't really know where to begin. I have this feeling that I know you, yet I've never been to America and I know it's your first visit. Not only do I think I know you, I've dreamt about you."

Catherine liked this man. She felt good sitting here with him yet she felt a fear.

"Does the name Gareth mean anything to you?" she asked slowly, not daring to look up at him.

"Gareth," he repeated. "No, I can't say that it does. Why?"

"I don't know. I don't know whether I'm going crazy or what."

"Why don't you tell me about it."

Rubbing her forehead wearily, she said, "I wouldn't know where to begin."

"Why not at the beginning."

Catherine felt warmed by his kind response and started at the beginning, in the elevator at Sak's Fifth Avenue, Beverly Hills. He let her talk and she related every detail right up to the moment when they met tonight. Leaning toward the fireplace, Alan knocked his unusual pipe gently against the hearth. She waited anxiously for a response. He took his time, bringing out his tobacco pouch and slowly packing his pipe. Then, leaning back and staring into the flames, he asked, "Am I your Lord David Strong William?"

Suddenly she realized that she didn't want him to be! How could this kind and gentle man be the ruthless Lord David? With tears rolling down her face, she looked at him hopelessly. He gently cupped her chin. His eyes looked deeply into hers. They were beautiful; Catherine had feelings about this man that she had never felt before.

"Please don't hate me, Catherine." Alan stroked her hair. She felt so confused that she began to sob like a child. He comforted her as his strong arms held her close. Kissing her gently, he wiped away her tears and told her that he would do all he could to help her understand the mystery.

The clock on the mantelpiece chimed.

"I must go now," said Catherine.

"Why should you go?"

"It's already midnight."

"Why not stay here? I'll have Gwyneth make up the guest room." The look on Catherine's face made Alan laugh. "Come now," he said. "This is 1984, and if you need a chaperone, I can assure you that Gwyneth will do a good job."

It did seem like a good idea; Catherine was feeling very tired. "Do you mind if I phone Frances? She'll worry if I don't."

"Certainly," said Alan. "While you do that, I'll go tell Gwyneth you're going to be our guest."

He left the room and Catherine picked up the phone. There was no dial. The operator answered and Catherine asked for the Blue Feathers Inn. It was Mildred who answered.

"May I speak to Frances O'Hara?" requested Catherine.

"Is that you, Miss, the American lady?"

"Yes, it is, Mildred."

"You had a telegram, Miss. It came this evening."

Catherine was curious and told Mildred to open it and read it to her.

"Oh, do you think I should, Miss?"

"Yes, I do. Now please read it." She could hear Mildred tearing open the envelope.

"It says," said Mildred, " 'I will be at the Blue Feathers tomorrow. Have some good news for you, Nickie.'" After reading the telegram, Mildred asked Catherine what she thought it might be.

Catherine smiled and told Mildred she had no idea and would she now put Miss O'Hara on the line.

"I can see her, Miss. She's by the fire with Lord Jason."

"Will you please get her, then?" asked Catherine, feeling impatient. She heard Mildred shouting in the foyer, and after a few seconds Frances was on the line.

"Hello. Is that you, Catherine?"

"Yes, Frances. I won't be back at the inn tonight." Trying to sound casual, she added, "I'll see you in the morning."

"Fine, Catherine. But where are you?"

"Honestly, Frances, I don't know. But everything's OK. See you in the morning. Bye now.''

Alan came into the room, carrying an old book. "Did you reach Frances?''

Catherine nodded, smiling at him. Alan smiled back and patted the settee with his hand. She went over and sat beside him.

"Feel like talking some more?" he asked.

"I'd like that. What are you reading?''

Alan stroked the old book gently, saying that he had something very interesting to show her. Feeling her heartbeat quicken, she watched him open the old yellow pages and run his finger through them till he found what he was looking for.

"Here now, read this," said Alan as he placed the book on her knee.

Lord David Strong William, having chosen for himself the maid of Manningstile Henlock as his bride, built for her a fine house. Waiting for his bride to come of age, he created the finest house in the shire. Having dutifully married this Welsh Lord, the maid kept secret a relationship with one named Gareth. When she was with child, Lord David believed he was not the father and turned his anger upon his young wife. After the child was born, he took it away to be brought up by a woodsman and his wife on one of his large estates. His anger and hurt never subsided, and because of his actions to all, he became known as Dark David.

Looking for the next page, Catherine was horrified to see that it was missing. She looked at Alan with bitter disappointment in her eyes.

"Do you know where the next page is?''

"No," said Alan. "I don't.''

"Well, does it say any more about Dark David?" He nodded, and she continued to read.

And with this summer's eve vow, she darkened the Welsh countryside. Lifting her hands high, covered with her Lord's blood, she threw herself down the steep cliff. It shall be recorded that the reliable churchmen of this village witnessed her curses that screamed from a broken heart. In his rightful line of heritage, Lord David Strong William, Brother of Lord....

Catherine stopped reading, her hands trembling; she looked at Alan for some consolation. He put his arms around her and they both stared at the old book.

Crying on his shoulder, she asked him, "What does it all mean? What's happening? Why me, why you?''

"I can't answer that," he said quietly. It was heaven to hold this girl who was the answer to everything he had ever wanted. As she clung to him, he knocked the old book onto the carpet. "Does it really matter, Catherine? Do you have to pursue something that might or might not have happened three hundred years ago?"

"I can't help it," she murmured. "It's a driving force. I wish I could forget it all and just stay with you like this forever."

Smiling, he gently pulled away. Still holding her shoulders, his dark eyes seemed to look deep inside her heart. "This is forever, Catherine; I want you to stay with me." He held her close again as she wept quietly.

The fire died down. Alan watched the flames diminish and felt content that the love of his life was fast asleep on his shoulder. Not wanting to disturb her, he laid her down gently and put a cushion under her head. Gwyneth came in to take the tray and asked if she should bring a blanket and a pillow.

"Yes, thank you," said Alan. "And bring a blanket for me. I'll just stay here in the chair."

Putting more coal on the fire, Alan then picked up the old book he had taken from his father's library and started to thumb through the pages. The unusual thing about this book was the fact that it was handwritten. Unfortunately, the book was started after the Strong William family had settled in Wales; prior to that time, there was hardly any record in the family archives. Throughout the generations, each eldest son had written a diary of the important events that had happened during his lifetime.

Alan wrinkled his brow. Why is that page missing? he wondered. Flipping through the book, his face softened as he saw his father's handwriting. His father's journal seemed lighter in tone and was full of family events, except for the war years. Now turning to the front of the book, he saw that two pages seemed to be stuck together. Gently, he pried them apart and was surprised at the newness of the paper. There was an ink blot that looked as though it had been made today. He tried to read the spidery writing, but couldn't make it out. He got up and went to the desk, put the book under the lamp, and searched the top drawer, taking out a magnifying glass. It looked like a woman's handwriting:

> *He who cannot find the page and does not wish*
> *to harm her,*
> *I speak to thee from days gone by and tell thee*
> *of thy karma.*
> *Thy cruel ways have now gone by and thou shalt*
> *make amends;*
> *Thou shalt know she too was paid, and then*
> *thy karma ends.*

Catherine stirred in her sleep, murmuring and calling out a name: *"Gareth."*

Who is this Gareth? thought Alan. If he stands between Catherine and me, I'm going to do something about it. Pondering that strange verse once again, Alan fell into a long, deep sleep, while Catherine tossed and turned, struggling through centuries of trauma that were now responsible for her tomorrows.

Chapter Six

Catherine woke early; the room was still dark. She didn't want to disturb Alan, so she lay there quietly, her mind pushing and pulling from reason to unreason. Raising herself so that she could see the dim profile of Alan in this chair, she thought she saw a strange light around him. She blinked her eyes—it was still there! Feeling a warm glow, she looked up and there was Gareth, urging her to leave with him. Speaking in a whisper, he told her that Patrick was waiting. She took his hand and they left quietly, not daring to waken Lord David Strong William.

In the garden outside, Megan asked, "Where is Patrick?"

"He is with thy mother; hurry now, before Lord David is upon us."

Lifting her up on the back of his chestnut horse, Gareth rode with her swiftly through the village to the Green Briar Inn. Fastening his horse, he led her through the back door into a tiny storage room. Her mother was there, wrapped in a shawl and holding baby Patrick.

"Daughter, thy wrongdoings cannot help thy bastard child," she hissed. "He shall find thee wherever thou hidest."

"Easy, old woman," said Gareth. "For we must hurry. Didst thou get the water and food?"

"Aye," she grumbled. "God be with thee, young fools, and may thy son live through thy curses."

Hastily kissing her mother, Megan took hold of the baby, who began to cry as he felt the warmth of his grandmother's body leave him.

"Sssh, little one," pleaded Megan as she followed Gareth into the night.

The lonely threesome rode through the night, coming into Cardiff in the early dawn. Needing rest, they stopped at the first inn and were thankful to sleep on fresh hay. They awoke to Patrick's cries. He was limping around on his tiny twisted foot needing food. Megan pulled out a thick crust of bread from her gown and gave it to the child.

Gareth looked weary; touching Megan gently, he said, "We had best be traveling again before Lord David's men are upon us."

Three days and three nights they fled from the pursuing soldiers. At last they arrived at their hiding place in a fishing village called Monretha, whence they planned to continue their journey by sea to escape the wrath of Lord David.

Captain Elvidge was uneasy. He knew that Lord David would not hesitate to cause him humiliation and deliver punishment if he failed to return with the woman and child. The rugged moors and thick undergrowth had impeded his pursuit of the pathetic runaways as they fled toward the sea coast. He and his soldiers had left without the usual provisions, so as dusk began to fall, they approached the village of Monretha and took lodging at a local tavern, the Mariners Inn.

Away from the discipline of Lord David's estate, the soldiers enjoyed the freedom of ale, food and village girls. Captain Elvidge planned to have his soldiers leave early in the morning, allowing small intervals between their departures to enable them to travel the treacherous sea road more easily.

Waking with the early light, the smell of wet leather and stale ale in his nostrils, Captain Elvidge alerted his soldiers to the task of the day. They were clumsy, slow and thick-headed; too much ale impeded the Captain's effort to continue the search for the runaways. Standing now, fastening his buckle and roaring his commands, the Captain belched and swore at the pouring rain.

Unknown to the soldiers, Megan and Gareth were not far away. After finding refuge at the village chapel, Gareth had ventured out to get milk for Patrick. Walking through the dark village, he quickly realized that the bawdy songs and loud voices coming from the tavern were those of Lord David's men. Not wanting to frighten Megan, he told her that the soldiers were in the village and that they should sleep only a few hours, then be on their way long before the soldiers arose.

Exhausted, Megan and Gareth fell asleep; fear twisted Megan's heart. She was weary and Patrick had been difficult. Continually crying his discomfort, he was making the escape even more harrowing.

It was Patrick's crying that woke Megan and Gareth. The rain was heavy and the sky was dark, the threatening clouds rumbling. Gareth immediately felt a sense of dread, realizing that they had slept too long. Trying not to raise any fears in Megan, he suggested that they move swiftly and leave the chapel, disregarding the rain, for he thought that the soldiers would surely search there. He had a friend of many years in the village who he was sure would shelter them awhile.

Meanwhile, Captain Elvidge commanded his men to search the village before they left. He himself talked to the fishermen. The villagers were sullen and uncooperative, which raised the Captain's suspicion. Leaving a guard by the boats and directing his soldiers to continue the search, he went back to the Mariners Inn to rest.

Hidden in the cellar of Gareth's friend, Henry Owen, Patrick began to cry. His crying turned to screaming as Megan tried to comfort him. They had decided to wait until the soldiers gave up their search of the village. They were warm and comfortable after a good meal provided by kindly Henry. Patrick at length seemed to respond to the need for silence, and feeling assured that he would be all right with Megan, Gareth kissed her tenderly and told her not to worry for he would be back soon. He was going down to the docks to find a boat for their escape.

After Gareth left, Megan felt comfortable and easy for the first time since they had escaped. Talking gently to Patrick, she watched him play, letting gentle, happy pictures of Gareth and herself filter through her mind. Suddenly, she heard heavy boots and loud voices. She held Patrick tightly, feeling disaster approach. All was quiet for a moment, and then the door at the top of the cellar steps burst open. It was Captain Elvidge, grinning broadly. He had found his master's prize!

Refusing to listen to Megan's pleas for mercy, the Captain took the child and handed him to one of his soldiers. Ordering Megan to follow him, the Captain left a guard by the cellar with orders to bring Gareth to him immediately when he returned.

Captain Elvidge had made no attempt to be discreet about finding Megan and Patrick. The village was immediately alerted, and Gareth soon discovered what had happened. He was alone and had no means of rescuing Megan and the child. He knew the soldiers would not harm her or the little one, so he decided to make his way back home and plan another attempt to rescue his love.

Gareth had long been Megan's sweetheart. When she had been chosen to be Lord David's wife, she had continued to see him in secret whenever she could. All had been well until she had become pregnant. Lord David's anger had been like fury from hell; somehow he knew that the child was not his. Yet he kept it and gave it his name.

He had even forgiven her for running away, now that she was safely returned to him. But unknown to him, Gareth continued to pursue Megan. Although he had nothing to offer her, he loved her and wanted her and the child to run away with him again. This time, he assured her, they would succeed.

Megan was torn; the decision was not an easy one. After Lord David's anger had subsided, he began to care for the child, treating him like a son. To stay with him would be wiser for Patrick's sake. But Gareth needed her too, and she loved him still, despite his desertion of her when the soldiers took them. He would come to her in the night and they would huddle together, planning their escape from Lord David's domination forever....

The light around Alan's head was stronger now. Catherine knew she had been back again, into the past.

Alan stirred, and she took off one of her blankets and put it around him. Kneeling by his chair, she looked at his face. His hands were sensitive; they could have been the hands of a pianist. Wanting to touch his face, she reached out, but was afraid to waken him. She was content to sit beside him and feel his strength. The light over his head now seemed to have the colors of a rainbow. It fascinated her: she reached out her fingers, wanting to touch the multihued aura. Suddenly, she realized that if she touched the arc above his head, she would have his blood on her fingers from another time—another life. It was important now to try and understand her relationship with this man.

I have loved him, she thought. Or do I love him now? Reaching out to touch his hair, her fingertips now a part of the radiance of his soul, she, Catherine, again became Megan.

Patrick was growing healthy and happy. Lord David had been away, as he was much of the time. She heard the horses arrive in the courtyard. Soon Lord David came up the stairs and into her room.

"Look what I have brought thee, Megan."

Like a child, she eagerly reached out for his gift. The candle was still lit and she leaned forward, her red hair hanging loosely over her bare white shoulders. She looked up and smiled shyly at Lord David as she took the gift, a lovely Celtic brooch. He had not been in her bed since she had betrayed him with the child. He looked at her lovely face but as he bent and kissed her, she recoiled and dropped the pin he had brought her. She saw his anger and held the sheet to cover herself. He tore it away from her and grabbing her hair, seemed to devour her with fierce kisses such as she had never known.

Her love with Gareth had been gentle—two young lovers exploring, both surprised by their own passion, but never venturing too far....

But this was different: David was a man and wanted his wife. He aroused in her the woman she didn't know existed. Forgetting everything, she responded to his awakening of her fervently....

The candle had burned low. She lay exhausted in his strong arms. Her life had seemed to change utterly in just a few minutes. Turning to him, she smiled and kissed his forehead gently. A look of pain came over his face, for he wanted his wife to love only him and be his alone.

"Dost thou love me, Megan?" he asked.

"Aye, my lord, and I promise thee I will lie in no other bed."

Her words infuriated him. He held her roughly and asked if Gareth's bed had given her more pleasure.

"Please, David, do not speak so cruelly. Let not thy words lie heavy in my heart. I loved Gareth as a girl, but you I have loved as a woman...and a wife."

Feeling bitterness but needing her love, this huge man wept. Trying to console him, she put her arms around him, rocking him like a baby. After a while, they lay peacefully together as man and wife, with all hurt melting away into the night.

Then it was dawn. Someone was knocking on the window: Gareth.

Lord David smiled as he opened his eyes and saw Megan at the window. Then he saw Gareth! Roaring like a lion, he reached for his sword, pushed Megan away and thrust his blade into Gareth's breast.

Gareth's eyes, his sorrowful grey eyes, bored into Megan's as he fell backwards into the courtyard below.

"*Gareth,*" she screamed. "*Gareth!*"

Lord David wiped his brow and looked with contempt at Megan. "Take thy bastard and never let me see thee again!" he shouted.

"Please, David, please listen to me." She knelt before him. Patrick limped into the room, hearing all the commotion.

"Mama, Mama." He pulled at her skirt urgently.

Still looking at Lord David, she ignored the child, and he went to play by the window.

"Come here, child and be with thy mother," roared David.

Running to his mother, the child began to cry. Megan held him tightly.

Two men, young and tall, suddenly ran into the room. One was Dylan, brother of Gareth, and the other his friend Timothy. Dylan's face was torn with grief. Blinded with tears, he let out a blood-curdling scream and thrust a knife into Lord David's heart. As the big man fell to the floor, he looked up at Megan, saying, "This is not the end." But it was, and the child played on the floor beside his body, laughing as he smeared blood on his tiny hands and face.

This macabre scene was too much for Megan. She ran sobbing and screaming down the stairs and out into the courtyard. Dylan pursued her with Patrick slung under his arm. She ran toward the cliff and in her tormented mind saw Lord David standing there saying, "This is not the end."

Lifting her bloody arms in the air to hold him, she leaped off the steep cliff. As she fell, she saw the sorrowful grey eyes of Gareth. The last voice she heard was Patrick's, calling, *"Mama, Mama!"*

Chapter Seven

Catherine awoke just before Megan reached the bottom of the cliff. Opening her eyes, she saw Alan standing there, smiling, with a cup of tea in his hand.

"How are you this morning?"

She shook her head. "I've got to be alone, Alan. Please take me home."

Looking hurt, he smiled again and asked if she would like breakfast.

"No, thank you. I must get back to the inn."

"What's wrong?"

Pulling her thoughts together, she tried to remember that she was Catherine Holmes from Los Angeles, California and had to see things the way Catherine Holmes would.

"Sorry, Alan. I had a rotten dream or whatever, and there's so much happening to me that I need to tell you...If you'll take me back to the Blue Feathers, I promise that when my friend Nickie arrives we'll all get together and I'll explain what I think I know."

"Fair enough," said Alan. "But please eat some breakfast first."

Riding along the beautiful Welsh countryside was a wonderful experience for Catherine, and she now realized that her dreams were not dreams at all. They were real happenings and she, through some mysterious fluke, was actually experiencing a previous life. The main characters were now alive as different personalities. She knew these lanes, she knew Manningstile Henlock. She wondered what all this meant. Why was this happening to her? What could possibly have triggered it all off?

Alan suggested that he stay and help get the group together.

Catherine felt relieved, glad that Alan was staying. She had a lot to say and do. Her mood gradually changed as they arrived in the village. Somehow she felt really close to Alan, yet it frightened her when she remembered what had happened in the early hours of this morning.

"I wonder what time Nickie will arrive?" she asked Alan.

"We'll soon find out. When we get back to the Blue Feathers, I'll phone the airport."

It was a beautiful morning, and the village looked like a picture postcard. Happy to arrive back at the inn, Catherine met Mr. Thornleigh at the door.

He smiled and asked, "Could I have a word with you, Miss?" Then, seeing Alan, he touched his cap and said, "Good morning, m'lord. I took the liberty of booking a room for your friend, who will be arriving in about half an hour, I'd say."

"That's wonderful, Mr. Thornleigh," said Catherine. "Did she call?"

"Yes, Miss, she rang about an hour ago. Should be well on her way now. And oh, Miss O'Hara is waiting in the sun lounge with Miss Sheridan."

"Who is Miss Sheridan?" asked Catherine.

"Local lady, a bit of a writer, among other things."

"Thank you." Catherine went to see Frances, leaving Alan chatting with the landlord.

"I'll be right in, Catherine. Just go ahead, I'll find you," Alan said, smiling.

Frances was talking, and the lady by her side was listening intently. When Frances saw Catherine, she got up, put her arms around her and introduced her to Miss Sheridan.

Catherine liked Miss Sheridan and invited her to join them for lunch. Then, looking at her watch, she explained that Nickie was arriving from the States in a short while and that she wanted to freshen up.

"Let's all meet down here at 12:30," said Catherine, and ran up the stairs to shower and put on her robe. About a half-hour later, the phone rang and Catherine felt excited when she heard Nickie's voice.

"Where are you, Catherine?"

Laughing, Catherine replied, "Come on up the stairs, second door on the right. I can't come down, I've just showered."

"I'll be right there. By the way, Catherine, got to tell you about this good-looking guy. I think I'm going to enjoy Wales. Be sure to be sitting down when I get there. I've got something to tell you that will flip your lid."

"Why? Are you pregnant?" Still laughing, Catherine put down the phone, wrapped a towel around her head and opened the door just as Nickie was about to knock. Both girls hugged each other as though it had been years since they had last met. Laughing and talking at the same time, they didn't see Alan watching them. Hearing his deep voice, Catherine's heart started to beat faster.

"Well, this is certainly a great reunion," he said kindly.

Nickie was surprised to see the man she had admired downstairs. "Aren't you going to introduce me, Catherine?"

Catherine invited them both into her room and offered to call downstairs for some coffee. Deciding it was too near lunchtime, they declined. Catherine didn't know whether to ask why Nickie was here or to start preparing her for all that had happened. Realizing she was not yet dressed, she excused herself and went to put on her jeans and shirt.

Relieved now that she could at last talk to someone about her fantastic news, Nickie shouted, "Hurry, Catherine."

"I'm coming," said Catherine, walking back into the room, looking lovely, her blonde hair shining. She reached out toward Nickie and told her how good it was to see her.

"Well, aren't you going to ask me why I'm here?"

"Why are you here?" asked Catherine, laughing.

Pushing the envelope into Catherine's hands, Nickie said, "Read this."

No one spoke as Catherine read the letter. With no emotion at all, she turned to Nickie. "This is absolutely incredible. My whole life has turned upside down. I feel like I'm on a merrygo-round. I don't think I can honestly take any more excitement in one day. What do you think of it, Alan?" she asked as she gave him the letter.

Alan stroked his beard and seemed to take his time digesting the contents of the letter.

"Were you close to your Uncle Alfred?" he asked Catherine.

"I've never heard of him."

Alan reached out and put his arm around her. Trying to sound lighthearted, he smiled and said, "Now, it can't be all that bad, can it?"

Feeling that her head might burst at any moment, Catherine said she must hurry and finish dressing because they would all be waiting downstairs for lunch.

After Catherine had gone into the bathroom, Nickie asked Alan what he thought of the letter. Pulling out his Mont Blanc pen and unscrewing the top, he started to write in his leather notebook:

1. Why has Catherine no knowledge of her uncle?

2. Who is Jonathan Whiteside?

3. Why must they meet specifically on August 8th following the uncle's death?

4. What are the conditions to be met before Catherine can claim her inheritance?

5. How did Jonathan Whiteside know that Catherine was in the United Kingdom?

6. How did he know that she was in Manningstile Henlock?

7. How did he know about Nickie?

All the time Alan was writing, Nickie watched him, a look of amazement on her face.

Alan turned and smiling, asked, "Something wrong?"

She told him how amazed she was that he could take an apparently simple letter and ask so many questions about it that she hadn't even thought of. "Oh, I'll admit it made me think a bit when they knew where Catherine was, and also about me, but apart from that, I never gave it another thought."

"That was the writer's intention," said Alan, filling his pipe again.

"The way you put it makes it sound real scary. What do you think Catherine should do?"

Putting the letter back in the envelope and into his inside jacket pocket, he said, "Well, Nickie, right now I'm not going to do anything till Catherine settles down and sorts out one or two things."

"You know, I expected her to be real excited, but it's like an anticlimax."

Alan told her not to worry and looking at his watch, called out the time to Catherine.

"Coming right now," she answered. "Has anyone called?"

"No," said Nickie, looking anxiously at Catherine.

"Shall we go then, ladies?" asked Alan, offering both arms.

Frances, happy to see Catherine coming downstairs, went over to meet her, saying that Mr. Thornleigh had come up with a good suggestion.

"What kind of suggestion?" asked Catherine.

"Well, I was telling him that we were all getting together for lunch, and he offered to let us have a private room just down the hall for no extra money."

"That's a fine idea," said Alan. "Shall we go?"

The table was set nicely and the paneled room was furnished with antiques. On the table were brass candlesticks holding tall, thin, blue tapered candles. Mildred came in and told Alan that Jason was on the line.

Excusing himself, Alan went to the desk phone. Jason wanted to know what was going on.

Before Alan could answer, Jason said, "I'll be right over," then hung up.

Joining the group still talking in the foyer, Alan told Catherine that Jason had just invited himself and asked if she minded.

"Who's Jason?" asked Nickie.

"That's Alan's brother," answered Catherine.

"This is getting better all the time," said Nickie, smiling.

"Now, let's see, how many are we?" asked Catherine, to no one in particular. Not waiting for an answer, she counted on her fingers: "Alan and Jason, Frances and Miss Sheridan, Nickie and myself; that makes six. Shall we all sit down?"

Alan sat by her and they continued talking, yet there was a feeling of apprehension in the room.

"Phone call for you." Catherine turned around when she heard Mildred's voice.

It was Jason on the line.

"Hello, Catherine, did Alan mention I was on my way down?"

"Yes," said Catherine. "We'll be having lunch in one of Mr. Thornleigh's private rooms. Will you be long?"

"No. As a matter of fact, I wanted to ask you if you would mind my bringing another guest. If you remember, I was going to bring him to dinner with you and Frances last night. His name's George Stern."

Catherine sighed. "What difference can one more make?" Then laughing, "It'll make odd numbers around the table." There was a pause.

"Not really," said Jason. "You see, through George I met this woman who's really into reincarnation. Before you say anything, I'll foot the bill."

"Haven't you heard?" said Catherine. "I've just come into an inheritance—if I fulfill the requirements."

"What on earth are you saying?" asked Jason, laughing.

"Oh, nothing. We'll talk more when I see you. How long will you be?"

Jason told her that he would be there in five minutes, as he was having a drink with his two guests in the Black Bull just down the street.

Alan was waiting at her side and smiled as she turned around. "I gather that was Jason. What's he up to now?"

"He wants to bring a couple of friends to lunch. They sound as though they might be interesting."

Joining the other guests, they sat down and almost immediately were drawn into the friendly conversation. Deep in thought, Catherine wondered whether or not this luncheon was such a good idea!

"Hello, everyone," she heard Jason say behind her a little later.

"Let me introduce Hilary and George."

"My word," said Frances. "Looks like we're having a party."

Everyone seemed in a lighthearted mood. Catherine had hoped that by talking everything out, she would have some answers. But it didn't look as though this group was in the mood to listen to her. Not wanting to change the party atmosphere, she threw herself into small talk and sipped her wine, which helped to mellow her piercing thoughts.

Lunch was delicious. The Welsh seemed to feed you as though it were your last meal, appetizing and fattening. Talking to George across the table, Catherine stopped abruptly when she heard Alan tap on his wine glass. The others stopped and waited to hear what Alan had to say. He took it upon himself to try and explain briefly what had been happening to Catherine during the past few days. There was perfect silence as he related the events. Catherine found herself enthralled; it was difficult to believe that all these things had happened to her in such a short while. Then Alan suggested that everyone at the table introduce himself or herself and give a bit of personal information. He volunteered to start.

"My name is Lord Alan Griffiths, and with me today is my brother Jason, who, I have no doubt, will tell you all about himself." Smiling, Alan continued. "I am not, and never have been, prone to having dreams...that I can remember, that is. But for some time now, I have been experiencing a haunting dream, and although I cannot remember exactly what it is about, I know that Catherine is a principal character in it. Considering that I have only just met Catherine, I realize my story seems incredible." He started to puff on his pipe; leaning back in his chair, he noted mentally that he had the full attention of everyone there.

"So that there can be no question about my behavior toward Catherine, I want you all to know something that I haven't yet told her."

Catherine furrowed her brow; everyone seemed glued to their chairs.

"I love Catherine Holmes and I want to marry her."

Catherine looked astounded. Nickie's jaw dropped. Frances clapped her hands in delight.

"Bravo, let's make a toast!" Jason shouted.

Miss Sheridan was terribly intrigued. After all, this was *the* Lord Griffiths, falling for an American girl he had only just met. George asked if he could give Catherine a kiss, and Hilary smiled like a cheshire cat.

After making this remarkable announcement, Alan leaned over to Catherine and whispered, "Regardless of anything or anyone, living or dead, I do love you." Then he kissed her, and Catherine made no attempt to stop him.

Feeling embarrassed, she smiled and tried to avoid the look on

Nickie's face.

"I am the not-too-younger brother of Don Juan," Jason said, continuing the introductions. "Incidentally, it was I who had the pleasure of meeting Frances and Catherine first. I am a writer and a bachelor, and my favorite hobby is psychic research. I have a flat in London's West End and came to my mother's to write at Cardiff House."

Frances took it to be her turn next and told everyone how close she felt to Catherine, and looking down to avoid Alan's face, she added, "And I feel very close to Alan, too. What is so exciting is that I was prepared for a perfectly ordinary holiday. As soon as I met Catherine, I knew that we had a deep affinity for each other. My mother was Welsh and my father was Irish. I'm a librarian and I have lived a happy life. I had my share of sadness, but I can honestly say I've been contented with my lot."

There was silence for a few moments, for Frances had put her feelings beautifully. Nickie thought, She seems younger once she starts to talk, and she really is a lovely woman.

"Just one thing more," Frances continued. "I have an intriguing hobby, if you can call it that. I have studied Tarot and I'm becoming quite good at it. Through practice, I have developed quite a sensitivity. I study and use the cards a lot."

Miss Sheridan sat upright in her chair. Her small, round body looked like a pleasantly plump teddy bear. Still wearing a small grey hat, she gave one the impression of being a nannie or something like that. Breathing deeply, she was preparing herself for her turn. Glad of the opportunity to let everyone know of her talents, she began:

"My name is Martha Sheridan. I have never married because I haven't had the time." This remark made the other women smile. "I have always been interested in history and used to teach at the village school here in Manningstile Henlock. I was to have been away today on business, but Miss O'Hara was rather insistent that I stay and join you. Penrithy Cottage, where I live, is one of the oldest cottages in the village and originally belonged to the village blacksmith. It was his daughter, Megan of Manningstile Henlock, who married into Lord Griffiths' family in 1502. As a matter of fact, I have done a lot of research on local history and have written articles that have been published in Cardiff and as far away as Harlech. I'm not a Spiritualist or anything like that, having been brought up as a strict Baptist; but because of the unusual happenings in my cottage and other places around here, I have become interested in the unknown."

Miss Sheridan's voice seemed to drop an octave as she said, "the unknown." Not sure whether she had finished or not, everyone remained politely quiet until Nickie took it upon herself to keep the party going.

"Well, I'll jump right in here," she said, smiling. "My name is Nickie Foster. I was born in Brooklyn, New York. I met Catherine when we were in school and we've been close friends for quite some years. I love her dearly and I came to Wales for the first time today to be the giver of what I thought was fantastic news. Anyway, I haven't had much time to discover how Catherine feels right now, but before she left the States, weird things were happening, let me tell you. God knows what it's all about. If I can, I'll help her sort things out."

Nickie was a pretty, vivacious girl with short, dark, curly hair and a smile as big as a sunrise. Rubbing her earring thoughtfully, she went on:

"Alan mentioned having dreams. I've also had dreams I can't really remember. Sometimes something has happened and it's as though I get a terrific insight just for a second or so and then it goes. I know this must sound crazy, but that's the best way I can describe it."

There was a good feeling now in the room. Everyone was excited, and after Nickie had finished, Jason asked Hilary if she would like to say a few words.

One word fitted Hilary: glamourous. She had big brown appealing eyes; her hair was light brown and pulled back into a sleek-looking bun. Her plain dark silk dress enhanced her slim legs, which were crossed comfortably. While everyone had been listening to whomever was talking, Hilary had been observing Catherine. Although Hilary looked like she had stepped out of a fashion magazine, she was obviously a woman with character. Speaking in a melodious English voice, she began:

"People find it hard to believe that I'm really Hilary Haddock. I've grown to like my name, although when I was young I hated it." Lifting up her left hand, she pointed to her wedding band. "I'm married to a journalist, Mike Wilcox, but I chose to keep my own name. Mike is on assignment in Canada. We are very much in love, and I work in a laboratory as a biochemist, which doesn't allow me much freedom to go on trips with Mike, although I have taken a few. Because of certain happenings in my life, I am a true believer in the law of karma and reincarnation. I would like to be a writer like Jason, but I don't seem to have the flair or whatever it takes. Anyway, I met Jason through George, who was helping Jason with his book. I was invited here at quick notice." She smiled at Jason. "And I'm very happy I was."

George looked like an athlete, not particularly good-looking, not as handsome as Alan, but definitely attractive. He was a quiet man and a school teacher. Coughing to clear his throat, he said, "I'm afraid there isn't much to tell you. I'm a bachelor. I don't like teaching, but they say I do a good job."

Nickie intervened. "What would you like to be, George?"

"A farmer, I think," he replied. Looking around the table to see how everyone reacted, he paused for a while, then, "I had some unexplainable things happen to me, but only when I was near certain people. At first I brushed them off, but then they happened more often."

"What happened?" asked Nickie.

"Well, I would somehow know a lot about someone, but it never made any sense."

"Like what?" asked Frances.

"Well, I can talk to a certain person and I'm immediately drawn to another time and place, and even though the person doesn't look the same, I know, I really know, that it's the same person I'm talking to. I really don't have anything more to say." He looked embarrassed and pretended not to be.

"You're all very kind to be here with me," Catherine said, "and I'm not sure what we should do next, but I have a feeling that we're all going to be a little wiser by the time we leave."

Frances broke the awkward silence. "I feel as though I'm part of a huge jigsaw puzzle, and every time I look at someone, I wonder how they fit!"

Alan took his cue from there and said that possibly Frances was right. Maybe in some spiritual way, their souls had been entwined. Jason said that maybe they should ask Hilary, as she was the expert.

"Thank you for your confidence in me, Jason," she said. "I don't pretend to know the answers, but I believe that the soul lives on through several lifetimes and through these lifetimes gathers experience. The law of karma is the law of cause and effect, which simply means that we reap what we sow. During these lifetimes, we have an impact on other souls and sometimes we are privileged to tune into past lives. At this point, I would take a guess and say that this is what has happened to Catherine. To understand karma, we must forget who we are now— our personality and present lifestyle—for if we are to believe in past lives, we must also understand that although the soul, or spirit, is still the same, the person we become, through the life we live at a particular time, is entirely different. It's hard to see yourself as a thief or murderer, perhaps. Or it may be difficult to see yourself rich, if you've never had a worthwhile bank account. And it can be almost impossible to see yourself as another sex."

At the word "sex," Miss Sheridan shifted uncomfortably and looked at her watch. Not that she intended to go anywhere, she was far too engrossed in today's happenings. Hilary asked if anyone had any questions.

Nickie was the first to respond. "Well, what do you think is happening to Catherine, then?"

Wetting her lips, Hilary thought for a moment. "It's not possible for me to say exactly what's happening to Catherine, but I can say that I've read many cases where people with traumatic past lives have been inundated with glimpses from the past; it's almost as though they have to find a way to understand and possibly make amends. The soul grows by these many experiences and in between lives chooses a certain life pattern which it knows will improve its journey. Listening to Catherine's story and oversimplifying her experience, we could say that something has happened in previous lives that has to be understood before she can progress. Another theory associated with reincarnation is that groups of souls interlock, as in a stage play, and each time a life is experienced, they play different characters. This is often referred to as group karma."

"Do you think we are all involved in Catherine's karma?" asked Frances.

"Who knows?" answered Hilary. "It's possible, I suppose. But it certainly would be gratifying to know for certain."

"I'm more interested in finding out whatever I can about Catherine," said Jason. If I should happen to be involved and find another me in her story, I would probably spend the rest of my life writing and trying to convince the world about reincarnation."

Miss Sheridan wanted to make sure that she wasn't being excluded from this exclusive group. After all, she thought, they are quite decent. Not too bad, really. Not having many friends always put her on the defensive, so if she could relax a little and show them she was enjoying everything, maybe they would include her in their research. Trying hard to wait for the right moment to say something worthwhile, she suggested that they could use her cottage anytime they all wanted to meet.

"How about hypnosis, Catherine?" asked George.

Everyone stopped talking and waited to see what Catherine would say.

"I don't mind," she replied. "As long as I'm in safe hands."

"Who would do it?" asked Frances. "Does anyone here know how to hypnotize people?"

George said that he had tried it on several friends and although he hadn't had a hundred per cent success, he felt that that was due to the subject and not necessarily his method.

Alan said that perhaps they were jumping the gun; before Catherine allowed herself to be hypnotized, she should have time to think it over. "How about all of us meeting this evening after dinner?"

They all agreed, and Miss Sheridan asked if they would like to come to Penrithy Cottage.

"All in favor, say 'aye,'" said Jason. The group voted in favor of meeting at Miss Sheridan's that evening.

Chapter Eight

As the group began to disperse, Nickie went over to Catherine. "Got a minute?" she shouted over the babble of the crowd.

Pleased at the opportunity to leave, Catherine smiled and excused herself from Miss Sheridan, who was busily trying to plan the evening. Reaching the door, she shouted "Bye" to everyone and said she would see them at Miss Sheridan's.

At the mention of her name, Miss Sheridan looked at the carpet rather coyly and was a little disappointed to find that no one was looking when she slowly raised her eyes again.

The men, who were still talking by the window, decided they would like to have a drink and asked if any of the women would like to join them. Miss Sheridan gave a tight little smile and said that she wanted to hurry along and pick up some pies and pastries for that evening on her way home. Alan offered to pay for the refreshments, and Miss Sheridan accepted the money, promising to give him the change later. The three men, Frances and Hilary went down to the bar.

Frances was feeling terribly excited and thought that this was the best holiday she had ever had. It was just wonderful to be so relaxed and not worry about time. Everyone was so very nice. Finding a big oak table by the window, they all sat down, waiting for Mr. Thornleigh to take their order.

"Well, what do you think of it all?" asked Jason.

Alan was the first to answer. "Quite frankly, Jason, I wish Catherine would drop the whole thing. I think she's had more than enough excitement for one day."

"Oh, I don't agree," said Frances quietly. "If she doesn't attempt to make any sense of it, she'll never be satisfied. When I met her in the railway refreshment room, she was in a bad way. Poor thing, I feel sorry for her...I think we should all do our best to help her straighten the whole thing out."

Mr. Thornleigh came over with the drinks and winked at Frances.

Wonder why he keeps doing that? thought Frances as she deliberately turned away.

Jason leaned over, his eyes full of mischief, and whispered to Frances, "I think old Tom there fancies you."

Laughing and blushing at the same time, she told Jason he must be out of his head. Just for sheer devilment, Jason asked Tom if he wanted to join them.

"Don't mind if I do," smiled Tom as he pulled over a chair from another table and tried to wedge it between Jason and Frances.

"Seems like you're all enjoying yourselves," said Tom, rubbing his hands on his trouser legs. Turning to Hilary, he furrowed his forehead as though trying to puzzle something out. Hilary smiled, and Tom, nearly shouting, said, "Now I remember where I've seen you, Miss! On the television, right?"

Nodding and still smiling, Hilary opened her cigarette case and offered everyone a cigarette.

"The minute I saw you, I knew I'd seen you somewhere before," said Tom jubilantly. "You're into all this psychic stuff, aren't you? It was a good program, I really enjoyed it. Don't know much about the subject matter, but I find it interesting."

Hilary thanked him and told him how much she enjoyed the Blue Feathers. "Is it haunted?" she asked.

Tom half smiled and rubbing his head, told her that people often said it was. This last remark got everyone's attention, including George's, who didn't have much to say about anything but was a perfect listener.

Anxious to know as much as possible, Jason asked if Tom could tell them some interesting stories about the inn.

Finishing his last drop of beer and wiping his lips on the back of his hand, Tom leaned back in his chair and said, "Funny you should ask that. Miss O'Hara here also wanted some information."

Frances interrupted him. "Please, why don't you call me Frances?"

"As I was about to say," continued Tom, "after Frances asked me, I decided to look in the old chest we have upstairs and see what I could find. I came up with some interesting things."

Unable to contain himself, Jason asked, "What interesting things?"

"For example, the Manor House, as it was called then, was built in 1493, or at least that's when the building started." Then, looking at Alan and Jason, Tom added, "By your ancestors, I believe, gentlemen.''

Deeply intrigued, both girls looked at each other excitedly. Tom continued.

"Lord Featherstone was granted the deed to the Manor House given as a dutiful and generous dowry on his betrothal to Mary Strong William, the beloved daughter of Lord and Lady Henry Strong William. Funny thing is, I know this was your family, Lord Griffiths, but there was a Lord David Strong William. I know you are Lord Alan Strong Griffiths, so I don't understand the relationship.''

Jason said, "Alan, Keeper of the Book, should know the answer to that one.''

"What does 'Keeper of the Book' mean?'' asked Hilary.

Alan told them that the eldest son was given custody of a family record book and it was his duty to enter all the family events during his lifetime from the time he came of age until his death.

"And it is now in my hands,'' said Alan solemnly. Crossing his legs and puffing on his pipe, he looked at Tom and said, "To answer your question concerning Lord Featherstone and our family name of Griffiths: It was Lord Henry Strong William, I think, who didn't have any sons, and in 1682 his daughter Mary married Lord Featherstone, whom she met when she was a ward of the court. He came from Lincolnshire in England. For a time Lady Featherstone became Keeper of the Book. In studying the records, I've seen evidence of a feminine handwriting. Before the birth of her child Rose, her husband died of a strange fever while in London. He apparently received care from the finest doctors, but they couldn't save him.''

"Whew, what a story,'' said Frances.

"This book,'' said George quietly. "How is it written?''

"Like a diary,'' said Alan. "But some of it is hard to decipher and part of it is missing.''

"Why is that?'' asked Jason.

"I'm not really sure,'' said Alan. "But now that I think of it, I'm sure that the missing part would answer some of our questions.''

No one spoke for a few moments, their thoughts like rapidly moving wheels.

"What happened to the Manor?'' asked George.

"No one really knows the whole story,'' said Alan. "After the death of her husband, Lady Featherstone left the village.''

"You say there was a child of that marriage?'' asked Hilary. "What happened to the child?''

"The child remained at the Manor House and the sister of Lady Featherstone brought her up. It was this child, Rose Featherstone, who married Lord Griffiths.''

"This is absolutely intriguing,'' said Hilary. "How on earth can you possibly remember all this?''

"My father would tell us both as boys about our family history and show us the family portraits over and over again. But there is so much mystery in our family. And now Catherine has appeared in my life and has become a part of the past and my present."

Upstairs, Catherine and Nickie were finally alone.

"There's so much to tell you, Nickie. This whole thing is getting deeper, and I just don't know my own feelings anymore."

Putting her arms around the back of the chair, Nickie was deep in thought. Not knowing what to say or how she could help, she asked Catherine if she had any scotch.

"No," replied Catherine. "It's better to go downstairs to the bar. There's no way to keep ice up here anyway."

Changing the tone of her voice, Nickie said, "Then let's go. After a good drink, I might come up with a brainstorm."

No one was in the bar. Tom Thornleigh came over and asked the girls for their order. He told them that he had enjoyed the "get-together" and was looking forward to this evening.

Tom Thornleigh ran a good business. There was no chore too demeaning for this kind and hard-working man. He had been a widower for a number of years and had a son working as an accountant in Cardiff. Being in the hotel business gave him the opportunity he needed to be among people. Nothing pleased him more than to see guests in the foyer walking up and down stairs or sitting in the bar with a drink. Tom liked to read; his favorite books were mysteries. This afternoon had a speck of mystery, thought Tom, and he was looking forward to helping solve this whole situation.

Listening to Catherine talk pleased Nickie. She thought it was good for her friend to unwind and relax for a while. Nickie didn't have any answers, but she was burning to ask a question. She chose a time when she felt Catherine had talked it all out.

"Who is your Uncle Alfred?"

"Honestly, Nickie, I never knew I had one."

Unwilling to accept this answer, Nickie asked Catherine to think—think really hard.

"It's no use, Nickie. I tell you, I don't know, and that's the end of that."

Scraping her finger around the top of the glass, Nickie said, "I don't think it is, Catherine. I know you're having these visions and things, but try to forget them for a minute and concentrate on reality—like now, for instance. It's 1984 and someone has left you something in a will. Now, this is a fact—It's happening right now. Just imagine there's a bent-over old man with wispy sideburns wanting to meet you at the classy Biltmore Hotel, near the ocean in California, and all he wants to do is to give little Catherine a bag o' money."

Catherine's face broke out in smiles. She couldn't help feeling how good it was to have Nickie around again. "What do you think about tonight?"

"Let tonight take care of itself. Now let me ask you a question. What do you think of Alan?"

Shaking her head slowly, Catherine hesitated, then said, "I've never felt this way with anyone else. I know there's something, but I honestly can't explain it. I know him, Nickie; I really know this man. But how can I? It doesn't make any sense."

"Well, that leaves me with a good second choice—that Jason isn't bad at all."

"How about George?" said Catherine, laughing.

"Well, I'll have to think about that. He's so quiet. You know, I nearly jumped out of my shoes when he spoke. Gotta admit he's got a deep, sexy voice, though."

"Look at the time," said Catherine. "We'd better hurry and get ready."

Both girls felt better now that they had had a good talk; Catherine felt nearly back to normal. Deciding to do her nails while Nickie bathed, Catherine put on the radio, and the song that kept haunting her—"Green, Green Grass of Home"—played very softly.

Back in her room, Frances kicked off her shoes and put her feet up on the bed. She tried to read a magazine, but her thoughts continued to explore the possible explanations for the coming together of all these people. Holding a wet washrag on her foot, which although swollen, wasn't paining her, she thought about Tom Thornleigh. He was a nice man and seemed to be attracted to her, or was that her imagination? Closing her eyes and lying back on the pillow, she smiled to herself, thinking what a fantastic holiday this was.

Arriving back at his cottage, Alan went to the library and opened the safe to get out his family record book. He thumbed through the old leaves, making notes now and then on a yellow legal pad. Gwyneth came into the room and asked Alan if he would like some refreshment.

He murmured, "No, thank you." She then went to add a log to the fire. "I'll be out for dinner this evening, Gwyneth," he said. "Why don't you go and visit your family?"

"Thank you, m'lord," said Gwyneth, grateful to have an evening off to spend some time with her sister.

Deeply involved in the book, Alan lit his pipe and eagerly searched for any clues that would help to settle the strange events of the past few days.

Kissing his mother politely on the cheek, Jason bent toward the fireplace to warm his hands. Rubbing them together, he asked Lady Margaret if she were still embroidering the same pillow case.

Glancing at him over the top of her reading glasses, Lady Margaret smiled and asked if Jason would be staying for dinner.

"No, thank you, Mother. I'm going to have dinner with Alan and some friends from the U.S.A. You know, Catherine and Frances, and some people from the village."

"How nice," Lady Margaret remarked. "Tell me, Jason, what are you up to?"

Jason pretended to look hurt. "Up to? What on earth do you mean, sweet Mother?" he asked, playfully tweaking her on the cheek.

"You know what I mean. But if you don't think I should know...."

Smiling, Jason said, "All right, Mother. I'll tell you." With that, he poured himself a drink and sat down on the couch. Approaching the subject carefully and doing his utmost to sound casual, he asked his mother if she knew any unusual stories about the family. Lady Margaret, looking over the top of her glasses again, asked him what kind of stories.

"About the past—ghosts, hauntings, or secrets of the Griffiths."

"You should ask Alan," his mother answered slowly. "He is Keeper of the Book."

"Have you ever seen the book, Mother?"

"Of course I have. Anyone can see the book, with the consent of the Keeper. Now Jason, why are you asking all these strange questions?"

"It's a long story, Mother, but you know the girls I brought to dinner? Somehow or other, the blonde American girl seems to be all entangled in our family. I know you'll think I'm crazy or something, but really, it's true—she and Alan have grown very close in a very short time."

Lady Margaret said nothing for a while and then, putting down her embroidery carefully, stood up and started to walk to the door that led into the hall. Seeing that Jason was still sitting on the couch, she said, "Come along now."

He thought they were going upstairs to the great hall, but instead they went down the corridor toward the west wing. It wasn't used much at all these days; Jason remembered running up and down here with Alan when they were children.

Taking a key from a chain around her neck, Lady Margaret opened the door to his father's old study. The room was impressive and looked as if his father could still be there. Everything was spotless. His father's carpet slippers were by the chair on the red oriental rug. The furniture still glowed warmly with the regular polish. Both Jason and Alan knew that their mother came to this room often. She asked him to sit down, pointing to a big dark-green leather chair heavily decorated with intricate brass studs. She herself chose to sit in an old rocker which his father had often used when he was trying to think.

Softly, Jason asked, "What are we doing here, Mother?"

Lady Margaret got up and walked over to the far wall near a fine Sheraton buffet and pointed to the pictures hanging on the wall. Jason felt himself go stiff—every hair on his back seemed to stand up. He was looking at two separate portraits: Catherine Holmes and his brother, Lord Alan Strong Griffiths, dressed in clothes of long ago.

"I've watched my eldest son grow and become more and more like Lord David Strong William, and I have often wondered who the lady might be. When I met Catherine, my heart nearly stopped beating...for this is a portrait of Megan of Manningstile Henlock, the young bride of Lord David Strong William."

"This is incredible," said Jason. "I don't understand. What does it all mean?"

"These portraits have always been in this room. They are very old and your father had a strong attachment to them. Your grandmother told your father that one day Lord David and Megan would meet again to fulfill their destiny."

"I don't understand."

"It has long been the belief that Megan and David died in torment. Their ancestors, our ancestors, have handed down strange tales through the centuries that tell of the agonizing attempts of David and Megan to meet again to live and experience the happy life they were destined to have. I thought Alan's likeness was unusual, but when I met Catherine, I couldn't help wondering whether there was some truth in what I'd heard."

"I really believe Alan has fallen head over heels in love with Catherine and she with him. But you know, Mother, the poor girl is afraid. I'm glad she has so many good friends around her. Do you know any of the stories you mentioned?"

"Not really, Jason. All I know is that they tell of the love, hate and anguish these two people are supposed to have experienced through the centuries."

"Are you talking about reincarnation, Mother?"

His mother frowned. "I suppose I am, Jason. How else can it all be explained?"

Chapter Nine

Singing as she put the finishing touches to her buffet, Miss Sheridan had decided that she was going to make the evening extra special and put out her best china. After all, she thought, it's not every day that Lord Alan and his brother come to Penrithy Cottage. Patting her hair and stealing another look in the mirror, she hurried to the door to answer the doorbell.

It was the American girl and her friend with Lord Alan and Jason. Good, thought Miss Sheridan, I can let them sit in the best chairs. Offering them a glass of sherry, she seated her guests and removed the cat from the rug.

The girls were interested in Miss Sheridan's collection of china figurines and followed her into the living room to see the contents of her fine china cabinet filled with the old Toby Jugs which were her pride and glory.

Meanwhile, the two brothers started to talk about the last few days. Jason wanted to know if Alan had ever really had a good look at the two portraits in their father's old study. Alan nodded without revealing any emotion.

Jason probed further. "Who do you think they look like?"

Alan replied that their father always said he thought Alan had the look of Lord David Strong William.

"But what about the woman?" asked Jason in a hushed voice.

"Well, what about her?"

"I swear it's Catherine Holmes."

"I know, I know," said Alan. "I've always known I would meet her. Let me show you something." And opening the family record book, he pointed out some very interesting details.

"You know," said Jason. "I've always wanted to look at this

book. Will you let me read it sometime?''

"Certainly," answered Alan. "When there's a need."

The girls came back into the room. Catherine looked beautiful in a simple white dress and pearls.

How lovely she is, thought Alan.

Nickie didn't wait to be asked to sit down; she sat right by Jason, who was obviously rather pleased.

Everyone arrived early or on time. Miss Sheridan was enjoying being the hostess, making sure that everyone felt comfortable. She had planned her little speech this afternoon. Not wanting to sound formal or pompous, she had decided she would make a better impression with the Lords Griffiths if she appeared pleasantly casual. In her efforts to be nonchalant, her nice little announcement came out rather abruptly. "Will you please get up now and go into the dining room." My word, she thought. I sound like an army sergeant.

Everyone admired the beautiful buffet she had prepared and picking up the bone china plates, started to help themselves to the appetizing food. Miss Sheridan had arranged the center bowl of fruit ten times or more, and that Tom Thornleigh messed it all up by taking out one of the apples underneath. Finger sandwiches, pickles, salmon and cheese all looked colorful along with homemade cake and sherry trifle.

There was an air of hushed excitement: the food was good; each person seemed to have a hidden secret and each of them wanted to know the others'. Finally, the dishes were taken away and everyone felt the mood changing.

Alan never seemed to let Catherine get too far away. She liked this and enjoyed the feeling of protection he gave her.

Nickie was enjoying herself, dividing her attention between solemn George with his cocker-spaniel eyes and the virile blond Jason.

Tom stayed close by Frances and they found a warmth in each other. Conversation flowed easily and they were comfortable together.

Hilary wove a thread of interest, moving around the rooms, joining in various conversations, easily and lightly adding a delicate touch of humor or a thoughtful remark.

Not wanting anyone else to handle her delicate china dishes, Miss Sheridan quietly pulled the kitchen door closed and started to clear up the kitchen. Her tidy habits soon got the kitchen in order. Loving every minute of all the intrigue and refusing several offers of assistance, she hummed a wartime tune, "There'll Be Bluebirds over the White Cliffs of Dover." Drying her hands, she untied her apron, took a second look around her spic-and-span kitchen and went smiling into the cozy living room.

Immediately taking command of the proceedings, she asked

everyone, "Well, when do we get started?"

There was a sudden silence, which made Miss Sheridan almost wish she hadn't said anything.

Jason got the ball rolling: addressing everyone in the room, but directing his question to Alan, he said, "Where *do* we start?"

Alan, realizing that they were expecting him to be Master of Ceremonies, quickly obliged. Holding Catherine's hand, which felt as cold as marble, he told them, "In the short time we've had, I've tried to do a bit of homework. You all know my feelings about Catherine, and it's for this reason I would like each of you to do your best this evening and suggest any ideas or theories you think may possibly help. The whole episode is both disturbing and exciting, and I think you'll agree that we must be prepared to venture into areas of philosophy that we may find difficult. But we're not exactly amateurs. We do have a good sprinkling of psychic and esoteric students, along with the fact that unusual happenings have actually occurred to some of us. This afternoon, Hilary gave us some basic ideas about reincarnation, and we found out that George is a hypnotist. Frances reads the Tarot cards, and the rest of us are very interested in Catherine. I feel that I may have something to contribute before the evening is over, but I don't feel ready yet to discuss my theory. So is anyone else willing to start?"

Martha Sheridan surprised everyone by speaking first. Keeping her hands together in her lap, she told them that her cottage had originally belonged to the village blacksmith who was the father of Megan of Manningstile Henlock. Having lived there for more years than she would like to say, she had grown to love her cottage but, as in any other love affair, she occasionally had times when she didn't understand what the house was trying to tell her.

"Let me explain a little more," she said. "It seems that every so often I hear strange noises which sound like people talking. At first I was afraid, but eventually I learned to accept the disturbances. I once had a friend who knew a medium from Cardiff and we had a seance."

"What happened?" asked Nickie, her eyes wide with anticipation.

"There were four of us and we sat around the dining table with a candle in the middle and before too long we all felt a very definite chill. Then Sarah Bingley, she was the Cardiff medium, sort of went to sleep and her guide spoke through her."

Jason found it hard to keep his face straight. He wanted to laugh, not at what had happened, but at Martha Sheridan's variety of facial expressions.

Continuing, Miss Sheridan told them that several messages had come through and then she fell asleep.

The mental picture of Miss Sheridan going to sleep in the middle of a seance tickled Nickie. Almost laughing out loud, she asked,

"Did anything happen?"

"They all got upset with me, including my friend, because I ruined their seance."

"How did you do that?" asked Frances.

"They told me that I tried to take over by talking in a funny voice and that they didn't appreciate my contribution. I didn't know what they were talking about and told them all I did was drop off and was probably talking in my sleep."

"It seems to me that you were the real medium and you went off into a trance," Frances said.

"Me?" gasped Miss Sheridan. "Never!"

Seeing that her remark had knocked Miss Sheridan off balance, Frances made a suggestion. "Why don't I get out my Tarot cards and see if they can help us understand what's happening."

Everyone agreed and watched as Frances took out her cards, wondering what she was going to do next. Frances passed the cards to Catherine and asked her to shuffle them well until she felt she wanted to return them.

Catherine took the cards, and half-smiling at Alan, slowly started to manipulate them. She placed one card in the center of the table and everyone leaned over to examine it.

Frances touched the card with her fingertips as though caressing some invisible energy and then said, "This is what covers you. A tremendous change in your life—sudden and unexpected. This will influence your life-style—home, work and relationships. You are in an important cycle: a karmic force will penetrate your subconscious and you will soon know the reason why. Don't try to hang on to old ideas or plans, for you are definitely undergoing a major change."

Catherine didn't speak.

Jason asked what the card was.

"This is the Tower, the sixteenth card of the Major Arcana, and the verse associated with the major symbol tells us:

> "*This karmic force will clear away
> The debris caused by yesterday.*"

"That sounds like reincarnation," said Hilary. "And I can sense that power, looking at the picture. You can almost feel the force as it strikes the tower."

Placing another card across the Tower, Frances again passed her fingertips lightly over it. Her voice, was very low, hardly audible.

"This is what crosses you for good or for bad. The Nine of Pentacles...." This card showed a lady with a long gown in a garden. She seemed to be holding a bird.

"What does that mean?" asked Nickie.

"A feeling of solitude, not able to reach her goal; or I should say her inner desire or purpose. I also see a possibility of unexpected money.''

The reading continued until Frances placed down the last card, saying, "This is the outcome." Smiling at Catherine, she told her that she was free to go in any direction and accept new responsibilities. "I would like to give you the verse for this Major Arcana card," said Frances.

"Free to choose your path at last,
You've learned your lessons from the past."

Still concentrating on the cards she had laid down, Frances told Catherine never to forget what it had taken to reach this point in her life and to think carefully before making any important decisions.

The whole thing had been fascinating. Every card that Frances had read seemed to fit Catherine's situation, and there wasn't a soul there who wouldn't have wished to have Frances read their cards.

"Thank you," said Catherine. "It's remarkable."

Tom felt a tenderness for Frances he couldn't explain. He wanted to hold her and protect her. Not knowing how to convey his feelings, he chose to squeeze her hand. Frances felt a great strength coming from this man.

Miss Sheridan thought that this would be a good time to put the kettle on and make some tea.

Alan watched her go into the kitchen and suggested that after they all had a cup of tea, perhaps George would like to see what he could do to help Catherine.

With the tinkling of teacups and saucers, and a cheery fire with small yellow flames coming from the red coals underneath the black, once again each person felt embroiled in their own private thoughts. Finally Nickie, who was anxious to get on with things, asked if everyone was finished.

While the women cleared away the china, George asked Catherine to relax on the couch. The lights were dimmed and the low flames threw dancing shadows high on the cottage walls.

Keeping his voice deliberately low, George talked to Catherine for quite some time. Alan was holding her hand; soon her breathing became steady and regular as though she were asleep. In the flickering firelight, George then changed his tone of voice and asked Catherine to go back with him in time. She appeared to struggle, and he asked her to relax. Tiny beads of perspiration appeared on her forehead as she rolled her head from side to side.

"Go back, Catherine. Go back to where it all began. What's your name?"

A child's voice answered. "Catherine...."

Jason began writing.

Nickie was afraid—afraid of what might be happening to Catherine.

Alan saw her concern and gave her a reassuring smile.

"What are you doing, Catherine?" asked George.

"I'm playing with Megan," replied the little girl.

"Who is Megan?"

"My dolly, silly."

"Why do you call her Megan?"

Now pouting, the child answered, "Because that's my real name."

Soothing her forehead and brushing away the damp blonde hair, George asked Catherine to go to sleep.

With a childlike sigh, Catherine put her thumb in her mouth and slept like a baby.

Waiting a few seconds, George repeated, "Catherine, go back again. Catherine, go further back."

The childlike body, still curled up on the couch, stretched out and the face looked almost lifeless as George coaxed her to go farther back in time.

"Where are you now?"

The voice of an old woman answered. "At the end of a long life."

"Tell me about your life. Who are you?"

Her jaw seemed to drop and the slight movements she made appeared labored, like those of an old woman. With a faltering voice, she whispered her name: "Lily."

Silence, not a sound.

"Go back, Lily. Go back to when you were happy."

Her body seemed to come to life, the heaviness disappeared. Her fingers began tapping.

"Why are you tapping your fingers, Lily?"

"Can't you hear the music? Isn't it wonderful?" a rich southern accent replied.

"Are you happy, Lily?"

"Oh yes."

"Please go back, Lily."

"I don't want to," she answered defiantly.

Persisting, now in a strong voice, George almost commanded her to go back. Not receiving any reaction, he asked once more. "Go back now."

Her hands now crossed over her breast; she nodded her head slightly and again her face seemed to change. One could almost feel the inner trauma as she flashed through cobwebs of past memories hidden from her conscious mind.

"What's happening now?" asked Tom, amazed at this phenomenon.

"Catherine is going on a journey back into her past life

experiences. And as you can see, she is reliving forgotten memories."

"Will she be all right?" asked Miss Sheridan.

"Yes, please don't worry," added George kindly.

Catherine's body movements had stopped. She seemed to be fast asleep.

George rubbed the back of her head gently and said, "Megan, Megan, can you hear me?"

The contrast in tone and speech was astounding. A rich Welsh voice answered.

"What is she saying?" asked Nickie.

Alan's face softened as he listened to this lovely girl speak in a beautiful Celtic tongue.

Miss Sheridan told Nickie that Catherine was now talking in Welsh.

George turned to Alan, asking if he would translate for him.

Nodding his head, Alan waited for George to ask the first question to 'his' Megan.

Before George spoke, Megan was talking.

Miss Sheridan put her head on one side as though she could understand this beautiful flowing, expressive language. She knew a smattering of Welsh and was able to pick up words here and there.

Frances, Tom, Hilary and Nickie were entranced. Nickie noticed a tear rolling down Alan's face, and when Megan began to sob, a deep and moving ache found its way into every heart there.

George looked helpless as Alan talked with Megan. He watched Catherine very carefully, taking her pulse and feeling her body temperature.

The fire had now burned down and had become a deep red glow which reflected on Megan's face and hair. Though most could not understand this Megan of Manningstile Henlock, they all felt the pain and passion of two lovers meeting again across the centuries.

George beckoned to Alan to stop. He was reluctant and said a few more words to his love. Jason, who also knew Welsh, was writing furiously. Miss Sheridan sat close by, holding out the palms of her hands as though trying to give the tragic lovers extra strength.

As Alan was trying to break away, Hilary bent over and whispered in George's ear. He nodded with approval, so Hilary asked Jason if he would try to bring Megan back to her next life—in Welsh!

Thoroughly enjoying every minute of this experience, Jason spoke in his natural tongue—gently at first—then more forcefully, as Megan gripped Alan's arms tightly. Slowly, they saw her change, and then Hilary asked, "Who are you?"

"My name is Emma, Madam. And who are you?"

Ignoring this question, Hilary asked, "Where are you, Emma?"

A tinkling laugh, followed by a perfect English accent. "At home with bonny Robin, waiting for my darling husband. Have you seen Guy?"

"Who is Robin?" asked Hilary gently.

"Robin is my darling, my baby, my son, and he is a gift from heaven," answered Emma.

Looking at his watch, George signalled to Hilary, and she immediately sat back in her chair as George brought Emma swiftly through the years back to Catherine.

Still caressing her with his hands, Alan looked relieved when George said, "Wake up, Catherine...glad to see you back."

Catherine opened her lovely eyes and was happy to see Alan close beside her. Smiling, she asked, "Did anything happen?"

"Did anything happen?" Nickie said. "No wonder you're such a good friend. You're so many people, that's why you have so much heart."

Kissing her softly on the cheek, Alan helped Catherine sit up. Miss Sheridan already had a glass of water in her hand to offer her.

Tom, looking somewhat embarrassed, smiled at Catherine and said, "Boy, was that something! You really gave me a turn once or twice."

Frances understood how he felt. "Me, too."

Kneeling on the hearth rug, Nickie was exuberantly enthusiastic. Looking at her watch, she was surprised that it was still early in the evening. "I don't know what's happening," she said, "but I can tell you all this: I don't know when I've enjoyed myself more than tonight."

Jason was flipping through the pages of his yellow legal pad, checking to see if he had everything written down legibly.

Lighting a cigarette, Catherine inhaled deeply and asked, "Will someone please tell me what happened?"

They all started laughing when they realized that the star of this performance didn't have any idea what had occurred.

"Before we get into this, do you mind if I put some more coals on the fire?" asked Miss Sheridan.

Nickie stood up to stretch her legs, debating whether to go over to Jason or George. Hilary was busy chatting with Frances and Tom, and Catherine and Alan were whispering to each other. Deciding to talk to George for a few moments because Jason was still involved with his writing, Nickie smiled and said, "You don't say very much, do you?"

George smiled back and feeling just a bit uncomfortable with this forthright American girl, asked, "What would you like me to tell you?"

Pretending to struggle for an answer, Nickie asked, "Are you really Henry Kissinger on a secret mission?" This broke the barrier and George laughed heartily. As he reached in his jacket pocket for his lighter, he accidentally pulled out a small black cap.

"Do you always carry that around with you?"

"No," he said, laughing. George was the son of immigrant parents who had experienced the brutality of the concentration camps. This was partly why he had studied hypnotism, for he knew that it was good therapy, having seen it used on many occasions for Jewish friends who had undergone the miseries of the war.

Nickie felt good listening to his rich voice. When you talked to him, he didn't seem shy at all.

"It's just that meeting a group of people all at once makes me behave differently," George said.

"Maybe you did naked temple dances in another life, and you're afraid someone might recognize you."

George liked Nickie and her ability to talk openly. Always involved with some project or other, he never seemed to have the time to socialize. He smiled as he thought of himself doing a temple dance naked. Nickie asked him why he was smiling. He just shook his head.

There was an awkward silence; Nickie was looking straight at him, wondering what was on his mind. Searching for something to say, he asked, "Do you ever have recurring dreams?" He seemed surprised when she answered yes.

"Well, why did you ask?" said Nickie.

"I can't answer that, but now that you've told me, I'd like to know what your dream is...if it isn't too personal."

Thinking for a minute, she said, "It's really hard to describe. You see, all the time in my dreams, I know that it's me. Now don't get confused. I don't know I'm dreaming, but in the dream I know I'm Nickie. Now this Nickie is quite a girl. she gets into all kinds of things."

Lifting one eyebrow, George asked, "What kinds of things?"

"That's the whole point. I don't know what kinds of things. But I do know they're vivid and I'm always myself, but also somebody else at the same time. Do you know what I mean?"

Nickie thought how good-looking George really was. She sat there and watched him as he thought about her dream. His skin was a nice shade of brown. Nickie let her thoughts wander. She saw him on the beach in his swim shorts. I bet he's a good dancer, she thought.

"So, what do you think?" she heard him say.

"About what?" she asked. "Freud's theory of dreams? I'm sorry, George. I was miles away."

"That's OK," he said. But tell me, where were you?"

"I was watching you dance in the temple."

They both started to laugh, but then Jason was clapping his hands, asking for everybody's attention.

"What do you all think about the experiment tonight? I suggest we discuss what we observed and see if we can understand it."

Everyone agreed that it was a good idea, especially Catherine, now that her reason for being in Wales was known by everyone she'd met. Maybe they'll come up with a simple solution, she thought.

Reaching for his notes, Jason told them he would refresh their memories by giving an outline of Catherine's regression.

"If you recall," he began, "Catherine first became a child and had a doll she called Megan. George took her farther back and she became an old woman, apparently at the end of her life. Her name was Lily. Again, Catherine regressed in that same lifetime, and we noticed an American southern accent. Here, Lily seemed to be happy and did not want to go back. Now the next episode was very interesting, for it appeared that Catherine was traveling back in time. It was like watching someone dreaming. She reacted to all her experiences, which were hidden from us.

"When she seemed to relax physically again, George called her Megan and asked if she could hear him. It was then we heard a new voice speaking fluent Welsh; not the Welsh language of today, but an ancient Welsh dialect no longer in use and known only to Welsh scholars. As you know, Alan conversed with Megan in this Celtic tongue. Hilary then asked George is he would try to bring Megan into the following life, still using the Welsh language, so that Megan would understand. We then met Emma, who told us about her son Robin and her husband Guy. That is a rundown of Catherine's regression tonight."

Hilary began the discussion by noting that although these lifetimes were touched upon, there were also others which Catherine seemed to pass through.

"Can anyone do this?" asked Tom.

Hilary went on to explain that everyone has the natural ability to regress, and that with practice some students are able to regress consciously and actually become aware of their past lives.

"Of course, it's far better with an experienced guide. Often, people realize the reasons for present life conditions when they discover the patterns of previous lives. It's been known to cure illness, develop awareness, activate previous knowledge and accomplish many other beneficial things."

"I understand what you've been saying about regression," said Frances. "but what I don't understand is why Catherine has been haunted and tormented by all these mysterious events, even to the extent of coming to a country she has never known."

"At least not in this life," said Alan quietly.

"I don't think I'm expressing my thoughts properly," said Frances. "My question is, why, without having an interest in reincarnation or past lives, is Catherine suddenly having her life turned around? For example, the voice on the telephone. As I understand it, Catherine was in no way even thinking of past lives; just an ordinary American girl busy living her life, and then for no apparent reason, all these peculiar things started happening to her.''

"I admit that Catherine's experiences are different from the norm," said Hilary. "If we are to believe in reincarnation, I think we also have to believe that for a reason we can't explain right now, Catherine's soul has some karma to complete. Not only that, but she is apparently in a cycle where the opportunity is imminent to fulfill her destiny. This could only be so if the other souls involved are also living now. And that is where she is at this time. Knowing, but not knowing—following a driving force. I think we can all agree that Alan is a part of Catherine's past, and maybe that's also true of some of the rest of us.''

Nickie stood up and walked over to the fireplace. "I'm sure that Lord Alan is the reincarnation of Lord David, but what I can't figure is: Who in the world is Gareth of Abergavennie? If Alan was Lord David Strong William, who killed Megan's lover, the theory of reincarnation doesn't make any sense.''

Smiling and bringing everyone's attention to Catherine and Alan, who were sitting close together holding hands, she continued: "Look at those two, they've only just met and they're crazy about each other. I would think that if we're to believe in reincarnation, Catherine would be ready to hit him over the head or something, wouldn't you?''

There was an obvious silent agreement. Everyone looked at Hilary for reassurance. Hilary took her cue and reminded everyone that many centuries had gone by since the souls of Alan and Catherine began their karmic journey.

"What does that mean?'' asked Miss Sheridan.

"How many lifetimes would you think there are in a span of 400 years? It could be that Catherine and Alan have gone through several lifetimes and have each paid their karmic debts. I'm sure that it hasn't been easy and that they have played many parts in the karmic drama, but nevertheless, everything goes in a complete circle. It would appear that they are now destined to love one another in this life.''

"I can accept all you've said up to now,'' Tom said, "but what I want to know is, who is Gareth of Abergavennie?''

No one could answer that question.

Then Frances suggested that the conversation between Megan and Alan under hypnosis might give the clue needed.

Catherine looked confused; it was obvious that she had no opinion. Jason looked steadily at his brother, his eyes questioning. Alan appeared reluctant to discuss the tender episode. Turning to Jason he asked if he would mind relating the gist of the conversation.

Jason nodded and turned his note pages. With his pen, he skipped along the lines, stopping at a certain point. Everyone waited to hear the words uttered across the centuries. Jason cleared his throat and told the group that the conversation was highly personal: Megan had told Lord David that she loved him, but he was apparently unable to accept this.

"My brother Alan was deeply touched by Megan's words, but Lord David found her vow of love unacceptable."

The group conversation continued in this way, and although no cut-and-dried answers were available, all of them felt personally involved. When Alan suggested that they would have to finish for the evening, the would-be esoteric detectives reluctantly agreed to call it a day.

Miss Sheridan's turn came at last. She glowed as everyone admired her cooking and her cottage and thanked her for her hospitality. The normally prim Miss Sheridan was warmly hugging her guests as they prepared to leave. It felt good to have friends; she was delighted that they were now calling her "Martha."

Offering to take everyone back to the inn, Jason invited them to pile into his Volkswagen bus.

Hating to leave Catherine, Alan said goodnight and whispered in her ear that he would be around for breakfast in the morning.

Chapter Ten

When they reached the Blue Feathers, they dropped off Catherine, Nickie, Frances and Tom, then continued along High Street to take Hilary and George to the Black Bull. Jason and Alan drove home silently to Cardiff House.

Hilary went straight to her room and called Mike. This was her favorite time of day when her husband was away. Curled up in the bed, she became a little girl, losing all her sophistication; she confided in him and eagerly waited for his advice on simple matters. Arranging to meet him that weekend in Tenby, she made several kisses over the phone, and he told her that he loved her and wished her a good night.

Frances and Tom decided to have a nightcap before going to bed. Mildred made an effort to be pleasant while taking their order.

Half smiling, Tom gave the order and Mildred turned to leave, but then came back, asking Frances when she would read her cards. Frances explained that there were so many unexpected things happening that it was difficult for her to make a definite time. But when Frances saw the disappointed look on Mildred's face, she suggested that the waitress come to her room after she had finished work.

Tom was displeased with Mildred for approaching Frances this way. Frances assured him that she was perfectly happy about the whole thing. Relaxing a little, he reached out and touched her arm. Frances felt the urgency in his fingertips and asked if there was anything wrong.

"Not really," he said. "But I can't help wondering if Lord Jason was Gareth of Abergavennie.''

"Then you do believe in reincarnation," said Frances.

"I suppose I do in a way," he answered. "Strange things happen on this earth and listening to Hilary and the others, I feel inclined to agree that it makes a hell of a lot of sense out of what happens in our lives." Changing the subject abruptly, he asked Frances what she thought of the Blue Feathers.

"I love it. I really do," said Frances. As she looked around the room, her eyes seemed to caress every picture on the wall. She told Tom that she really felt as though she were home.

"When are you leaving Manningstile Henlock?" he asked.

Her face seemed to drop. She sighed and told him that she still had a few weeks to go. "It seems as though I've been here forever and it feels good. You're a lucky man, Tom Thornleigh, to be able to call this beautiful place home." She noticed that his hand seemed to be shaking a little. "Is there something wrong?"

"No," he said quite definitely. "It's just that I've never met a woman like you and I wouldn't like to see you ever leave the Blue Feathers. You seem to fit in just right. I suppose what I'm trying to say is...I'd like to keep company with you." His chin seemed to rest on his chest as though he were afraid to look at her.

Frances felt his strength. The warmth of this big man was a good secure feeling. It flashed across her mind that it could never be the same as it had been with Martin; but Tom was very kind, and she was at a time in her life where she might really enjoy "keeping company" with this man. As she touched him, he raised his head, his eyes anticipating rejection. Frances leaned over and kissed his cheek.

"I like the idea, Tom. Let's see how it goes, shall we?"

Immediately, he put his arms around her and gave her a big bear hug.

As Mildred brought in the drinks, her mouth opened and she nearly dropped the tray when she saw Mr. Thornleigh and the guest being familiar. Placing the drinks on the table and trying not to look Tom in the eye, she mumbled, "Will that be all?"

Both Frances and Tom laughed out loud at Mildred's reaction and with another squeeze of the hand, sealed the bargain. They talked about their childhoods, their likes and dislikes, exploring each other for the first time. It felt comfortable for both of them, and their closeness was only disturbed when they heard Mildred making all kinds of noises to attract attention.

"What is it?" asked Tom irritably.

"I'm finished work now," said Mildred, "and I was wondering if the lady would be doing my cards."

With a sigh of patience, Tom looked at Frances, who was already saying yes. Kissing Tom lightly on the cheek, she said goodnight and invited Mildred to come up to her room. Tom sat for a while, trying to believe what had happened. He felt like a boy again and could hardly wait till morning.

Frances read the cards for Mildred, who sat like a frightened bird, moving her head up and down or sideways to respond to a question. Frances had lots of patience and tried to make Mildred understand the significance of the reading. Eventually Frances finished, and Mildred thanked her and wondered if Frances would read the cards for her mother. Refusing gently, Frances told Mildred that she was on holiday and had lots of things she would be doing.

"Are you and Mr. Thornleigh courting?" asked Mildred.

"Kind of," answered Frances, who knew it wouldn't be any use trying to explain further.

Undressed and in nightrobes, Catherine and Nickie were talking about everything that had happened to them.

"What do you make of it all?" asked Nickie. "Here you are, no nearer to finding out why these things have happened. What are you going to do next?"

Catherine thought for a moment before she answered. "There's got to be a reason for everything that's happened to me and somehow or other I'm going to find out what it all means. Then there's the letter from that Jonathan Whiteside about an Uncle Alfred, whom I didn't know I had, leaving me something in a will. And to top it all off, I, Catherine Holmes, have fallen in love with a Welshman."

In a voice of mock correction, Nickie said, "Welsh *Lord*, if you please," and then started giggling, which made Catherine laugh. Lying on the bed, they howled with laughter like two schoolgirls in tenth grade.

Feeling in a much better mood, they decided to go to bed and meet for breakfast in the morning. Then Catherine remembered she had made arrangements with Alan.

Nickie jokingly remarked, "Well then, I'll just have to sit at another table," and went off to her room.

The closet door wasn't closed properly, so Catherine went to shut it. As the closet didn't contain many clothes, she noticed a small door at the back. It was narrow, with a porcelain knob. Turning the knob, she was surprised when the door opened, and even more surprised to find another door of heavy dark wood with a big heavy handle behind it. Not knowing why, she pushed this door and it opened very slowly. Half afraid to go any further, she saw a dim yellow light that looked like a candle. Not moving, frozen to the spot where she stood, she heard a voice:

"Come along, Megan, and close the door quickly."

Not knowing why, she followed the directions of the urgent appeal. Feeling a restriction around her legs, she noticed two things: first, she was wearing a long bodiced gown, deep violet in color, and strange-looking shoes; and second, before her were steps going down. A hand reached out as though to help her. Feeling a fear she'd never known in her life, she tried to scream, but nothing happened.

The voice said, "I have brought him, Megan, and he is weary after his long journey. He has promised to wed us tonight."

She descended the rough stone stairs into a small underground storeroom. As she stepped into the light, she saw a tiredlooking priest in a rough brown gown tied at the waist. There was Dylan, Gareth's brother, and Timothy the woodman.

"SSHH," said Gareth in a loud whisper.

They all looked up at the wooden boards above them. Heavy footsteps were pacing up and down; voices could be heard and then the roaring laughter of Lord David Strong William.

In a hushed whisper, the priest asked, "Who art thou, maid?" Anxious glances passed among the three men.

"Megan of Manningstile Henlock," she answered quickly. "Prithee, Father, what is this night about?"

The priest beckoned her to sit on the sacks filled with grain, then said, "Since thou art with child, am I to assume thou art carrying the child of Lord David Strong William?"

"Nay, Father, I think not. This sin I shall carry with me to my grave, but there is naught I can do. I am helpless that such cruel fate should be my master."

"Tell me more, child," asked the priest.

Gareth turned fiercely to the priest and said, " 'Tis my doing, Father. Megan cannot burn in hell, for I too am a sinner."

Megan fell to her knees, bowing her head to the priest. "I shall find absolution in freeing my conscience. Bless me, Father, for I have sinned."

The priest patted her bowed head and gently waited to hear her confession.

"Since I was a child, I have known that one day I was destined to become the wife of Lord David. In my innocence, I clung to Gareth of Abergavennie. In our need for each other and in our secret hiding place, we gave comfort to each other. One night, I came to our secret place and was violently molested by a devilish stranger. It was fated that I know not the father of the child I carry in my womb. The only sign I know I carry in my heart."

"What is this sign, child?" asked the priest.

Speaking in a hushed voice, she told the priest that she could never tell, for it was too terrible to speak of.

Nodding his head, the priest lifted her chin and looking into her young face, said, "Then Gareth of Abergavennie is not the father of thy child?"

Megan nodded and with a whimper, cried, letting her tears fall on the rough cloth of the priest's robe. "I have never loved Gareth in the way thou mightst think, Father never."

Gareth put his arms around Megan and rocked her gently as though to give her comfort. "Megan speaks the truth, Father; we were children together. We built dreams, and my love is such that I would die on this spot for her, but it has never been violated."

"Is this so, child?" asked the priest.

"Yes, Father," she replied. "I do love him, but not as a husband; ours has been a childish love, born in the rain that understands the need of flowers, in the wind that carries the pollen. I cannot tell thee more, Father, for my lips and heart understand a love that does not need the bonds of marriage. I love Gareth as myself and David also."

The priest raised his hand in blessing and kissing his beads, went into silent prayer.

Dylan knelt on the floor beside Megan and put his arms around her and Gareth while Timothy looked on and witnessed the terrible sadness of these three friends huddled in this dark hiding place.

As the priest finished his private prayer, he sat back on the sacks and asked Megan whether Lord David was aware of her unborn babe. Megan nodded and told the priest of Lord David's anger.

"As his wife-to-be, I must respect and honor my Lord, for I fear the child within me. He hath consented to accept the child on condition I see no more of Gareth and my friends. Wilt thou give us thy blessing, Father, for if anything happens to me, I wish it that Gareth take my child."

The priest, with his face by the candle, looked like a saint as Megan pleaded.

"Please, Father. Join us in holy wedlock so that I know my child will have a father."

"But what of thy coming marriage to Lord David?" asked the priest.

Megan knew that the priest was bound by his faith and would not consent if he knew the truth of her plot. She desperately searched her heart for the right words to say to this man of God.

"As I am not yet the bride of Lord David, I wish to marry Gareth of Abergavennie."

"So it shall be, child, if that is thy choice," answered the priest. "Kneel here, children."

With joy in their hearts, Megan and Gareth knelt before the priest, and the dark room filled with grain became a magnificent cathedral. The priest solemnly unwrapped the chalice from its protective cover and with Dylan and Timothy as witnesses, joined Megan of Manningstile Henlock and Gareth of Abergavennie in holy wedlock.

"Go back now, sweet Megan. Tarry no longer," pleaded Gareth

when the ceremony was done.

Megan held him close and reached out her other hand toward Dylan. "Hold me, dear companions, for I fear and loathe my return."

"Hurry, Megan," Gareth said anxiously. "I will be back and thou shalt know when I am near. Look for the stave at thy window and thou shalt know of my presence."

With that, Megan knelt before the priest, who touched her head in a special blessing. Murmuring her thanks, she hurried back up the stairs and reaching the top, locked the door and went to the window. She could see the faint outline of the three men and the priest. She then retired to her bed. Touching her bare finger, she could actually feel a wedding band, and in her heart she felt secure as only a woman can with a father for her child.

As Catherine sat on the bed, she saw the whole thing happen and knew that the priest would never be seen again. Feeling cold, she reached out to light a cigarette, then called Alan at Cardiff House.

"Hello," said Lady Margaret. "Who is this, please?"

Not realizing what she said, Catherine answered, "Megan."

Putting down her book, Lady Margaret answered, "Wait a minute, please. I'll get Lord Alan for you."

"Thank you."

"Hello." It was Alan's deep, rich voice.

Catherine told him about her flashback, then said, "Alan, it was different this time. I saw it all happen. It was real. I can't stay here any longer. I'm sure Tom will understand. This place is doing things to me. I'll get a room at the Black Bull."

"Don't move. Stay right where you are. I'm coming over," said Alan and then put the phone down.

Catherine went over to turn on the television. There was John Wayne in an old cowboy movie. Normally, she couldn't stand old movies, but this was good. It reminded her of home. She was Catherine Holmes and Megan belonged in another time, in another world.

It wasn't too long before Alan arrived. As soon as Catherine opened her door, he took her in his arms and she clung to him like a lost child.

"Come home with me, Catherine. We'll collect your things in the morning."

She scribbled a note and left it on the door so that everyone would know where she was in the morning. She was happy to be leaving the Blue Feathers.

In the car on the way back to Cardiff House, Catherine asked Alan if he could understand what was going on. If the story were true, it didn't make sense.

Alan was quiet and his face was set firmly as though he were only half listening. When he did speak, they were nearly there. He reached out and touching her arm, said, "Before you go to bed, I'm going to try and sort something out. Hopefully, it will put an end to all this."

Catherine looked at him in surprise, but already they were driving up to Cardiff House.

Chapter Eleven

Lady Margaret was at the door to greet them. Before Catherine could apologize for causing any inconvenience, Lady Margaret anticipated her feelings. Putting her arms around Catherine, she told her how happy she was to see her and that she had had one of the guest rooms made ready for her. This warm, affectionate welcome put Catherine immediately at ease. Turning to her son, Lady Margaret suggested they all go into the library where there was a nice fire.

Alan loved this part of the house and seemed to cheer up the minute he walked in. Making sure both women were seated comfortably, he then went to pour drinks.

Staring into the fire and wondering whether or not she was going insane, Catherine looked weary and forlorn. Now that the three of them were relaxing, Lady Margaret looked at Catherine with a direct and open approach.

"I believe you are back home, Megan."

Instead of soothing her, this remark made Catherine terribly afraid and looking at Alan, she wondered what would happen next.

Leaning over and speaking with a gentle voice, Alan said, "Don't be afraid, my darling. I'm sure that what Mother has to say will help us both come to terms with our lives."

Lady Margaret was a beautiful woman and her dark eyes and strong features were softened by her winning smile.

"I don't really know where to begin, for the beginning goes so far back. Perhaps I should start by telling you that my life has also been affected by the history of this family. I know for certain that in a previous life I was Rose Featherstone, first daughter of Mary Strong William, my mother, and Lord Henry Featherstone, my father. My grandfather, Lord John Strong William, was the last male to carry on the family name."

"But how can you possibly know that you were actually Rose Featherstone?" asked Catherine, wanting to believe Lady Margaret, but finding it difficult to accept her certainty.

"I know, my dear, because when I was about your age, I too was haunted and terrified by reincarnational memories and visions."

Catherine remembered Lady Featherstone being mentioned when they had all met at the Blue Feathers. Turning to Alan, she said, "Wasn't it Rose Featherstone who was raised by her Aunt Amelia, her mother's sister, and then married Lord Griffiths?"

Alan assented, adding, "It was Rose's mother who apparently disappeared after her husband, Lord Henry Featherstone, died, leaving baby Rose in her sister's care."

"Before I can say more," said Lady Margaret, "I must know that you believe, for by believing, this family can rid itself of its karma. You, my dear, are only one part of this ancient story. I have waited many years to see the karmic debts paid by the ancient line of Strong."

Catherine nodded as if in agreement, which encouraged Lady Margaret to go on with her story.

"Let me tell you then of my life as Rose Featherstone. It has taken years to put the pieces together, but at last I feel my purpose in this lifetime is approaching.

"I was born in 1684 and baptized Rose Featherstone. I've told you of my parents. My Aunt Amelia was a widow who lived with them, caring for me as a baby and doing the needlework. My parents were young and very happy. Our family lived in the Manor House in the village of Manningstile Henlock, which you now know as the Blue Feathers Inn.

"The Inn was named that because the coat of arms belonging to my father's family contained three blue feathers. My father went to London and contracted a strange fever. His death came quickly, and the shock almost killed my mother. Her devoted sister Amelia helped Mama through the bereavement and took care of me, the baby. No one knew what happened to my mother; but I do." Pausing to light a cigarette, Lady Margaret lifted her feet onto a tiny satin-covered stool and continued.

"The Strong family can trace its ancestry back to the ancient Celts. The first Strong was an ancient warrior who was known for his strength and valor. He was the leader of his clan and was called William of Garth. They were a peaceful clan, living a simple life in the Welsh hills. They worshipped ancient gods and celebrated their holy days acknowledging the earth, sun, moon and stars. It is written that terror and evil came upon them when they were attacked in the night by painted warriors from the sea. The attackers came silently and without mercy and murdered every woman and child as they slept peacefully. The men were killed also after much fighting. William of Garth awoke to see his attacker raising an axe over his body. With all the strength he could muster, he fought off the screaming, painted warrior. Like a man possessed, the attacker continued to scream his curses and wounded William. As they struggled in the dark, William realized that his wife and son had been brutally murdered and were lying nearby in their own blood. An unknown power then possessed William and he killed his attacker. William searched the village, but there were no survivors.

"His ears were deafened by the warriors retreating down the hillside, screaming jubilantly as they made their way to the sea. William wept like a child; even now it is said that when the moon is full, William's cries of agony can be heard on Garth Hill. Burying his dead, he made great vows of vengeance. In his sorrow, his mind became demented, and this young warrior, broken and alone, remained as a hermit for many years.

"One day a traveler came by. This was the first person that William had seen since the massacre of his tribe. Raising his arms high and screaming his agony, he started to attack the innocent stranger. But seeing that it was a woman had a strange effect on him, and he fell on the ground, weeping and wishing to die. The woman, whose name was Blodwin, gave William solace and helped his aching heart and tortured soul to heal. Regaining his strength, he learned to smile, but could not forget his hate for the evil the painted warriors had brought upon his kin. Each day, like a young tree, he grew stronger and enjoyed the companionship of Blodwin, who had brought him back from the dead. His scars were healed and he now had a desire to live and fulfill himself.

"Feeling his need, Blodwin encouraged William to go and seek a new life away from the horror of Garth Hill. Knowing that Blodwin was now a part of his life, he asked her to go with him and seek a new clan. Their journey took them over the Welsh mountains, along flowing rivers, through forests and green fields. Blodwin looked at the stars and guided their journey as they passed through hamlets and forest clans.

"One night as they prepared to sleep, Blodwin told William that the following day they would reach the place where they would live, and that he would become a fine warrior and a chief of the clan. Blodwin was tranquil; to William, she did not seem as though she came from the earth. He would watch her perform quiet ceremonies and study the stars and moon. Always she was right. He learned to rely upon her judgment, and she filled his heart with a great love.

"The following day, they came out of the forest and arrived in a small village. Blodwin appeared to know the friendly faces that greeted them warmly. William was happy and when Blodwin presented him to the elders, he realized she had taken him home.

His days and nights were filled with happiness, and Blodwin became his second wife.

"He was industrious and gained the confidence of the village elders. Occasionally, he would feel the pain from the past, especially when Blodwin gave birth to his first son. Visions of his murdered wife and baby would come into his mind and he would feel anger rise within him. The people of the village were good and kind; they worshipped in the way he had seen Blodwin worship on their long journey. Many questions were unanswered: Often he had asked her of her family and home, and where she was going when they first met. She would smile and tell him that she had been sent to find this wild and unhappy man and would say no more.

"When their child was one month old, William was summoned by the elders to come to them alone when the moon was full. Blodwin prepared him: bathed and scented his body, placed spring flowers in his hair and made for him a suit from the skin of a deer. On his wrist she put a bracelet of beaten copper and she felt a fierce pride well up in her breast for this handsome, darkbearded warrior who was her man. William went to the elders and before any word was spoken, became involved in a ceremony. He was asked to kneel; flower petals were poured on his head and water from a crystal stream was given him to drink. At last peace came into his heart as he sat with the elders, waiting to hear why he had been summoned on that summer's eve.

"He learned that the village elders were full of wisdom and had knowledge that came from other worlds. They could foretell the future and knew of his past. Eager to learn and become one of them, he promised to tell no one but his eldest son of the mysteries revealed to him. The Chief Elder told him that when he received the gifts unknown to other men, he would also have to accept knowledge of his karmic path. Once he had this knowledge, there would be no going back, and he was given twenty-eight days and twenty-eight nights to consider his choice.

"When the given time was over, William presented himself once more to the elders and told them that he was ready to accept the great powers and knowledge of his karmic path. He lay on a stone slab under the full moon. The elders gathered around him silently. Each one touched him on the forehead between his brows; he heard them chanting melodiously. Someone placed hands on his head and he fell into a deep sleep. It was during this sleep that his higher mind became known to his consciousness, and all manner of wisdom was given to him.

"He would be known now and in generations to come as Strong. This name would continue for all time and each son would pass it on to his son. If karma was not fulfilled, the line would be broken and each generation would be asked to pay the karmic debt, and restore the family name to honor.

"From this day forth, he would keep a record of his life and of his family. Each first-born son would continue to keep this book from generation to generation. The first-born Strong would be born with hidden powers and as he grew, they would develop as he learned to use them wisely. If a girl child should be born, the Keeper of the Book must make it known to her that she must reveal the book to her eldest son when he became seventeen years of age. 'Until the rightful male is ready to be the Keeper of the Book, *no woman shall look upon its pages.*'"

Until now, neither Catherine nor Alan had spoken, for they were listening to every word Lady Margaret was saying. Alan, seeing that Catherine wanted to say something, asked his mother if Catherine could speak for a moment.

"Sorry," said Lady Margaret. "I should have known you would want to ask questions."

Catherine thanked her and said, "Surely it hasn't been possible for each eldest son to produce a son? You said that William was told that if a girl was born, the Keeper of the Book, who was her father, would tell her that *her* son at the age of seventeen would then become the Keeper of the Book. But what happens if the daughter of the Keeper of the Book doesn't have a son?"

"When William became a member of the elders, you remember, he was also given the knowledge of his karmic path."

"Yes, I remember," said Catherine.

"Well," said Lady Margaret, "he knew then that the bloodline would be broken because of past karma, and that until the karmic debts had been paid, the book was destined to become dusty and unused. The Higher Order still exists, and each member is a Keeper of the Book. When one line is broken, it is then the responsibility of the Order to watch over that book until the rightful heir is ready to learn its secrets. Alan is a member of that order, although he will never speak of it nor of its members. He is active and has great knowledge."

Catherine looked at Alan, and his eyes smiled back at her as if to reassure her that all was well.

"So when there's no son to become Keeper of the Book, the elders of the Higher Order take charge of it till the rightful heir comes along," said Catherine.

"Yes," said Lady Margaret.

"But I thought Alan said everyone in the family could have access to the Book."

"Only if the Keeper knows it is right for them to see it," said Alan. "There's a small verse in the book that says:

> Only when a need is there
> Should the seeker look.
> Within these pages secrets hide

For the Keeper of the Book.''

The fire was low, and it was well after midnight. Lady Margaret suggested that they all get some rest and talk further in the morning. "Come along, Catherine. Let me show you to your room."

Saying goodnight to Alan, the women went upstairs. Catherine's room was cheerful, with tiny rosebuds on the wallpaper and gleaming white enamel paintwork. Catherine loved the room immediately and knew that she was going to sleep well that night.

Back at the Blue Feathers, Nickie was the first to see the note left on Catherine's door. Smiling, she went downstairs to see if she could find Frances, who was already eating breakfast with Tom.

"My, you're up bright and early," she said to them.

"We've already been for a morning walk," said Frances cheerfully.

"I saw Jason looking for you, Nickie," said Tom, holding Frances' hand.

"You did?" said Nickie, already on her way out to find him.

Jason was reading the morning paper in the foyer when Nickie put her hands over his eyes. Laughing, he said, "This has got to be Nickie Foster."

Pretending to be disappointed, Nickie asked how he could tell.

"Easy," he said, "I can smell your perfume."

Mmm, thought Nickie, He's a lover. "Well, your brother has escaped with Catherine, Frances and Tom obviously don't want my company, and I think George and Hilary are over at the Black Bull. So what do you think we should do?"

Jason suggested that they should escape and take a run out for breakfast. "Let's go to Southworth's Cafe on High Street. They make the best porridge."

"Best what?" said Nickie, giggling. "Porridge?"

"You know what porridge is, surely."

"Let's go and try it. But first let's tell the others where we'll be."

"You know, this is almost like a family affair. Tell me, Nickie, who is Gareth of Abergavennie?"

"I'll bet it's you," she said slowly.

On the terrace at Cardiff House, Lady Margaret, Catherine and Alan had just finished breakfast.

"Do you two want to go out somewhere?" asked Lady Margaret.

Catherine looked disappointed. "Oh, I thought we were going to talk some more."

Lady Margaret looked happy that Catherine showed an interest. "If Alan doesn't mind, I would love to finish the story."

Putting his arms around his mother and Catherine, Alan said, "Certainly. I think we should finish it and bring Catherine up to date; then perhaps I'll stand a chance of spending some time alone with her.''

Feeling his hands on her, Catherine couldn't remember when she had ever felt so loved and secure. They went into the Morning Room, which was aptly named. Overlooking a beautiful flower garden with green grass lawns, it was a picture. The furnishings were light and pleasant and instead of family portraits, there were watercolors and bright soft cushions. Once they were all settled, Lady Margaret went straight into her story, beginning again with Mary Strong William, who became Lady Featherstone, her mother in a past life.

"In this life as Rose, I was the only child. But I want my story to begin with Mary Strong william, the daughter of John Strong William, who had no son. This woman was my mother and she married my father, Lord Henry Featherstone, in 1683. Shortly after that, in the following year, I was born. My mother knew that her father was Keeper of the Book and that the book was never intended for her. So when her father, John Strong William, was dying, she made plans to read the book before it disappeared into the hands of the Higher Order.

"She discussed her intentions with her sister, the widow Amelia Dodsworth. Amelia tried her best to discourage Mary. Nevertheless, Mary was determined to read the book, not believing that any harm could befall her. Her father died in the night but before he passed away, he told Mary that he knew of her plan and begged her not to read the book. He had hardly breathed his last breath when she went down to the library to find the forbidden record. My mother was never the same woman again.''

"What happened to her?'' asked Catherine.

Lady Margaret looked sad. "Mary wrote a letter to me to be read when I was sixteen years of age. She left it with my Aunt Amelia. When I read that letter, it told Amelia to sell the Manor House and provided adequate money for Amelia and me to live comfortably. Mary revealed everything in this letter, explaining how she had been warned by a stranger not to read the book when she first made her plans, long before her father died.

"One night while her father was away, this stranger called at the Manor House and talked to my mother for a long time. Amelia remembered this part of the story and told us how Mama looked as if she had been crying. As the stranger left, she heard Mama calling, 'Nothing will change my mind!' The stranger stopped at the door and before leaving, asked her to reconsider her decision, for if she carried out her plan, he could only promise her certain disaster. Not long after, we heard of father's death. Mother became sick and nearly died herself, but Amelia told me when I was older that fate was not that kind. She recuperated and then left.''

Lady Margaret was silent and Catherine asked, "Where did she go?''

"That is a long story and not mine to tell. But we now come to my life; that is, my past life as Rose Featherstone.''

Intrigued with the mystery of Mary Strong William, the mother of Rose Featherstone, Catherine felt compelled to ask Lady Margaret once more about the Higher Order.

"Why is this one family, the Strongs, so important that an entire group of people observe its activity throughout the generations just to protect that one book?''

Alan smiled as he reached for his pipe and pouch. "Perhaps I can explain. You see, Catherine, the Order is comprised of highly evolved souls; each member is aware of his own karma within his own family line, and each member is a Keeper of the Book. They all protect each of these records and are constantly aware of each family through the generations.''

Catherine's eyes got wider. "You mean that the story your mother has told about William is not the only story, that there are other families under the same influence?''

Tapping the stem of his pipe on his teeth, Alan nodded and went on to tell Catherine that the Higher Order was spread all over the world and consisted of small cluster groups, one of which he had been a member of since he was seventeen.

"What's the purpose behind all this?''

"These highly evolved souls have always been concerned about the total balance of man and the earth. Since time began, we have followed the ancient laws of nature and esoteric philosophy. Each of us is aware of our own family and its moral progress through the centuries; so all of us are Keepers of the Book and protectors when the karmic path changes in any one family.''

"This is fantastic,'' said Catherine. "It's also frightening to think that this kind of thing is in existence in this modern world.''

Alan gave a deep sigh and said, "Perhaps there would be no modern world as you know it but for the constant activities of the Higher Order.'' Shrugging his shoulders, he then hesitated as though he wanted to say more, but decided it wasn't the right time. Breaking the conversation, he looked at his mother and asked if she would like to continue.

"First, I think we should have some coffee.''

"Good idea,'' agreed Alan.

Catherine asked if she could use the phone to call Nickie.

Tom Thornleigh answered and recognized her voice immediately. He sounded bright and breezy and told her that everyone had missed her at breakfast. "By the way, Catherine, a Jonathan Whiteside called.''

Catherine felt a tightening inside. "What did he say?''

"Oh, just reminding you of your appointment in California on the eighth, that's all.''

"What's the date today?"

"August fifth."

"That gives me only three days to get there," said Catherine, to no one in particular. Remembering that Tom was still there, she thanked him for taking the message and said she would see everyone later. Alan saw that she looked pale and asked if anything was wrong.

"You know the letter I received from Jonathan Whiteside about the will? Well, he called me at the Blue Feathers to remind me about the appointment back in the States."

"Oh, I shouldn't worry about that," said Alan. Then, turning to his mother, he asked, "Are we ready to carry on?"

Pouring another cup of coffee from the elegant silver pot, Lady Margaret continued with the story of her life as Rose Featherstone.

Chapter Twelve

Nickie and Jason had breakfast together at Southworth's. Over coffee they talked about their lives and the fascination they shared in the story of Megan.

Strolling down High Street toward the Blue Feathers, Nickie was delighted with everything she saw. They heard a car horn and looking back, saw Hilary and George, who stopped the car and asked where they were going. Jason and Nickie didn't have any plans, so they all decided to go to the Blue Feathers and see if Catherine and Alan had returned.

Sitting outside the inn, Tom and Frances were deeply involved in conversation. Everyone got out of the car and went over to join them. Nickie noticed that Frances' foot seemed to be swollen and asked if it bothered her much.

"Not really," said Frances. "It just seems to come and go."

Pulling out a chair, Jason asked if it was all right to join them and they readily agreed.

It didn't take a minute until they were all deep in conversation about Catherine. Hilary mentioned that she was leaving soon and going down to Tenby to meet Mike for the weekend. George said that he would like to book in at the Blue Feathers for the weekend. Unfortunately, the inn was fully booked, and Tom was having difficulty trying to accommodate his regular guests. Jason thought of a bright idea and invited everyone, including Tom, to come to Cardiff House for the weekend. Tom looked undecided; Frances could see what he was thinking.

"Come on, Tom," she urged. "It'll do you good and we can be together without any interruptions. The inn will be all right."

Thinking it over for a moment and rubbing his chin, he said, "I could ask Mary and her husband to look after things...OK, let's get in a holiday mood." He hugged Frances, and she had never felt happier.

"If I didn't want to see Mike so damn much, I would have loved to join you all for the weekend," said Hilary, laughing.

"So it's agreed then?" asked Jason.

Everyone was delighted.

"I'd better call Cardiff House and have them get ready for us. Now let's see, how many will there be? Ladies first: Catherine, Frances and Nickie; then there's Alan, myself, George and Tom, and Mother makes eight. Excuse me for a second." As Jason got to the door, Nickie called him back and asked if Martha Sheridan might be invited. "Of course, I had completely forgotten poor Miss Sheridan. "Why don't you call her on the other phone, Nickie?"

Nickie went directly to Mildred and asked if she would get Miss Sheridan on the house phone.

"Is there anything wrong, Miss?" asked Mildred.

"Why? Should there be anything wrong?"

"No, I suppose not," said Mildred sourly. "I was only asking."

"Well, Mildred, I'm only answering...Hi! Is that you, Martha?" For the second time in less than a minute, Nickie was asked if there was something wrong. "No, Martha. There isn't anything wrong. Jason asked me to call and invite you to Cardiff House for the weekend. Can you make it?"

"Can I make it?" asked Martha, not believing her own ears. "I wouldn't miss this outing for the world. Tell him I'm coming. Oh, but how will I get there?"

"Why don't you pack your overnight case and I'll call you back with arrangements," suggested Nickie.

"Tell Jason thank you," Martha shouted into the phone, then immediately hung up. This is like a dream come true, she thought. Fancy staying at Cardiff House with Lady Margaret. What would everyone think when she mentioned it casually in the corner shop?

When Jason called home and told his mother that they had house guests for the weekend, she was delighted. Assuring Jason that the staff would prepare immediately, she suggested that dinner that evening would be a nice way to start off the weekend.

"By the way, are Alan and Catherine up at the house?" asked Jason.

"Yes, and could you have someone at the inn put her things together and bring them with you?"

"Will do, Mother...see you sometime this afternoon. Bye."

Lady Margaret smiled as she put the phone down. Jason had always been this way, extroverted and enjoying company just as she did. Alan was like his father, more selective, more inclined to live a peaceful life. Except for those trips he took now and then, he was nearly always home or at his cottage.

Joining Catherine and Alan in the Morning Room, she found them standing by the window with their arms around each other. They made a perfect pair, she thought, and hoping that all this disruption would soon come to an end, she told them about the weekend.

"By the way, Catherine, I took the liberty of making arrangements for your belongings at the inn to be packed. Jason said he would bring them this afternoon sometime."

"That's fine, Lady Margaret. I hope he's not too late, so I'll have a chance to hang my dress before dinner."

A twinkle came into Lady Margaret's eye. "How would you like to choose a dress from my collection?" she asked. Then laughing, she said, "Oh, please don't think I'm trying to lend you one of mine. I have several, all different sizes, upstairs. I'll let you select your own."

"What a lovely idea," said Catherine. "When can I look at them?"

Feeling that this would be a good time to be on his own with Catherine, Alan volunteered to take her upstairs and show her the gowns while his mother went to inform the staff of the weekend guests. Alan noticed how beautiful Catherine's hair looked as she walked upstairs with him. The light shining through the stained-glass windows reflected on her blonde hair. She looked as pretty as a picture.

Walking down the long, impressive wood-paneled corridor, Catherine said, "It's bigger than any hotel I've ever stayed in." Ahead of them was a fine porcelain vase filled with flowers, and Catherine had a fleeting memory that she knew this vase, then the thought went as quickly as it had come.

"Here's the room," said Alan, unlocking the door.

Catherine gasped. "This is absolutely beautiful!" It was decorated in purple and pink; splendid, but delicate. "It's fit for a princess."

"Then why don't you use this room for the weekend," said Alan, delighted that he could please this lovely girl who had won his heart more than once. Accepting his offer, she tried the bed, which felt soft and comfortable. Alan walked over to the bed and looked at her as she lay back, laughing. He wanted to hold her; he wanted to marry her, but this was neither the time nor the place to tell her that. He opened a huge mahogany closet with three doors full of gorgeous gowns in all colors and sizes. Taking one out at random, she held it up to her and asked Alan what he thought.

"You'll look adorable in anything you choose," he said kindly. "Why don't I leave you for a few minutes so you can try on as many as you wish? Just give me a call. I'll be downstairs; when you're done I'll take you for a walk through the grounds."

Giving him a hug, she agreed that it would be fun to explore the closet. Giving her a kiss, he left her.

Cardiff House seemed alive and Alan had never been happier. He whistled as he went downstairs again. He could see his mother talking to the staff. There was excitement in the air.

Catherine pulled out a royal blue dress and held it up to her. Looking through the mirror, she noticed that something was pinned on the back. It read: *Lady Charlotte, 1899 Engagement Party.* How interesting, she thought. She then pulled out another gown from farther down the rack. The style was different. It didn't have the same sleeves as the first dress. This one was gathered around the waist, forming a kind of bustle at the back. Again there was a label; this one read: *Beatrice Griffiths, 1865 Coming Out Party.* The next dress she saw was of deep, rich, brown velvet, beautifully made, with intricate designs stitched in gold thread. With it on the hanger were two frilly petticoats. Knowing she needn't search any further, Catherine looked at the label and this time she read: *Alice, Wife of Edward Strong Griffiths, Washington House, 1876.* Knowing it would fit, she decided to try the whole ensemble. Taking off her jeans and sweater, she stepped into the white calico petticoat. Unfastening the dress, she heard someone call her name....

"Alice, how long are you going to be? You know our guests will be here any minute now."

Edward was irritable as usual, and Alice knew that this evening was important to him. He was eager to settle his business and return to Boston. Edward had never been the same since his quarrel with and separation from his elder brother. There had been a violent argument in the study. Edward's voice had been loud as he had accused his elder brother of some misdoing. Shortly after this, they had moved to America, and the once loving and attentive Edward had grown cold and distant.

"Please, Alice," he said, as though conjuring up every scrap of patience he could muster.

Reaching for her shawl, Alice got up from her dressing table and taking a last look in the mirror, asked, "What time are your guests arriving, Edward?"

Putting his gold watch back into his waistcoat pocket, he corrected her mildly, "*Our* guests, Alice."

The West Coast of California was a far cry from her beloved Wales. Boston had taken her a little time to get used to, but this sleepy Spanish town was unlike anything she had experienced before. It was early evening in mid-December and flowers were blooming in the garden. Never having been in this type of climate, Alice found it fascinating. The hotel had all the amenities; it was only five years old and the proprietor had equipped it with modern furnishings and conveniences.

On reaching the lobby, two men with tall hats came through the front door. Anxious to greet them, Edward passed Alice on the stairs. They were shaking hands when Alice reached the bottom of the stairs. Edward introduced them and suggested that they indulge in an aperitif and a cigar until the owner, Mr. Washington, joined them. Alice was happy with this arrangement. It meant that she could have a few moments to herself.

"I think I will walk in the gardens before dinner, Edward."

"Fine, fine, my dear," said Edward, as though relieved.

As she made her way through the dining room toward the garden, she went through the door onto a patio and deciding this was a good place to observe everything, sat in the window seat.

Mrs. Washington came in from the garden with a small Chinese boy carrying a pile of plates so high that he could hardly see over the top of them. Ignoring the boy's discomfort, Mrs. Washington saw Alice and stopped to admire her dark brown velvet dress.

"You look as pretty as a picture sitting there, ma'am," said Mrs. Washington kindly. Then, turning to the boy, she asked him to hurry and put flowers on the table before dinner started.

Looking over towards the stables, Alice wondered if Emmanuel the stable boy might be on the grounds. Since she had arrived, he had given her lots of attention, and Alice was flattered by his smile and uncouth manner. He was a fine handsome figure of a man. When they had arrived a month ago, he had been overly attentive, smiling such a smile that Alice blushed to recall it. Then she heard the little Chinese boy.

"Excuse, please, Miss." Pointing to Edward, the little boy nodded his head and hurried away.

Seeing that impatient look again on his face, she went to join Edward and his guests.

The dinner conversation was dull: finance, property and finance again. Feeling herself dropping off to sleep, Alice opened her eyes wide and...

...still holding the brown velvet dress, Catherine decided that she would wear it this evening for dinner. Hearing a tap on the door, she answered, "Please come in." Expecting Alan, she was surprised to see Lady Margaret.

"Have you decided which dress you're going to wear, Catherine?"

"Yes, thank you, Lady Margaret...this one," Catherine replied, displaying the brown dress happily.

Lady Margaret approved, and Catherine put her arms around Alan's mother, thanking her for the dress, for the beautiful room...and her heart thanked her for Alan.

Together they went downstairs.

Chapter Thirteen

Linking her arm in Alan's, Catherine walked with him through the spacious gardens. After a while they sat on a bench near an impressive circle of oak trees. Alan was quiet for a while, content to have his arm around Catherine's shoulders. The sun was shining, yet the air was cool. Finally, he spoke.

"Have you decided what you're going to do about Jonathan Whiteside?"

Catherine's eyes seemed to be searching every leaf on the nearest tree as she pondered that question. "I have a feeling I ought to see what it's all about. What do you think, Alan?"

Giving her a friendly hug, he said, "Catherine, you've got to do what you feel is the right thing."

"Can you come to the States with me?"

"I don't know, dear. I'd like to go with you to the ends of the earth, but I'll have to think about this one."

"Why?"

He laughed and said he would think about it and talk to her later that evening. "We'd better get back to the house. It's three o'clock, and our guests will be coming soon."

With that, they strolled back, laughing and talking and looking forward to dinner.

Frances felt herself becoming more and more attached to Tom. It seemed as though her life was just beginning. It didn't seem possible that she had only known him two days. This whole thing was so foreign to her nature: Normally, she was shy and rather introverted, but since meeting this wonderful man, she felt young again inside and out.

The whole day was perfect: the kind of day you would like to put in a picture frame and keep forever. Tom could not remember when he had felt happier. Talking to Frances and being near her made him feel protective and comfortable. Each hour they had together felt like a year. Yet Tom felt a fear in his heart, the fear of losing Frances. He didn't know why he felt so apprehensive; this feeling marred the joy that was flooding him. The simplicity of it all, he thought. No middle-aged man had ever enjoyed sitting in a park as he had this morning with Frances. They had planned to have afternoon tea together before getting ready to go to Cardiff House. The minute he saw her face smiling at him, he knew he had known her somewhere before. Collecting his thoughts, he was amazed at his own deep sentiments: How could he have known her before...before *when*?

Frances came down the stairs; her limp seemed to have gone. As she walked over to him, she ran the last few steps and suddenly she was in his arms. He was like a mountain. She felt secure, and they held each other tightly without saying a word.

Tom buried his head in her hair and whispered hoarsely, "I can't let you go, love. I can't, do you understand?"

She pressed his shoulders with her fingers, as if to say 'yes.' He went to kiss her, and tears were on her cheeks.

"What's this?"

"I don't know, Tom. All I know is that I love you."

Laughing and almost crying himself, he lifted her up in the air and said. "I won't let you down till you say you'll marry me."

"I will, I will," shrieked Frances as she struggled to put her feet back on the ground.

Hearing her answer, Tom held her close; so close that it seemed as though they were breathing together. "When, sweetheart?"

"Whenever you want, Tom."

"You mean that?" When Frances kissed him, he knew the answer.

Their laughter aroused Mildred's curiosity and peeping into the hotel lounge, she couldn't believe her eyes.

Whatever next? she thought. I don't know what's happening to Mr. Thornleigh....

Nickie was having a long serious conversation with Jason, who was so pleasant to be with. He was bright, intelligent and had class, but Nickie's thoughts kept wandering: She wondered where quiet moody George might be.

"You know," said Nickie, "when I think back, everything started with Catherine. But during our talks, dreams have been mentioned several times; yet no one has discussed their dreams. Know what I mean?"

"Interesting," said Jason. "I think you have a point. Maybe we should suggest to everybody tonight that they tell us about their dreams and then maybe we'll find some ends we can tie together.''

"Do you think George will be coming?" asked Nickie, a little too casually.

Jason laughed. "Does it matter?"

"Not really. I was just wondering."

Nickie felt a bit of a fool, and so obvious! She hated to be obvious. The likely choice, if she had one, would be Jason, but George was somehow very special....

George and Martha were chatting in the hotel foyer when Jason arrived. "Where is everyone?" he asked. Then, seeing Martha, he took a step back and said, "My, how lovely you look!"

Martha's heart gave a twitter. She had really made an effort. She managed to get a hairdresser's appointment and wore the dress she had worn for her niece's wedding in June. This whole day had been perfectly exciting for Martha. She had spent time finding her weekend case and wiping every cosmetic jar before she carefully packed it for the weekend. Not being entirely satisfied with her nightwear, she had gone to the drapery shop and spent more than she really wanted to on a pink fleecy nightgown with a matching robe. After all, she had told herself, it's not every day one gets an invitation to Cardiff House.

George looked good in his dark suit, thought Nickie. Sighing inwardly, she wondered why she was always attracted to dark moody men. He smiled and came over to give her a kiss. Always selfassured, Nickie returned the kiss in a lighthearted way and decided to stay real close.

Mildred came in and announced a phone call for Lord Jason. Thinking it was his mother, he went to the desk to answer.

A strange voice asked, "Is that you, Jason?"

"Yes," replied Jason, curious to know who was speaking.

"This is Mike, Hilary's husband. I was supposed to meet her here in Tenby, but as yet I haven't seen her. I wondered if she had been delayed at your end."

"Not that I know of," answered Jason. "Hang on, I'll ask the others." Seeing Tom coming from the bar with Frances, he shouted, "Have either of you seen Hilary?"

"Not since she left," said Tom.

Speaking now to Mike, Jason told him that as far as he knew, Hilary had left, and no one had seen her since.

"That's strange, it's unlike Hilary not to let me know."

Giving Mike his phone number at Cardiff House and asking him to call if he should need him, Jason said goodbye and hung up. Rounding everyone up, Jason suggested that they leave, as Lady Margaret always liked to serve dinner promptly.

Waking up from a short nap, Catherine stretched and began to feel excited when she remembered the weekend ahead. She really loved her dress. As she sat at her dressing table finishing her make-up, she ran her fingers slowly over the gold thread....

Feeling nervous, Alice sat in her favorite corner of the window seat. Edward was still in San Francisco, and these past few weeks had been heavenly. After waving goodbye to Edward as his carriage drove away from the stable, she had stood there for a while, gazing at the mountains, glorious in the morning sun. Her eyes squinted in the strong sunlight. She didn't see Emmanuel until he was standing right beside her.

His dark, wavy hair glistened. His smile was seductive and in a deep voice with a strong Mexican accent, he asked if the man who had just left was her husband.

Hesitating, and surprised that he had spoken to her, she reluctantly answered, "Yes."

"How long he go away, lady?"

Shocked that he should ask this question, Alice started to walk away.

Emmanuel laughed loudly. Then, changing his tone of voice, he beckoned for her to follow him. He took hold of her hand, and she allowed him to lead her to the stable door.

"You like horses?" When she nodded, he asked, "Would lady like to ride?"

Feeling that the conversation had gone too far, she shook her head. He roared with laughter.

"You come ride with me at noon today. I find nice chestnut for you." With that remark, he turned around and went into the stable.

Alice just stood there. When he looked back and saw that she hadn't moved, he began to laugh. Not knowing how to deal with such a man, she started to run back to the hotel, still hearing his laughter as she ran through the garden.

Going up to her room, it seemed that her heart was beating faster. This man did things to Alice which she found difficult to understand. Telling herself that he must be mad to expect her, a lady, to go riding with a stable hand, she managed to laugh out loud, trying to reassure herself that the fool was out of his head. Fussing with her hair for a few minutes, biting her lips and rubbing her cheeks to put a glow on her face, she went downstairs to have her morning coffee. Once again, she sat in the window seat, letting the morning's episode run through her mind over and over again. Suddenly conscious of someone staring at her, she looked up. He was standing at the end of the garden, smiling. Impudent servant, she thought.

He waved, and once again she heard the roar of his laughter as he went about his work. Her hands were shaking as she put down her cup and saucer.

The proprietor's wife, Mrs. Washington, came through the glass door with her little boy, Johnny.

"How are you this morning, Lady Griffiths?" she asked. "Can I get you more coffee?"

"Thank you, that would be nice."

The little boy stayed with Alice as her mother went back to the kitchen. Not uttering a word, he just stood there staring at Alice, who slowly began to feel uncomfortable. When Mrs. Washington returned, Alice tried to sound as casual as she could and asked if there were horses available for riding.

"Oh yes," answered Mrs. Washington, happy to be of service to this foreign lady.

"Well, I would like to ride today at about noon. Will that be possible?" Mrs. Washington said she would make the necessary arrangements. "Thank you. Of course, I will need an escort, in case I get lost or the horse is unruly."

"Certainly, madam. I will take care of it for you."

Alice thanked her and went upstairs to her room. As soon as she closed the door, her poise left her. She was trembling but full of anticipation. Having changed into her riding gown and fixed her hat with a scarf, she heard a knock at her door.

"Come in, Mrs. Washington."

The door opened and Emmanuel stepped inside. "Are you ready, Lady Griffiths?"

Taken aback at seeing Emmanuel in her room, she said, "Yes, thank you," and walked to the door.

With his back to the door, the large man looked at Alice and laughed as she tried to open it. "I'll scream if you don't let me out," she cried.

Lifting her up in his arms as though she were a·feather, he held her close, speaking softly in a foreign language.

"Let me down, you pig!" she cried, her hat now fallen to the carpet. "I'll beat you if you don't let me go!"

Once again he roared with laughter.

Feeling frustrated and angry, Alice started to hit him with her riding crop.

He stopped laughing, ripped the crop from her hand and started to kiss her on her face and neck. Her body went limp and she showed no more resistance. Carrying her to the bed, he threw her small body on it.

Terrified, she looked up at this huge man who was still grinning and untying his leather breeches. She lay there, unable to move, fearing his animal passion, but anticipating a kind of love she had never known....

When it was over, she turned over on her stomach. A tear trickled down her cheek.

He dressed quickly and fastening his boots, lifted his leg onto the chair and with a mock bow, asked if madam would be riding tomorrow.

After he had gone, Alice bathed, put on her dress, and smiling a strange smile, was ready to go downstairs....

As Catherine came down the stairs, she looked magnificent, her blonde hair a perfect contrast to the dark brown velvet dress.

Alan ran up the stairs to meet her, sensing something different. "Catherine, your hair is beautiful."

Lady Margaret, standing at the foot of the stairs, was amazed to see that Catherine had put up her hair as they wore it in the eighteen-hundreds.

There was a promise in the air that night at Cardiff House. Everyone was dressed in festive style. They enjoyed excellent champagne and a wonderful dinner of roast duckling in orange sauce. The dinner conversation was pleasant, but the "TomFrances announcement" was the highlight of the meal.

"I would like to tell all our friends here tonight that Frances has consented to be my wife," Tom said proudly.

Immediately there were handshakes and kisses. Frances gave off a glow that radiated throughout the room. Nickie almost felt envious of the romance that Tom and Frances were experiencing. I never get anyone who looks at me like that, she thought. Will I ever?

The maid approached Jason, telling him he was wanted on the phone. It was Hilary's husband, Mike.

"Hilary eventually made it. She hadn't been feeling well and missed her train connection."

"I hope she's all right."

"That's why I'm calling. I put her to bed right away. She doesn't have a temperature, but she's a little delirious, I think."

Jason felt perturbed and was genuinely concerned. "Is there anything I can do?"

"Well, she arrived at the hotel here and as you know, I had been waiting for her. She walked right up to me and asked me to go to Cardiff House with her. Remember now, I didn't even know there was a Cardiff House, so I said, 'Hilary, what's the matter with you?' She gave me a strange look and said, 'My name is Blodwin, and the group is now together and we must go.' "

"Is she all right?" asked Jason.

"She's OK now, but she had me worried for a time. She keeps insisting we go to Cardiff House. Have you any idea what's going on?"

"How far away are you from Manningstile Henlock?" asked Jason urgently.

"Oh, I should say about an hour or so drive, why?"

Jason thought for a moment and then asked Mike if he would care to come to the house for the weekend if Hilary was feeling well enough.

"Hold on a sec," said Mike. "I'll go ask Hilary and see what she wants to do."

"Hello." Jason heard Hilary's voice.

"Well, hello, Hilary, are you all right?"

"Yes, I think so. I felt kind of strange earlier on, but now that Mike's here, I'm feeling much better."

"Would you like to bring Mike up to Cardiff House? Do you feel up to it?"

Sounding her usual self, Hilary told Jason they would leave within ten minutes.

Jason decided not to go into detail about Hilary or Blodwin, so he told his guests that she and her husband Mike were going to join the party later on in the evening.

Everyone was happy and left the dining room to retire to the huge lounge, fondly called the Tapestry Room by Lady Margaret and her family.

"Are you coming to the States with me to see Jonathan Whiteside?" Catherine asked Alan.

"If you want me to," answered Alan kindly.

This news made her happy; soon she was joining in different conversations and enjoying many compliments on her dress. The women were impressed by her hair, especially Nickie, who knew that Catherine hadn't a clue when it came to fixing her hair.

There was a settling down. Cardiff House felt warm with friendship; hearts were happy, and the evening crept on silently. The huge room with the glow from the fire dancing on the walls; glasses of wine reflecting light; soft piano music playing Chopin: a perfect setting for future memories.

Feeling in the perfect mood, Tom lifted his glass and said, "Here's to Gareth of Abergavennie."

Lightheartedly, the others lifted their glasses too.

Then Tom said, "But who *is* Gareth of Abergavennie?"

Jason suggested that the only one who could possibly know was Megan.

Catherine felt a chill but managed to smile.

"I think it's you," said Frances, pointing her finger at Tom good-naturedly.

There was a stillness, as though everyone was considering the possibility, simply because this was the first time anyone had suggested Tom's being a character in Megan's life.

"Why me?" asked Tom, putting his arm around Frances.

"Let me hypnotize you, Tom," said George.

This question created excitement; Martha Sheridan was the first to give encouragement. "Come on, Tom. After all, you've nothing to lose."

Soon they were all trying to persuade Tom to lie down and let

George take him back in time. Not wanting to admit he was afraid, Tom said, "Eh, folks, it was only a joke, really it was."

"But suppose it *isn't* a joke and you really *are* the reincarnation of Gareth?" said Nickie.

"To be honest," said Tom, "I think Jason is Gareth."

Listening carefully to everything, Martha asked if she could make a suggestion. Eager to hear what she had to say, Frances said, "Listen, everybody! Please, let's be quiet for a moment and hear Martha's idea."

Martha got up from her cozy chair as though ready to recite a poem at the village fair. Both hands clasped in front of her, a shy flutter of the eyelids gained the attention she desired.

"I agree with having another hypnosis session, but I have this strange feeling: almost like someone is telling me inside my head that we should have a seance."

Before anyone could speak, the maid announced that Mr. and Mrs. Wilcox had arrived. Alan and Jason both jumped to their feet to greet Hilary and her husband.

Mike Wilcox was a friendly man who looked as if he might be a professor or an inventor; youngish, but with the unkempt look often developed by those who are always preoccupied with work. Hilary looked her best, an emerald green dress and simple jewelry making her appear as though she had stepped out of *Vogue*. It was difficult to imagine she had had problems earlier, thought Jason.

"Feeling better now?" he asked her.

Hilary nodded. Mike instantly liked the guests at Cardiff House and was glad he had come. Nickie told Hilary that they were considering a hypnosis session or a possible seance.

Jason could see that Hilary and Mike were quite relaxed and offering them a drink, asked, "Now what's this Mike told me? Don't you think we have enough mystery and intrigue without bringing in another character?"

"Another character?" asked Alan.

"Yes," said Jason, in a deep dramatic voice. "And a Celt, no less."

Lady Margaret asked Jason what on earth he was talking about.

"Why don't you tell them, Mike?" Jason replied.

Brushing his hair back with his hands and balancing his drink on the arm of the chair, Mike smiled and looking as if he needed approval from Hilary, told them that she had said she was someone named Blodwin.

Before Mike could go any further, Catherine almost shouted, "Blodwin?"

The flames in the fireplace suddenly diminished and burned with a bluish pallor. The atmosphere changed abruptly from that of a cozy gathering to a room chilled, full of eerie vibrations. Alan stood up; he seemed taller somehow. The lights were dim, and

Lady Margaret was humming a strange tune. Without conscious thought, the group held hands and slowly everyone joined Lady Margaret in an old Celtic chant, forgetting everything that had been said. Catherine tried to see what Alan was holding as Tom gripped her hand tightly. A rich melodious voice asked all heads to bow. Speaking through Martha, the voice continued:

"Thou, whose paths have crossed through many centuries, now reach the time chosen to free thy souls from past karma. It hath taken many lifetimes, and through the grace of the Universal Spirit, thy blemishes will be lost in the compassion thou mayst have for one another. Listen well to the Keeper of the Book. He who shall next inherit this earthly title waiteth to be born, and his mother will be the maid Megan of Manningstile Henlock, rightfully united with her kindred spirit.

"All hatred, curses, bloodshed and evil thou hast shared and the lessons of many lifetimes have now brought thee all to this one place. For this is the holy ground where Blodwin brought William of Garth to the elders for his initiation. Blodwin, not born of this earth, fell in love with the mortal, William of Garth, and in giving birth to their son passed on the wisdom of the elders which had come down through many generations. 'Tis now time to reveal thine identities to each other so that thou mayst progress and go thy separate ways. Blodwin, the Higher One, will now speak to all gathered here."

Expecting to hear Hilary speak, heads were raised slightly. Hilary's face could be seen in the firelight, but she did not utter a word.

Lady Margaret again started her chant and the room became icy cold. A circle of light formed above their heads; the energy could be felt by all. Lady Margaret's chant became louder; everyone felt compelled to join her. As they did so, the light became stronger and brighter, descending to the center of the room. As it reached the carpet, the energy took shape and form. Lady Margaret stopped singing and so did the others. Everyone stared at the form as it developed. The figure of a tall, slender female with hands outstretched, dressed in a cloak and hood, swayed and moved as though gaining strength. Then it spoke in a hollow voice.

"I am Blodwin; I have walked among thee through many lifetimes, trying to help thee on thy karmic path as I did with William of Garth many centuries ago. 'Tis now the hour, and with the Keeper of the Book, Alan Strong Griffiths, who is the seed of my first William, each of thee must see the paths thou hast trodden. When this hath been done, thy reward will be peace, if what is revealed to thee can be accepted. Be warned that it taketh but a fleeting moment for this to be, although to thy consciousness 'twill be long and weary. All will be well with thee, for thou art in the presence of the Masters."

Coming as from nowhere, hooded figures materialized in the circle. Blodwin continued:

"Each elder here present hath shared thy karmic path, and 'twill be through their consent and love that thou shalt be privileged to make amends." Then, with a forceful voice, Blodwin commanded, "Be thou cleansed of all negative experiences gathered throughout many lives! Prepare thy souls for freedom!"

On this command, the members of the group felt a coldness engulf their bodies as though they were being bathed in icy water from the bowels of the earth.

"The Keeper of the Book will also gain his freedom, if he endureth the pain of his past. Each of thee must take this journey alone, but thou shalt return with joy and freedom of spirit if thou followest the paths shown thee by thy Masters."

With this, each Master left the circle and slowly approached his chosen one.   Fear and apprehension surged through each body; because their hands were joined, this vibration was equally felt by all.   As the elders approached, they felt a darkness come upon them. It was like going into a black sleep, back through the grave to face an unknown reality.

The hooded figures now absorbed the waiting souls as they wrapped their cloaks about them.

Cardiff House was locked in time.

Chapter Fourteen

MARTHA

Martha was aware of a deep voice. Although she felt afraid. she knew that she was safe. As her Master walked over to her in his flowing robe, she felt the robe spinning around her body like a cocoon.

"Be still, Martha, and relax. Thou art protected. Now I will show thee thy progress through eternity."

It seemed as if she were going back in time; the Master would point out different episodes. It was like being at a theater. As each scene appeared, the Master would reveal the circumstances until she began to see a definite pattern being woven.

And then "Martha" was no more. She was a beautiful young woman and knew that she was in her home. It was a pleasant room; she could hear children laughing and playing. Engulfed in selfishness, she was envious of a friend who was visiting. This friend seemingly had no obligations, but the soul of Martha felt that she had more than her fair share. The face of her husband was full of love and hurt; she heard children crying now and saw that she had deserted her family and comfortable home. The rest of that life was a miserable record. She saw a classroom full of children, but it was more than that—it was an orphanage. A child was being brutally whipped; another child was tied to a chair. A big heavy woman with her teeth clenched and saliva coming from the corners of her mouth was shouting obscenities at the innocents. Realizing that this beast was herself, she recoiled and begged to be shown no more.

She felt the gentle hands of her Master and heard him say, "This must be; thou must see and recognize thy karma."

As other events from previous lives were revealed to her, she wanted to escape; it was hell, yet she knew there was no escape. The only mercy would be forgiveness. Now came a sensation of change; a transformation of energies into something totally different. She was hearing her own voice, merciless, deep and masculine. She (he) was passing sentence on a young boy who was guilty of stealing a loaf of bread for his brothers and sisters. She was this brute of a man, showing no mercy and condemning the boy to ten years imprisonment. Ignoring the cries of his mother and the appeal of the boy's father for mercy, the judge walked away from the bench.

Not knowing how her spirit could hold together, Martha was transported once more, out of this agonizing situation. She was in another country. She spoke in another language, yet understood every word. Obviously wealthy, she was childless and barren.

The next episode was almost unbearable. She was paying money to an evil-looking man, dirty and unkempt. In the room was a young woman, who was her maid. The girl had given birth to a baby and wanted her child more than anything in the world. The girl's name was Marie and while pregnant she had applied for work.

Martha knew her own name was Dorothy Fenshaw; she was married to a rich industrialist. When she hired Marie, she knew of the girl's predicament and promised her food, shelter and protection after the baby arrived. This, of course, had never been her intention. She wasn't able to give her husband a child; this situation provided the ideal opportunity to take the baby from this poor, pathetic creature and keep it as her own.

The filthy yellow-toothed man was Marie's father, whom Dorothy Fenshaw had contacted and offered money to allow her to keep the newborn baby. He readily accepted the money and knocked Marie to the ground when she tried to reclaim her baby. Mrs. Fenshaw had the man drag the screaming girl out and take her away. If he or Marie were ever to return, she told them, she would have them both put away forever: the man in jail for attempted murder and robbery, and the girl in an asylum.

The soul of Martha experienced great agony, for she was now taken beyond Dorothy Fenshaw's knowledge. She watched the painful scene as the man drank incessantly; he wasted every penny he had been given for the sale of his grandchild. Finally, poor Marie committed suicide after being raped by her own drunken father.

Throughout this journey back into her past lives, her Master's voice guided her and helped her to understand her own lack of love and charity. She saw how she had been blessed with a beautiful husband and children and how, through her own selfishness, she had deserted them. Her Master pointed out scenes from the lives of her husband and children after she had left. They were pitiful; she felt a shame that tore her heart. The lives of her family had deteriorated after her disappearance. She recognized the impact we have on others' life paths.

Again she was shown scenes from the cold, inhuman orphanage and her mistreatment of little children. If her soul could have wept, it would have filled oceans. Going back to the courtroom and to miserable scenes of her life as a man and a judge, once again she saw the wretched lives of people who had suffered because of her terrible lack of mercy.

The life of Dorothy Fenshaw was no better as the stolen baby grew into manhood. More and more every day, she was reminded of his cruel ugly grandfather. Then there were times when she saw the gentleness and beauty of his mother, and always when she reached out to embrace him, she would be haunted by the memory of Marie's face. She would see again her tears and agony and remember her terrible suicide. And the boy could never understand the strange moods of the woman he called mother.

The next scene was almost unbearable: her son had experienced bad dreams since childhood, but she had never shown any interest or tried to help him. When he was fully grown, he finally told her how he had had this same dream from early childhood. He would see a beautiful young woman preparing to commit suicide and she would always call his name for help. In the dream, he would try but could never find her. He would waken in the night, perspiring and shaking.

Dorothy Fenshaw, on the verge of insanity, murdered her son when he was nineteen years of age. She was sentenced to death and unable to endure her guilt and anguish, committed suicide in her cell.

Martha knew it was after this particular life that she had had to learn many lessons before being given the privilege of life again. For a long time she had experienced total darkness in the black womb of the universe, like a star waiting to be born. Then, once more the opportunity of fulfilling her karma was given to her.

She saw herself as a poor young woman who had been in domestic service since a child in the Welsh city of Harlech. The master of the household raped her while the mistress was away. Not being completely without mercy, he gave her three gold crowns and dismissed her before the pregnancy became obvious. Walking on foot for many miles and several weeks she acquired work at an inn in Abergavennie. Her labor pains began in the night and afraid to ask for help, she delivered herself in the stable where she worked. Driven to near distraction, she felt helpless seeing her three newborn babies lying in the straw. Her plight was sorrowful, for she knew she could never exist with three babies.

The last born was smaller than the first two boys. It was a little girl, which she named Megan. The two lusty boys were plump and robust. She had to make her plans quickly for fear she would be seen. Sobbing with grief, she held her two sons to her breast and fed them till her milk was running from their tiny lips. Wrapping them first in her petticoat and then a sack hanging from the barn saddle hook, she placed Megan in a safe corner and went out into the village to dispose of her sons. Holding them close, she looked for a place to leave them. She came to a bakery and could feel the heat of the oven as they baked their bread during the night. Making sure they would be found, she left the two boys there, then ran back in the dark to Megan with tears streaming down her face. Her heart was broken and aching for her sons. Picking up Megan, she hastily prepared to leave Abergavennie and set off on foot southward.

Many events flashed quickly by. Martha relived the anxiety of carrying the baby day after day. Almost starving, she arrived at last in Manningstile Henlock. She asked at the blacksmith's where she might find work. This kind man could see that her child was not very old and offered her room and board if she would keep house for him. The blacksmith became her husband and Megan's father. The village took kindly to her, and she lived many happy years as a blacksmith's wife.

One day, when Megan was about seven years old, a new family with two sons, Gareth and Dylan of Abergavennie, moved into the village. No one knew, nor did her husband ever ask, who Megan's father was. When she would attempt to tell him, he would say, "Hush, my love, thou art now mine and so is sweet Megan. My life started upon the day thou didst arrive."

So as the boys grew up and played with Megan, the three became inseparable. But fear and guilt began to grow in the mother's heart, and many of her actions and remarks seemed unreasonable and unkind. For as all the children grew, she saw that her sweet Megan did not look at Gareth of Abergavennie with the eyes of a sister....

There was a blackness and Martha was alone, terribly alone. She was begging for forgiveness; her spirit was tortured with constant memories. She heard the voice of her Master, telling her to reach out and take hold of his hand. Doing this, she saw the darkness disintegrate and she felt a great need to try again.

Feeling peace now and a renewed need to live, she mentally conversed with her Master, seeing her present life in full perspective. Twice she had nearly married, but each time she had suffered the humiliation of being left alone. Knowing that she had to overcome her feelings of rejection, she turned her life around, trusting the feelings that told her to find her vocation in teaching. Martha did so and felt a reasonable satisfaction in her years as a teacher. She had often suffered loneliness in this life and had devoted herself to helping, not only her pupils, but their families. Lately, she had experienced thoughts of self-pity and often wondered why she had never married and had children. Now that she knew her karma, she felt a warm pulsating energy around her. It was like being born again. She pushed her head up into the light. There to help her was her Master, and there was the unspeakable joy of knowing she could try again.

He spoke: "Thou hast trodden thy karmic path, and the pain thou hast suffered is the hell thou needst no longer fear. The previous lessons will remain in thy higher consciousness, but their memory will now be erased forever. In thy return, thou shalt feel a great love and compassion for all thy fellow men. Joy will be thine, and to those who receive thy kindness, awareness will be given. Be peaceful now; take a new karmic path so wide, so generous, that others may find peace and fulfillment through thee."

Feeling the hand of her Master upon her head, Martha sank into the sweetest sleep, that sleep which gives the soul perfect rest.

TOM

It was almost too much for level-headed Tom. As the figure of the Master approached him, he gripped Frances' hand tightly. As the Master's robe wrapped about him, he could hear himself screaming for Patrick. The old woman was holding little Patrick, fondling his golden curls, tears surging down the creases in her face like rivers going to the sea. Recognizing Megan's mother, his heart sighed with relief.

Tom's journey into his past had been easy, like putting on an old shoe. He slipped with ease into forgotten memories. His Master smiled as Tom's spirit explored freely. His character had not changed, and in each of his lives, simple lessons were learned. Tom felt himself in flight; he could move at will. As he looked down, he saw cameos of previous lifetimes. When he felt a desire to know more, he would find himself slipping easily into the past experience. His Master was beside him and Tom smiled, knowing that he had always been with him. The abbey he saw below caused a great surge of happiness. Desiring to discover the joy beating in his soul, he descended, and inside the ancient walls he heard his brothers chanting.

"Brother Francis," someone called.

Turning, he saw the old Abbot in his grey robes. This round, jolly, fat priest hastened to greet him warmly. Uncertain of what was happening, Brother Francis asked his forgiveness for not announcing himself properly. With tears in his eyes, the old Abbot welcomed him back home.

"It has been too long, Francis. Didst thou find the answers?"

Brother Francis shook his head and Tom's consciousness was confused. He felt pain and uncertainty.

"Hast thou made peace with thy conscience, son?" asked the

priest. "Canst thou look upon thy sister now and know her to be a bride of Christ?"

Instantly, Tom knew why he had come back to this time and this holy place. Weeping, he dropped to his knees and confessed that his self-inflicted penance of six dark months in a tiny cell had not changed his feelings toward the nun, Sister Patrick Thomas. The old Abbot's smile drained from his face. His hands were shaking with emotion as he placed them on the young priest's head. He was grieved to hear of the young man's torment and his desperate need for advice but he felt helpless to guide him.

"Let us kneel together, my son, and ask God for direction."

As the old Abbot said his prayers, Brother Francis saw Sister Patrick Thomas kneeling before the altar. She was not aware of his presence. She prayed several times a day to gain strength and ask that she be rid of the need for earthly love.

Brother Francis left the old priest, still in prayer, and walked quietly to join her at the altar. When they saw each other, they embraced, and all who saw them were shocked and whispered of shame and excommunication.

Hearing the raised voices, the old Abbot opened his eyes and forgetting his feelings of love, pointed his finger and told the young priest and nun that they would both go to hell unless they repented and never saw each other again.

Upon hearing this and seeing their accusers, they knelt silently together as the voices got louder. Asking silently for forgiveness, the priest and the nun kissed at the altar and then left the abbey as Francis and Patricia. Leaving their beloved Church, they went out in the world together to raise a family. Seeing his past lives and their simplicity of purpose, Tom would remember events instantly as they flashed before him. Life with his beloved Patricia was only marred by his conscience. Their life together had been perfectly matched. Realizing that his karma was to forgive himself, he viewed his past experiences in perspective and knew that he and Patricia were bound together for all time.

As the vision faded, he felt compelled to hold onto the warmth and love he had shared with this woman. He looked in desperation at the Master, who shook his head. The agony of separation tore his heart. Like a sleep within a sleep, Tom felt very cold. This time he was not a spectator, he was Dylan of Abergavennie.

Hearing loud voices, he and Timothy ran up the stairs. The sight before him was pitiful. Never had he seen such horror! Lying in a pool of his own blood was his brother Gareth. This young, vital man had been struck down by Lord David, who was standing there with his hands covered in blood. Poor Megan was distraught, her deep sobs echoing loudly. The sight of the child laughing and playing in Gareth's blood was too much for Dylan and blinded by his tears, he lunged forward and killed the murderer of his brother.

Still in her nightgown, Megan ran out of the house into the cold night air, sobbing and screaming, unable to bear all that had happened. Dylan ran to get her with young Patrick in his arms. It was too late! As she reached the edge of the cliff, he saw her smile strangely and open her arms as though to embrace someone. Still smiling, she plunged to her death down the steep cliff. There below in the moonlight he saw the smile of death on Megan's face. With this terrible burden of grief, Dylan took the child to his grandmother's cottage and as they sat by the peat fire, told her the terrible tale. Overcome by remorse and grief, the old woman gazed at her grandson and the last of her three children.

The old woman came over to the broken man and putting her withered arms around him, rocked him like a baby. They both fell asleep, and the fire died. In the cold grey morning, Dylan once again witnessed death. The old lady had paid her karma.

FRANCES

Still holding Tom's hand, she saw the hooded figure approach. She immediately thought of the Hermit and her fear and apprehension melted away. The Hermit was the ninth Tarot card in the Major Arcana and carried a lamp which glowed with friendly yellow light. Remembering the verse in her book, she repeated it in her mind:

> *Look up, dear friend*
> *And see the light;*
> *It shines by day and shines by night.*

The Master came nearer; Frances could see his aura. Again she thought of the Hermit. She had learned the key to this card by heart:

> *Ask and it shall be given you;*
> *Knock and it shall be opened to you.*

As she felt herself enveloped in the Master's cloak, she was consciously aware that the pain in her leg had completely gone. The Master spoke to her:

"I am your Master and I will be with you as you experience your life's journey. Have no fear; my name is James and when you think of me I will be ready."

James the Master appeared to grow smaller as he went farther and farther down a long narrow tunnel. Frances knew that she was meant to follow. Suddenly aware of great speed, she saw herself in numerous lifetimes.

In a tiny, whitewalled room, kneeling in front of an ebony cross, anxiety filling her heart, she asked for forgiveness for a love that

was all-consuming. She, Sister Patrick Thomas, had met Brother
Francis on only a few occasions. But the love she felt for him was a
full and overwhelming love that had occurred instantly upon
meeting him. Many hours had stretched into many months of tor-
turous indecision, until finally Francis had imposed upon himself a
penance of isolation and continual prayer. This he did for both of
them. When it was over, their love was still as overpowering, so
they gave up their vocations, he as a priest and she as a bride of
Christ.

In their freedom as Patricia and Francis, their love blossomed
and they had children and a wonderful marriage. But they were
never able to fully ease their consciences. Patricia often wondered
why she had changed direction in life. Not that she regretted her
marriage and love, but she suffered from constant guilt that she
had gone in the wrong direction. She would often pray for
punishment.

Reliving these past memories, she asked James, her Master, why
she had suffered such torment and guilt. She could hear his answer
and learned that thoughts were living things: She had designated
her own punishment to be reflected in her next life.

Back now, traveling at great speed through the long narrow
tunnel, she felt her personality change and an excruciating pain in
her leg. She was a child, a little boy, frightened when the man hurt
her mama. Patrick had fallen down a steep staircase. Papa was nice
to Patrick when Mama wasn't near. He would play and hug and
shower kisses, but as soon as Mama came, he would change.
Patrick loved Papa and could not understand his Mama always
telling him how really nice Papa was and how Patrick should love
him.

Next, Frances witnessed a gruesome scene, seeing it as the little
boy Patrick saw the terrible tragedy. Two Papas were lying with
Patrick on the floor and Mama started to make loud, horrible
noises and run away. Patrick became afraid as his Uncle Dylan held
him too tightly, chasing Mama. Patrick never saw his Mama again.

This last scene left Frances trembling and even now, as it faded
from her, she could feel the terrible pain which she had brought
with her into her present life. Was she still punishing herself for
breaking away from her Church?

"This is the question you should have asked a long, long time
ago," she heard the Master say.

"I set my foot in the wrong direction?" she asked sadly. "And I
carry the pain today?"

Pleasant memories came now of Uncle Dylan, so good and kind.
As she lived the youthful past of Patrick, Frances realized that
there was more to know of this life, but her Master indicated that
this was not the time. She appealed to him, and he gave her a little
longer—just fleeting glimpses, hard to decipher. She, Patrick, a

grown man now, was in love with a ballerina. She gasped as her mind tried to tie these things together. Her visions faded. She left the tunnel behind and knew that she was returning to her Francis, the priest; her kind and loving Uncle Dylan; her husband-to-be, Tom Thornleigh. She had indeed come home and left the ballet for good.

Unlike Martha, Frances and Tom, the rest of the group had experienced something entirely different. As the Masters came toward them, they all felt themselves being lifted higher and higher. They heard the chanting of the elders and although not aware of each other, they all heard Blodwin's voice:

"Thou art now encircled by the elders. Each soul present hath lived many lifetimes. In some way, thy past lives hath touched upon one another. 'Tis written that the Keeper of the Book will find his peace when there is peace among thee. Thine origins are from this ancient place. Each of thee hath known these worn stones and solemnly vowed thine allegiance to one another. Thy roots are to be found in the Higher Order: each of thee chose a life path that would eventually fulfill a Karmic Circle. This circle is not yet complete, but as thou findest thine individual purposes, thou shalt be blessed with peace and inner satisfaction. On the last night of this year, December 31st, thou shalt gather here once more, in perfect peace and harmony, to gain further knowledge of thy purpose. And each of thine earthly lives shall find contentment."

Blodwin's image began to break into tiny colored lights. Around her was a brilliant aura. Once again the chanting could be heard, and a sensation of unbelievable speed, as though they were taking flight through the universe. Stars and moons whirled past; incredible beauty and heavenly music accompanied them. Glimpses of past lives flashed by which they would instantly recognize and immediately forget, for this was not their time. A cold darkness came upon them: it was night and the moon was full. Ancient stones cast strange shadows as the moonlight fell upon them. They were participating in a ceremony, each robed and devout. In a fleeting second of time, everyone present knew that Blodwin's words were wisdom and truth.

"Before I release thee," said Blodwin, "I will leave in each of thee the knowledge of thine ancient heritage and purpose. But beyond this thy memory will be veiled; thou shalt now pursue thy purpose and achieve tranquility of soul." And once more their conscious minds were severed from karmic memory.

Chapter Fifteen

Jason was the first to awaken. His eyes opened and he was happy to feel himself back in this world again. He saw his mother staring into the fire. Tom was kissing Frances tenderly on the cheek. Slowly, the room came to life again, and Jason felt that a good stiff drink would raise everyone's spirits.

It looked as if Martha had been crying, but there was a certain glow that indicated tears of happiness. His brother Alan was looking at him curiously, and this made Jason feel somewhat uncomfortable. Alan looked away and seeing that Catherine was stirring, stroked her hand gently and waited patiently until she spoke. Mike looked more tousled than before, not understanding all that had happened. He rubbed his hair and told anyone who might be listening that he had had a damn good sleep. There were smiles from the others, but each one was wondering if their experience had been just a strange dream.

Then Nickie said, "God, what a trip! I'm sure I flipped out."

Catherine leaned over and handed Nickie a lighted cigarette. "I think all of us have had a very personal experience. I know I have; maybe it would be better if we didn't go into detail." No one spoke, but heads nodded in agreement. Catherine then turned and said, "What do you think, Lady Margaret?"

"Perhaps you're right, dear."

Jason, trying to inject life into the party, readily agreed, and going over to the desk, switched on the radio. The tension slowly vanished as everyone began talking, glad that they wouldn't have to discuss Blodwin's message. Jason asked Nickie if she would like to dance; the music was slow and he held her close. Pulling away, Nickie glanced at George, who seemed to be involved in a deep conversation with Catherine. Jason admired Nickie's dress. Normally she would have enjoyed his compliment, but somehow she felt a pull toward George and wished he would at least acknowledge that she was alive.

Lady Margaret came in with the maid, carrying delicious snacks, and invited everyone to help themselves.

"Would you like a sandwich?" asked Jason. Nickie thought this was a good reason to stop dancing and accepted his offer.

Martha felt a deep contentment. Thinking over what had happened, she felt her life fall into place. There was so much she wanted to do. As she sat, she felt content and secure, not afraid of tomorrow.

It was like one big family gathering. But Catherine had questions left in her mind. She had to go see this Jonathan Whiteside, although she hated to leave Wales, which she already loved dearly. California, her home, her job (if it were still there), seemed to belong in a different world. Jason asked her what she was thinking. Smiling, she told him she was thinking of her trip back to the States.

"Will you come back?" he asked, concerned.

"Yes, I think I will."

Alan had overheard the conversation and reassured Jason that he could bet his life on it.

Watching Alan and Catherine together, Jason thought how attractive Catherine was. Then, of course, he was always attracted to good-looking women.

Hilary was feeling tired, so Mike suggested they go to bed. Excusing themselves, they left with Lady Margaret, who wanted to show them their room.

"What do you think happened tonight, Hilary?" asked Mike when they were alone.

Not wanting to talk about her experience, Hilary answered casually that she had fallen asleep. Mike thought this was funny and putting his arms around her, asked if she were feeling any better.

Mike fell asleep first. He hadn't been in bed five minutes before Hilary could hear him breathing deeply. As she lay there, she could see the moon through her window. The bed was marvelous. She felt lucky to have Mike as a husband: he was both kind and considerate. As she drifted into sleep she thought, This weekend is going to be fabulous....

Frances and Tom sat close together on the couch and talked in whispers, taking great delight in analyzing their past lives.

"It's still hard for me to accept all this kind of stuff," said Tom. "But seeing that both of us had the same things happen to us, and that wouldn't be easy to do, even if this whole thing was a joke...."

Frances snuggled closer. "It seems like you've always been here to protect me, Tom. Funny, isn't it? First, you were my kind Uncle Dylan, then you were my Francis, and now I'm your Frances."

"How's your foot, dear?"

Wiggling her leg and feeling her ankle, Frances looked at Tom with wide eyes and told him that she couldn't feel a thing.

"I suppose that falling and damaging my leg when I was baby Patrick, and the guilt of going in the wrong direction as Sister Patrick Thomas account for my leg. And isn't it strange that I've always wanted to be a ballerina, and when I was Patrick, the woman I fell in love with was a ballerina?"

"Do you really love me?" asked Tom, feeling uncertain again.

"Of course I do, Tom. Now there you go again. I'm convinced that you're also the reincarnation of the original Doubting Thomas."

George watched Nickie as she laughed and talked, envying her ability to be so comfortable among people. He always felt awkward in company and admired people like Nickie who could appear confident and poised in front of strangers. Why did she keep looking at him?

Nickie had a strange feeling when George looked at her; then she saw Catherine on her way to the kitchen. Going over to join her, she asked Catherine if she had a minute.

"Anything wrong?"

"Not really. It's just that I have a funny feeling about George."

Catherine started to laugh. "You must be joking. You, Nickie Foster, losing your grip?" Nickie was always self-confident, especially around the male sex. Hearing Nickie talk like this amused Catherine. But Nickie looked serious.

"Look, Catherine, I'm not kidding. This guy kind of gives me a guilt complex, if you know what I mean."

"Well, I saw Jason trying to get acquainted. And you seemed to be acting cool, not your real self. Don't you like him?"

"That's something else. I kind of like him, but I get a creepy feeling when he gets too close."

Catherine thought the conversation was amusing and didn't take Nickie too seriously. "Your trouble is that you can't make up your mind which eerie feeling you like best."

"Maybe you're right. I think I'll have a drink and then toss a coin."

Both girls went back into the room with the others. Nickie felt in a better mood. The music was playing softly, and Jason asked Catherine to dance. Alan was talking to his mother, so Nickie decided to make her move.

"Shall we?" she asked George.

George straightened his collar and struggled up out of his chair.

For a moment, he looked at his hands and appeared to be deliberating where to put them. Nickie laughed and snuggled a bit too close for George's comfort. The wine made her feel romantic; she asked George if he enjoyed dancing. He gave an embarrassed chuckle and as if to prove he did, pulled her close.

Deciding to be frank, she whispered, "Have you any idea why I'm so attracted to you?"

His answer surprised her. "Maybe it's because I'm so goodlooking. I do this to all the girls." This remark seemed to break the ice; they both relaxed and enjoyed being with each other.

Jason was friendly and extroverted, yet rather secretive, thought Catherine. He wasn't at all like his brother: his friendliness was genuine, yet Catherine found him difficult to understand. People like Alan you know right away, but the Jasons in life are different: they have a way of being extroverted, yet you end up not really knowing anything about them.

"What time is it?" she asked, trying to see Jason's watch.

"Oh, it's not midnight yet, Cinderella. By the way, Alan told Mother and I that he was going to the States with you."

Although Alan had said he would go, hearing this from Jason made her feel very happy. "Let's go talk to your mother awhile, shall we?"

Jason, smiling, said, "You mean let's go over to my brother. All right, we'll do that—if I have to."

It seemed as though Alan were waiting for them: they didn't have the opportunity of talking. Alan took Catherine off to dance, leaving Jason with his mother.

"Time to put out the lights," said Lady Margaret, smiling at Catherine and Alan. Not realizing that everyone had gone to bed, they had been swaying gently to the music for a long time. Lady Margaret had been patiently waiting for them to finish so she could say good night.

"Oh, good night, Mother. Don't worry, I'll turn off the lights."

Smiling graciously, Lady Margaret left them both alone. They decided to have a nightcap before retiring.

"Have you any idea what this whole thing is all about?" asked Catherine as Alan gave her a drink. He didn't answer, so she asked again, "What's this whole crazy thing about, Alan?"

His answer was plain and straight to the point. "Will you marry me, Catherine?" His eyes were intense and seemed to penetrate so deeply that she found she had to look away. Holding her chin and turning her face toward his, he asked once more, "Will you marry me?"

"I don't know. I think that once I get away from Manningstile

Henlock and back to the USA again, I'll be able to look more objectively at everything.''

"Don't you love me?"

"Yes, Alan, I do, but I think you understand that I can't commit myself to anything until this whole crazy thing is sorted out."

Stroking her hair, he smiled gently and said, "Then I'll wait. I've waited this long; a little longer won't make that much difference."

Frowning, she asked, "What do you mean?"

"Let's leave it at that. So when are we going to the good old USA?"

That remark didn't sound right coming from Alan, and Catherine laughed. "Whenever you're ready, m'lord."

"Why not Sunday?"

She nodded gravely and Alan said, "Well, Sunday it is. Now let's get some sleep, for I can feel some other ideas coming to mind." He kissed her passionately for the first time, and she felt compelled to agree with him, for the same thoughts were in her head, too. Walking her to her room, Alan held her close and then reluctantly said goodnight.

Closing her door behind her, she breathed a big sigh and got ready for bed. She lay there for a while and could see that the moon and stars were huge; her room was flooded with bright moonlight. This room felt so good, yet she couldn't sleep. Her mind was running at great speed, one thought merging into another. Flashes of her life at home came to her: she saw her apartment and Bartholomew sitting in the window. He never learned, thought Catherine. Oh no, he knocked over her crystal vase! In her mind, she chased him and could hear Vera Harris outside on the veranda asking Bartholomew what he was up to. Vera was her next-door neighbor and had agreed to take care of the cat in Nickie's absence.

My God, thought Catherine. This is actually happening! It's not my imagination. Opening her eyes, she lay and thought about it awhile. She had actually seen Bartholomew's kittens. Two black, one tiger and a tabby. She had seen the cup with lipstick that Nickie had left on the coffee table, and when she had looked outside, it had been raining. Thinking more about this, she remembered it was daytime and Vera was home. She would phone right now.

"Hello, operator, I want to make an overseas call." Lighting a cigarette while the operator got through, Catherine sat upright. I'm fully awake, she thought, convincing herself.

"Hello." She heard Vera's voice.

"Hi. This is Catherine—Catherine from next door."

"Oh, you're home already?"

"No, Vera. I'm still in Wales."

"Is something wrong?"

Catherine thought for a moment and asked, "How many kittens did Bartholomew have?"

"Five. But one died. I thought Nickie was over there with you."

"She is."

"Surely you haven't called me to ask how many kittens Bartholomew had."

"Listen, Vera, please, this is important. I know you'll think I'm crazy, but please, just listen. Has it been raining?"

Vera gulped. "Yes," she said.

"And did Bartholomew have two black, one tabby and one tiger?"

"Yes, but why?"

Trying to keep her voice steady, Catherine asked, "Would you mind going into my apartment and seeing if my crystal vase is broken on the carpet by the window?"

"Are you serious, Catherine?"

"Believe me, I am."

As Vera went to check on the vase, Catherine closed her eyes. She saw Vera button the top of her blouse as she went out the door. She saw her smile at one of the neighbors. She sneezed; then, opening Catherine's door quickly, glanced over to the window. Catherine saw the broken vase again.

"Catherine, are you there?" Vera was back on the phone.

"Oh yes. I want to thank you for taking care of Bartholomew. Guess I'll go now. Bye."

"Wait a minute, Catherine," shouted Vera, but the phone was dead.

Catherine went looking for her cigarettes. Dear God, what's happening to me? Am I turning into some kind of freak? Wide awake now, she turned on the radio and a couple more lamps and decided to manicure her nails. The closet door was open and she noticed on the upper shelf an assortment of hats—some with feathers, others with faded flowers and ribbons. The radio was playing music from *My Fair Lady* and Catherine thought of Eliza Doolittle, all dressed up at the races. She couldn't resist trying on some of the hats.

She tried on several before her eye caught the dark brown velvet hat. It had a dusty pink ribbon and dark brown feathers that looked as if they had been dipped in oil. As she examined the hat, she saw the initials "ASG" inside. Realizing it matched the gown she had been wearing, she put it on and heard the little Chinese boy tap on her door.

"Missee, Missee, buggy readee."

"I'll be right down. Thank you." Checking again to see that her hat was on straight and pulling on her gloves, Alice went downstairs.

Mrs. Washington greeted her and told her that Emmanuel was waiting with the buggy at the side of the hotel. Glancing out the window, she saw Emmanuel holding the reins and chewing a piece

of straw. Her heart missed several beats. As she came out of the
side door, he gave her his big smile. He didn't move as she waited
to be helped into the buggy. There was a loud voice: Mrs.
Washington.

"Emmanuel, help the lady!"

He got down slowly and with a mock bow, helped Alice into the
buggy.

"Where does fine lady want to ride?" he asked.

Clearing her throat, she told him that she would like some ocean
air. It was all downhill to the ocean. They passed some fine homes,
but they weren't anything like the houses she was accustomed to.
The scenery was beautiful. The sleepy little town was protected by a
mountain range, and the sky was so blue she could see every detail.
The houses stopped and the road narrowed. It looked as though the
road had been cut through a vineyard. Emmanuel waved at some of
the Mexican workers, who yelled back in a language she didn't
understand. They were now passing small adobes and wooden
shacks.

Emmanuel stopped the buggy. Jumping off, he said, *"Un
momento,"* and disappeared into one of the small shacks.

Children came running to the buggy. They laughed and pointed
at Alice's hat. This made Alice very uncomfortable; she was angry
that he had left her alone like this. The sun was hot and she began
to feel great discomfort. She tried to talk to one of the boys.

"E-man-yoo-ell—please," she told the boy. He started to giggle.
Alice repeated her request, and the children tried to copy what she
was saying. Feeling tears come to her eyes, she was feeling almost
desperate when at last she saw Emmanuel strolling toward the
buggy.

"How dare you keep me waiting here like this!" she cried.

He didn't like her tone of voice and glared at her angrily. He
jerked the reins fiercely and shouted, "Hidee—*up!*" The two horses started to gallop.

Alice had to hold onto the bar. She shouted for him to stop, but
he kept his eyes in front. Sobbing now from fear and frustration,
she prayed that this nightmare would end.

Finally Emmanuel brought the horse to a stop, then jumped
down and put out his hand to help her. He pointed to the ocean; the
spot was secluded. She felt the breeze on her face. She turned to
look at him, and he sat down on the sand, pulling her down beside
him. Crying now as he held her roughly, she realized he was wild,
like an animal; she could expect neither mercy nor respect. He
started to stroke her face. She tried to pull away. He slapped her
and then started to kiss her. The more she relaxed, the gentler his
kisses became. Soon she responded, and he was whispering words
of passion she couldn't understand. Strange, she thought, the
language of love can always be understood....

The ocean was choppy and the wind was high. They were surrounded and protected by the cliffs. "You love me, fine lady?" Emmanuel asked her.

Pulling away from him, she asked to be taken back to the hotel. "I see you later, *si*?"

Unable to say yes or no, she murmured, "Maybe."

He let her go, his laughter becoming one with the wind and the gulls. Going back to the hotel, neither of them spoke. As she got out of the buggy, she realized she was covered with sand. Taking the back entrance, she went up to her room, afraid she might see Mrs. Washington or some of the guests.

Breathing a sigh of relief, she sat in the rocking chair, wondering if Edward would stay away longer than he had originally planned. She took off her clothes and shook them outside the window. She did not want sand in her room. He was standing outside and as he saw her shaking the petticoats, he roared with laughter. Then, throwing her a kiss, he went away, whistling. She knew she would be seeing him later. Alice decided to have her afternoon nap. Lying on top of the bedcover, she closed her eyes and felt the strong arms of Emmanuel around her once more....

"Catherine, Catherine, are you all right? You're absolutely freezing!"

Opening her eyes, she saw Jason. "What's the matter?"

"You must have been dreaming. You were shouting someone's name."

"What was the name?" she asked anxiously.

"Emmanuel. Shall I stay with you till you drop off?"

"Oh, no, I'll be OK. I guess I just had a bad dream." She fell into a deep sleep and Jason stayed with her, watching till dawn brought the first light of day. The maid brought in the morning tea and said, "Good morning," as she opened the drapes.

Catherine felt good and got out of bed, taking her tea over to the window. The view was glorious. She saw Alan ride up to the house. His horse needed a good rubdown. Alan must have been riding him hard, thought Catherine. Opening the window, she called to him. But when he looked up, she thought she saw Emmanuel's face.

Hurrying now to get dressed, she put last night behind her, for she was eager to see Alan. Nickie was already eating when Catherine got to the dining room.

"Boy, do these Welsh know how to eat breakfast! I've had a bit of everything: sausage, bacon, eggs, tomatoes and whatever these are."

"Those are kidneys," said Jason.

"Kidneys?" she gasped.

"Yes," said Jason. "They're delicious."

Breakfast was delightful; everyone helped themselves from a long buffet filled with silver dishes. Each dish was piping hot, and to finish, there was homemade jam on toast lashed with thick dairy butter.

The day was pleasant for everyone. Cardiff House sat on onehundred-ten acres of Welsh beauty. Part of the land had a secluded beach. On this marvelous estate, there were riding trails, picturesque walks, tennis courts and a bowling green. The magnificent house boasted a fine library and also a fine collection of paintings. The game room had a billiard table, and every game imaginable was stored neatly on shelves indexed by Lady Margaret especially for house guests. There was an exquisite music room with a grand piano. The weekend guests were invited to enjoy all the facilities, meeting at one P.M. for luncheon and eight sharp for dinner.

"I need to talk to you, Nickie," said Catherine.

"That's fine with me. Let's sit out here on the side lawn. Now, what's on your mind?"

Catherine started to tell her about her strange experiences.

"I thought you'd be used to being Megan now," said Nickie.

"That's the whole point, Nickie. This time I'm not Megan, I'm Alice."

"Alice?" Nickie laughed till she ached. Even though Catherine was confused, she couldn't help laughing with her.

"Oh, and there's something else," said Catherine. "I'm going to the States tomorrow."

"The States?" said Nickie, not believing her ears. "But honey, we've only just arrived, and apart from you going spooky, everything's been perfect. Now why go and spoil a good thing?"

"Don't forget my mysterious date with Jonathan Whiteside."

Nickie knew that Catherine had gone through hell and wished there was something she could do to help. "OK, then I'll go with you. Maybe we can come back together someday. What do you think, Catherine?"

Before Catherine could answer, she saw the men strolling toward them.

"Have you seen Frances?" asked Tom.

"Last time I saw her, she was with Lady Margaret, Hilary and Martha, looking at the paintings," said Nickie.

Leaning over to Catherine, Tom gave her a big hug. Without thinking, Catherine hugged him back. He smiled fondly and said he was going to find Frances.

"Have you noticed George's legs in those white shorts of his?" asked Nickie as she watched him walking toward them.

"Can't say that I have," said Catherine, amused at Nickie's way of putting things.

Hilary and Mike were coming back from riding. Hilary looked

magnificent in her riding clothes, and Catherine commented on her ability to look well-groomed whatever she was doing.

"You know, Catherine, I have to agree. I suppose that's what happens when you're confident and know you have your man."

"Come on, Nickie, do I detect a little envy there?"

"You bet you do. I'd give my eyeteeth to be a sex symbol."

As Jason walked over, he overheard her remark and told her that she could keep all her teeth.

"Now I'd say *that* man knows what he's talking about," said Catherine, smiling.

During lunch, everyone was obviously having a wonderful time. Lady Margaret told them that cocktails would be served about six-thirty, followed by dinner at eight. Catherine thought it would be a good time to tell them that she was going back to the States in the morning with Nickie. Jokingly, Nickie asked if they would like to keep the party going and all come over to the States.

Frances felt genuinely sad that her friends were leaving so soon, but when she remembered her own announcement, she cheered up. Trying to keep the excitement out of her voice, she said, "Well, I have some news for everyone, too. Tom and I are getting married in September and we would like all of you to come to the wedding."

Tom looked proud as he confirmed the plans and told them it was going to be nothing but the best.

After a round of congratulations, Nickie insisted that her invitation was still open. "Who's going to come back with us?"

"Well, I am, that's for sure," said Alan.

Determined to keep in contact with her new friends, Martha said, "I'll see you all at the wedding. You will be back, won't you?"

"Certainly," said Alan.

"Why don't you come with us, George?" asked Nickie. I have a guest room and you're more than welcome."

George looked embarrassed as Nickie kept looking at him, expecting a direct answer. Before he could say anything, Jason looked at George and said, "I'll go if you will."

"I'll think about it," said George. "I really can't say one way or the other right now."

Nickie felt a deep disappointment, but not wanting to display her feelings to everyone, she changed the subject.

The evening was pleasant, but there was an air of sadness. The group had begun to rely on one another and it seemed that they'd always been together. Alan had gone to Cardiff after lunch to get the airline tickets and upon returning, told them they would be leaving about midnight.

"Why don't you try to have a nap?" he told Catherine. "It's going to be a long night."

"I couldn't possibly sleep. I should be packing right now."

"Me, too," said Nickie.

The two girls excused themselves and went upstairs to pack.

"Do you think Jason is coming with us, Catherine?"

"Of course he is. Alan got his ticket."

"But what about yours and mine? We've made arrangements to go back at different times."

"Don't worry. Alan's taken care of everything."

"Including you, by the sound of it," said Nickie, laughing.

The travelers said their good-byes to everyone. There were hugs and kisses and promises that they would all keep in touch.

"Don't forget, George," said Nickie. "You're welcome anytime. Here's my phone number. Just give me a call whenever you're in California."

Thanking her, George folded the paper carefully and put it in his wallet.

Hope he doesn't lose it, thought Nickie.

They hadn't been in the air too long before everyone was asleep. Catherine was trying to imagine what Jonathan Whiteside would look like. Nickie was thinking about George. Jason was happy to be going to America and Alan was already fast asleep holding Catherine's hand.

Chapter Sixteen

The flight was uneventful and they landed on time at Los Angeles, where they spent the night. Catching the first available flight to Santa Barbara, they arrived with time to spare. Santa Barbara was strikingly beautiful.

Waiting while Alan and Jason rented a car, Catherine and Nickie went to the newsstand. Nickie was looking for information on Santa Barbara. She was amazed that after living in California all these years, she could discover a place like this existing so near Los Angeles.

Alan and Jason walked over, saying they would have to wait about half an hour, so Nickie pointed to an interesting sign, "Peter's Flying Machine." It was the airport restaurant.

"Good idea," said Jason, and the four of them went upstairs.

The waitress was friendly and suggested that if they took the scenic ride in Santa Barbara, they would get a good idea of what the city was like. They finished their drinks and went down to get the car.

"What a beautiful city," said Jason. "I feel as if I'm on the Mediterranean."

"Yes, it does have a definite Spanish flavor," said Alan.

Feeling somewhat nervous, Catherine reminded Alan that Mr. Whiteside had mentioned only three reservations, so what should they do?

"We'll deal with that problem when we come to it," said Alan.

"This is dreamy," said Nickie. "Just the place I would choose for my honeymoon."

As they drove along Cabrillo Boulevard, they were impressed by the natural beauty of the coastline and buildings. The palms were magnificent and the harbor looked inviting with its clean boats and fisherman hauling in their ropes.

"I think we'd better make our way to the Biltmore," said Alan, glancing at his watch.

After driving along the shoreline, hugging the beach most of the way, they were thrilled when they saw the setting of the hotel. Everyone seemed at ease except Catherine. Her palms were wet with perspiration and she continually touched her hair as they made their way to the dining room.

It wasn't until much later that Catherine remembered their strange meeting with Jonathan Whiteside. When they arrived in the hotel lobby, it was full of people going different ways, but Alan walked straight up to a silver-haired man and introduced himself.

"Mr. Whiteside?" asked Catherine nervously, joining Alan.

"Yes, I'm Jonathan Whiteside. It's good to see you. Did you have a good flight?"

Smiling, Catherine nodded and introduced Jason. Mr. Whiteside didn't seem at all concerned that she had brought three friends with her. Somehow it wasn't the sinister meeting she had imagined.

The lunch was superb, but they hadn't yet talked about the letter or the will. Nickie kept nudging Catherine under the table, as if to say please get on with it. Wetting her lips, Catherine looked anxiously at Alan.

Alan grabbed the cue and in the smoothest way possible, said, "Well, Jonathan, you wished to see my fiancee about her Uncle Alfred's death."

Mr. Whiteside wiped his mouth with the crisp, white napkin, dabbing the corners carefully. He looked at Catherine and asked if they would like to go to his room.

Before answering, Catherine looked at the others, who gave a nod or a smile of approval.

It seemed to take ages before they eventually reached the room. Nickie found it hard to contain herself. As she sat down, she said, "Please, let's get down to facts. I can't stand this waiting. What's it all about, Jonathan?"

Jonathan pulled out his briefcase and started to search through papers. Catherine lit a cigarette; Alan reached over and touched her hand.

"Your Uncle Alfred was the older brother of your father," Jonathan began, looking at Catherine.

Catherine interrupted, "But my father didn't have a brother."

"He did, Catherine," said Jonathan. Continuing, he went on to tell her that her father had been adopted as a baby. "Alfred, the older brother, was only sixteen when their mother died in childbirth. Alfred watched your father, Richard, grow up and accept a new family as his own. Shortly after their mother died, your grandfather passed away, overcome by grief and sorrow at losing his wife and baby. Alfred, the elder brother, went to India and prospered. He would send anonymous amounts of money to your father's new parents. This enabled them to educate your father, but he unfortunately never knew that his benefactor was his brother Alfred. It was Alfred who provided for your college education."

"I always wondered how Daddy could afford to pay my college fees. But didn't he know where the money was coming from?"

"No, he understood that it was an inheritance from his mother's side of the family in Canada."

Nickie now spoke. "But why didn't Catherine's father ever investigate where the money had been coming from all those years?"

Pausing to clear his throat, Jonathan continued. "I was a close friend and colleague of your Uncle Alfred after he prospered in India. He came to Manchester, an industrial city in the north of England, and became a wealthy man in the cotton industry. I had met Alfred as a boy while I was in school in India; he was a student at the same time. Our meeting was not by accident, for we were, and I am still, members of a worldwide order."

Remembering their experience with the elders and the message Blodwin had given, Catherine asked, "Not Blodwin's order? I mean, the Keeper of the Book?"

Jonathan looked into Catherine's eyes and she knew she mustn't pursue this line of questioning.

"Although your parents died suddenly in an auto accident, Alfred, though considerably older, lived on for quite a number of years."

"And all this time he knew about me?" asked Catherine.

"He certainly did, and helped you in many ways."

Seeing her doubt, Jonathan reminded her of past incidents.

"Remember when you needed a car badly? You had had three used cars and each one had let you down. You were suddenly able to buy a new car at half price. In fact, you bought the car for exactly the amount you had in your savings. Then, before you took your trip to Paris, remember how you desperately wanted to continue your schooling? You received a letter informing you that you had been selected by the Board of Governors for a free all-expenses-paid trip to Paris."

"But that came from the school," protested Catherine.

"Influenced by your uncle, my dear," said Jonathan. "Now before we digress again, I would like to tell you the conditions of your uncle's will."

So far, neither Alan nor Jason had spoken; they too were eager to hear about this strange will.

"It begins with a verse," said Jonathan.

"Sweet daughter mine of yesteryear,

I say goodbye with one more tear;
To clear the karma from your way,
Listen now to what I say:
You shall meet him with the sign,
For he has kept it through all time;
When you know him, face him, then
Do not let it be again.
Marry him who loves you now;
Be careful now to keep this vow.
When you know the rightful one,
You'll be blessed with ancient son.
I will to you my own, my kin:
You will find him, sweet Catherine."

Jonathan continued with the body of the will, mentioning property, business and finance.

After he had finished, Catherine said quietly, "I'm afraid I don't understand." Looking over the top of his glasses, Jonathan started to explain in layman's language what the will was all about.

"The verse seems like a riddle," he said. "But the rest looks comparatively simple. Your uncle has left you two pieces of property: a house, a very fine one, in San Francisco, and a small hotel in England. The money is by no means a huge amount, but enough to take care of you for the rest of your life. It will be paid to you in small annuities and will pass on to your son when he is seventeen years of age."

"What is this property in England?" Catherine asked.

"Before I answer that, Catherine, I am waiting for certain papers to come from your uncle's bank. They should arrive within the next two or three days. Until then, why don't you stay here in Santa Barbara and relax for a while."

"Sounds fascinating to me," said Nickie.

Jonathan looked at Catherine, who nodded with a half smile. He told them that he had booked accommodations at a local inn called the Washington, and they could drive over anytime they were ready.

Jason was the first to stand and shaking hands with Jonathan, asked if he would like to join them for dinner later.

"Wonderful idea," said Jonathan. "Have you anywhere particular in mind?"

Jason said he had heard of a good place in Montecito.

"That's right on my doorstep, you might say," answered Jonathan.

"Good. Then we'll pick you up at about 7:30. Now, which way do we go?"

After getting the directions, they all said goodbye and enjoyed a pleasant scenic ride to the hotel.

"This must be it," said Nickie, pointing to an attractive white building.

The young girl at the desk greeted them warmly; it was almost like coming home. Checking them in, Maggie introduced herself, and Jason was quick to detect the traces of an English accent.

"I was born in Coventry. Do you know it?" she asked.

"Quite well," said Jason. "I stayed at the Leofric just last year."

"How old is this place?" asked Nickie.

Maggie then went on to give them a brief history and pointed out the various amenities. As she showed them the parlor, Catherine felt strange and began to shiver. Maggie began talking about the original owners in 1871 and pointed to the pictures on the wall.

"Are you all right, Catherine?" asked Alan.

Wiping her forehead, she said, "Yes, but I have the feeling I've been here before."

"Here we go again," said Nickie.

Maggie, not quite sure what to do, went ahead, with Jason's approval. They went into the Victorian living room.   Catherine felt everything spin around; then, seeing a door, she walked straight outside.

"There's the dining room," said Maggie. Breakfast is served between eight and ten and lunch from 12:30 to 2:30."

Catherine was sitting on the porch, staring across the garden. Maggie wasn't quite sure what to do next. Seeing her hesitate, Alan went out and took hold of Catherine's arm.

"Thank you, Maggie. The hotel is beautiful."

Catherine and Alan walked back into the hotel.

"Your rooms are in the oldest part of the hotel," Maggie continued. "I have a room each for the ladies and a room with twin beds for you and the other gentleman. Will you come this way, please?"

Maggie took Alan and Jason to Number 1, which was a charming old room upstairs at the back. It had little nooks and corners and was decorated just perfectly.

"It's like going back in time," said Jason.

"Please don't say that," said Nickie, laughing as she tried to peer over Jason's shoulder into the room.

"Your rooms are just down the hall," said Maggie to the girls, looking at her keys. "Miss Holmes, Number 7, and Miss Foster, Number 4."

Nickie didn't wait for Maggie to show her. She took the key and was off down the hall. "I love it, I love it!" they could hear her shout.

When Maggie opened Number 7, Catherine felt weak.

"If you prefer another room, I'm sure Maggie can find one," said Alan.

Catherine knew that she had to stay in this room. She couldn't run away. "I'll be all right. It must be all the excitement." Seeing Maggie's worried face, she added, "This is lovely, Maggie. Thank you."

"I'll bring up the bags," said Jason. "And how about us having a drink in the garden? Do you have any ice, Maggie?"

"Yes, we do. I'll show you the machine when you come downstairs."

Alan was concerned, but Catherine didn't want to spoil the weekend. "I'll be all right, honey, really I will. Why don't you go have a drink with the others. I'll try and rest before we go to dinner."

"Are you sure? I'd much rather stay here with you."

"No, really, I mean it, Alan. I'll be OK."

Kissing her gently, he drew the curtains, and she was asleep almost immediately.

Downstairs, Nickie was in good spirits. "Where's Catherine?"

Alan explained that she was resting, so they went to join Jason, who was in the reception area talking to Maggie.

In Room 7, Alice knew she had fallen hopelessly in love with the wild Emmanuel. She also knew he completely lacked any sensitivity: he was like a wild animal. Thinking of Edward, she let her mind go back to Wales, wondering what had happened that night when Edward and his brother quarreled. Remembering, she thought of Charlotte, Richard's wife. She had been crying and Richard had seemed angry with her.

Hoping that Edward wouldn't return for a few days, Alice started to imagine how Emmanuel would look dressed properly and with the manners of a gentleman. It was too much to hope for. She unlocked her door, ready for him to come in from the back stairs. He didn't knock; she ran to him. Pushing her away, he wiped his hand across his mouth and muttered something in Spanish.

"Are you all right, Emmanuel?"

"I tell you, woman, I am plenty mad." Pointing his finger at her, his dark eyebrows merged together. "You never come to the stable for me. Never. Do you hear me?"

Not understanding the reason for his anger, she tried to smile. He slapped her across the face.

"Don't you laugh at me, fine lady! I finish with you, then I go find real woman for my bed."

Crying now, shocked to hear him talk like this, she ran to him. "I love you, Emmanuel, please don't hurt me like this!"

He held her from him, his strong hands gripping her shoulders painfully. He looked at her and began his horrible laughter. Unable to move, she struggled and pleaded for him to stop. Shoving her back, he said, "I go now, and I don't want to see your ugly face again. You hear me, woman?''

Confused by his attitude and cruel words, she asked, "What have I done? You know I love you, Emmanuel. Why do you treat me in this cruel way?" He didn't answer, so she went on. "You told me you loved me."

He roared with laughter again. "Me love you? I can get a real woman anytime I want. Your petticoats are like a fancywrapped gift with nothing inside. You hear me, woman? I said, *nothing*! Now get out of my way and go back to that stupid husband of yours."

She tried desperately to hold on to him, but he shook her roughly and threw her on the bed. He left the room and as the door opened, she could hear him laughing all they way down the back stairs. Humiliated and broken, she stayed in her room without food or drink for two days.

When Lord Edward arrived, Mrs. Washington anxiously told him about his wife's condition. "She won't let us in to make the bed, nor accept any food. Maybe she has a fever."

Edward quickly went up the stairs. Banging on the door, he insisted that Alice let him in. All she would say was, "Go away. I want to die." Realizing he had a key, he opened the door and was shattered by what he saw.

She had torn her clothes and thrown them all over the room. She looked wretched. Her hair was loose and unkempt; the room smelled foul. Her eye was black and swollen. Edward couldn't believe what he saw.

When she saw him, she was ashamed and began to cry.

He held her close, rocking her like a baby. "My sweet darling, what have I done to you? How could I be so thoughtless, to leave you in this way? Are you sick, my love? My poor demented love, how wicked I am, punishing you for my own misdoings." Still holding her, he asked if she could ever forgive him. She was unable to speak, so he sat her in the chair and went to fetch hot water and fresh linen. Rolling up his fine shirt sleeves, he began to clean up the filthy mess. When he had made the bed, he bathed her like a child and as he brushed her hair, whispered soft words of comfort.

Opening the windows, he saw Emmanuel and waved down to him. Pulling the bell rope, he waited for the Chinese boy to come upstairs. He ordered broth and weak tea and taking off his soiled shirt, sat in the chair, trying to understand why Alice, his sweet Alice, was in this terrible condition. Collecting her town clothes from the floor, he found a piece of paper with Alice's handwriting:

My Dearest Love Emmanuel:

My heart aches for you. Why won't you see me? I have waited till past midnight for you to come to my room. I love you and I cannot rest till I hear your voice again. I need your strong arms to hold and comfort me. Edward will be back soon and we must be honorable and speak to him of our love, as you promised.

Yours,

Alice

Edward had never felt such anger. He looked at the bed and saw Alice, asleep now like a babe. It wasn't possible that she could have let that uncouth stable hand put his hands on her. *Dear God, it wasn't possible*! The thoughts that came into his mind were agonizing. He broke down and cried. His sobs were overheard by Emmanuel, who was listening outside the door. The stable boy went down the back stairs, grinning and whistling....

Chapter Seventeen

George woke suddenly. His body was wet with perspiration and still shaking. His dream was still vivid in his mind. He could remember every detail; he could still smell the room. Each word of Alice's note was like a hammer in his head. Murder was in his heart and he saw his hands trembling. My God, he thought. How could I possibly dream a thing like that? Feeling a sudden urge to talk to Catherine, he called Lady Margaret at Cardiff House. She answered the phone as politely as she would have at one in the afternoon, although it was one in the morning.

"Hello, Lady Margaret. I have to get hold of Catherine. Can you tell me where she is, please?"

"Yes, George. She's with Nickie, Alan and Jason in America."

"I know, I know," he said quickly. "But can you tell me where?"

Smiling, as though George were actually in the room, she replied, "Yes, as a matter of fact, Jason called me earlier this evening. They are staying in a small hotel in Santa Barbara, California called the Washington."

"Do you know the number?" George asked urgently.

"Oh, yes, the boys always leave me telephone numbers wherever they are; they know how I worry."

"Lady Margaret, could I please have the number?"

"Oh, certainly." She gave him the number, repeating it several times.

George thanked her and sitting on the bed, decided to call immediately.

Catherine heard the phone ring several times. Picking it up, she heard Maggie.

"I have a call from the United Kingdom for you, Miss Holmes."

"Oh, thank you, Maggie. Will you put it through, please?"

"Catherine, is that you, Catherine?"

Recognizing George's voice, she said, "Yes, George. Where are you?"

Ignoring her question, he started to tell her about his dream. She gripped the phone tightly, for as he spoke, he described exactly what she too had dreamed.

"My God, George," she said when he had finished. "You've described the dream I just had, the same names, the same everything; you woke me from that very same dream." There was silence. They could both hear the faint hum of the long distance wires.

"I've got to see you, Catherine, right away."

As though she hadn't heard, Catherine said quietly, "Then I really was Alice and you were Lord Edward...?"

"Catherine, can you hear me? I have to see that place! I have to come to the Washington. I'm catching the first flight out. Nothing makes any sense in my life. I have to find out! Will you still be there?"

"Yes. I think I understand, and I know I'll feel better when I see you."

Breathing a sigh of relief, George said goodbye, glad that Catherine didn't think he was crazy.

The pressure of her experience and the familiarity of the room didn't worry her quite as much since she had talked to George. As she stood by the phone, her hand still resting on the receiver, she felt suddenly light and in a much better mood. The terrible feeling of depression had left her and now she was aware of a burning curiosity. Laughing to herself, she thought of Nickie's face when she told her about her dream and about George. Oh yes, especially George.

Slipping her shoes on, Catherine went downstairs to find the others. Maggie told her they were out in the garden.

This place is unbelievable, she thought. It's just so lovely.

Standing on the veranda, she saw them sitting on the lawn. Alan waved and walked over, still looking concerned. Nickie was obviously enjoying herself. She asked Jason to pour Catherine a drink.

"Guess who's coming to dinner tomorrow night?" asked Catherine mysteriously.

"Who?" asked Nickie.

"Ah, ah," said Catherine. "Guess."

The men smiled and let Nickie pursue the question. "Oh, come on, Catherine, tell me, please?"

"Tonight at dinner."

"No, now. Come on, Catherine."

"*No*! I want to tell you all tonight."

Relaxing in the warm sunshine, they chatted about Jonathan and the will. Announcing that she wanted to wash her hair before dinner, Nickie went back to her room.

Wrapping her hair in a towel, Nickie thought she would have a cigarette before she used the hair dryer. Life had become so exciting since she received the letter from Jonathan Whiteside. Now that she was away from Wales, she knew how much she missed George. Normally, she would have enjoyed every minute with Jason. He was fun to be with, but George aroused something she hadn't known before. Her mind went back to Cardiff House and she felt sad that she wasn't there. Putting out her cigarette, she lay on the bed, listening to the birds. Closing her eyes, she heard Edward and Richard quarreling.

They were in the study; her heart was heavy with guilt. Creeping down the stairs, she heard the voices getting higher. She heard Edward appealing to Richard.

"You have it all wrong, Richard. Believe me, I have never touched Charlotte. I love her as a sister."

Richard was furious. "God damn you, Edward! I saw you with my own eyes. You were holding her! Deny it if you can!"

Edward tried to convince him that Charlotte had been acting strange lately, and that he had done all he could to avoid her approaches.

"You're talking about my wife, Lady Charlotte, and what you have done is unforgivable!" Richard shouted.

Unable to tell his brother about Charlotte's behavior, Edward was lost for words.

Charlotte felt worried and did not want the conversation to go too far. Primping herself before she tapped on the study door, she walked in and smiled sweetly at her husband and brother-in-law.

Richard glared at Edward and in a dark voice, told him that this was the end of their relationship. He never wanted to see him again.

Memories of a happy boyhood flooded Edward's mind as he tried to reason with Richard. Feeling that this was the right time, Charlotte moved toward her husband. As he put his arm around her, she asked, "Now why are you silly boys quarreling?"

Unable to contain his emotions, Edward burst out, "Why don't you tell your husband the truth? Tell him why and how you have pursued me, causing distress to Alice and myself. Go ahead, Charlotte; *tell him the truth!*"

In mock surprise, she dabbed her eyes with her lace handkerchief and asked Richard why Edward was saying all these cruel things to her.

Richard's voice turned icy cold. "Edward, I expect you to leave with your wife and never return to Cardiff House." As Edward started to leave, Richard added, "If you do come back, I will kill you."

Charlotte thought it best to continue being upset till Richard's anger cooled down.

Now that Edward had left the study, Richard pushed her away. Knowing her personality well, he spoke harshly to her. "Are you damn well satisfied, you whore? I know what Edward says is true, but I wouldn't admit to him that my wife is such a bitch."

Fluttering her eyelids and trying to soothe him, she was pushed out of his way as he left the room. Lucky it wasn't any worse, she thought. Maybe I went too far this time....

She had been a barmaid who was more than generous with her favors when she had met Lord Richard. His desire for her had been unquenchable, and she had played the game well, refusing to associate with him unless they were married. After their marriage, Richard had become a bore to her, but she was only having fun with Edward. Poor Edward was far too serious, and his dull wife Alice, with her pious ways, made her sick. Deciding to change into a pretty dress and have some of Richard's favorite wine brought up, she thought about her early bawdy days.

She had made more money in the hay than in the bar, and Richard had known this when he married her. Thinking that possibly she had gone too far this time, she planned the kind of evening she enjoyed when Richard was too busy or interested in other things. When he went away, sometimes she would go back to Cardiff and enjoy once again the noisy, drunken, promiscuous nights that had once been her world. Occasionally, she would get pangs of conscience. And Edward—Edward was so damn stupid, she thought. Why didn't he behave like all the others?

She wasn't about to let him snub her, so she set out to seduce him. Surely he couldn't prefer that miserable-looking wife of his; she should have been a nun. When Edward had ignored her, Charlotte found it difficult to understand and pursued him constantly. If Richard hadn't come in suddenly as he did, she might have succeeded with her plan. She never could get along with Alice, who came from an aristocratic family. Truth was, Charlotte wasn't really interested in Alice's dull husband. She would have laughed at him if he had shown any real interest. But he shouldn't have been so obviously uninterested. Now Richard had told them to leave and she would be Lady Charlotte, the mistress of the house. Once he had got over his upset, Richard would be fine, thought Charlotte, and she would be free to run Cardiff House her way.

God, it made her feel miserable seeing Alice and Edward leave and Richard treating her coldly. The house was empty; she had never felt so bored. The weeks rolled by and she was now planning to leave Cardiff House forever....

The phone was ringing.

"Hello." It was Catherine.

"Hi, Catherine."

"I just wanted to remind you we'll be leaving for Montecito in about an hour."

"Thanks, Catherine. God, I had a weird dream. I was Lady something-or-other and there were two men."

"Mmm, sounds interesting. What happened?"

"Well, I think I was a bit shady. I know I was married to this wealthy guy called Richard, can you imagine? Anyway, I started playing around with his brother, whose name was Edward. And listen to this: It seems I was trying to make it with him. Now believe it or believe it not, this character ignored me!"

"Wait a minute, Nickie, I'm coming to your room." Catherine hung up and went rushing down the hall in her bathrobe. As soon as the door was opened, she asked, "Where were you in this dream?"

"Jeesus! Oh no, no, I don't believe it!"

"Where were you?"

"*God Almighty, I was in Cardiff House!*" Pacing the floor, puffing nervously on her cigarette, she looked at Catherine, all calm and composed. "Look here, Catherine. I don't mind *you* having these weird dreams, but it's not for me. God, this really freaks me out. Oh shit, Catherine, maybe I should go see a psychiatrist."

"Calm down, honey, no need to get excited."

"Excited!" yelled Nickie. "Here I am, ready to go out of my mind, and you tell me not to get excited! Let me tell you, Catherine, it takes a lot for me to lose my cool, but I can feel myself flipping already. That broad Charlotte was me, Nickie Foster!"

"Say that again," said Catherine.

"Say what?"

"Her name."

"Charlotte." Flopping back in her chair, Nickie asked Catherine for a glass of water.

Turning on the faucet, Catherine tried to sound casual and asked, "What was Charlotte like then?"

"She had on a low-cut velvet dress. I had—I mean, *she* had—a good figure and her hair was jet black with pearls threaded through. I *saw* her, Catherine, know what I mean? *I was Charlotte!*" Catherine offered her the water glass. Pushing it away, Nickie said, "Hey, I need something stronger than water. Look, Catherine, let's get ready and then talk it over with Jason and Alan, shall we?" "Yes, I think that's a good idea, Nickie. See you in a little while. Give me a call if you're ready before I am." Kissing Nickie lightly on the cheek, Catherine went back to her room and thought very seriously about Nickie and her transformation into Lady Charlotte Griffiths.

The men were already waiting when the girls went downstairs. Catherine put her arm through Alan's and they went to the car. Nickie started in right away with her experience.

"Can you imagine, this happening to me? Me, of all people. If I was Charlotte, the wife of this Lord Richard, and Catherine was Lady Alice, married to Richard's brother Edward...who do you think was Emmanuel?"   "You've got me," said Jason, shaking his head.

As they drove, everyone appeared to be thinking hard, trying to put the pieces together.

Licking her lips, Catherine said, "Listen, everybody...I have something to tell you that'll make your skin crawl."

"Oh, Jesus," said Nickie, "I don't know if I can take any more."

"Well, take a deep breath, Nickie...Guess who called me this afternoon?"

Alan suggested Jonathan.

"No, take another guess."

Lighting a cigarette, Nickie mumbled, "I can't stand it, honest to God."

Catherine waited a moment and then said, "George."

"*George*?" shrieked Nickie. "Why did he call *you*?"

"Well, he had this dream. And the strange thing is, our dreams were identical. In fact, when he phoned, he woke me from the same dream. George is Lord Edward." With that, Catherine sat back and lit a cigarette.

"George is Lord Edward?" said Nickie. "George? Do you know what that *means*?"

Jason said, "Sounds like you and old George had an affair, you naughty girl."

Nickie leaned back and inhaled her cigarette deeply. "My God, Catherine. No wonder I've had this strange feeling about him. Can you imagine? But say, you know what this means?"

Jason laughing, said, "No, what does it mean?"

Slowly and deliberately Nickie said, "There are still two guys we can't account for—Emmanuel and Lord Richard. And we have two guys right here!"

Everyone thought for a minute, then Jason said, "Don't forget, at Cardiff House it was a totally different lifetime; now we're talking about something that happened in the 1870s."

"How do you know it's the 1870s?" asked Catherine.

"Because Maggie told us about Mrs. Washington, the original owner, and you mentioned her, Catherine, when you were telling us about your dream."

"But what are you trying to say?" asked Nickie impatiently.

"What I'm trying to tell you," said Jason, "is that you haven't considered Tom, Mike, Hilary or my mother."

"Or Martha," said Catherine.

"I don't get it," said Nickie.

Alan said, "They're trying to tell you that it's possible to be a different sex in another life."

"This is too much for me," said Nickie. "But what I would really like to know is, why is all this happening to us? Let's face it—it doesn't happen to the average person. Why us?"

"That's a good question," said Alan. "Maybe it's because in different lifetimes we've all touched upon one another, and perhaps this is the first lifetime we have all been together at the same time. This could be our only opportunity to know this." Continuing, he said, "Maybe it does happen to other people. It's happening to us, but no one else knows about it. So, other people may also experience a similar situation but be reluctant to reveal it publicly."

"Mmm," said Nickie. "I guess you're right."

"Here's the Biltmore," said Jason, leaning toward the window. "I'm feeling peckish and ready for a good dinner."

The doorman took the car, and they met Jonathan just inside the foyer. They were taken immediately to the impressive dining room. Nickie commented that it reminded her of the library at Cardiff House.

"I'll have the information for you by tomorrow, Catherine," said Jonathan. "I hope you can keep yourselves occupied in the meantime," he said, smiling.

Nickie couldn't wait to tell Jonathan about the Washington Hotel and all that had happened. Expecting him to ridicule the idea, Catherine was surprised that Jonathan took a great interest. Too soon the conversation changed and the men got involved, talking about politics and elections and other things. Occasionally, they would politely draw the girls into conversation, which Catherine didn't mind, but Nickie was restless.

"Is someone ever going to ask me to dance?" she asked.

Jason stood up and they walked over to the dance floor.

Catherine and Alan got up to dance. He held her close and whispered, "I love you, Catherine." She responded by stroking the back of his neck. "Do you like idea of living at Cardiff House? It's a far cry from California."

She hadn't thought about living in Wales. Although she had thought a lot about marrying Alan, this hadn't occurred to her. "Sounds OK to me," she murmured. "Wish my life would settle down again. I just can't understand it all."

Alan held her closer, wishing he could say something to help. "You know, darling, you have to believe me when I tell you that everything's going to be fine. Trust me, Catherine. I know what I'm talking about. And another thing, young lady: I'm not going to let you out of my sight till it's over."

Jonathan was like a watchful uncle, encouraging them all to enjoy themselves.

Nickie couldn't help thinking about George. She saw the women looking at Jason. He really was good-looking. Oh, hell, she thought, I may as well enjoy Jason.

Arriving back at their hotel, they all decided they would get a good night's sleep. Alan kissed Catherine tenderly and reluctantly left her. When he got to his room, Jason was already in bed, sitting up reading the L.A. *Times*.

"Well, what do you think of all this, Alan?" asked Jason.

"It makes me realize there's more to life than we think."

"You're pretty serious about Catherine, aren't you?"

"I've never been so serious in my life."

Jason asked Alan what he thought of Nickie, but Alan was cleaning his teeth and didn't hear him. Going to the bathroom door, Jason told Alan that he wouldn't mind living in the States. "I could write here. After all, I'm on the doorstep of Hollywood."

"What about Nickie?" Alan asked, wiping his mouth on the towel.

"Oh, there's nothing serious between us. We're more like good friends, if you know what I mean. Wouldn't you like to settle here?"

"Not bloody likely. Nothing could take me away from Wales— nothing."

"Well, nothing ever happens back there in the valley, except for an occasional trip to London or a flight to Europe. But here is the center of it all—it all happens here in California."

Alan sighed. "You know, it's all a matter of what you want out of life. As for me, when I marry Catherine, I'll have it all."

Jason shrugged and went back to bed as Alan got into the shower. When he came out, Jason was fast asleep.

Chapter Eighteen

The champagne had made Nickie sleepy and she was too tired to take off her make-up. Catherine didn't feel sleepy at all, so she decided to get a book out of the hotel library. The hotel was quiet; no one was about. The office had closed. Catherine felt good being alone. She wanted to think. She chose a book, went to sit in the window seat and opened her book.

Frantically turning the pages, Alice looked for the note she had written to Emmanuel. Heaving a sigh of relief, she found it inside the book and once again looked out the window. They were ready to leave; ready to go back to Boston.

Since that terrible night, she hadn't seen Emmanuel close enough to talk to. He would always avoid her and then she would hear him laughing. She had been in an awful state the night Edward had come back and was glad that he had no idea of what had happened in his absence. Edward had been so kind, telling her that she had had a fever. She loved Edward very much, but Emmanuel seemed to possess her soul. If only he would speak to her, hold her one more time, it would be heaven. She held her hand on her stomach, as though protecting the seed that had been planted there. She heard the Chinese boy.

"Missee, please come to your room."

Taking one last look from the window seat, she went back upstairs. Edward was lying on the bed, looking as though he had been in a terrible fight. Mrs. Washington was wiping his head with a wet towel.

Alice asked, "What happened?"

The Chinese boy said he had found Edward on the ground by the bushes.

"Where by the bushes?" asked Alice, feeling her anger rise.

"By the stables, missee."

Bending over Edward, she felt a tenderness that she hadn't known before. "Please tell me, darling, what happened to you."

His head was bleeding and as he opened his mouth to speak, she could see that he had lost a tooth. Edward squeezed her hand and whispered that all was well.   Mrs. Washington beckoned Alice to the door and suggested she let Edward sleep for a while.

"But we are leaving today," protested Alice.

Mrs. Washington said that she had called for the doctor and suggested Alice ask his opinion when he arrived.

Sitting alone with Edward, stroking his hair gently as he slept, Alice knew that Emmanuel was responsible for Edward's condition. Feeling her anger rise and her affection disappear, Alice vowed she would have her revenge on Emmanuel—child or no child.

Edward continued to sleep. His face was bruised and swollen. The doctor arrived and strapped his shoulder.

"Looks like he's broken his arm," he said to Alice. "Has he been in a fight or something?"

"Oh no, Doctor. Lord Edward was out riding and had a nasty fall," she answered, feeling her rage mount inside.

"Well, he'll have to rest for a few days. I'll come back and see how he is."

Alice went down to see Mrs. Washington and asked if she could borrow a horse. She was escorted to the stable by the little Chinese boy. She didn't see Emmanuel and asked the other stable hand where he was.

"He go home, miss; his mother sick."

Determined to find him, she asked where his home was. The stable hand directed her toward the ocean, the same way Emmanuel had taken her that day. Mounting the horse, she rode him around the corral to see how responsive he was. Then asking the stable hand to have him ready in an hour, she went back to Edward. He was still asleep, and there was a Chinese woman sitting by the bed.

"My son asked me to look after your husband," she said, smiling. "My son like him very much."

Alice was grateful and put her arms around the kind woman. She saw the empty bowl and asked her if Edward had finished it.

"Yes, missee; then he fall asleep again."

"What is your name?" asked Alice kindly.

My name is Gospel." It was the first time in days that Alice wanted to smile.

"Gospel, you say?"

"Yes, missee, I read the gospel since I was little girl and that's how I got my name."

"What is your son's name?"

Gospel's face softened. "His name is Lookjun." Then, with pride, she added, "After the two apostles."

Explaining that she had to go out, Alice asked Gospel if she would stay with her husband. Nodding her head, Gospel agreed.

It was late afternoon as Alice rode past the fine homes and down to the Spanish community. This time she had no fear and ignored the children who were curious to see a fine lady. She knocked on the door of the shack she had seen Emmanuel enter on the day he took her to the ocean.

"Is Emmanuel here?" demanded Alice of the old woman who appeared at the door. The woman shook her head and tried to close the door. "Where is he?" Pushing the door open, Alice walked straight past a heavyset young woman asleep on a bed of rags and again asked the old woman where Emmanuel was. The old lady started to weep and wail, but Alice relentlessly went on.

"I want to know where he is. Isn't he your son?"

A man came through the door and in broken English told Alice that the woman did not understand English.

"Then why did the woman start to weep when I asked for Emmanuel?"

The man looked tired and beckoned her to leave the room. Following him outside, she listened in astonishment as he told her that the old woman was Emmanuel's mother and the other one was his wife, who had just given birth to a dead baby. It was her eighth child.

"There is much sorrow in this house tonight, lady, for Emmanuel was found dead by the ocean."

Alice was stunned. His baby leapt in her womb. "This is nonsense," she said. "Now tell me where he is."

The man said no more but, turning, directed her to follow him.

"Where are we going?"

"To the Mission. The brothers are preparing him for burial."

Knowing that she would never be satisfied until she knew the man spoke the truth, she prepared to follow him. Not saying another word, she rode past the hotel and up to the Mission to savor her revenge.

It was getting dark. She saw a priest talking to a group of men, so she dismounted. Normally, she would have been hesitant, but now she walked boldly up to the priest and asked if Emmanuel's body was in the Mission.

The priest looked concerned and couldn't understand why a fine English lady would be asking for a dead stable hand. "Yes, he is here."

"I want to see his body," she said defiantly.

Father Jose looked perturbed; taking her to one side,

he told her that Emmanuel had suffered a brutal death and he didn't think it wise for her to see the body. Refusing to listen, she told the priest that it was important for her to see the body and that she wanted him to hear her confession afterwards.

Taking her through the courtyard, she was impressed with the peace she felt. Father Jose led her into a small stone building. She recognized Emmanuel's boots and large strong legs. He was covered with blood, as though he had been attacked and knifed by many people. Her courage diminished and she felt nauseous, but she had to see his face. Forcing herself to look at him, she felt her own blood drain.

As she came to, the priest was rubbing her hands and face. "You fainted, *Senora*," he said. "Are you ready to confess now?"

Nodding meekly, she told him of her association with the dead man and that she was carrying his child. The priest showed great compassion and after confession was over, Alice was able to face the truth. She knew that she had to make some major decisions. Father Jose offered her refreshment and said that one of the men would take her back to the hotel in a buggy, but first she must rest awhile.

"Apparently you do not know how Emmanuel died," said the priest.

"No, Father, I don't."

"I believe you, child. Emmanuel was a wild one: even by his own people he was not liked. He was found in one of his favorite spots on the beach by two of his sons. They dragged their father's body all the way back home and then came to the Mission for direction. Now why don't you go home, child, to your husband. Ask forgiveness and go back to your own country and try to forget."

She now felt a need to return to Edward and was happy to leave the memory of Emmanuel with the good priest.

It was dark when she reached the hotel. When she got to Edward's room, Luke-John was asleep on the floor by his bed. Edward opened his eyes and smiled at Alice. Her heart was so full of love that she broke down and sobbed. Not moving his body, he reached out to touch her, and she knew that all was forgiven.

Catherine wasn't sure whether she had slept or relived her past. She looked around at the room and felt a great warmth and happiness. Humming a tune, she was no longer afraid to go back to her own room. As she fell asleep, she could feel a deep-down happiness and joy of the soul.

The phone rang in Jason's room.

"It's me, George."

Jason had been fast asleep and nearly dropped the phone. "Well, hello, George, where are you?"

"I''ve just arrived and I'm checking in," he answered.

"What room have they given you?"

"Number 33. It's in the next building. Look, I'll go and unpack and meet you for lunch."

"Will you call the girls?"

"Yes, I'll do that before I go to my room. See you later."

George was fascinated with the hotel and found everything just perfect. He left his bags in his room and took a stroll around the gardens. Wanting a cup of coffee, he went back in and asked Maggie. They talked for a while, and he told her what was happening back in England. The telephone began to get busy, so she excused herself and George sat in a comfortable easy chair. He suddenly felt tired. He hadn't slept and was anxious to see everyone. He closed his eyes...

He didn't want to open them again. The words in Alice's letter seemed to burn his soul. Edward felt a strong compulsion to throttle Emmanuel. He thought of Alice in that man's arms and began to weep like a child.

"It's my own fault, my own damn fault. I treated her badly and used her as an outlet for my own anger. My sweet Alice. Please God I haven't lost her," he cried. Looking at her wasted body and thinking of the misery in which he had found her, his heart ached. He felt torn apart.

Mrs. Washington knocked on the door, and he asked her to please send someone to stay with his wife. The landlady readily agreed to watch over Alice herself. Thanking her, Edward set out to find Emmanuel.

Emmanuel swaggered down the dusty road, grinning. The hot sun shone on his black hair. His large white teeth had sent many a shudder down a man's spine. He was sick of the white woman: all she did was speak fine words. Her body didn't speak. It was like a ship waiting to be launched. Thinking of her thin bony body, he laughed aloud and hurried home to Maria, who had blood in her veins and a tongue she kept still.

His wife Maria was breastfeeding little Antonio. Picking up the child with one hand and ignoring his cries as he struggled for more milk, Emmanuel shooed him outside and closed the door.

"Please, no, Emmanuel, our baby will come soon. Already I feel pains."

Shoving her onto the bed, he took off his belt and gave her a lash. "Be quiet, filthy cow! You want me to beat you?"

Crying for mercy and in great pain, Maria wept as he took her savagely.

Outside, Maria's brother was talking to his friends. He knew that his sister had started with the child a few hours earlier. Hearing her cries, he burst into the room and tried to drag Emmanuel away. But he could not match Emmanuel's strength and staggered as he was kicked in the groin. He yelled for help, and the other young men rushed in. They were too late. Emmanuel was fastening his britches and Maria was giving birth to a dead child.

"See you *manana*," said Emmanuel as he left whistling. He would now go down to the ocean and sleep on the warm sand. It didn't stink like the hovel he lived in or the lousy stable. Satisfied, and completely without remorse, he went to his favorite spot for his *siesta*.

After being directed to the beach, Edward could see Emmanuel lying on the sand. He went over and asked him to stand up like a man. As he walked to Emmanuel's other side to get out of the glaring sunlight, Emmanuel tripped him and howled with laughter as Edward fell. Then, before Edward could rise, he was upon him, kicking his face and head with his heavy boots.

Edward attempted to get up and felt iron fists pounding his flesh. Sand was in his eyes and mouth, yet he fought back. Emmanuel's mocking laughter spurred him on. Seeing his own blood in the sand, then blinded from sand and cuts, Edward heard voices, loud voices, and the thudding of feet on the sand. He heard Emmanuel roar like a wounded lion. The words he heard were incomprehensible to him. There were many voices, and he trembled with fear as he felt himself being lifted up. He thanked God as he felt the hands lower him gently onto dry clean sand. Emmanuel's screams deafened his ears, and then suddenly there was silence.

Still unable to see, Edward felt around him with his hands. A voice spoke close to his ear. He couldn't understand what the man was saying, but he knew he was in safe hands. They lifted him again gently, but each step they carried him caused excruciating pain. He knew he was now in a buggy. The voices were murmuring in the background. He could hear and feel every creak and turn of the wheels. It was agony. His pain overcame him and he remembered no more until he saw Alice's face and felt her loving touch.

"Wakey, wakey," said Nickie. "I knew you'd come. Why don't you be honest and tell me it's because you can't resist me?"

Jumping to his feet, George kissed her lightly on the cheek. Then he saw Catherine with Alan, and Jason shaking his head.

"Tired, old boy?" asked Jason.

"I suppose I am. And also very hungry."

"This place makes the finest crepes you've ever eaten," said Alan.

The five of them went into the dining room for lunch and George told them of his latest experience.

"God Almighty, that was dreadful," said Jason. "But how do you feel now?"

"It's funny you should ask that, because I feel remarkably

good."

Catherine and Nickie remained silent, both touched by George's story. Catherine wanted to caress him tenderly, feeling like his Alice must have, all those years ago.

Jonathan joined them in the dining room and after meeting George, listened with interest to his story.

"What does it feel like," he asked, "to know about yourself from another life? Can you look at it objectively or do you feel guilt and remorse?"

"Neither," George answered. "It's as though I were looking back at your life, for example. I see it, and in the capacity of a counselor I can see where I went wrong, but I definitely don't feel any impact on myself."

"What do you think, Nickie?" asked Jonathan.

"Well, it's pretty much the same with me. It hasn't had any effect on how I think and feel now. I keep thinking of Charlotte and trying to figure out what part of my present personality fits in with her. Maybe I'm looking for a tie-up, a link, some similarity, but Charlotte was Charlotte, and I'm Nickie."

Catherine said, "I feel the same way as Nickie and George. For instance, I don't feel regret for the weakness I've found in my past lives. I do feel that I'm still growing and can learn from past knowledge, but I don't regret what has gone. It's as though it all had to be. My only concern is, where it is all leading to? Maybe I'm wrong, but for some reason I feel that I'm involved in a different way. I know the others have had past traumas, but I feel that I have more to come."

Jonathan could feel the tension and changed the subject. "Well, Catherine, your property in San Francisco is a large house that's been converted into apartments. It's in the hands of a realty company that manages it and collects the rents, so there's no immediate concern about that. Your other property is pretty much the same. It's an inn in England called the Rose & Crown that's being run by a man and his wife. They have been there for many years, so again, there's no need for any immediate action. Your annuity will begin on your wedding day. May I suggest that you visit the Rose & Crown and stay there for awhile. It's a charming bed and breakfast place and was built in 1572. I'm sure that if you relax, everything will sort itself out."

"I like the idea," said Nickie. "Don't you, Catherine?"

Before Catherine could answer, Jonathan said, "I forgot to mention something important: I have here $10,000 in cash to take care of any immediate expenses."

"I want everyone to come to the Rose & Crown with me," said Catherine. "And I'm paying!"

"I'm flying to New York," said Jonathan. "Why don't you all come with me and get your flight connection from there."

"Good idea," said Jason.

The rest of the day was busily filled with packing and taking a last look at beautiful Santa Barbara.

Chapter Nineteen

Jenny and Bill Jackson were thrilled to receive a cable from Jonathan Whiteside, telling them to expect the new owner from the United States. A request for six rooms created a lot of activity, and giving the brass that extra polish was not considered a chore by Jenny. The small staff was notified of the special visitors, and Jenny told Bill that she hoped it wouldn't rain.

Traveling from the airport, the friends went through the busy city of Manchester and were soon climbing the northern Pennines. The scenery was stark and magnificent. Here and there were green rolling hills and over the horizon, the tall thin chimneys of the cotton mills. Slowly, these too disappeared, and they were passing through villages.

"I love it here," said Nickie. "I feel as though I belong."

Soon Alan stopped the car. They were enchanted when they saw the small inn. Standing alone on the crest of the moor, it had magnificent sweeping views of the surrounding moorlands. Heather and gorse were richly intermingled with buttercups.

"Is this it?" asked George, unbelievingly.

"Certainly is," said Alan. "Now let's investigate the Rose & Crown."

Catherine was dumbfounded. She had never expected anything like this. The architecture was Tudor and the sign outside read, "Established 1572."

"It looks as though it's straight from a picture postcard," said Catherine.

A man and a woman came out the front door. The woman was half-running to the car, and the man took large, long steps. Holding out his strong hand, he greeted his visitors with the genuine warmth of a Lancastrian.

" 'Ow d'yer do?" Bill said. "This is my wife Jenny. And which o' you two lovely ladies is our new boss?" His manner was forthright and honest. Catherine liked him immediately.

"I guess it's me," she said modestly.

"Well, come in, ma'am, and let us show yer the Rose & Crown."

Cobbles and red brick made a fine entrance into the old inn, where wood beams and old furniture were warm and friendly. The leaded windows sparkled with filtered sunshine. Jenny, obviously proud and wanting to show off the inn, pointed past the old wooden bannister rail which extended into a large lounge with an Italian marble fireplace. The walls were covered in dark green fabric which blended perfectly with the green carpet. Antiques and old pictures were dotted here and there, and over the fireplace was a striking oil painting.

Jason felt the green velvet armchair to be inviting, and had to try it out. Nickie was mesmerized as her eyes took in every single detail. The rich royal-blue velvet drapes tied with golden cords were held just far enough back from the tall windows to retain privacy. The color and texture of the drapes were perfect, but somehow they didn't seem quite right, thought Nickie.

"Why don't yer make a point o' comin' in fer afternoon tea at four o'clock?" asked Jenny. "Mr. 'Owarth, who teaches at the school, comes in every other day ter play 'is violin."

"We've sumtimes 'ad the mayor 'ere with 'is wife, an' we'd be right proud ter 'ave yer this afternoon," said Bill.

"Fantastic idea," said Alan. "I'm sure we'd love to accept your invitation." Turning to the girls, he asked, "Right, ladies?"

They agreed readily and Jenny confirmed it, saying, "This afternoon it is, then." Looking at Catherine and Nickie, Jenny said to the men, "I bet the ladies cud do with a cuppa tea right now, is that right, ladies?"

"Sounds wonderful," said Catherine, and Nickie sat on the settee carefully.   Bill turned to the men and asked, " 'Ow would yer gentlemen like ter go in the bar fer a pint while the lassies 'ave their tea?"

"Marvelous idea," said Jason.

"This way, gentlemen," said Bill. "And mind the step; don't want yer to be fallin'."

In this friendly atmosphere, the girls relaxed and waited for Jenny to bring in the tray. The men had to bend their heads as they went into the bar. A fire was burning in the brick fireplace. The pungent smell of hops rose from the cellar steps. A couple of local villagers were playing cribbage, and a dog came over to welcome the three men.

"Feeling better, George?" asked Alan.

"Yes," said George slowly but not convincingly.

Jason was quick to perceive the change in George's mood and said, "Come on, old boy, get it off your chest. What's wrong?"

"I've been thinking about my life as Edward and I feel as though I need to talk to Nickie privately about one or two things. Would you mind?"

"Of course not," said Alan. "Why should we mind?"

"Well, I didn't want to spoil our stay at the Rose & Crown."

Jason frowned and asked, "Isn't that why we're all here, to get this whole thing settled once and for all?"

"Yes, but I want to be considerate of everyone's feelings."

"That's decent of you, George," said Alan. "Now how about that pint?"

Looking more like himself, George smiled, "This one's on me."

Jenny came into the lounge, which they fondly called the Green Room, carrying a tray with fine china cups and saucers. A typically English selection of delicious cakes and pastries was beautifully arranged on a three-tier cake stand. The napkins were folded like rosebuds, and the finger sandwiches looked scrumptious.

"I thought we were just going to have a cup of tea?" said Nickie, overwhelmed by what she saw. "Mmm, I must try this one," she said as she helped herself to a sandwich.

Jenny smiled. She was hoping that she had made the tray attractive enough to tempt the girls.

Catherine felt a warmth from this friendly woman and gave her a hug, which was a good enough reward for Jenny.

"I can't get over this place; it's darling," said Nickie, stirring her tea.

Catherine was investigating the choice of cakes and pastries. "I know I'm going to put on pounds if this is a sample of what we're going to get," said Catherine.

Soon Jenny came in again with an old flowered teapot. "More tea, ladies?"

"Thank you, Jenny," said Catherine. Then, touching Jenny's hand lightly, she asked, "Why don't you call me Catherine? And this is my best friend, Nickie."

Blushing and thrilled to have this privilege, Jenny said, "Thank yer kindly, ma'am, I mean, Catherine. When yer through, just let me know an' I'll show yer ter yer rooms."

Nickie looked around at the many beautiful things in the Green Room. "You know, Catherine, I could live in a place like this. What are you going to do with it?"

"With what?"

"The Rose & Crown."

"Oh, I don't know, Nickie. I still can't believe it's mine. It hasn't sunk in yet."

"Well, it is, honey."

"Let's go find the men," suggested Catherine.

As they went across the narrow brick hallway, they could hear
Alan laughing. It sounded like music to Catherine. The dog ran up
to greet them as Catherine stood in the doorway, taking in the
charming atmosphere of this quaint pub. Nickie, seeing the piano,
dashed over and started to play. Very soon, everyone was singing,
including Bill, as he worked at the bar.

A few more locals had come in and the news soon got around
that there were two American girls staying at the Rose & Crown
and one was the new owner. Very soon, everyone was talking, some
were singing, and a casual drink turned into a friendly party.

Nickie soon exhausted her repertoire and asked if anyone else
would take over the piano. There was no trouble in getting a
volunteer, and very soon everyone was joining in a singalong.

Feeling that this was an opportune time to talk to Nickie, George
went over to her. "I'd like to talk to you alone for a few minutes,
Nickie."

Her eyes sparkling, she asked him to sit down.

"Not here."

Sensing that he was serious, Nickie got up and went into the
Green Room. They sat together on the settee, but George didn't
know where to begin.

Nickie held his hand and, looking at him directly, said, "I know,
dear, I really do."

"I can't help wondering what happened to Charlotte and Edward," George said in a low voice.

"I don't think we'll ever find out. Now that we're away from the
Washington, I feel that maybe there aren't the vibrations to help
us. Do you know what I mean?"

George didn't answer, but Nickie thought he looked as though he
had an idea.

"Can you think of a way?"

Nodding his head, he replied, "I think so. I'd like to try hypnosis. Would you mind?"

"Not really. Why should I? I won't feel a thing."

"Come on," said George. "Let's go to my room."

"Great. I thought you'd never ask." Hesitating, she said, "Do
you know where your room is yet?"

"Damn," said George, laughing. "I have no idea. Let's tell the
others that we're checking in."

While Nickie got the keys, George went to the bar and told
Catherine and Alan they would be up in his room.

It was like a dollhouse upstairs. Each room was identically
decorated with Victorian blue-flowered wallpaper. On each floor
was a bathroom at the end of the hall. A big brass bed with an old-
fashioned dresser was in each room, complete with antique water
jug and bowl. Nickie was enchanted and couldn't believe her eyes
when she saw the large porcelain chamber-pot under the bed. On

the nightstand was an old-fashioned lamp and a candlestick in case the lights went out, Jenny had told them.

Bouncing on the big feather bed, Nickie squealed with delight.

"The only place we can work," said George seriously, "is the bed."

Facetiously, Nickie remarked, "If you insist."

George told Nickie that it was important for her to relax and be serious.

Making herself comfortable, she closed her eyes and listened to his deep, soothing voice. He took her back until she became Charlotte once again.

Quickly taking her through the quarrel between her husband and Edward, he asked, "Now that Alice and Edward have gone, what is it like at Cardiff House?"

It was an English voice that answered, but with a noticeable accent which George found interesting.

"Miserable," she replied.

"Do you miss your sister-in-law, Alice?"

"Yes. She was dull, but I miss her."

"Are you and Richard friends now?"

"Not really. He never speaks to me unless we are in bed."

"Go forward, Charlotte, another five years, and tell me what is happening."

Her breathing started to get irregular, so George asked her to go ahead a little farther. She calmed down and he asked, "Are you all right, Charlotte?"

"I suppose so," she answered miserably.

"Is something wrong, Charlotte?"

"Richard has a mistress, and I feel hurt and unwanted."

"Who is she?"

"A woman from the theatre, all dressed up in fancy clothes."

"But you have fine clothes, too, Charlotte," said George.

She rasped back at him, "He hasn't bought me a dress in years! He won't let me dress like a lady anymore."

"Why is that?"

"He said that I act like a servant girl, so I deserve to be treated like one. Truth is, he blames me for Edward and Alice and it's only partly true."

George began to feel tense and chose his words carefully. "Tell me, Charlotte, who is to blame?"

"Him, himself," she answered. "He was peeved when Edward left and he was always talking about Alice. Then about a year ago, we had a dreadful row and since then he has treated me like dirt."

"Why do you stay, then?"

"Because I'm going to outlive him, you just wait and see."

"Tell me, Charlotte, what happened to Alice's son?"

There was a pause. "Which one?"

"The oldest."

"Oh, you mean Jose? He's a priest. He gave up all his inheritance and went to the Church. He's beautiful, so handsome with his dark, curly hair. Such a waste."

Taking her farther forward, he asked, "How old are you now, Charlotte?"

A weak, faltering voice replied, "I don't really know. Eighty, I think, or thereabouts."

"Where are Alice and Edward?"

"Long gone, long gone. Sweet Alice, she was an angel."

George felt that this was all he needed to know. Bringing Nickie back, he thought about Jose and his vocation.

George enjoyed sharing the experience with Nickie, and she had a good feeling inside when she heard Charlotte's comment about Alice.

"Glad you did it, George?"

"Yes, I think I am. I'm not quite sure why it was so important to me, but it was. Thank you, Nickie."

No one had ever moved her like George. She wanted to hold him in her arms like a little boy and straighten his curls, but he seemed oblivious to her feelings. She heard Jason's voice in the hallway and then a knock on the door.

The tiny room was soon packed to the brim as George and Nickie talked to the others about Charlotte.

"Catherine, I've just got to go and see your room," said Nickie.

"Well, it's just like this one; exactly the same."   "And so is mine," said Alan.

"You realize that this is our third inn?" said Jason.

"Mmm...the Blue Feathers, the Washington House, and now the Rose & Crown. I love every one of them," said Nickie sentimentally.

"Don't forget afternoon tea, girls," said Alan, looking at his watch."

"Are you coming?" asked Catherine.

Alan looked at George and Jason, but neither of them looked enthusiastic.

"OK, OK," said Nickie. "We get the message, don't we, Catherine?"

"We thought we'd like to have a walk on the moor," said Alan. "So if you don't mind, I'll stay with the boys...."

The girls enjoyed afternoon tea. They didn't see Jenny and when they asked for her, the waitress told them that she was working in the kitchen. The painting over the white marble fireplace was rich in color. Both Nickie and Catherine were fascinated by it.

"They have a dining room upstairs," said Nickie. "Let's have a look."

It was rather like a dining room one would find in a large home, formal but friendly. The walls were half-paneled with mahogany and there was an unusual brass plaque of something that looked like three feathers. There was a wedding cake on a special table beside the sideboard and the table was set, ready for a reception. A maid came to set out wine glasses and they asked if they could see the kitchen.

"Just through that door, miss," said the maid, and the girls popped their heads through the doorway.

There was a perfect old-time country kitchen, complete with an old-fashioned ice box still in use. On one wall there were shelves up to the ceiling, packed with everything imaginable. Fancy cakes, just decorated, pies and homemade bread. It was a hub of activity. Nickie noticed the window, unusual for a kitchen.

"See the window, Catherine?"

It was a round stained-glass window which looked as though it belonged in a church or a chapel rather than a hotel kitchen. the cook was friendly and said hello. Catherine pointed to the door, asking where it led to.

"Oh, that's Bill and Jenny's private room."

Strolling back downstairs, they bought postcards, then went out to the cobbled porch to sit on the park-like bench and write to friends back home.

The afternoon was pleasant for everyone; they decided to dine at the Rose & Crown. Nickie tried a few times to get into the bathroom to wash and finally decided to do it the old-fashioned way. Remembering the kitchen, she walked down the next flight of stairs with her large jug. She asked for hot water. The waitress was amused by the idea of seeing an American do this. "Even English people don't do it any more," she said, laughing.

In her room now, Catherine could hear Nickie next door singing and dropping things. As she brushed her hair, she tried to think and put everything into perspective. Who was Gareth of Abergavennie? Was it George or Jason? And who was Emmanuel? Her head seemed to spin whenever she tried to concentrate on this mystery of reincarnation. Someone tapped on the door. It was Jason, asking if she were decent.

"Yes," she called. "Come in."

Watching her as she finished putting on her necklace, he thought how beautiful she was and how lucky Alan was to have her love.

"Are you serious about my brother?"

"Why do you ask?"

"Oh, I don't know. But you really seem to hit it off well, you two."

He went to see if Nickie was ready. Her door was partially open, and he asked if he could come in. Nickie, shoving all kinds of things into her purse, asked him what kind of writing he did.

"All types, really. I'm busy writing different articles and slowly but surely I'm putting a novel together."

"What's the story about?"

"Oh, it's an adventure, a touch of mystery, and I think there's one murder."

"What about love?"

"And a bit of that, too."

I wish he'd buzz off, thought Nickie. Then: What's the matter with me? He's not bad at all, but somehow I just can't get turned on to him. I like him more from a distance; when he comes up close, he doesn't do a thing for me. Finally Jason left, returning to Catherine's room.

Catherine was surprised to see Jason again. As he watched her through the mirror, she could feel his eyes and was uncomfortable.

"What's the matter, Jason?"

"Oh, nothing. Can't a fellow look?"

"I suppose he can." Then, changing her tone of voice, she said, "But nothing more."

Not to be put off, he said, "I'll give you time, Catherine. You might change your mind."

They both laughed, and he held the door open for her as they left the room.

"Come on, Nickie," Jason said in the hall. "We're ready to go down to the bar."

"OK, be right with you." Walking downstairs, Nickie saw a little dust on the bannister and wiped it away with her hand.

"What are you doing?" asked Catherine in amazement.

"I just can't stand to see this place anything but perfect, I guess," said Nickie, still looking for dust.

Waiting in the hall while Jason went to check on Alan and George, Catherine saw a page from an old guest book framed and hanging on the wall in the brick hallway. Curious to see what it said, she read: "*August 8th, 1601, J. E. Hornby - Somerset County.*" Once again, she had the same sensation she had experienced several times when Megan's tale had forced its way into her mind. The more she looked at the page, the stronger the feeling: her back and shoulders felt prickly. She felt that if she turned around, she would see the Rose & Crown as it was in 1601.

"Catherine, are you OK?" Nickie saw a look almost of fear on her friend's face. Wanting to make light of it, she waved her hand up and down in front of Catherine's eyes which did, in fact, help her bring her thoughts back to the present.

"Good evening, ladies."

Nickie had to look twice before she realized this was Jenny. "You look wonderful, Jenny. I hardly recognized you. What a transformation. What's your secret?"

Jenny was genuinely flattered. Always busy around the inn, she never had the opportunity of dressing up. She had planned to look her best this evening for the new owner.

"Yer like it then?" she asked shyly.

"Oh, it's not just just your dress," said Catherine. "It's everything about you. You look lovely, Jenny."

Bill came over and holding Jenny close, gave her a big hug. "I agree. She's the belle of the ball."

The men now joined them and Alan asked, "Shall we go into the bar?"

As they went in, Catherine asked Bill what he could tell her about J. E. Hornby.

"Well, Jenny 'ere is the local 'istory buff an' I know she'll luv tellin' yer about Jack Hornby." With that, he followed the others. Catherine and Jenny went in after him. The men stood up as the women joined them at a big table by the fire.

After their orders had been taken, Catherine said, "I want everyone to listen, please. I'm going to ask Jenny about some of the inn's history and in particular, Jack Hornby."

"Who the hell is Jack Hornby?" asked Nickie.

"Better still," said Alan, "how do *you* know about Jack Hornby?"

"I don't know if anyone has noticed the old guest page framed in the hall. Well, when Nickie and I were waiting just a short time ago, I looked at it and then I started to get that strange feeling of going back in time."

"Oh no, not again," cried Nickie.

Bill and Jenny looked confused, so to avoid a lot of explanation, Jason said, "I'm sure Jenny can tell us about Jack Hornby."

In her rich north country dialect, Jenny told the oldest story associated with the Rose & Crown, for there were many.

"Jack Hornby came from a rich family and on his way to Manchester, he stopped for lodging here at the inn. The innkeepers then were Samuel Nuttall and his wife Sarah. They had two children, Marion and Tobias. The inn was very much like it is today, and Jack Hornby enjoyed his short stay. Promising to return on his way home, he then left for Manchester. It was a long, hard ride in those days along these wild moorlands. The innkeeper and his wife were concerned about his welfare and safety, for there were highwaymen who would often rob the lonely traveler. Anyway, he came back in about three weeks and lodged again at the Rose & Crown.

"The story goes that Marion and Jack fell in love and planned to get married. He left again for home, arranging the wedding date. The day before the wedding was to take place, a tragedy occurred. Marion was cleaning the window, sitting on the ledge with her back outside and her legs forward into the hall. She lost her balance, fell back and dropped three stories to the cobbles below.

"Jack Hornby arrived as planned. Finding his intended dead, he took the room which was to be their bridal suite and lived there the rest of his life. Fifty years ago, there were many reports from guests sleeping in that room that it was haunted. I've even seen an old paper with the story that a man was asleep in bed and was awakened by rustling noises. He swore he saw a white light and a young woman dressed as a bride standing at the foot of the bed. Other reports say that a man was seen coming through the wall, carrying a bag. Others have been awakened to the sound of crying. But we haven't had anyone report a ghost or any noises. It seemed to stop forty to fifty years ago."

"What a romantic story," said Nickie. "I'd love to see the room."

Bill moved uncomfortably and glancing at Jenny, said, "Well, the room's not 'aunted anymore, yer know. As Jenny told yer, we've never 'eard of anyone seein' or 'earin' anything."

Nickie crinkled her nose, which always indicated deep thought. "I wonder why no one has experienced the ghosts recently?"

"Because they're not 'ere any more," Bill said emphatically.

"Where is the room?" asked Nickie, straightforwardly.

Jenny told her that it was at the bottom of the hall on the third floor.

Catherine started to smile. "I'm on the third floor and at one end is the bathroom, so that means I'm in that room."

"We can move you, ma'am, if you prefer another room," said Jenny, concerned.

Nickie was thoroughly enjoying the conversation.

"I'm staying right where I am," said Catherine.

"Shall we go in for dinner?" asked Alan.

"Good idea," said George, holding Nickie's arm.

Nickie wanted to touch George's hand to let him know that she was aware of his nearness, but then decided otherwise, not wanting to scare him off.

Dinner was excellent, with fresh homegrown vegetables and homemade dessert. It was the kind of meal that induces sleep.

Finishing her cigarette, Catherine excused herself and Alan left with her. At her door Alan held her gently and kissed her good night.

During dinner, Catherine had felt a strong need to leave and go to her room. She didn't feel afraid, even after she found out that she was in the old haunted guest room. Climbing into her comfortable bed, she snuggled her head into the pillow facing the window. It began to rain, and she could see the rain trickling down the leaded glass. Downstairs, she could hear them singing in the bar, which apparently was an English tradition. This was the first time in a long while that she could unwind and feel relaxed. So much had happened to her, and now it was difficult to believe that she wouldn't have to worry where her next dollar was coming from.

Reaching out to turn off the light, Marion felt the hot wax of the candle burn her fingers.

Unable to go to sleep, Marion let her mind drift back over her first meeting with Jack. To begin with, it had been Mr. Hornby, but then both had experienced an overwhelming sense of belonging to each other. At every opportunity, Jack would seek her out, finding any excuse to talk. She in turn would do likewise, seeking his whereabouts and then finding any reason to walk near him. This need to be near each other grew in a short time. Marion let her mind go back to that sunny afternoon she was walking back from the village.

The provisions were heavy for her slight build. Jack had been riding and stopped to give her assistance. They had sat beneath the tree at the corner of Rivington Lane. He had asked so many questions and as he talked, she felt that she had never seen such beauty in a man before. Her thoughts were higher than the tree. His voice was like music. He kissed her hand; then, helping her up, his arms went around her.

They were still for a moment; when she sensed that he was letting her go, she held on to him. This unlocked their passion for each other, and he kissed her on the cheek and on her bare shoulders. His hands were running through her hair. Feeling the strength of his body against hers unleashed a deep desire, and she responded eagerly. He suddenly pulled away, and she was aware of being separated from him. She threw herself against him, urging him on. She heard him say her name several times.

"Marion, Marion, my love, will you marry me?"

Over and over again, she whispered, "Yes, yes."

Then his voice seemed to change. She was frightened. The sun had gone, the room was dark, and *Catherine was not alone*! The man in her bed was still kissing her; her nightgown was torn, and the man beside her was naked. Feeling his flesh next to hers, she tried to scream, but her voice was paralyzed. With all the strength she had, she struggled and hit him several times.

Now fully awake, she managed to scream and the man left swiftly, disappearing into the night. Looking for her robe and thankful that she had wakened before he had actually raped her, she put the lamp back on. Her bedroom door was still open and there was a dim light in the hall. She could hear Nickie's voice talking to someone—Alan.

"Nickie! Nickie!" she cried.

As soon as Nickie and Alan heard Catherine's call, they ran, for both could tell that something was wrong. When they entered her room, Catherine began to cry. It took some time to calm her down. Telling them what had happened felt odd, for she first had to start with the dream. They listened patiently, but Alan's anger was surfacing.

"Please, don't tell anyone," pleaded Catherine. "Please, Alan, don't. Promise me you won't."

Holding her and listening to her crying aroused the worst in him. He went downstairs, having given his promise, and ordered a pot of tea from Jenny, who willingly put the kettle on right away.

As Nickie helped Catherine change her nightgown, she suggested that perhaps it was only a dream; after all, they had been talking about ghosts and things and maybe her mind had triggered off the nightmare.

Alan came in with a tray. "Feeling better, my love?"

Smiling, she nodded her head and told him that it must have been just a bad dream.

Nickie was quiet but she felt her blood chill as she saw red finger marks on Catherine's shoulders and arms. Nickie smiled and asked if Catherine would like her to stay the night.

"I think I would," she said. "And if I start dreaming, please wake me up."

"Sure will, honey. Now lie down and I'll just get my pajamas. Stay with her a moment, Alan, will you?"

As Nickie walked to her room, she was terrified. Catherine had *not* been dreaming: the red marks and the torn nightgown were sufficient to convince Nickie that *someone had been in the room with her*!

Reluctantly, Alan left the two girls, and Catherine asked for a cigarette.

"Want to talk about it?" asked Nickie, as she handed over the packet.

"You know, Nickie, I became Marion just like I became Megan. And there's something else."

"What is it?" asked Nickie, getting undressed.

"Remember when Megan told the priest she was raped in the cellar and said she would know him by a sign?"

Nickie nervously waited for her to go on.

"Well, it was the same man in my dream tonight...with the same sign."

Nickie thought for a moment. "How could you know that, Catherine? Megan lived a long time before Marion, so how could the same man attack her? I think dreams have a way of conveniently fitting things together sometimes. This Jack Hornby was on your mind before you went to sleep and your subconscious associated him with the other guy."

"I don't think so."

"What was the sign anyway?"

"I don't want to talk about it any more," said Catherine, finishing the conversation abruptly.

Realizing that Catherine had closed up, Nickie put out the light and curled herself up, ready to go to sleep. Already Catherine's breathing was even; she seemed to be fast asleep in no time. Reaching out her hand, Nickie felt a need to comfort her.

"Keep yourself warm, child," Sarah said to her daughter. The bed was next to the fireplace and her husband Sam had made a good fire to last through the night. Marion had insisted on washing her hair in the rain barrel, and her mother had told her she would get sick. Her fever seemed unusually high and Sarah was hoping that Sam would come home soon.

Weary and tired, Sam opened the door and a rush of cold air invaded the room.

"Close the door, Sam. Marion needs to keep warm."

Bending over his daughter, Sam looked at the girl as she slept and asked Sarah what she thought was wrong with her.

"She's got a fever. I think she's worried about Jack."

"Do you think he'll come back for her?" asked Sam, yawning.

"Oh, I'm sure he will." Then, looking down at Marion, her face softened. "Isn't she lovely, Sam?"

"Yes, Sarah, she's a bonny lass and looks like her mother did all those years ago."

As Sam sat down, Sarah knelt beside him. "Are you glad you married me?" His answer was a smile and a kiss.

As Sarah prepared his supper, good wholesome broth and fresh bread, she thought of her many happy years with her husband and the joy of Marion and Tobias.

"Where's the boy?" asked Sam, referring to their son.

"I haven't seen him, dear, since he was chopping wood earlier this afternoon."

"That boy worries me, Sarah. I feel it in my bones; he's up to no good."

Tobias was a strange boy, small in stature but broad and heavy. As Marion had been born in the middle of a hot summer's day with the sun shining bright, Tobias had arrived in the night when the moon was hidden. Sarah had inherited an inborn fear from her mother that Tobias would be a strange and moody boy. This had proved to be so. Every time Sam questioned his son's actions, there was trouble. Loving both her husband and her son often made situations difficult. Always protective of the boy, Sarah tried many times to explain to Tobias how he should behave in public. Marion was close to her brother; he would respond to her more than anyone.

Tobias came into the warm living room for his supper. Ignoring his parents, he went over to where Marion was sleeping. His speech was slurred and his leg dragged as he walked. Poor Sam wondered how this insolent, unpleasant being could possibly be their son. As a small child, he had been almost uncontrollable, and it made Sam's heart sick when he saw how the boy treated his mother. Tobias grunted and looked at Sarah. She knew he was concerned about his sister.

"She will be all right, Tobias. Don't worry yourself. Sit down and have your supper."

Tobias made an attempt to awaken his sister. Marion opened her eyes and smiled.

"Tobias, why did you disturb your sister?" asked Sam.

Scowling as he sat at the table, Tobias gulped and slurped his broth. When the bowl was empty, he took his bread and wiped it on his tunic. He then shoved the bread into his mouth and pointing to the pot on the fire, grunted.

Sarah got up immediately and began to fill his bowl with more broth. Sam's anger was fire inside him. Closing his eyes, he silently prayed for perseverance and strength. Tobias knew how he disturbed his parents and everyone else, for that matter. The only one he liked was "his Marion."

Sam asked Marion, who was now sitting up in bed, when she expected Jack Hornby to return.

"Very soon, Papa."

Sarah lifted Marion's chin and looked into her face. "You're looking better, child."

"I feel better, Mama. Tomorrow I will help you in the kitchen."

Tobias was happy to see Marion. He went over to the bed and started to dance a jig. Sarah was glad that his dark mood had left him. Marion was clapping her hands as Tobias tried to please her with his grotesque dance. Sam found the whole thing unbearable. Pushing his chair away from the table, he left to find some chores to do.

Sarah's heart was heavy. Tobias had stopped dancing. He left the room, and Marion had fallen asleep again. Going over to cover her, Sarah held her daughter close. Her heart ached, for she knew that Marion would soon be gone.

Chapter Twenty

Alan had gone to his room. Filling his pipe, he let his thoughts flow freely. He recalled his mother telling Catherine about her life as Rose Featherstone, the urgency in her voice as she had asked Catherine if she believed in reincarnation. Trying hard to remember exactly what Lady Margaret had said, her words came clearly to his mind:

"Before I can say more, I must know that you believe, for by believing, this family can rid itself of its karma." Alan could see in his mind's eye the tiny satin footstool and the embroidered slippers his mother had been wearing that night. His mind drifted as he thought of the story of William, the first Keeper of the Book. His mother had said, *"No woman shall look upon its pages."*

Thinking of that evening, he remembered how beautiful Catherine had looked and how his mind would drift away from the conversation as he sat there watching the woman he loved. It had been important for his mother to talk to Catherine, and he knew that when she took Jason to his father's study to show him the portraits, she believed Catherine to be Megan of Manningstile Henlock.

My poor Megan, thought Alan, as he remembered the conversation they had had while she was under hypnosis. The phone rang.

"Hello, is that you, Alan?" It was Jonathan Whiteside.

"Yes, how are you, Jonathan?"

"Fine. Are you in bed?"

"No, I'm just relaxing. But surely you didn't call to ask me if I'm in bed."

"No, I'm sorry," said Jonathan. "I would like to see you."

"When? Where are you?"

"I'm right here in the Rose & Crown."

Surprised, Alan said he would meet him in the bar in five minutes. Hurriedly, he slipped on his sweater and went downstairs.

Two pint glasses were on the table.

Thought you'd like a Black & Tan," said Jonathan.

"Thank you. What brings you here to the Rose & Crown?"

"It's time for us to talk," said Jonathan seriously. "The reason I'm here is to assist Megan as she comes to terms with her karma." He reached out his hand, making a secret sign.

Alan was overjoyed to meet a brother of the Higher Order.

"I'm really grateful, Jonathan. I know we're going to need your help. Catherine has gone through so much, I just wonder how she keeps on going without cracking."

"Don't worry about that. She is strong in mind, body and spirit."

Alan's voice was low. Tapping his pipe gently on his palm, he looked directly at Jonathan and said, "Catherine was nearly raped tonight."

"I know. I got here as early as I could."

"Why?" said Alan.   "Why should this happen again?"

Jonathan's voice was stern. "It wasn't again. The act did not take place."

There was silence between the two men. Then, "It was Jason, wasn't it?" Alan asked reluctantly.

Nodding his head gravely, Jonathan told him that what he had to say next was vitally important. "As Keeper of the Book, Alan, you know that these things must occur in order to clear the karma of everyone concerned."

"Yes, but there are parts I either don't know or can't understand."

"Yes, but that's because certain knowledge has been temporarily removed from your higher consciousness. Very soon your powers will be restored. In the meantime, I must explain about your brother. But not the whole story, for you too are involved in this karmic pattern, and to complete the esoteric mystery, you must be ignorant of certain events until the right time."

"But why Jason?" asked Alan, his voice heavy with disappointment.

"Drink up and try to relax while I fit in one of the jigsaw pieces," Jonathan said. "Your brother Jason represents the negative energy which has worked and will continue to work in opposition to the esoteric need for truth and balance. He has great power for evil, and can manipulate others to do his will. For example, the attack on Catherine tonight was not done with Jason's conscious knowledge."

"I don't understand. What do you mean?"   "Wait a moment. Let's order another drink before we go any further." Summoning the barmaid, Jonathan asked for two tots of whiskey and a couple of chasers.

Deeply concerned, Alan thought of his brother and all the years they had been together. Boyhood memories came easily into his mind, and it was impossible to think of Jason as being evil.

"Alan." He heard his name spoken sharply. "Listen to me carefully. Certain energies have been veiled in your higher consciousness. What I have just told you about Jason is not new to you. You have known this since you became the Keeper of the Book. Less than two weeks ago, you knew exactly what I know now. Without the esoteric power, you have come to another level of thought and on this level you are more prone to negative energies and emotions. Soon you will be back onto a broader plane and what you feel now will be insignificant. Believe me, Alan." he reached out and gave Alan his hand.

In that fleeting second, Alan regained his normal level of awareness. His mind expanded instantly. His vision pierced the normal perception of man and he saw his life and purpose. Looking down on himself, he understood the limitations under which he was laboring. Feeling again the magnificence of his entire being, he saw with exquisite rapture his love for and etheric ties with Megan. The vision of Jason was before him. He became aware of Jason's evil purpose, but from his level of understanding, far beyond human comprehension, Alan felt only unbounded love and compassion for his brother. It was at this point that Jonathan released his esoteric influence, and once again Alan was imprisoned within his ordinary senses. He was now prepared to listen carefully to his esoteric colleague.

"The brother you know as Jason still exists. At conception his soul entered your mother's etheric body, already occupied by an evil soul. In her womb two fetuses were formed: your brother was to be the twin of an evil being known as Kradeno. In these forms, they would have experienced the powerful forces of good and evil and learned to manipulate these energies in the human body. But gaining strength as the fetus grew, Kradeno drained your mother, Lady Margaret, of all her physical strength. He actually murdered his brother in the womb by depriving him of sustenance from his mother. Kradeno became twice the normal size. He did this by bloating his body with evil and extracting all the nutrients from your mother's body for himself.

So your brother did not enter the fetus for fear of killing his mother, although he knew that the birth of Kradeno would totally destroy the karmic pattern, and that if allowed to remain alone in the fetus, he would ultimately cause mass destruction. Each one that you know in your karmic group would be marked to die in some foul way. But there was nothing he could do physically to oppose Kradeno. Only through the constant healing prayers of the

Order did Lady Margaret survive, for Kradeno's plan was to cause her death as well after she gave him birth."

Somewhat confused, Alan asked, "Who is the person I know as Jason?"

"Jason is the earthly form of Cimraknus, a highly evolved soul whose purpose is to correct the karma created by this group over many centuries."

"And what is the purpose of the evil soul?"

"His purpose is to destroy the positive energies that have accumulated and utterly annihilate all that we know as love. But for the help of the Higher Ones, Kradeno would have already put an end to the progress that has been achieved. He is always prepared to take on human form and destroy everything that is good and positive."

"But why?"

"As long as the evil one can reincarnate, he can postpone his inevitable destruction. He has taken many forms. He uses the body to serve his evil intent and then leaves it to suffer the consequences of his despicable actions. Your brother Jason now sleeps peacefully, and he will have no memory whatsoever of attacking Catherine."

"Where is the evil soul at this moment?" asked Alan.

"Its power is resting for the present, but as long as its negative energies are among us, we may all be influenced. Fortunately, we have the assistance of a being who is Jason's higher self—the Master Rhaydhonasie. Through the grace of this evolved soul, all will yet walk the path of karma."

"I'm still concerned about the girls. I know they will be curious and determined to investigate the attempted rape." Refilling his pipe with tobacco, Alan leaned back in the chair, waiting for Jonathan to advise him.

"Don't worry, Alan. Rhaydhonasie will erase the event completely from their minds, so that they will not remember a thing about it."

Relieved to hear this, Alan asked, "What will become of Jason?"

Emptying his whiskey glass and taking a long drink from his chaser, Jonathan continued.

"A new Jason will evolve after the karma is complete. A gentle soul waits to come in. He will be given the gift of a long earth life of happiness. So don't worry about your brother; the best is yet to come for him."

The night ended late for both men, but Alan felt much better and thanked Jonathan for his help and caring. He was thankful also that Catherine would have no memory of the attack. Smiling to himself as he got ready for bed, he thought how Nickie would have loved to investigate the attack on her friend.

Catherine woke first and wondered why Nickie was in her bed. Shaking her gently, she heard Nickie groan.

"What are you doing here, Nickie?"

Nickie opened her eyes and saw Catherine and wondered the same thing. "I don't know, Catherine. What happened last night?"

Catherine sat up straight and pushing her hair back from her face, looked at Nickie. "My mind is a blank. Do you think we drank too much wine?"

"Beats me. But you can bet we'll soon be hearing about it if we did."

"I'm feeling hungry. Mmmm, smell that bacon."

With their minds on breakfast, both girls got ready quickly and went down to the dining room.

"I just love this place," said Nickie. "Everything looks so nice and clean."

The dining room had one large refectory-type table at which all the guests sat. If someone came in and it was crowded, they had the choice of collecting a breakfast tray from the kitchen or waiting until someone had finished.

Jason was sitting reading the paper; Alan got up to greet the girls. George came in shortly after.

Trying to sound casual, Catherine said, "I must have been terribly tired last night. I don't remember much after dinner." Then, looking up, hoping someone might fill her in, she saw Alan wink at her.

"Both you and Nickie could hardly keep your eyes open, and as I wasn't sure which was Nickie's room, I bundled her in with you."

"So that's how it happened," said Nickie. "Trust me to let a good-looking man put me to bed and I go to sleep."

"By the way," said Alan to everyone, "did anyone know that Jonathan checked in late last night?"

"He did?" said Nickie. "Where is he now?"

Walking into the dining room, Jonathan said, "Here he is. Good morning, everybody."

"How did you get here so quickly?" asked Nickie.

Helping himself to the breakfast buffet, Jonathan casually remarked, "I took the Concorde."

"Really?" asked Jason. "God, I'd love to fly that way. How was it?"

"It was marvelous. Smooth and impossible to realize how fast you're flying."

"It's good to see you," said George. "How do you like the Rose & Crown?"

"From what I've seen, I like it very much."

Catherine was looking out the window, enthralled with the

beautiful view. "Just look at the gorse and heather," she said, pointing to the moors. "I want to walk on the moors. Anyone else want to come?"

"I want to write some cards this morning," said Nickie.

"And I'd like to look around the inn some more," said George.

"Well, how about you guys?" asked Catherine, looking at the three men left.

"I'd love to, Catherine," said Jason, "but I must go into Bolton to the news office and I won't be back till after lunch. Sorry."

"That leaves you and Jonathan," said Catherine, looking at Alan. "Are you going to give me an excuse?"

"I think we can make it," said Jonathan. "But you'd better wrap up warmly; it gets awfully cold up on those hills."

"Meet you downstairs in about ten minutes," Catherine said, hurrying away.

"Want to come for a walk on the moor, Tobias?" Marion asked.

Eagerly, he came stumbling down the stairs. Marion thought that any minute he might fall.

"The bluebells are out in the dell, Tobias. Want to come and pick some with me?"

Beaming with pleasure, happy to have the full attention of his sister, he began to jump up and down, making a terrible noise.

"Shh," said Marion. "You know Papa will be angry."

At the mention of Papa, Tobias' noises became even louder.

As Marion had predicted, Sam came from the kitchen and shouted at Tobias to be quiet. Tobias made ugly faces at his father and Sam cuffed him, which made the boy run out of the inn, screaming loudly. Sam shook his head wearily as Marion gave him a kiss and ran out to join her brother.

Marion loved to run in the heather, her hair blowing free. Tobias ran behind her, his foot dragging and his heavy body panting with the exertion. Reaching the crest of the hill, Marion lay down and pulling wild flowers, threw them up above her head. Tobias tried to catch the petals with his clumsy hands like a child tries to catch soap bubbles.

"Toby, I'm going to marry Jack. Isn't that wonderful?"

Tobias glowered and made grunting noises. It was obvious he didn't approve.

"Now, now, Toby. This is going to make your Marion very happy. Please be happy for me. I know you'll learn to love Jack as I do."

Lifting his heavy forearm as though to hit her, Tobias made a low moaning sound, as though in agony. Rolling over on his face, he pounded the grass with his huge fists. Marion tried to soothe him. Trying to brush his tears away, he pushed her to one side and ran off into the trees.

Poor Toby, she thought. I hate to leave him. I must talk to Jack about his future. Standing now and brushing the grass from her dress, she started to call for her brother.

"Tobias. Tobias, let's go home now."

His reply sounded like the howl of a wolf in pain.

As she returned to the inn, she looked back to see if he was following, but there was nothing: just the lonely wind sweeping over the moor.

It was later that night when she heard Tobias downstairs. Creeping quietly, she went to talk to him and was distressed to see him guzzling ale. When he saw her, he tried to do his jig, but fell on the brick floor, laughing and sobbing.

Soon her mother came down to see what was happening. Nothing could be done to move the drunken boy, now unconscious, so she gently covered him with a stable blanket.

The next day, Marion thought of all the preparation for Jack's arrival. Soon she would be a bride and live in Somerset County. She loved working in her father's inn, meeting travelers and helping Mama keep everything clean and bright. They always had plenty of food on the table, and when Tobias was good everything was fine. Going now to make the beds, she saw Tobias at the top of the stairs. When she called to him, he ignored her. Wanting to be friends and talk to him some more, she ran upstairs and the housemaid said, "Good morning, Miss Catherine. Hope you have a pleasant day."

Catherine felt good, her arms linking the arms of Alan and Jonathan. The moorland air was keen; one could see for miles high on the Pennine Chain. It was the first time she had seen the Rose & Crown from a distance. Its black-and-white Tudor architecture stood out against the stark background of the moorland.

"Why don't we walk down to the village?" asked Catherine. "It's about two miles; are you men up to it?"

"Let's go," said Alan.

Their conversation touched on many things; Alan felt relieved that Catherine didn't ask anything more about last night. Jonathan asked Catherine what she intended to do with the Rose & Crown.

"I like it exactly as it is. I wouldn't change it for the world. Jenny and Bill are perfect innkeepers—they've put so much of themselves into the pub that I'd like things to just carry on as they have been. It's hard to believe that I can come and stay anytime I want. It's wonderful! Did you have something in mind, Jonathan?"

"No, I'm happy to see things left exactly as they are."

Arriving in the village, the men decided they would browse in the newsagent's shop, while Catherine explored the small gift shop.

The North of England, high up in the moorlands overlooking the industrial valley towns, was not on the accepted tourist route.

Dampness seemed to cover everything, including the dark cobbles and stones, making them look like black glass. The rich north country dialect was friendly, and Catherine became aware that everyone she spoke to was ready to smile or give a helping hand. She could feel the hard-working spirit prevalent in the neat sparse homes. The old ladies still wore shawls as though they were the protectors of long-gone mysteries of yesteryear. Their faces were gentle but strong, deeply lined with years of hard labor like the crags around their homes. Looking at them, Catherine felt a deep respect for the Lancastrian heritage.

Catherine bought small brass plates with imprints of the Bolton Town Hall, the Sixty-Three Steps at Barrow Bridge and Rivington Pike. She left the shop, looking for Alan and Jonathan, the old-fashioned doorbell ringing as she shut the door.

"We found a delightful tea shop just down the street," said Alan. "Shall we try it?"

"Great idea," said Catherine.

Another bell tinkled as they opened the door to the tiny cafe. A pleasant plump lady welcomed them and showed them to a heavy oak table. She offered them a wide choice of homemade scones, pastries and cakes. The selection was overwhelming and the temptation too great. They all made their selections, and the shopkeeper came back with two large plates brimming full.

Catherine spent the next few minutes thoroughly enjoying her cream cake. "I keep thinking of Frances and Tom," she said. "Especially the wedding." Then, changing the subject quickly, she turned to Jonathan. "What is happening to me? Can you tell me?"

"Don't worry about it, my dear," he answered. "Everything's going to be fine."

"But how do you know that?" she persisted.

Alan intervened. "Catherine, darling, why don't you stop worrying right now and eat your cream cake?"

After they had finished, Jonathan said, "Well, shall we start back? Remember, it was easy coming to the village, but now we're full of cream cakes and the walk back is all uphill."

Chapter Twenty-one

Nickie bought her postcards in the lobby and decided to write in the Greem Room at the desk by the window. This room felt very special to her and as she sat there, her eyes devoured every single object in the room. If this was my place, I'd make it my home, she thought. I'd close the door on the world and enjoy every single minute here. There were many old photographs placed here and there, and the large oil painting over the white fireplace was magnificent. She began to write, the painting still on her mind.

Dear Sir:

How can I ever thank you for the beautiful portrait of my daughter and her husband-to-be. Mr. Hornby told me of your generosity and that I was to consider the painting a gift. Such a gift has never been mine, sir; my husband and I will treasure it always. May I offer you our humble hospitality. Please feel free to accept lodging at the Inn at your convenience. I do hope that you will be with us to honor the bride and groom on their wedding day.

Yours,

Sarah and Sam Nuttall

After finishing her letter, Sarah looked around the room.

Everything was gleaming and the painting was so impressive. Talking with her husband Sam had been good. He felt the same way she did about Marion's wedding to Mr. Hornby. Both were happy for the couple but also a little sad, for they had always hoped that when Marion married, she would continue to work at the inn. But Mr. Hornby came from a wealthy family; Marion would be leaving the Rose & Crown.

Sarah's thoughts continued to drift. Tobias always lay heavy on her mind. Poor Tobias. He had the body of a man and the mind of a spirited child. She knew that Sam was bitterly disappointed with him. When Tobias was small, Sam had had such fine dreams, but as the child grew, she watched Sam's dreams disappear. Secretly dreading the day the Marion would leave, Sarah wondered what would happen to Tobias. At times he was uncontrollable, and Marion could persuade him to do things that no one else could. Sarah was constantly tormenting herself thinking about Sam and Tobias after Marion left. Talking to the priest helped, so she decided that she would arrange a meeting, hoping he would be able to give her some direction. Feeling cold, Sarah got up to go to the fireplace, once again looking at the beautiful painting of Marion and Jack.

"It is a lovely painting," said George. "Thought you might like to have lunch with me. The others don't seem to be back from the village yet, and I'm feeling hungry. How do you feel?"

"Hungry. Let's go." On their way to the dining room, Nickie asked, "Well, what have you been up to this morning?"

"I had a chat with Bill and Jenny and learned some interesting facts."

Nickie's face lit up. "Mmm, such as?"

"Such as, today is or would have been the anniversary of Marion's wedding to Jack Hornby."

The waitress asked for the order twice before Nickie realized she was there. "Oh, I'm sorry," she said. "I'll take the roast pork, with stuffing and apple sauce. Thank you."

"The same for me," said George. "And two glasses of Chablis."

Eager to continue the conversation, Nickie asked George how he knew about the anniversary.

"I told you," he said, smiling. "Jenny and Bill told me this morning."

"How exciting. I wonder if anything will happen."

"What do you mean?"

"Well, I wonder if Catherine will get a ghostly visit tonight or whether I'll meet Mr. Hornby arriving with his bag."

"You really enjoy all this kind of stuff, don't you?"

Sipping her Chablis, Nickie's eyes were shining. "You bet."

George's expression changed.

Hesitating before he answered, he told her he had gone to the bar for a beer earlier this morning and had experienced a weird feeling.

"What do you mean, weird?"

"It was as though something were about to happen, something terrible. I can't explain it any better."

"Well, don't worry about it. I often get to feeling that way."

The lunch was good and wholesome and as they were having dessert, Alan popped his head in the door. Nickie yelled over, "Come and join us."

Bringing extra chairs to the table, Jonathan and Alan ordered coffee while Catherine ran upstairs to change her clothes. As she came back down, she met Jason in the hall.

"Hi, just returned?" she asked.

"Yes, I had a nice morning in Bolton. It's a very pleasant town. We should have dinner there sometime. What do you think?"

"Sounds like a good idea."

When they arrived in the dining room, Nickie suggested that they all go downstairs to the pub. Everyone agreed.

It was late afternoon and Catherine and Nickie were sitting in the Green Room. Nickie had told Catherine about the anniversay and it sent a chill down Catherine's spine.

"You really love this place, don't you?" said Catherine.

"I sure do. I feel like I know every inch of it. I'm going to hate it when we leave, you know." She paused, then, "What are we going to do next, Catherine?"

"That's what I've been asking myself. I really don't know."

Nickie lit a cigarette and sounding like a mother, said, "You're going to go away and get married and live in a fine house."

Catherine laughed. "You make it all sound so simple. And speaking of getting married, don't forget we'll be going to Tom and Frances' wedding soon."

"Hey, that's right! You know, Catherine, being over here in England is like living in another world. But I kind of worry a little about everything back in the States, you know, the apartment and God knows what else...."

"Come on now, don't worry, you haven't been here all that long!"

"Oh, I realize that, but I still worry...God, I really love it here. Can you imagine waking up to all this every morning, Catherine? Wouldn't it be wonderful?"   "When's your birthday, Nickie?"

"Jeez, it's tomorrow," said Nickie, her mood quickly changing. "I'd forgotten all about it; we'll have to celebrate."

"Come with me...Come on," Catherine repeated as she saw Nickie hesitating.

They went through the hall, out the back door and down to the bottom of the garden. In a small copse was a tiny cottage with a thatched roof and small windows. The door had a brass knocker.

"Oh, Catherine, look at this!" cried Nickie in ecstasy. "Just look at this! Have you ever seen anything so *beautiful*?"

Catherine took a large old-fashioned key out of her purse and opening the door, said, "Jonathan gave me the key this morning. Apparently it's part of the property and it's mine."

It was unfurnished, but everything was spotlessly clean. It had a small brick fireplace and two bedrooms. The old-fashioned bathroom had stained-glass windows.

Nickie was overwhelmed. As she walked from room to room, she became even more ecstatic. "What are you going to do with it, Catherine?"

"Jonathan told me that it's a special guest cottage. It's been used by a writer for about four years, but he recently left to go live in London. Now it's yours. Happy birthday, honey!"

Nickie was speechless. She stood perfectly still and stared at Catherine. Tears ran down her face.

"It's your birthday present," said Catherine. "I want you to have it. Of course, you'll have to furnish it, but you can visit anytime you want."

Nickie found her voice at last. "You mean it, Catherine? You really mean it? Am I dreaming? Am I in another life?"

"No, you're not dreaming. Rose Cottage is yours. It's your birthday gift from your newly wealthy friend. Now, wasn't it worthwhile looking after Bartholomew?"

Hugging, kissing, crying and laughing all at once, Nickie asked, "Did you say I can visit *anytime*?"

Nodding her head, Catherine said, "Yes, and here's the key."

Letting out screams of delight, Nickie started running through all the rooms and Catherine ran after her, laughing.

"You've got to be crazy, Catherine!"

"What do you mean?"

"You said I could *visit*. I'm *moving in*!"

Catherine suggested she think it over. "Are you sure you'd really want to live out here on the moors?"

"I've lived here before. Now I'm coming back home," said Nickie, holding her key tightly.

Jason had enjoyed his trip into Bolton. He had met his secretary at the Swan Hotel and they had enjoyed a good lunch. After making a few phone calls, he went to visit Hall-ith Wood, Crompton's home. It was quite a place, built about the same time as the Rose & Crown, he surmised.

Samuel Crompton had built the first spinning wheel, which had made the cotton industry prosper. In the house were furnishings belonging to Crompton, even his pipe. Jason had the feeling that any minute Mr. Crompton himself would come in the front door.

Taking his car, he then went to visit Smithills Hall, another fine

Tudor building. Part of it was used as a restaurant, and he thought how nice it would be to bring the others one evening for dinner. Driving around the ring road, he passed the beautiful Mossbank Park and decided he would take a look at an old church in Deane. Then, going back into town, he visited the old Bolton parish church there. There was a little pub by the Swan with a chair hanging up on one of the beams. One of the locals told him that during the Reformation, a man had sat in this chair and had his last drink before having his head chopped off.

Ordering a beer, Jason thought of the past few days. He thought of Nickie and Catherine. He found it difficult to understand his own needs and desires. Sometimes he felt like settling down and being a country farmer, and at other times he enjoyed wheeling and dealing and being the typical playboy. If his mother and brother knew of his business interests, they would be amazed. He always told them that he was writing and would go off to submit his work to newspapers and publishers. But Jason had become exceptionally rich and owned properties all over England and Wales.

It was odd, he thought, how he could complete a transaction. He had the ability to separate his emotions completely from his business dealings. Once he decided he wanted something, he would always get it, regardless of the cost. He was ruthless. He used another name and had learned how to be another person. It was a great life: he loved being able to disappear when the going got tough. Even his secretary, who traveled anywhere he wanted, didn't know him as Jason. Chuckling to himself as he looked at his business card, he thought how well this name had served him through the years: "*Lloyd Richards*."

George saw the girls in the back garden and waved through the window.

Nickie was obviously excited and couldn't wait to tell everyone about her Rose Cottage.

Catherine went upstairs to get ready for dinner, leaving them together, happy that she was able to give something worthwhile to Nickie. She needed to think things through, to find herself again. Everything was going at such a fast pace, her whole world had turned around. All at once, she was close to people she had never known...or *had she*!

Jonathan was reading a book when Alan knocked on his door. Happy to see him, Jonathan invited him in.

"I've been thinking about Kradeno and Cimraknus," said Alan. "I think I understand how they have influenced Jason. You know, he's been quite a mystery over the years not only to me, but to my mother. Nothing you can put a finger on, but I know he lives another life away from Cardiff House. I think Lady Margaret knows also but doesn't say anything. When it first began, he was away at college. I used to question certain things, but never got a direct answer. Good old Jason has an elusive way with him, but I knew, I felt it in my bones. Anyway, I didn't come to talk about Jason. I wanted to ask if Kradeno had anything to do with Megan being raped and the birth of Patrick.''

"I'm afraid so," said Jonathan. "You know that if Kradeno fathered a child, his seed would be evil."

"Yes, that's what I thought. But there seems to be a gap after that lifetime. Remember, after Megan we were made aware of Lord Edward and Alice, his wife, going to California. So what happened to Patrick, I'd like to know? And, for that matter, what happened to Emmanuel?''

Jonathan thought for a moment and then said, "This is why you have all been brought together, for when the mystery is solved, then all karma will be paid."

Alan looked concerned. "But what about Frances? If she was Patrick, the seed of Kradeno, is she now affected in some way?''

"No. Let me explain: The soul of Frances was also Patrick, who was the son of Megan.''

"I understand; please go on."

"Well, Frances is not blood-related to your family, right?''

Alan nodded. "Then what you're saying is that there is a possibility that the evil born in Patrick has continued through the generations in our family.''

Jonathan agreed.

Alan thought about this for a moment and then said, "The fact that the soul of Frances was Patrick, and that she, as a man, fathered one of my ancestors means that the evil was passed down to his son and continued in that way in my family. Then Frances incarnated later in a different family which excluded her from the evil influence of Kradeno.''

"You're getting better at understanding."

"But surely the soul of Frances would have been influenced in some way, regardless of what family she incarnated into?'' Lighting his pipe, Alan waited for Jonathan to answer.   "When Frances was Patrick, he passed the seed of evil to his son, allowing Kradeno to continue his career of pain and destruction. Once Patrick had died and left this earth, Kradeno was no longer interested in his soul, for he needs a living body to create his evil and terror. Whoever inherits the evil seed is released once he dies. Nevertheless, the soul has been influenced and through many successive lifetime experiences compensates for the actions of a previous lifetime, thus repaying karma.''

"So Frances has had to repay karma through her lifetimes, but does not pass on the evil seed. Each lifetime her soul can improve, but the lineage of Patrick is born capable of doing Kradeno's work willingly.''

"That's about it," said Jonathan.

"So Jason is in fact under Kradeno's influence?"

"I'm afraid so."

"But why not me? I'm the eldest son."

"Because you are the Keeper of the Book."

Catherine was resting on her bed, listening to her small radio and enjoying a cigarette. The music was soothing and she thought of Nickie and how happy she was. Her facial mask was beginning to tighten, so she put her cigarette out and lay back on the pillow to allow the mask to work....

"Stop it, Toby, you're hurting me."

Tobias chuckled and held his broad hands tightly over Marion's eyes.

"I know who you are, you silly boy," she said.

He grunted and let go.

"Why did you run away, Tobias, when I was telling you about Jack and me?"

He started to jump up and down, saying "No, no, no, no!"

"All right, Tobias, I won't mention him again, I promise."

He put his arms around her and started to cry.

Marion knew he was feeling great pain at the thought of her leaving and this caused her pain, too. She wanted him to be happy and share in her joy.

"Why don't you help me, Tobias, and then we can go to the moor?"

Smiling again, he took her broom and started to sweep the hall vigorously.

Papa had said that she and Jack could have this room for their wedding night and Marion wanted everything perfect. Polishing the brass bed and changing the linens, she replaced them with beautifully embroidered sheets and pillow cases which she had made and stored in her dowry chest. It was sheer delight for Marion to prepare this room.

Not thinking, she said, "Doesn't it look lovely, Toby? I know Jack is going to love this room."

Tobias began his low murmuring and Marion realized he was jealous, so trying to behave as though she hadn't noticed his change of mood, she said, "When I've washed the windows, we'll go outside and pick some wild flowers."

He didn't speak. Standing there looking sullen, he watched his sister open a window. She began to sing a song, but he didn't like her reason for being happy.

Sam came upstairs to see how the room was getting on and noticed his son's dark look and the contrast of Marion's sweet, happy face.

"Oh, Papa, it's you," she said with surprise.

"Who did you think it was—Jack?" he asked.

Tobias thrust forward. His anger was evident. He didn't want his sister to leave him. He didn't like them talking about this Jack. He wanted her out of this room that she intended to share with the strange man. He wanted her to come and play outside on the moors. He hated the room and his father walking up to him.

Marion shouldn't smile at anyone except me, the deranged boy thought. It wasn't fair. As anger blinded his vision, he suddenly lurched forward and pushed his beloved Marion out of the window. He thought it funny to see her legs and petticoats fluttering as she fell three stories to the black, shiny cobbles below.

As Marion felt Tobias strike her back, then felt herself falling into emptiness, she reached out to Gareth of Abergavennie, whose smile still held for her the promise of long ago. As he held her in his arms, she knew he would take her gently into dark oblivion and then she would have to search through time to find him once more....

Then Tobias' father was beating him and yelling words he couldn't understand. He ran downstairs to finish playing with Marion, wanting to play tag on the moor. Sarah heard Tobias' yelping and the terrible sound of Sam's crying. Lifting her skirts, she ran up toward the bridal suite. Tobias passed her on the stairs, running like a wild animal, calling his sister's name. As Sarah reached the top story, she saw Sam kneeling with his elbow on the open window ledge. Instinctively aware of tragedy, she screamed, *"Where's Marion?"*

Sam didn't answer.

Screaming and demanding an answer, she ran to the open window and saw her daughter broken and crumpled on the cobbles below. She felt nauseous and vomited as she saw Tobias kissing Marion's blood-stained face and pulling at the limp body, shouting, "Come and play, Marrie, come and get flowers with Toby."

Each parent was severed from the other by the horror, unable to communicate, each cut off and alone in their individual nightmares. Then Tobias, looking up and seeing his parents at the window, called, "Mama, Papa, come play with Toby, come now, pleeese?"

It was still early. The help had not yet arrived. Sarah felt the sudden impact of fear: she knew that Sam was unreachable. Closing the window and leaving him collapsed on the floor, she hurried downstairs, collecting cleaning rags and a wooden bucket. Running outside, she threw the rags and bucket on the cobbles. Then, holding Marion's sweet blood-stained face to her breast, she rocked her like a baby, allowing her tears to flow freely, first crying inwardly and then letting nature open the shocked emotional barriers to relieve the flood of agony from a mother's heart.

Soon she heard Joshua's feet on the cobbles. He was coming to work in the kitchen. Not raising her head, she continued to hold her baby.

Joshua looked up as Sam opened the window and screamed for Marion, who was now in her mother's arms. Seeing the wooden bucket and cleaning rags, Joshua thought that Marion had fallen from the window.

It was pathetic to see Sarah holding her daughter. Marion could no longer feel her mother's comfort or the call of her father, which she always answered so readily.

Joshua touched Sarah gently, but she no longer responded. Seeing Sam staring down at the horror below, Joshua ran in through the back door and up the stairs, his only thought to get Sam away from the open window. It was as though Sam were sleepwalking. He responded to Joshua's guidance without uttering a word. Joshua took him down into the tavern and tried to give him a drink, which dribbled over his closed lips.

"Sam, Sam, this is Joshua. Sarah will need you." Sam seemed to come alive at the sound of Sarah's name. "Stay here, Sam, and I'll bring Sarah to you."

Sam put his head on the oak table and cried like a baby. Joshua ran outside.

Sarah was still holding Marion, whose eyes were still open wide. He found it difficult to release Marion from Sarah's grip. Then, laying Marion's head gently down on the ground, he took Sarah, who was sobbing quietly, to her husband.

When they saw each other in the tavern, they embraced, and the blood of their daughter, which had collected on Sarah's dress, dripped between their two bodies onto the brick floor.

It was obvious to Joshua that Marion had been cleaning the window and had fallen to her death. Picking up the cleaning rags and putting them neatly into the wooden bucket, he put the stable blanket over Marion and went into the tavern where Sam and Sarah were now sitting dry-eyed, holding hands and sharing their pain silently.

Walking back now to the kitchen, he heard Sally's scream outside. On her way to the kitchen, she had seen Tobias kneel in the pool of blood, putting wild flowers in Marion's hair. Not understanding what was happening, she bent over them and saw that Marion was dead, her eyes open and sightless. Tobias was laughing.

Joshua came and shooed him away, telling him that Marion was tired and didn't want to play for a while. Tobias left, pouting, and then, leaping into the air, ran away to the moors.

Covering Marion again, Joshua shook the hysterical Sally and told her to take care of Sarah and Sam while he went to report the tragic accident.

As she walked down the hall, Nickie could hear Catherine calling.

"Gareth, Gareth, where are you, Gareth?"

Nickie felt her blood turn cold. "Megan's" haunting voice was terrifying. She ran into Catherine's room, not knowing how she was going to handle the situation.

Catherine was now sitting up in bed. Her facial mask had cracked, which gave her a macabre look in the darkened room.

Nickie's scream woke Catherine, who got up to go to Nickie, but Nickie was already halfway down the stairs.

George could hardly believe his ears when he heard Nickie screaming. As she passed his door, he ran out and took hold of her. Struggling like a frightened rabbit, her head buried in his chest, she pointed back at Catherine's room.

Catherine was coming down the hall. George laughed out loud when he saw her facial mask.

"Come on now, Nickie, everything's all right. You didn't see a ghost. See, Catherine's here."

Still scared and holding on tight to George, Nickie peeked over his shoulder and saw Catherine looking astounded at all the commotion. "I'll be with you in a minute, George," she said. "Just let me rinse this off. Take care of her. I won't be long."

Hearing Catherine's voice, Nickie felt some of her tension leave. George was talking to her. It felt good to be in his arms. She could feel his lips moving near her face and she knew that everything was all right. Looking up now, she saw George smiling at her and telling her that Catherine would be here shortly. Gently, he kissed her forehead. Putting her arms around his neck, she lifted her face and he slid his lips onto hers.

When Catherine came out with her shiny, squeaky clean face, she was still bewildered. But she could see that she wasn't needed.

Chapter Twenty-two

Alan phoned his mother.

"Hello, Alan dear," she said. "How is Jason? Is he behaving himself?"

Realizing now more than ever before that his mother always asked about Jason in this concerned way, he tried to put her at ease, telling her that everyone was having a marvelous time at the Rose & Crown.

"When are you coming home, dear?" she asked.

"Well, Mother, I'm not quite sure, but it won't be long."

"Cardiff House isn't the same without you boys," she said. "And how are Catherine and her friend?"

"Oh, they're fine, Mother. I'm hoping to bring Catherine back with me. This isn't definite, but I hope it can be arranged."

They said their good-byes, and Alan stripped off to shower in the old-fashioned bathtub which had had the modern addition of a hose-type shower. Alan was a "shower thinker," not a "shower singer," and the water wasn't running very hot at all....

It felt hard and cold on his face as he rode over the Pennine Chain. Marion, his sweet bride-to-be, had been on his mind constantly since early this morning. When he awoke, he was sure she was calling him. It didn't sound as if she were saying "Jack," but he knew she needed him and the horse could not go any faster.

Jack Hornby couldn't understand his desperate need to get to the Rose & Crown. All had been well until he had felt the need to stop for refreshment at the King's Head. Dismounting his horse, he felt Marion's scream rip through his body to such an extent that he doubled over in pain.

From that moment on, he wasted no time: riding his horse as fast as possible, he feverishly made haste, anxious to reach his bride-to-be. The rain came down heavier and the dark, forbidding clouds whipped up into green-black whirlpools in the dark northern sky. As if eager to participate in the wild storm, the wind lashed, knifing his face with its icy edge. Unable to think, unable to ease his aching body, Jack Hornby rode on toward a love that had gone beyond the darkness of the lonely moor.   Alan's consciousness was deeply stirred by the psychic trauma; his body was now cold from the icy moorland rain. Shivering, he stepped out of the shower and reaching for his robe, collapsed in his chair. Trying to focus in on two levels of consciousness, like a child desperate to remain in a dream, he closed his eyes and felt a warm towel being placed around his drenched hair. He reached up behind him with his hand and affectionately said, "Marion, Marion, my love."

But the rich north-country voice that answered was not his Marion. He stood up and felt the water from his boots surge down his legs. Sarah was standing there, holding the towel, and Sam was beside her, holding the wet cape he had taken from Jack when he had arrived almost unconscious at the inn. Feeling the dreadful misery of Marion's parents, he knew that something was terribly wrong.

With the rain glistening on his face and beard, he asked, "Where is Marion?" It seemed that Sarah was anticipating his question: her answer was an agonized flood of tears. "Stop weeping, woman, and tell me—where is your daughter?"

Unable to contain herself, the wretched woman ran out of the room, leaving Sam to relate the horror of Marion's death.

His voice cracked and harsh, hard working hands rubbing constantly on his coarse tunic, Sam told the man who was to have been his son-in-law how Marion had been cleaning the window of their intended bridal suite when she lost her balance and fell to her death below.

Heaven showered its mercy upon the grief-stricken Jack by erasing all emotion. He was instantly emptied: Sam's words went through him without any response, leaving an echo of a love born yesterday and to be fulfilled in a century many lifetimes away.

Smiling, Jack walked past Sam and reaching out his arms, walked upstairs to his room with his bride at his side. Marion's tinkling laughter and provocative smile warmed his heart; as she ran ahead toward their room, he watched with love and joy his sweet bride, her gown of white muslin flowing behind her. As she opened the door, she threw him a wild flower from her hair. With a shout of laughter, he ran in behind her, closing the door on the world....

"You're dripping wet, you'll catch your death of cold," said Catherine, reaching for the towel left on the chair. "And I'm ready for my dinner. I thought you had dropped off to sleep and I got tired of waiting.''

Alan felt elated. Apologizing for his lateness, he kissed Catherine, twirled her around and poured them each a glass of sherry, telling her he would be exactly five minutes.

The afternoon had gone slowly for George. His depression was growing and he felt the need to be alone. Finding himself a comfortable chair in the Green Room, he listened to the local schoolmaster, Mr. Howarth, play his violin.

Sinking back in his chair, George closed his eyes as the music of "Greensleeves" haunted his memory from long ago. Dividing the relaxing atmosphere of the Green Room from the brick hallway was a mahogany bannister, near the reception desk for guests. He could faintly hear hushed conversations as Mr. Howarth played his afternoon music. Unmistakably, there were footsteps, heavy and laboring, slouching down the brick hallway....

"Is that you, Tobias?" asked Sam sharply. There was no response; Sam felt nervous. He knew it was his imbecile son and he also knew that if he saw him, he would kill him. "Get out of my sight, you soulless creature! Begone or your ugly life will not be worth living!''

Having made the fire safe, Sam got up from his knees and looked across the Green Room. Tobias was standing there in the yellow candlelight. His thick lips were parted, showing his big yellow teeth. Sam noticed the ugly green saliva trickling down from the corners of his mouth. A window suddenly smashed inwards with the force of an unearthly wind. The beautiful statue of Saint Joseph was lifted up in the air from the old wood chest that had held his mother's dowry. It swayed insolently as it came toward him.

Unable to look away, Sam could hear Tobias' evil laughter. "Stop this, Tobias! You hear me? Stop it, I say!" As the statue floated in front of his face, it suddenly crashed to the floor with tremendous force.

Trembling, Sam forced himself to look at his son and saw an ugly green light growing around him. As the light grew larger, a foul smell pervaded the room. Sam felt stifled and struggled for breath.

Tobias raised his hands above his head and thick blood oozed down his arms and onto his clothing. He began to step forward and Sam felt his feet turn to lead. A deep, resounding voice came from Tobias:

"I am Kradeno. Thou shalt hear me."

Then the vision of his dead daughter appeared and the possessed Tobias held her slender body close to him and kissed her, covering her beautiful face with the vile green saliva. As Sam was trying to move forward, the voice spoke again.

"I am Kradeno, and this worthless scum thou hast fathered shall be my instrument."

As he said this, the body of Tobias began to expand. As it grew, thick green slime poured out of its nose, mouth and ears. Tobias' eyes became larger, eyeballs protruding with the sickening force of the slime as it tried to find a way out through them as well. "He is damned and will continue to serve me. Lay not thy hand upon him or thou shalt meet a miserable, agonizing death." The voice grew louder; Sam's ears were deafened by thunderous laughter. He started to cross himself; as he put his hand to his head, Kradeno said, "Thou needst holy water, but I will give thee better."

Once again, the vision of Sam's daughter was shown to him. She walked toward him, and as he reached out to touch her, his ears were again deafened by the horrid laughter of Kradeno.

Another window broke as a surge of evil energy burst into the room: its force was so great that Sam fell backward, hitting his head heavily on the floor. Then the force hit him in the belly, causing excruciating agony. He saw again the form of his daughter: now she too was forced backward. Suddenly her stomach was ripped open. Grinning, Tobias dipped his fingers into her bloody body and commanded Sam to do likewise.

Refusing, Sam felt appalling pain as his first finger was suddenly broken off. Kradeno grabbed it and dipped it in the gaping gore-spouting stomach, commanding once again that Sam do as he ordered. Sam struggled to his knees, begging for mercy and experiencing relentless pain. Horrified, he did as Kradeno bade. Upon opening his eyes, he saw that his beloved daughter was gone. Tobias was bending over him.

"Papa, Papa, love Toby now pleese, Papa. Love Toby."

Sam was in agony. His finger lay on the floor in a pool of blood.

Tobias put his arms around Sam who, recoiling from his embrace, screamed to all the heavenly angels for mercy and comfort from this torment.

Tobias picked up his father's finger and licking away the blood, began to coo and kiss the dismembered digit as though to give it comfort.

Calling upon the heavenly hosts, Sam prayed for everlasting peace. He cried for the soul of his daughter; he asked to be with her. Pleading for mercy, he picked up the fallen statue of Saint Joseph and brought it down with all his strength on his son's head.

The voice of Kradeno spoke with Tobias' last breath: "Pray, old man...never stop...for when thy miserable end is nigh, I shall be upon thee. Live in fear and know that hell awaits thy miserable soul. As long as fear lives with thee, thou art mine when thy time endeth." A sickening gurgling sound came from Tobias, and his head rolled over to face his father.

Tormented beyond human endurance, the broken man was lost between heaven and earth. He saw the image of Sarah before him, and her love leapt in his tired heart. Offering his last breath to his God, he let go, waiting for death.

Suddenly the room was flooded with golden light and Cimraknus towered above him.

"Samuel, when thou openest thine eyes, thy son Tobias will no longer be. Do not look for him. Because of thy faith, thou hast won light and life. Never look back in fear, for it will surely be thine end. Go to Sarah, revere the memory of thy children and give love and care with all thy heart to Jack Hornby, who will rely on thee for the remainder of his earthly journey."

Determined to follow the guidance of this glorious being, Sam walked straight ahead, knowing that the body of his son no longer lay on the floor. In true faith, he went to give Sarah comfort and to care for Jack as long as he lived.

George awoke with perspiration on his brow. He sat still and, as the memory of Sam flooded into his consciousness, he realized the part he had played in this karmic drama. Something told him that fear is the honey of evil; fully awake, he knew that fear existed everywhere, but that he had never known what it meant since he had paid the price as Sam.

"What is it George?" Nickie was stroking his hair at the temples. "What is it, my love?"

George detected the tenderness and concern in Nickie's voice. He put his hand to his shoulder, touching her. Behind him she was murmuring in his ear.

"I'm fine, Nickie; what's wrong?"

She came from behind his chair. Her face was white.

Frowning, he held her hands. "Nickie, dear, what is it?"

Her lips trembling, she stroked his hair with a worried look on her face. "Your hair, George, your *hair*!"

Putting his hand to his head, he asked, "What about my hair? What's wrong, Nickie?"

Unable to tell him, she pulled her compact from her purse and held it up so he could see. He stared at the reflection, rubbing his fingers through his hair over and over again. It was pure white!

"What happened, George?" asked Nickie anxiously. "Please tell me."

His voice faltering, his heart beating faster, he related the experience of his past life as Sam. As he began to tell her of his gruesome encounter with Kradeno, she listened, horrified and spellbound. She held his hand with loving care, yet her concern was not for George but for Sam, her beloved husband.

Kneeling beside him now, she rested her head on his knee,

listening to every word he said. She felt a contact with the past. . . .

Sarah felt overwhelming compassion for Sam. "But where shall we tell everyone Tobias is?"

Still shaken from his terrible meeting with Kradeno, Sam tried to steady his voice and calm Sarah. "My dear wife, it was Joshua, not I, who presumed that Marion fell out of the window." He felt Sarah flinch when he mentioned their daughter's name. "When Joshua found her, he thought she had fallen. So let it be that way, Sarah. We have suffered sufficient pain."

Raising her tear-stained face, Sarah asked, "But what of Tobias? How can we explain where he's gone?"

Wiping a tear from her cheek, Sam said, "No one can explain that. If we tried to, we would be accused of witchcraft. Leave it be, Sarah...we can say that he disappeared shortly after Marion's fall, which is true."

Sarah nodded slowly in agreement. "What of poor Jack? What will become of him?"

"We will take care of him, Sarah, and love him as our daughter would have. I'm afraid he will never be himself again. The poor man is demented. We will find in him the love of Marion and the misery of Tobias, our sad inheritance."

Sarah noticed for the first time that her husband's hair had turned white. Realizing the depth of his grief for their lost children, she promised faithfully that she would never permit fear to remain under their roof. And to ensure the safety of their immortal souls, she would let the priest have as a chapel the small room next to theirs, which was once the nursery of Marion and Tobias. "When it becomes hallowed, we will have daily Mass, and no evil will come under this roof."

Feeling well pleased with Sarah's solution, Sam prepared to face the world, knowing that Cimraknus would dwell in their household, protecting them from Kradeno's fearful threat.

"So that's why the kitchen has a round stained-glass window." said Nickie. "It was originally a chapel. Isn't that fantastic?"

George felt relieved. His tension had melted away. His white hair did not concern him: he considered it a small price to pay for the blessing of Cimraknus.

"Can you imagine what a fabulous movie this would make?" asked Nickie. "And as for your hair, George, it looks terrific, sexy even." Taking a good look at him, she nodded her head in approval and kissed him with the tenderness of Sarah and the need of Nickie.

Jason was pleased with himself. Nothing ever worried him, but lately, since his arrival at the Rose & Crown, he had felt a certain resentment toward George. He was the one who always got the girl. Catherine was out of the picture, but Nickie was free: a little loud, but not bad at all. He liked his women to be discreet and submissive. Nickie was neither of these, but nevertheless he wouldn't mind taking her to Brighton for a weekend...on business, of course. Shrugging his shoulders, he let his thoughts dwell on Dottie, the bosomy barmaid downstairs. He began to whistle a tune.

During dinner, Jason felt uneasy when the group started to relate their past-life experiences. He felt a sudden jolt when Nickie asked, "Where do you come in, Jason?" Not giving it much thought, he answered carefully, "I think I must have been Joshua, who else?"

Giving his remark some consideration, Nickie asked everyone, "Well, who was Tobias?"

At the mention of this name, Jason felt a cold shudder up his spine.

"What's the matter?" asked Catherine.

"I don't know...but just the sound of that idiot's name gives me cold chills."

"Why don't we drop the subject?" asked Alan. "Have you heard about Nickie's birthday tomorrow? What shall we do to celebrate?"

"*Whooppee!*" cried Nickie, happy that they were interested. "How about a picnic on the moor?"

"That sounds great," said George. "And by the way, congratulations again, Nickie. I hear you are the proud owner of Rose Cottage."

Having momentarily forgotten her inheritance, Nickie now understood why she was in such a good mood. "Yeah, I can't believe it. When I have it all furnished and fixed up, I want everyone to come and visit."   The conversation slowed down and everyone seemed tired, so they said their goodnights and went back to their rooms, ready to celebrate Nickie's birthday in the morning.

Jason remained downstairs, keeping his eye on the barmaid and giving her a wink at every opportunity. He felt sure she was getting his message. Strolling over to the bar, he asked her for a drink and invited her to have one with him.

Knowing that he tipped well, Dottie readily agreed. Leaning over the bar with a provocative smile, she enjoyed listening to his cultivated accent and fancied the idea of a toff like this making a pass at her.

"How about me meeting you after you finish?" he asked.

Giggling a little, she nodded her head like a child asked if she would like candy.

Patiently waiting, he tried not to watch her too much, for her coarse mannerisms put him off. Then, not wanting everyone in the bar to know why he was waiting, he whispered that he would be in his room when she had finished. Leaving a five-pound note on the counter, he told her to bring a little something with her to help the party along.

Chapter Twenty-three

Everyone went downstairs early to breakfast to celebrate Nickie's birthday. Jenny had put a candle in the middle of Nickie's sweet roll. As she walked in, they all sang, "Happy Birthday," and Jason was the first to get up and give her a kiss. Handing her a beautifully wrapped gift, he asked if she would like to take a ride over the moors to see the museum and church in Bolton.

In her happy mood, Nickie thought it a wonderful idea. Jason was somewhat disappointed when she extended his invitation to everyone.

"Where's Dottie this morning?" asked George.

Jenny shook her head, obviously not too happy about her barmaid's absence. "Last night she was in the bar till nine, and she usually goes to bed early so she can be on breakfast duty," said Jenny. "I 'aven't seen or 'eard from 'er. I swear, these lasses from Manchester are always the same. They come lookin' for a job in the country and always prove to be unreliable."

"Now, now, Jenny, take it easy," said Bill. "Dottie's been a good girl; maybe she's not feelin' well. She'll turn up. Just yer wait an' see." With that, he started to pick up the dirty dishes. Jenny put on her martyr look and continued to serve her guests with a fixed smile.

Talking to Catherine and Alan, Jenny said, "Yer picnic lunches may be a bit late. I'm afraid I'm goin' to 'ave to do 'em all meself."

Seeing that this obviously bothered her, Alan said, "You're right, of course, you are short-staffed. Why don't we have our picnic some other time?" The question had been directed to everyone and they agreed.

Wondering whether or not she might have upset the new owner

and the gentleman, Jenny was quick to apologize for her attitude and tell them she didn't mind at all. Alan insisted she needn't bother and that everyone would eat in the village. Thanking him for his consideration, she went round to Nickie and kissed her lightly on the cheek and wished her a happy birthday.

Suddenly, there was a commotion: people were shouting, and a woman screamed, "Oh, my God!"

"What the hell's going on?" said Nickie.

An English bobby was standing in the dining room with a note pad in his hand and his chin strap tight on his chin. Nickie noticed that everytime he spoke, the strap went up and down.

"Good mornin', all. I'm Constable Turner of the Lancashire Constabulary. Are you ladies and gentlemen all residents of the Rose & Crown?"

"Yes, why, Bert?" asked Bill.

The constable coughed, a little embarrassed. "I'm on official duty, Bill, and I'm Constable Turner now."

"What's wrong?" asked Jenny irritably. She didn't want any peculiar goings-on in her inn, especially with the new owner here.

"A murder, Mrs. Jackson, that's what's wrong," he answered in his best official voice.

"A murder?" yelled Nickie. "Who, for God's sake? Oh, God, it isn't Jonathan, is it?"

Coughing again and brushing his moustache, Constable Turner replied, "A lass by the name of Dottie. Worked here, didn't she, Mr. Jackson?"

Shocked and unable to comprehend, Bill nodded. His thoughts were on Dottie, who was always so full of life. He couldn't believe that she was dead or that anyone would murder the poor lass.

"I knew, I just *knew* when she didn't come in fer work that somethin' was wrong," wailed Jenny.

"Was she supposed to be working, then?" asked Constable Turner, proud of his ability to question. Now fancying himself a detective, he said to everyone in the room, "When did you last see her?"

Everyone started to say something at the same time, and realizing he'd gone about it in the wrong way, he wished the detective would hurry and come in.

"Let's have some order, please," he requested. Already he had lost his authority and people were ignoring him. A short, stocky man with a red face and a Scottish accent entered the dining room.

"I'm Detective MacIntyre. Are you the proprietor?" he asked Bill.

"Yes, and this is my—"

Cutting him short, Detective MacIntyre asked if he had a room to spare for questioning.

Jenny was mentally calculating which rooms would be presentable when Alan cut in. "Begging your pardon, officer, but won't this room do?"

Taking off his raincoat and nodding to Bert, the detective pulled out a chair. Bert took off his helmet to reveal a shock of sandy hair that resembled a Betterwear brush.

"I'd like you to give my constable your names and addresses, please," said the detective.

Alan intervened. "Before you go any further, Detective MacIntyre, would you mind telling us why we are being questioned?"

"Somebody's been murdered and the girl worked here, I believe."

"Yes, but what *happened*?" asked Nickie, unable to keep still.

In a dull monotone, MacIntyre told them that Dottie had been found about a mile away on the moorland, naked, raped and strangled.

Jason was the first to speak. "But why are *we* being questioned? After all, it could be a?yone in the village...or someone from the city."

"Perhaps so, sir, but nevertheless, it's my duty to question you folks. After all, every one of you is a stranger in these parts."

No one could argue with that, so they answered his questions, one by one.

"What a birthday," said Nickie. "Jeez, what shall we do now? It's like an Agatha Christie story."

Soon they heard the ambulance siren and voices and people moving about.

When Jonathan arrived for breakfast, Nickie immediately told him the story. Jonathan's expression remained the same throughout. The sound of the siren broke up the conversation, so everyone started to leave.

Alan took Jonathan to one side and asked, "Do you know what happened?"

Nodding his head, Jonathan looked grave. "Brace yourself, my boy. It will soon be over."

Puzzled by Jonathan's remark, Alan thought about Jason and was disturbed. "Want to sit out on the front bench and have a smoke?"

"Good idea. Let's go."

Outside, enjoying the fresh moorland air, Alan bluntly asked, "It was Jason, wasn't it?"

"Well, yes and no."

"Yes and no?" repeated Alan. "What do you mean?"

"Jason raped her, impregnated her with Kradeno's seed and then left her. Within five minutes of the assault, he had forgotten it."

"Then who murdered the girl?"

"Kradeno himself. Not satisfied with the limited degree of lust that Jason had for her, and not wanting his seed to remain in this woman, he, the evil being, killed her. Not Jason.''

Thinking of the terrible death the girl must have experienced, Alan was about to ask something when Jonathan said, ''The girl was unconscious through shock after Jason left her. It was at this time that Kradeno finished her.''

''How do you know this? How do you know Dottie didn't go through hell with this evil force before she died?''

Sighing as though it were easy to understand, Jonathan said, ''When your brother left the Rose & Crown with Dottie, I saw them from my upstairs window. I hurriedly dressed, but by the time I reached the area, I saw Jason making his way back. I could see that he wasn't aware of his actions. I continued down the road until I saw the girl and the evil energies surrounding her body. Believe me, she was not conscious at the time. Kradeno had materialized and had his hands on her neck when I arrived. I was too late. He disappeared, leaving the body in a ring of black energies and his seed unable to grow in the dead girl's womb. But because of my presence, Kradeno was unable to complete his evil intention; he was forced to kill her immediately. So she died, without terror, completely oblivious to his presence.''

''But why would he fear you? Surely a human being wouldn't deter him.''

''You forget,'' said Jonathan kindly. ''Members of the Higher Order also have...powers.''

Still distressed at Jason's actions. but relieved that he hadn't actually murdered the girl, Alan felt at a loss. He sat for awhile and quietly smoked his pipe.

The detective left in the car, leaving Constable Turner behind to wait. Bill asked if he would like a pint before he left.   Once again taking off his helmet, which represented officialdom, Bert said, ''Aye, Bill. Thank you. Hope you didn't mind me being a bit sharp before.''

''No, Bert, you an' I went to school together. I know there's times when y' 'ave t' work fer yer livin'.''

This broke the ice and the two men laughed and enjoyed their pint.

''Eh, that lass was in a bad way, Bill,'' said Bert.

''I know,'' said Bill. ''Y' told us.''

Shaking his head as though to erase the sight of the girl's body, he continued, ''No Bill, you don't know one half of it. The girl's stomach was all bloated—it looked like someone had used a bicycle pump on her...and then she just kind of...broke open.''

''I thought yer said she was strangled?''

''She was, and also brutally molested. The detective said I was to keep it quiet, so keep your mouth shut, won't you, lad?''

''Not a word,'' said Bill sincerely. ''Not a word.''

Alan eventually broke the silence between Jonathan and himself. "Will this ever end? How long will Kradeno attach himself to our family?"

"When he is recognized by the sign, then he will return to the bowels of the earth until he is able to rise again and once more attach his evil influence to humanity."

"Is someone living now destined to know this sign?" asked Alan, trying his utmost to understand the karmic mystery. Before Jonathan could reply, Alan spoke again. "What am I saying? We know for sure that Megan knew the sign. Does that mean Catherine will be the one to discover the secret of Kradeno? My God, Jonathan, do *you* know the answer?"

Jonathan did not speak. He leaned over and touched Alan on the forehead, between his eyebrows. A blinding light severed the veil momentarily, and when Jonathan released his touch, Alan knew that he himself would be involved. But how, he didn't know, for once again his consciousness was veiled.

"Want a stroll?" asked Jonathan.

Declining the invitation, Alan said he was waiting for Catherine to some outside. Thanking him for his help, he watched Jonathan's easy walk as he strolled off toward the village.

Nickie saw Alan sitting on the bench, so she came over to him.

"Wasn't it terrible? That poor girl...it's hard to believe she's dead. I keep thinking of how happy she was last night....You know something, Alan?" He raised his eyebrows. "I'm not in the least afraid. I figure it's got to be some maniac in a car that saw her, pulled her into the car, drove her out to the moors and then attacked her."

Her mood changed then. "Alan, I've been wanting to ask you something. Remember the night when George hypnotized Catherine, and you and she were talking when she was Megan?" When he acknowledged her question, Nickie went on.

"Jason was taking notes because you were talking Celtic to each other. What did Catherine—I mean Megan—say?"

Alan thought about that night. Not knowing why, he thought that possibly an answer might lie in the conversation between Megan and himself. "Let me think about it, Nickie, and look over Jason's notes, and maybe we can talk about it some other time. Do you mind?"

"Of course I mind, but I suppose I'll have to go along with you, won't I?"

Smiling, he said, "I suppose you will."

Jenny had finished her inventory lists. Checking once more before discussing the contents with Catherine, she admired her presentation, looking forward to the compliments she hoped would be forthcoming. Handing her inventory sheet to Catherine, she waited patiently for Catherine to comment.

Catherine glanced at the contents of the neatly handwritten papers. Noting Jenny's nervousness, she complimented her efficiency and told her that she was busy right now but would examine them in detail later.

Jenny winced as Catherine folded her lists. She would have preferred to discuss one or two things now, like the chipped vegetable dish and the need to have a larger table for Mr. Howarth's violin.

"Thank you again, Jenny, I'm sure I'll find this very helpful," said Catherine.

"For the past six or seven months, I've not overspent my budget," said Jenny proudly. "I 'ope everything is to yer satisfaction, miss. Bill and I work real 'ard to keep the place nice."

"It's beautiful," said Catherine, "and I wouldn't want it any other way. I hope you and Bill will keep looking after the Rose & Crown for me."

It was more than she had expected to hear. Overwhelmed, Jenny started to cry a little. Then, dabbing her eyes with her handkerchief, she said, "Thank you, miss. I didn't want to bother yer, but Bill and I will be proud to continue on here."

Relieved that the interlude was over, Catherine went to see what everyone was doing and where they might be going this afternoon. Alan was busy talking to Jonathan, Nickie and George were in a quiet corner of the bar, and Jason was coming down the stairs behind her.

"Want a spin, Catherine?" he asked.

"What I really want to do is go to a book shop."

"Well, I know where there's a pretty good one in Bolton."

"Sounds good to me. I'll meet you at the car in a couple of minutes."

When Catherine reached the car, Jason was already sitting in the driver's seat, ready to go.

"Jump in," he said, and Catherine sat back, ready to enjoy the scenery of Rivington.

"I found a delightful route on my way back yesterday. Shall we try it?" asked Jason. "It might take a little longer, but it's well worth it."

"Sounds fine to me."

"Now don't go to sleep on me," said Jason, laughing. "I want you to enjoy the ride."

"OK, I promise I won't close my eyes," said Catherine, feeling more relaxed with Jason than she had ever been.

Jason turned on the car radio, which made a nice background for his attractive voice. "Now we're riding over to Belmont and if you look over to your left, you'll see the reservoir." He continued to point out interesting places, and soon they were driving into Bolton.

The book store had a good selection and Catherine felt unhurried. Jason also enjoyed browsing around and left Catherine entirely alone, hoping she wouldn't be too long so that he could spend more time with her before going back to the Rose & Crown. Finally, she made her selection and they went out into the busy street.

"How about some coffee?" he asked.

Walking to the corner of Bradshawgate and Churchgate, they went into the Swan Hotel. Making themselves comfortable, they sat back in the easy chairs and Jason offered Catherine a cigarette.

"It hasn't been too easy for you, has it?" he asked.

"Well, I don't think it's been easy for anyone, really. Look what happened to poor George. It's incredible, yet he's taken it so well."

"It must have been bloody awful," said Jason, "to turn his hair snow white. Let's change the subject. How do you like your Rose & Crown?"

"I still can't believe it's mine."

"What are you going to do with it?"

"Leave everything as it is and concentrate on my life. Your brother and I are very much in love. We both feel this, but there's also a barrier between us. Until that has been removed, we can't fully belong to each other."

Jason watched as Catherine spoke. The sunlight from the window shone on her blonde hair and her eyes were the deepest blue he'd ever seen. As she talked, her hands moved gracefully, and when she smiled, he felt a need that could never be fulfilled.

"What are you staring at?" asked Catherine, laughing.

"Oh, this and that; wondering when we'll vacate ye olde Rose & Crown and join Tom and Frances for a drink at the Blue Feathers."

"Yes, I'm looking forward to seeing them again. Frances must be busy planning her wedding."

"By the way, Catherine, what were the books you bought?"

A little embarrassed, she told him that she had gotten two books on reincarnation. "You know, Jason, I've been thinking. Although you too are a part of everything that's happening, you seem to be on the outside."

Frowning, his voice lowered, Jason asked her what she meant.

"Well, I don't really know how to explain it, but let's say you haven't lost one blond hair yet."

More relaxed now, he told her, "And, young lady, I don't intend to."

"Jason?"

"Yes, Catherine?"

"What do you think the sign is?"

"I've no idea at this point. I'm curious to know."

Catherine suggested they go back the short way, so Jason reluctantly took her arm and they returned to the car.

"You look a little tired. Why don't you lean back and have a nap and I'll wake you when we reach the inn?" Jason said.

Grateful that she wouldn't have to make conversation, Catherine relaxed. Yawning, she asked how long it would be before they reached the Rose & Crown.

"Not too long. Do you mind if I put the radio on?"

Soon she was asleep, and as he drove, Jason looked over frequently, admiring her lovely profile.

It was getting foggy as they started to climb. Jason's thoughts started to focus upon his strange life. As a boy, he remembered quite clearly having a fantastic vision: the figure of a man framed in gold light, hovering in his bedroom. He was only thirteen when this happened and he could remember not having any fear. The figure gave off a beautiful glow. Then the form spoke to him:

"I am Rhaydhonasie, thy Master. Once again, thou hast the ability to choose thy path."

Jason knew that here was all that was good, and the room became a dancing rainbow. As the different colors pulsated around him, he felt warm and happy. He could actually taste the different colors. Each time he would do this, he would feel transported and see his own body sitting on the side of the bed.

The thought of numbers came into his head and he heard music. It was a child's paradise. He felt free to explore its boundaries. One thought and he would become the essence of each individual experience presented to him. Then suddenly, he heard again the voice of Rhaydhonasie and felt the powers of esoteric vision lessen.

"Thou shalt know fear which is reached by the sweetest path known to man—temptation. Know it and turn away when 'tis presented to thee. All manner of earthly pleasures may be thine, but in return thou wilt lose thy soul. Call for me when decision tortures thy mind and I will remove the evil forces destined to lurk beside thee in this life."

Then the room darkened and the young boy trembled. Kradeno materialized. He was huge, and Jason the boy felt small and insignificant. Treasures beyond imagination were presented to him and then withdrawn. He felt himself lifted into the air: Kradeno was holding him in the palm of his hand. As the voice of Rhaydhonasie echoed through the room, commanding him to leave, Kradeno invited the boy to come with him. Through the window Jason could see everything he had ever wished for, his for the taking. Once again, Rhaydhonasie ordered the evil one to leave. With a loud, thundering scream he was gone.

After this initiation, Jason learned to use both powers to his own advantage. On occasion, Rhaydhonasie had warned him of his evil ventures, but Kradeno would always give him the comfort he desired. Gradually, down through the years, Jason's constant acceptance of temptation weakened him. He found that he could no longer stop Kradeno. He would appear without request, and it became more difficult for Jason to bring Rhaydhonasie into his life, for he was afraid of Kradeno's anger.

While in college, he settled for Kradeno exclusively. Living was so easy with Kradeno's simple methods. As he looked back on his life, Jason realized that he no longer had any control, and although he could use the negative energies anytime he wished, there were times when he, Jason, disappeared somewhere in a void, only to be brought back and forced to face whatever chaotic circumstances had been created during his "absence." This became more and more difficult.

He knew that Kradeno had murdered Dottie. It was not Jason's intention to harm her, yet he now had no control over the evil that was gradually suffocating him. Wanting to change his life around, he began to think of Cimraknus, the good spirit that he knew inhabited him also.

The car started to swerve from side to side on the narrow road. He concentrated on the golden light he had seen as a boy. The car began to shudder, and Catherine woke up quickly. The control panel reflected the fear on Jason's face. Too afraid to say anything, she watched silently. A foul smell filled the car, and she could feel an evil force stirring.

Jason shouted, *"Cimraknus!"* and the car door was suddenly flung open.

Catherine felt a hand pushing her. She screamed, "Jason, please, what's happening?"

A horrible face suddenly filled the windshield. Jason managed to bring the car to a stop. Hideous laughter filled the car. Jason slumped over in the driver's seat, apparently unconscious. Catherine leaned over to see if he had been injured. Touching his hair, she froze in terror.

The car was flooded with an eerie green light and she could see the head of a serpent jerking out of Jason's forehead between his eyes. His head was suddenly full of white maggots crawling hungrily down his face. Then Catherine heard the voice of Kradeno:

"Woman, once more thou hast seen the sign."

She was petrified with horror and tried to draw away. As she did so, the head of the serpent jerked farther out of Jason's forehead. Its evil mouth yawned open and its sharp tongue darted out at her.

"Be still, Megan of Manningstile Henlock!" it hissed. "Through the ages, thou hast destroyed my seed with thy pious ways."

The limp body of Jason convulsed with tormented laughter. Catherine felt the centuries swiftly envelop her body until she was back in the cellar, totally immobilized by the head of the serpent. She thought she heard Jason's voice calling from eternity, "*Rhaydhonasie*," and then she knew no more....

"Wake up, Catherine, we're nearly there."
Shaking with terror, she opened her eyes, the dream still vivid in her mind. The car was slowing down as Jason turned off the road. "Are you all right?" he asked.
Unable to speak, she nodded her head. Fumbling for her purse and parcel, she scrambled out of the car as quickly as possible. She ran toward the warm lights of the inn, then through the hallway and up to her room. Taking off her shoes, she collapsed on the bed, murmuring over and over again, "Rhaydhonasie, thank you...Rhaydhonasie, thank you...."
Jason parked the car, got out and lit a cigarette, breathing deeply of the cold night air. He felt good. The moon was full. he wanted to collect his thoughts before he saw anyone. It was obvious that Catherine was distressed. As long as she thought she had had a dream, all would be well. He knew in his heart that Kradeno was now uncontrollable. But Rhaydhonasie had kept his promise, the promise he had made to Jason as a boy. Reliving those minutes of horror in the car made the hair on the back of his neck bristle. He remembered Kradeno's stench. Somehow he had stopped the car in the fog and saved both their lives. He knew that Catherine had seen Kradeno. Regaining consciousness and seeing the terror on Catherine's face had prompted him to put his arms around her. He realized that she had mistaken his embrace for an attack and had fainted.
Cimraknus had been released by Rhaydhonasie after Jason had appealed for help. Cimraknus had told Jason that he had much to accomplish, but that his earthly time was limited. Somehow, Jason did not fear the short life now left to him. Then, Kradeno's threat had scorched his eardrums:
"Never shalt thou call upon the Higher One! His protection may be thine, but I shall destroy thee if thou shouldst consider changing thine evil ways."
Jason now understood that Cimraknus was with him, but that the curse of Kradeno would be carried out and end the misery of generations. But first Jason had to correct many things. He prayed that he would be given the time.

Alan and Jonathan took a walk over the moors. Alan felt disturbed and angry that he hadn't stopped Catherine from going with his brother. He told Jonathan how worried he was. Jonathan tried to calm Alan, telling him that Catherine was undergoing a transition of consciousness and although it was traumatic, she would be all right.

Alan felt his anger rise again. "If Jason harms her, I'll kill him."

"Jason is also undergoing a transition from darkness to light. Then his soul will find peace."

"What about Catherine? For God's sake, if what I understand about Jason is true, he's practically insane," said Alan, desperate to know Catherine's whereabouts.

"Soon your consciousness will regain its normal level and you will see with clarity all that has taken place."

Catherine had been sleeping for three hours. When Nickie discovered that she had gone off with Jason, she began to feel tense and nervous. She spent the afternoon with George, and they took the time to talk and find out more about each other. Nickie was convinced that she belonged at the Rose & Crown. George had been somewhat of a mystery until she found out that his parents had suffered and died in World War II at the hands of the Nazis. His uncle and aunt had brought him up; he had been a brilliant student, gaining his Ph.D. in psychology.

Their togetherness was like coming home for both of them. Nickie and George warmed to each other, learning that they were much alike in many ways, although their personalities were totally different. They discussed his work with hypnosis, which she found quite fascinating. She admired his nonchalant attitude, especially in regard to his whitened hair.

Nickie wanted to take a tray up to Catherine, but Alan suggested that she let her sleep.

"Maybe I'll just go and cover her up then," she said to Alan, who agreed and offered to walk upstairs with her. "Do you think she'll be all right alone?"

Alan knew that Nickie would never sleep worrying about Catherine, so he said, "If you think it's best, why not spend the night with her? Call me if you need me."

"Why don't you sleep in my room next door?" said Nickie. "I'd feel much better if you did."

They said goodnight and Nickie closed the door quietly.

Catherine was awake first.

"Oh no, it's you again," she said, amused to see Nickie curled up in her bed.

"Oh, hi, Catherine, feeling OK, honey?"

"Never felt better, and I'm as hungry as a horse."

There was a knock on the door. It was Jenny. "There's a call f'yer, Miss Catherine."

"I'll be right down," said Catherine, putting on her robe.

"Hello. Oh, hello, Frances! Yes, everything's fine. What can I do for you? Oh, you are? That's great! Sure will. Got it. Bye now!"

Running back to her room, Catherine told Nickie that Frances and Tom wanted to be married this weekend because of certain arrangements with the Blue Feathers and they wanted everyone there.

"Whooppee!" said Nickie, kicking her legs up in the air. "I just adore weddings, don't you?"

Alan immediately began making plans for them to leave the Rose & Crown and travel to Wales. The wedding announcement cheered everyone, and the girls busily discussed what they would wear, letting the men get on with other details.

Chapter Twenty-four

Jason wanted to travel alone. It was a long journey to South Wales and he needed time to be with himself. His behavior was normal around Catherine because he thought that everything had been obliterated from her mind. He said his good-byes and told them he would see them at the wedding. "I'll be at Cardiff House, Alan," he told his brother.

It was good to be free and away from everyone. He opened the car window wide to let the fresh air blow free in his hair. Last night's terror lay heavily on his mind. He knew now who he was and what was ahead for him. Now that he had called upon Rhaydhonasie and received the protection of Cimraknus, he was doomed to experience the full wrath of Kradeno. It was important that he reach Cardiff House as quickly as possible. There was much to do before the wedding, before the others arrived.

After several hours of driving, Jason gained more insight into his past lives. As he searched with his conscious mind, he felt an increasing anxiety. Having come to terms with himself, he wanted to do all he could to end the torment that had followed the life paths of those he had loved and hurt down through the centuries. Aware that he was now spiritually vulnerable, he knew that through his past misdeeds Kradeno could and would soon take total possession of his thoughts and actions. In the time left, not only would he have to reveal his past sins, but also obtain compassion and forgiveness from those he had placed on the road to hell.

Focusing now on his plans and feeling a deep-down satisfaction, he asked aloud for Rhaydhonasie's help during his last days. First, he would attend to all his business interests and the distribution of

investments and monies, then he would prepare to face the past
karma of all those who had been affected. Just about an hour's
drive and he would be home. Resolving to erase all that Jason was
and had been, he glanced at the clock, eager to get home and see his
mother before she retired.

Trying to understand the law of cause and effect, Jason became
aware of a familiar vibration. He knew that Kradeno was close.
Cold fear made every nerve in his body tense. Weakly, he called on
his higher Master. A hideous laugh deafened his ears as, with every
atom of strength he could muster, he held the golden light in his
mind's eye. A voice clear and commanding cut through the
maniacal laughter and told Jason to stop driving. Immediately, he
felt an unearthly pressure surround his body. He managed to bring
the car to a stop. In the passenger seat, Tobias was grinning at him.

Cimraknus spoke to Jason. "This pathetic creature once encased
thy soul. His demented spirit was a result of Kradeno's work
through many lifetimes."

At the mention of Kradeno's name, a revolting gurgling sound
came from the back seat. Afraid to turn, Jason watched as Tobias
licked his thick lips. As mucus from his nose settled on his
protruding tongue, he repeated Megan's name and the gurgling in
the back seat grew louder.

Cimraknus told Jason to release his voice and cry for
Rhaydhonasie's help. "Do not be afraid. Reach out."

Jason struggled. He could feel the words deep in his heart. His
breath was becoming shorter as he made an intense physical effort
to speak. Kradeno's evil force thrust him painfully back in his seat.
He felt his eyeballs burn as Emmanuel suddenly towered above
him, laughing wildly.

"Imbecile, thou art *this*!" screamed Kradeno.   "There is no
hope in heaven or hell for thee against my revenge. I promise thee
everlasting hellfire!"

Jason was beyond wishing for death; his agony gave him the
strength at last to call out, "Dear God, help me, please! *God, help
me!*"

Total peace filled his heart and soul. The demon Kradeno was
suddenly no longer there. Tobias and Emmanuel disintegrated, and
Jason knew that although he had lost his earthly rights, somewhere
he would earn peace after he had walked through hell. What he had
experienced was only a glimpse of things to come, but his heart was
filled with hope, for he knew that after his penance, Rhaydhonasie
would not forsake him.

Lady Margaret immediately saw a change in Jason when she
opened the door. As he bent down to kiss her on the cheek, she
could feel a difference and she reached out a hand to caress him.
Normally he would have pulled away, but now he smiled. He felt

very tired and asked his mother to excuse him.

Unfastening his shirt, he glanced in the mirror and looked at his reflection. HIs face was somehow different, but he couldn't decide what the change was. Thinking now of Cimraknus, he ignored the negative energies building in his room. Too tired to acknowledge the evil that attempted to surround him, he prepared for bed and slept deeply through the night.

Sitting close to George in the back seat, Nickie listened carefully to Alan and Catherine discussing the Rose & Crown and all they had experienced.

"Why doesn't someone ask about Tobias?" asked Nickie. "Or Emmanuel, for that matter?"

No one answered, for they had all been avoiding this question.

"And what I'd really like to know is," everyone spoke together, "Who is Gareth of Abergavennie?" This added a lighter tone to the conversation and everyone laughed.

"How do you fit in, Alan?" asked Nickie.

Alan thought for a moment. "I know this may sound strange, but I'm not quite sure."

"As far as I can see," said Catherine, "you and Jason must fit in, but there must be a reason for us not knowing where at this time."

George was enjoying Nickie's closeness. "How about dropping this discussion. Let's look forward to the wedding. I'm sure all of us will have to come to terms with this karmic drama eventually."

"I agree," said Catherine. "So what shall we talk about?" Not hearing any response, she turned to look at Nickie, but she and George were rediscovering their past love. Almost envious, she reached out and touched Alan's hand. He responded and held it tightly. To hell with it, thought Catherine. Thinking of Frances as a bride, she fell asleep.

Excited that she had guests, Lady Margaret was in the garden early, picking flowers for the breakfast table. It wasn't until 10:15 that the first sleepy guest came down for breakfast.

"Good morning, George, dear. How are you?"

George liked Lady Margaret and spent some time talking to her about the Rose & Crown and the karmic experiences. She listened with interest, wishing it was all over and done with. Alan and Catherine made a lovely pair; she wished it was their marriage on Saturday instead of that of Frances and Tom. Then, reprimanding herself for such thoughts, she poured George another cup of coffee and gave him the morning paper to read. Jason had risen early and was already up and about. Soon her son Alan would be down with his pretty Megan. She was really looking forward to seeing everyone again and waited patiently as the clock chimed 10:30.

The phone rang and Lady Margaret answered it. "Good morning, Cardiff House."

It was Hilary. Sounding excited and happy, she asked if everyone was back. Lady Margaret chatted with her and invited her up to the house.

"Wonderful idea. Thank you, Lady Margaret. Mike and I will be there in a short while."

They said good-bye and Lady Margaret went back to the dining room, hoping to tell someone about Hilary's arrival.

Alan saw his mother and embraced her, telling her how wonderful she looked. Catherine greeted her warmly and Nickie gave her a hug.

"It's good to have you all back," Lady Margaret said graciously. "I do so enjoy having you all here at Cardiff House."

"I wonder how Martha is," said Nickie.

Smiling, Lady Margaret told them that she and Martha had become good friends.

"That's marvelous, Mother," said Alan.   "Yes, I think so too. Martha is going to move into Cardiff House very soon."

"She is?" said Alan, pleasantly surprised. "I like that idea."

Feeling quite pleased with herself, Lady Margaret knew that Alan worried about her being alone and would spend more time in his cottage if she had a companion.

"But what about her cute little house?" asked Nickie.

"Martha and I have decided to use it as a village museum. Both of us have collected quite a few interesting old things like documents, photographs and parochial records. We think it would be a nice attraction and we could convert the parlor into a tea shop."

"You have been busy, Mother. I think your project will be great. By the way, where's Jason?"

"Goodness knows. He was up and about early. I believe he left."

Sitting at the window, Catherine saw a small European car come up the winding driveway. She watched as Lord Alan's two dogs ran yelping toward the car.

"Hilary and Mike are here!" Waving through the window, she caught Hilary's eye, and she waved back enthusiastically.

"We brought Martha along," said Hilary. "Frances and Tom said you were coming to the Blue Feathers, so they're waiting there."

It was a warm and friendly reunion; they were all happy to see each other again. The room filled with friendly conversation and laughter; they decided to go to the Blue Feathers that afternoon. Alan took Catherine to one side and told her that he wanted to go to his cottage for a while.

"Can I come?"

Kissing her gently, he whispered. "I would love to be alone with you, but I'm afraid I have some work to do. I'll meet you at the Blue Feathers."

"What kind of work?"

"Oh, boring little details. Go and enjoy yourself, and I'll see you later."

Jonathan was waiting by his car when Alan finally got away. "May I go with you to the cottage?" he asked soberly. "Your higher consciousness will be restored very soon now. This is why you feel the need to be alone, but I've been sent to be with you at this time."

Appreciating this information and happy to have Jonathan around, Alan readily agreed. "The cottage is small, but I have two bedrooms. What about the others?"

"I've already told your mother that I have important work to do and that I'll be there for the wedding."

"Fine," said Alan. "Shall we go?"

Catherine felt uneasy without Alan, but nevertheless she tried to get into the mood and enjoy meeting everyone again.

Hilary offered her a Sobranie cigarette and they sat in the window seat together. "I really missed you all," said Hilary. "And it's so good to see you."

"Thank you. We missed you and Mike. I'm glad we're all together again."

Hilary was anxious to find out what had happened since she last saw them. With Nickie's help, Hilary was brought up to date. The only thing Catherine didn't mention was her experience with Jason in the car coming back from Bolton.

Mike and George were talking to Lady Margaret. Mike was explaining the tough work of journalism and how he preferred the small-town newspaper.

"I was born in Liverpool and life was hard for my parents. Only my mother is living now. She worked long hours during my school years, giving me the encouragement to overcome my poor background and strong Liverpudlian dialect."

"What happened to your father?" asked Lady Margaret.

"He was killed in World War II. To cut a long story short, I feel that I would like to fulfill my mother's dream as she helped me fulfill mine."

"What was her dream?" asked George.

"To have a little cottage in the country, plant geraniums and sit on the village green, you know what I mean?"

"It's a lovely dream, Mike," said Lady Margaret kindly. "But why would you want to give up your kind of work to work on a small-town newspaper?"

"Oh, my job was marvelous before I got married. But I'm always away from home and hardly ever see Hilary, or my mother, for that matter. And there's another reason. I like the idea of getting close to people. Living in a small community gives one the chance to really belong. It can get very lonely in the large cities."

"I know what you mean," said George. "I've always fancied myself as a farmer."

Lady Margaret was intrigued by the conversation. "You are a schoolteacher by profession?"

Sighing, George nodded.

"It's strange, isn't it, how we can be one thing and have a deep desire to be something else? Maybe you were a farmer in another life?"

"Maybe so," laughed George.

Hilary and Catherine finished their talk and came over to join the group. Looking at her watch, Hilary suggested that they had better be going, as Frances and Tom would be waiting.

"Why don't you come with us, Lady Margaret?" asked Catherine.

Never having visited the Blue Feathers, Lady Margaret thought it would be a good idea.

"So that makes six of us," said Mike. Two cars should do it."

"I'll give Frances a call and see if it's OK for us to go over now," said Nickie.

Tom answered the phone and was happy to hear Nickie's voice. "Don't forget to tell the menfolk that my stag party is tonight."

When they arrived at the inn, Catherine was impressed with Frances. She looked beautiful. "Love is good for you."

Frances agreed. "I can hardly believe I'll be Mrs. Thomas Thornleigh tomorrow. I know I'm not going to sleep tonight. I haven't seen Alan yet. Where is he?"

Catherine told her that he had gone to his cottage and would be down later. Frances had prepared sausage rolls, finger sandwiches and homemade apple pie. The reunion was a happy one.

"If the boys are having a stag party, how about us girls getting together?" asked Nickie.

"Sounds good to me," said Catherine. "How about you, Frances?"

"I'd love to."

When Jason had left earlier, he had been careful not to wake his mother, who was an exceptionally light sleeper. The dew and the morning mist gave the lawn and flowers an ethereal look. As the first morning bird greeted him, tears came into his eyes. Soon all this would be no more; it didn't seem possible that evil could lurk within such beauty. He had left a note for Alan and taken the cottage key. He needed to be alone to think things out. As he drove away, he thought of poor Catherine and the terror of the ride back from Bolton. Thinking about that experience, he felt the car begin to sway from side to side, as though a strong wind were trying to push it over.

"Cimraknus, help me see this through," he asked.

Instantly, he heard low, horrific laughter. Then his neck was jerked back sharply.

"*Rhaydhonasie!*" he shouted. He was trying to steer the car, his head still pulled back by the evil force of Kradeno. He could feel the car going out of control.

"*Rhaydhonasie, pleeeease . . . .*"

A golden light fell upon his head and face and he felt his neck muscles ease as he gradually brought his head forward again. Concentrating on his inner eye, now flooded with light, he put his foot on the accelerator. Speeding down the country lane, he felt the evil energy strengthening again. Twice he heard the terrible gurgling in the back seat. As he drew into the cottage driveway, he relaxed for a moment. Putting his hands to his head, he began to sob.

The cottage had a damp feeling. He turned on the gas fire and put the kettle on the stove. Finding a sweater of Alan's, he then made a pot of tea. There was something very special about this cottage. He felt safe and secure there. He got out his pen and began to write down a list of important things he had to do.

Alan had seen Jason's note and decided not to tell his mother. Talking to Jonathan in the car, he told him that Jason had left early in the morning with his key and to expect him there when they arrived.

The cottage door was slightly ajar. Alan looked in apprehensively. Jason was asleep in the chair and the room was damp and very cold.

Jonathan grabbed Alan by the arm. "Wait a minute." He walked in, holding his head as though listening for something. "Wait there," he called back to Alan at the door.

Going over to Jason, Jonathan stretched out his arms before him, then brought one hand quickly back to his mouth and licked his fingertips as though he were burned. Alan watched in amazement. Jonathan said something in a low voice, and Alan felt the cold air return to normal.

"You can come in now," said Jonathan.

"What the hell is going on?"

"This room was a psychic booby trap. And the energies were coming from Jason's subconscious."

"You mean Jason meant to harm me?"

"No, but Kradeno did."

At the mention of his name, Kradeno's evil laughter burst out of Jason. His body shook hideously. Alan stepped forward to help his brother, but Jonathan held him back and passed through the negative barrier surrounding Jason, saying some strange words.

"Everything will be fine now," said Jonathan. "Please don't ask me any more questions. Let's get on with bringing back your higher sensitivity; then you can help me to help Jason."

Alan was appalled at seeing Jason this way, with his body limp and his jaw hanging loosely.

"Lie on the couch and relax," Jonathan directed.

Alan loosened his tie and took off his shoes. Jonathan brought over a chair and asked him to close his eyes and concentrate on his voice. Alan did as he was asked and waited to hear Jonathan speak. All he heard was a hushed chant; he felt himself slipping away, still waiting to hear Jonathan's voice. Instead, he heard many voices and each time they spoke, he could see changing colors. They were vibrant; he felt himself wrapped tightly in each piercing ray. He felt his mind shoot upwards and like a fast-traveling meteor, felt his whole being change into swiftly moving light.

He was no longer aware of his body. There was a huge tree before him, masses of vibrant colors swirling in small clusters on each branch. The urge to take one, then two, came over him. Each time he did this, he felt stronger. The pulsating colors were his to take and as he took them, he became aware of a greater strength building within him. He felt his mind expand into knowledge. A sensation of speed followed, and he was taken through a long tunnel. Everything he saw registered in his conscious mind. It was as though he were a magnet, picking up every scrap of wisdom in the universe. Now, feeling totally filled, he heard music such as he'd never heard before and began to feel a heavy sensation. He felt cold as he struggled back to re-enter his physical body. His thoughts were no longer limited; his spiritual vision was limitless. He heard Jonathan's voice: "Be still for a moment, and you will retain all the wisdom you have gathered."

When he opened his eyes, he knew that he was at last his true self. He wondered how he had possibly existed before within the vibratory limitations of his physical body.

"Welcome home," said Jonathan, smiling. "How are you, brother?"

"I know who I am, thanks to you, Jonathan. It's good to be back. Thank you for staying with me." All his questions were answered now, and he was even more amazed at how he had previously been content to accept his limitations. Smiling at Jonathan and with no immediate concern for Jason, he filled his pipe and savored again the unlimited powers he had voluntarily relinquished so that he could participate in the search for karmic release. His mind went over all that had taken place. He saw himself groping, trying to find answers. It all seemed so easy and natural now, and he knew that his love for Megan was rightfully Catherine's.

"So everyone thinks the same as I did?" said Alan.

"Exactly," was Jonathan's reply.

"Surely my mother must have some idea of what is happening to Jason."

"I think she must, for her own knowledge of previous lives is astounding. Believe me, the story of Rose Featherstone is full of intrigues that would amaze you."

Jason stirred. Alan poured him a scotch.

"Are you OK, old man?" he asked.

Jason felt cold and stiff; he took the drink from his brother. Alan turned up the gas fire, understanding Jason's torment. "It's all right, Jason. I know, I understand."

Breaking down, Jason cried like a child. "You couldn't possibly know, and I couldn't possibly explain...."

Speaking firmly, Jonathan told him, "We do know, Jason, and as long as you are willing to make amends, we can help. It's not going to be easy, but if you're sure you want to see this thing through, your brother and I will help."

"My choice is limited," said Jason bitterly. "If I choose the right way, my only promise is eternal damnation; if I choose to continue the way I have been going, I get the same result in the end."

"What is it you want to do, Jason?" asked Alan gently.

"God knows, I want to set everything as right as I possibly can. I've caused death, unhappiness and destruction in many lifetimes, and I know that if I don't deal with it in this life, I'll be doomed...or I should say, destined to hurt you all again."

Both men of the Higher Order knew that his intentions were honorable. Alan asked, "If I were to tell you that your soul can avoid total obliteration, would you submit yourself to the guidance of Rhaydhonasie?"

Jason swallowed hard and nodding his head slowly, agreed to undergo the trials ahead of him. In the bright morning the cottage was sunny. Beside him stood two men ready to give him strength, and in his heart he knew that Cimraknus would also protect and help him endure the unknown evil. A foul smell suddenly filled the sunny room, as once again Kradeno laughed at another promise....

Fear gripped Jason's heart; Jonathan and Alan raised their arms above his head, creating an arc. The evil influence tore out of the room, leaving the cottage door open and the fragrance of flowers filled his nostrils, dispersing the stench and his fears.

"There is much to do," said Jonathan. "After the wedding celebration we'll have the time to deal with it, so please be prepared to spend some time with Alan and me. This must be completed before we meet Blodwin on New Year's Eve."

Chapter Twenty-five

The three men made their way back to the Blue Feathers. Jason's mind was busy making his future plans and he decided he would start putting them into action as soon as possible.

Catherine was happy to see Alan. As she held his arm tightly, he could sense her concern. There was much handshaking and Tom and Frances were the perfect hosts.

"Did you know you're going to a stag party tonight?" asked Nickie.

"Is that so?" said Alan. "Sounds good to me."

Jason, feeling his normal self, thought it a wonderful idea and asked what the ladies would be doing.

"Don't worry about us," said Nickie. "I've got it all arranged. We gals are going to get together at Cardiff House."

Soon the welcome-home party began to break up. Tom was busy at the bar and Frances was already part of the working staff, controlling the books and front desk.

"How I managed without her, I'll never know," said Tom proudly. "Frances does a great job and everybody loves her." Then, looking round to see if Mildred was listening, her regular hobby, he whispered, "Even Mildred."

After the men left for the stag party, the women got together and relaxed. Catherine missed having Alan near her. They had been separated practically the whole day, and she had grown used to having him with her nearly all the time. He promised he would see her before he went to bed, and she was looking forward to this.

"You seem different somehow," said Nickie to Martha.

"I do?" she asked. "How?"

"I don't know really, but there's a happiness around you that I never saw before."

"I know what you mean," said Hilary. "I feel it, too."

Martha seemed more confident and not as eager to please. "I suppose it's because I'm living a dream. I've always wanted a good friend and now I have Margaret."

Lady Margaret smiled as Martha went on.

"My life is full of all the things I ever wanted to do, and living here with the companionship I now have is what I call a perfect situation."

Lady Margaret agreed. She felt the same way. Once this karma thing was out of the way, she could foresee happy times ahead.

Hilary waited for the right moment and when no one else was talking, said, "I have an announcement to make." Gaining everyone's attention, she continued. "I'm pregnant."

"*You are!*" screamed Nickie. "How absolutely *fantastic!* When can we plan a baby shower?"

"What's a baby shower?" asked Hilary.

"You mean to say you don't know what a *shower* is?" asked Nickie. Looking around, she could see that only Catherine and she knew what she was talking about. "In the States, when someone is expecting, all the friends and relatives get together before the baby arrives and have what they call a shower. Everyone brings presents for the new baby."

"That's lovely," said Lady Margaret. "I shall plan to have a shower for Hilary."

"When is the baby due?" asked Catherine.

"Next June, the doctor thinks."

"How do you feel?" asked Nickie.

"Oh, I get sick easily, but the doctor thinks it'll go away soon."

"I want lots of babies," said Nickie.

"Lots?" asked Catherine, raising her eyebrows.

"Well, at least three."

The conversation was warm and friendly, and Catherine thought of having children. In her imagination, she could picture Alan as the perfect daddy. She wished this whole karmic drama was over, so that she could start living a normal life. It was like waiting at the edge of a cliff, knowing that something was going to happen, but not knowing when or what.

Lady Margaret brought in the family album, starting first with her wedding pictures. There were pictures taken outside in the garden and the house looked exactly the same; only the young people from another generation looked different.

"Gee, I like the way they used to dress," said Nickie. "Here, look at this one." She showed a photograph of a young man to Catherine, who had to look twice, he was so much like Alan. A tender look came into Lady Margaret's eyes.

"That's my husband," she said with quiet pride.

"I remember that handsome man. He used to ride around in the village and charm all the girls," said Martha.

Turning the album page, they saw pictures of the honeymoon taken by the seaside. It was easy to see that Lady Margaret and her husband were well matched. As they continued to look, there was a sudden change in hairstyle.

"What a contrast," said Hilary, turning back to see the previous pictures, in which Lady Margaret's hair was long and taken up in the back.

"Oh yes, I had my hair 'bobbed.'" Going through the photographs brought warm memories back to Lady Margaret.

"Gee, Lady Margaret, is this you?" asked Nickie, pointing to a very pregnant lady.

"Yes, I was huge, as you can see." Pointing to a small boy, she said, "This is Alan. He was a lovely little chap."

"I can't get over how big you were," said Nickie. "Just imagine, Hilary."

Hilary asked if Jason was a big baby.

"Not particularly," said Lady Margaret. "When I was pregnant with Alan, I hardly experienced any problems, but with Jason, I had a terrible time. I lost a lot of weight." Pointing to the picture, "See my face and arms? But my stomach was tremendous. In fact, when I was about six and a half months, I used a wheelchair part of the time, it was so difficult to walk."

Catherine was fascinated with the photographs of Alan growing up. He hadn't changed much; she wished she could have shared some of those childhood years with him.

Frances had brought her final list of things to do and asked Nickie if she could think of anything else to put on it. Earlier that afternoon, Lady Margaret had invited her to stay. She had brought her things and was hoping the party would break up soon so that she could check everything.

"Where are you going for your honeymoon?" asked Hilary.

"Tom and I thought we would love to go to the Lake District."

"Oh, you'll love it," said Hilary. "I think it's the most beautiful place. I just feel so peaceful there."

Lady Margaret, being an excellent hostess, could tell that Frances was ready to leave, so she asked kindly, "Would you like to go up to your room now, dear?"

"Thank you, I would, Lady Margaret," answered Frances. "Will you all excuse me?"

"I think I'm ready, too," said Catherine, and the others agreed. The three girls went up to bed, and Lady Margaret and Martha spent another half-hour chatting and drinking cocoa.

The following morning, Nickie was up bright and early. Knocking on Frances' door, she said good-humoredly, "It's a lovely day for a wedding."

"Thank you," called Frances. "Be down soon." Stretching lazily, she glanced at her watch. In three hours exactly, she would be Mrs. Thomas Thornleigh. Wriggling her toes, she propped herself up on the pillows. Looking at her legs, she saw a remarkable change. One leg had always been considerably thinner than the other, but now it seemed quite normal.

There was a tap on the door. It was Lady Margaret with the maid. They brought in a breakfast tray complete with a pink rose.

"This is lovely. Thank you so much."

Placing the tray on Frances' lap, Lady Margaret told her that she had plenty of time to get ready and to call whenever she needed help.

"Catherine promised to help with my hair," said Frances. "And I'm sure the others will be here as soon as they have eaten."

Kissing her lightly on the cheek, Lady Margaret left Frances, who was already digging into her cereal. The phone rang. It was Tom.

"Hello, sweetheart. How are you this morning? Remember, we have a date."

"I feel so happy, Tom. So wonderfully happy. How did your stag party go?"

"It was a beauty," said Tom. "I bet there's some thick heads this morning."

Frances laughed and told him how pleasant her evening had been and how she missed him. "Got to go now, dear."

"Must you?"   "I'm afraid so, darling. I have so much to do."

Giving an exaggerated sigh, he said, "All right, if that's what you want." And then, softening his voice, he said, "I'll see you in church, love. Bye-bye."

Frances had never felt happier in her life. It was just too perfect. Something had to go wrong, she thought. She caught a glimpse of herself in the mirror and decide that something had! As soon as she got out of the bath, Nickie, Hilary and Catherine were there, all of them offering help. It was like a room full of schoolgirls, giggling and all talking at once.

"Well, come and take a look at this," said Nickie, looking out the window. Alan was getting out of the car, and Catherine's heart missed a beat as she saw how handsome he looked. "What is he doing here?" she asked.

Frances was now finishing her final grooming, nervously twitching at her gloves. She said to Catherine, "Oh didn't I tell you? He's giving me away."

Catherine wasn't quite ready yet. She had been busy helping the bride. She didn't want Alan to see her till she was dressed, so she told Nickie, who was already on her way down, to tell Alan she would see him at the church.

The wedding ceremony was simple and the bride looked happy and radiant. George was the best man and Jason was a splendid usher. Lady Margaret added that touch of elegance to the proceedings. The entire village seemed to be packed into the tiny church.

Afterward, as confetti was thrown, Tom called out, "Everyone's invited. See you at the Blue Feathers."

"Throw your bouquet," shouted Martha to Frances.

Frances gave it a kiss and tossed it into the happy crowd. Two hands caught it; one was Catherine's, the other Nickie's. As their eyes met over the yellow tea roses, they both felt love in their hearts for each other. Nickie, who was an expert at relieving tense situations, said, "Does this mean we're going to marry the same man?"

After the newlyweds left for their honeymoon, everyone relaxed and made their way back to Cardiff House.

"I need to talk to you, Alan," said Catherine. Pulling her back onto the couch, he put his arms around her and asked what she wanted.

"I've been thinking. I should go back to the States and see to everything."

"Are you coming back for good?"

"If you want me to, I will."

His answer was clear as he held her close and kissed her.

"Can you come, darling?"

"Not really, Catherine." Seeing that his answer disturbed her somewhat, he added, "Before New Year's Eve there's a lot to do. It's far more serious than anyone knows. Jonathan and I are going to need all the time we can get."

Holding his hand, she told him that she realized something serious had to be settled. "And after that—then what?"

"You and I will be married."

"But—"

He interrupted her. "No buts, young lady. You can rest assured I'll be waiting and counting every minute till you come back. Now let's get serious, shall we?"

She nodded, enjoying his being in command.

"You'll have to decide what to do with your apartment and property in San Francisco. Have you given it any thought?"

"I don't have very much furniture, but what I do have I can give to Vera and I can also let her have Bartholomew. I don't know what to do with the house in San Francisco. I love to visit, but I could never imagine me settling there."

"You mean *us*. It's presently rented out, isn't it?"

"That's what Jonathan said."

"Well, why don't you leave it as it is and ask him about selling it or something?"

"I like that idea. So when I come back...then where will I live?" she said with a twinkle in her eye.

"Right here in Cardiff House. And after we're married, we'll live in the cottage. How about that?"

"I just wish I didn't have to leave you...."

They talked for a while, sipping wine and watching the fire.

Nickie and George came into the room. Catherine thought that this would be a good time to find out how she felt about going home. Nickie listened to Catherine and Alan as they talked about their plans, and when Catherine asked, "Are you coming back?" Nickie answered with a smile.

"Have you forgotten? I happen to own a nice piece of property now and I'd like to spend some time there."

George felt panic. He had never thought of Nickie leaving. He could hear Alan telling them that he and Catherine intended to get married at the beginning of January.

Listening to Alan talk this way, full of confidence, made Catherine feel excited; she began wondering what she would wear and where they would go for their honeymoon.

"I'll find a job in Bolton somewhere," she heard Nickie say.

Catherine sensed a touch of loneliness in Nickie's voice and felt sad. She asked Nickie, "Are you sure you want to come back right away and live here? Wouldn't you rather just come for vacations?"

Nickie hadn't really given it a lot of thought. If Catherine was married, she would be entirely alone. But putting on a brave face, she told them, "I guess I'll just think things out and then make my decision." Tears were pricking her eyes. She asked Alan if a girl could get a drink around this place.

George felt as though he had both feet in his mouth. Realizing the depth of Nickie's feelings, he knew he had not made any commitments. Taking a deep breath, George asked, "Are you really intent on becoming an old maid in Rose Cottage?"

Nickie wasn't prepared for that kind of question. She was immediately on the defensive. "What do you mean?"

"Well, now that I have a couple of witnesses here, I'd like to ask you if you'll marry me."

It was the first time Catherine had ever seen Nickie completely dumbfounded. Nickie's lip began to quiver, and George took hold of her. She put her head on his shoulder and crying, said, "I never expected such a romantic proposal...In fact, I didn't expect a proposal at all."

George kissed her as Alan went to pour drinks for everyone.

"Here's a toast to Nickie and George," he said.

Raising his glass, George smiled. "And here's another toast to Catherine and Alan."

It was a sad good-bye for the girls. They were the last to leave

Cardiff House after Hilary and Mike had left for home. Lady Margaret was crying and Martha kept dabbing at her eyes with a handkerchief. Alan and George took the girls to the airport and as the plane climbed into the sky, Alan whispered in his heart, "Soon my love, very soon...."

"It doesn't seem possible, Catherine, does it?" said Nickie, gazing out of the plane window.

Pulling out her cigarettes, Catherine asked, "What doesn't seem possible?"

"All that has happened. We've only been in the air an hour and already Cardiff House seems centuries away."

Inhaling deeply, Catherine agreed. "We've both found love, Nickie, and come hell or high water, I intend to be back as soon as possible."

"Me, too. You won't catch me letting Geroge get away."

The stewardess offered them drinks. Opening her packet of nuts, Nickie asked Catherine why she thought New Year's Eve was so important.

"I don't really know, Nickie. But Alan said it's very important."

Offering Catherine a nut, Nickie said, "Do you really think Blodwin will come back?"

"I guess so," said Catherine, feeling nervous at the idea of going through again what they had experienced before. "Let's not talk about it. What's the movie?"

Nickie looked through her program. "It's a thriller, *Twins of Evil*, with Peter Cushing. An English movie made in 1971."

"That's all I need," said Catherine, laughing. "Will you hold my hand?"

Back at the airport, Alan and George were feeling lost without Catherine and Nickie. They had a drink in the airport bar, then, shaking hands, exchanged phone numbers. Promising to keep in touch, they parted.

George felt empty. Nickie had filled his life with love and laughter. The only thing that made the whole affair bearable was the fact that she had accepted his proposal and that he could look forward to living the rest of his life with her.

Chapter Twenty-six

Alan focused his mind on Jason as he drove back from the airport. It began to rain. He felt a deep, compelling need to return as soon as possible. At the traffic light in Manningstile Henlock, he saw a lonely figure walking out toward the main highway. It was now raining heavily, but the walk was familiar.

Stopping the car, he called, "*Jason!*" The man kept on walking. Now he was sure it was his brother. "*Jason!*" he called again.

Jason turned as Alan got out of the car. He was grinning and laughing. The rain was running down his face. When he saw Alan, a voice spoke, but it wasn't Jason's voice.

"Be damned and away with thee!"

Alan reached out to touch this creature. As he did so, the man he knew as Jason started to run away, dragging one leg behind him.

Running after him, Alan shouted, "Kradeno, it's not your time! Get out and leave my brother alone!"

The evil soul reached out as if to attack Alan, but he instantly directed higher energies toward this pathetic creature. Immediately, the body of his brother dropped to the ground. Alan picked him up and carried him back to the car. Laying him down gently on the back seat, he drove to his cottage without looking back.

Wondering where Jonathan might be, Alan arrived, at the cottage. He saw the light was on, and then Jonathan came out with a raincoat over his head.

"Help me get him out," Alan said. He and Jonathan carried Jason into the warm living room. Taking off Jason's wet clothes and covering him with a blanket, they sat down and began to plan their next move against Kradeno.

After the wedding, when everyone went back to Cardiff House,

Jason had gone to Alan's cottage. Locking himself in, he had sat down at the desk and begun to sort out his papers. He felt an urgent need to get everything in order. Having redirected his properties, money and business interests, he had put everything into his brief-case, ready to take to his attorney on Monday. Then he had decided to walk into the village and pick up a newspaper. He had sensed the negative energies gathering around him shortly after leaving the newsstand. Hurrying back, he had pulled up his collar as it began to rain. His body felt painful; he could actually feel his flesh being torn and the warmth of his blood on his shirt. He was about to call on Cimraknus, but it was too late. He could feel the evil of Kradeno possessing him....

Jason opened his eyes and was relieved to see Alan and Jonathan with him.

"Where am I?" he asked faintly.

"You're all right, Jason. You're back at the cottage. Can you tell us what happened?" asked Alan.

Jason related the incident and started to shiver. Jonathan gave him a hot drink and reassured him that neither he nor Alan would leave him. Alan telephoned his mother; he knew that she wouldn't be as curious and ask too many questions, now that she had Martha with her.

"Yes, this is Alan. Just wanted you to know that Jason is with me at the cottage. We plan to spend a few days here together with Jonathan."

"How nice," she answered. "Keep in touch. Martha and I are busy getting ready to open our village museum."

Alan said good-bye, then sat beside Jason on the couch. "Want some clothes, old man?"

"I think so," said Jason, smiling. "It is a bit restricting lying here naked." Pulling the blanket around him, he followed Alan into the bedroom and got dressed. The three men then sat and talked about Jason's future.

Arriving home in North Hollywood, both girls were quiet. Everything seemed so huge. The roads were wide, the automobiles were large and there were so many people. As the cab weaved its way through the traffic, the driver's American accent sounded strange to them after spending so much time away. Nickie was the first to try and get things back to normal.

"Who's going to be the next president?" she asked the driver.

Half smoking and half chewing his cigar, he told her he didn't know and wasn't very interested.

"This is home," she said to Catherine. "Democracy and all that. He doesn't give a damn."

"Nickie...I'm missing Alan already."

Trying to cheer her up, Nickie said, "Look, Catherine. Soon you'll be seeing Bartholomew and his—I mean her—family, so you'd better cheer up, right?"

Appreciating Nickie's efforts, Catherine decided to try and enjoy her homecoming. Unlocking her apartment door, Catherine could see how well Vera had looked after things. There was Bartholomew surrounded by four darling kittens. Vera had heard the girls arrive, and they ran to greet each other warmly.

"You're not going to believe what I have to say," said Nickie.

"I'll believe anything," said Vera, laughing. "What is it?"

"You are now looking at a nearly married woman, and the lucky man is an Englishman, no less."

Screaming with delight, Vera yelled, "I *don't* believe it! You've got to be kidding me!"

"No, honest. And Catherine is going to marry a Welsh lord!"

"Eh, you guys, you're having me on."

"No, it's gospel, I swear," said Nickie.

"When is all this going to happen?" asked Vera, fixing the rollers in her hair.

"January," replied Catherine. "For both of us."

"Let me fix you some coffee," said Vera. "And then I want you to tell me everything, and I mean *everything*!" Vera went into the kitchen and started to make the coffee.

Catherine whispered to Nickie, "For God's sake, don't mention reincarnation or anything like that, will you?"

"Of course not. You think I'm crazy?"

"We have two days before the full moon," said Jonathan. "I have to leave tomorrow, but I'll be back in time."

Jason looked concerned.

"Don't worry," said Alan. "I'll be with you. Nothing can possibly happen till the right date."

Jonathan put his overnight bag on the table and shook hands with both brothers. "If you should need me, call this number." Handing Alan a piece of paper, he said good-bye and left.

"Go back to sleep, Jason. You need the rest."

"I think I'd prefer to get into bed," said Jason.

"Good. Why don't you turn in now, old boy?"

After Jason was settled, Alan brought out the book. Lighting his pipe, he turned to where the page was missing. Uttering a spell in ancient Celtic, Alan put a protection around himself and the cottage. Calling now upon the wise souls who had initiated his forefather, William of Garth, Alan left his earthly body, rising to the higher levels of consciousness. Freeing himself from earthly thoughts, he sought the wisdom of the Masters. Jonathan was already there; his aura enlarged to embrace Alan's spirit.

Cimraknus spoke: "The missing page of thy book was removed

by thy brother under the influence of Kradeno. It told of Gareth, and this knowledge would have revealed the path of evil intent. The higher powers will be made available unto thee to ward off Kradeno's evil. At the full moon, the one known as Jason will be exposed and his past presented with such reality that he may choose to retain his evil ways and lose his soul, or to attempt to withstand the temptation. This choice will require our strength in aid of him, for it means the loss of all he hath ever known."

The radiance of Cimraknus gradually faded and his energies joined the mystic circle of the Masters. Pulsating among them now was a light whose brilliance was beyond human comprehension. As the violet glow extended itself into infinity, the voice of Rhaydhonasie revealed its wisdom:

"He, known as Alan, with the help of him we calleth Jonathan, will be assisted by Cimraknus, and to this trinity of esoteric energies I will direct power which may be used as they will to save the soul of Jason. But only with his full consent may the higher powers influence and counteract the evil of Kradeno. Prepare thyselves, ye three, for the full moon, for it is then that Kradeno will feel the surge of negative energies and make ready to take the sacrifice of this wretched soul. Terrible sights and sounds will be manifested by him. Only when Kradeno hath fulfilled his promise of everlasting hellfire, can the soul of Jason be saved. The oil of mercy will be poured generously on his scathed soul if he withstandeth his karmic fate."

Rhaydhonasie's pure light began to subside, and the Masters, blessed with eternal truth, merged back into their chosen paths on earth.

As Alan opened his eyes, Jason was sitting in the opposite chair. His legs were crossed and his eyes had a distant glaze. Before Alan could question him, Kradeno roared with laughter. The room shook with evil vibrations.

"So, thou art returned, high master?" he said scornfully. "In what direction dost thou intend to place thy puny opposition?"

Now in full possession of his original powers, Alan could see the discarded entity that was his brother Jason, hovering weakly beside the physical body like a dim candle glow. Kradeno's strength grew with Jason's fear, but Alan's aura rejected the evil emanating from Kradeno.

Trying to eliminate the shield of protection around Alan, Kradeno manipulated Jason's body as though it were a puppet, first moving his arms and legs in a grotesque manner, then causing horrible gurgling sounds to come from his lips. Finally, Jason's body was lifted high in the air, then dropped back down into the chair with terrific force.

During this terrible scene, Alan did not move. Calling on Cimraknus, he felt peace envelop him. As a spectator, he watched without fear the macabre efforts of the evil one. Calling inwardly to Jonathan, he felt the contact, then a sudden impact of energy. He knew that Jonathan was aware of his need. As the now silent Kradeno waited, Alan felt a trinity of energies building in the room. They were like steel, and it was obvious that Kradeno did not have the power to move. The furious Kradeno growled, "What is it thou wishest to know?"

"Why do you seek the soul of my brother? Why can't you leave him in peace?"

"He belongeth to the demons. He shall yet serve me again."

The body of Jason, like a rag doll, was again lifted up in the air and allowed to drop suddenly.

Alan got up to help. In that second of lost concentration, Kradeno roared free of the mystic triangle and was gone. Alan carried his brother back to bed and bathed his bruised body. Fortunately, Jason did not regain consciousness, and Alan slept in his room all night, praying that Jonathan would return soon to help him watch over his brother.

The following morning, Jason was still weak and sore, but his spirits were bright. He asked to be alone. He did some writing and made several phone calls.

Alan knew that tonight would begin the fight for Jason's soul. He wanted to talk to him, yet he was afraid to create any fears of what might come. Sitting in his chair, he prayed for Jason, asking that he might choose the right path when the time came. His thoughts then drifted to Catherine, his precious Catherine. Fondly, he thought of her love for him and her reluctance to leave. Reaching for the phone, he asked for the overseas operator.

"Hello, darling," he said as soon as he heard her voice.

"Oh, Alan, it's you. I'm so happy you called. What are you doing?"

Smiling, he told her that he was calling her. Both were laughing and trying to speak at the same time. Catherine finally spoke first.

"I love you, Alan, and I can't wait till I come back."

"When will that be?"

"Soon, darling, very soon."

Alan told her all the news except about Jason, and they said good-bye reluctantly, with Catherine promising to call when she was ready to come back to Wales.

Jason came into the room carrying two mugs of coffee. His steps were slow, and Alan noticed that he had lost a lot of weight. "I have to talk to you," he said.

"Fine, old boy, I'd like that. Come and sit down." Alan watched as Jason stirred his coffee; his hand were not steady and he seemed drawn and pale.

"How's mother?" asked Jason.

"Oh, she's wonderful now that she has Martha's companionship."

As Jason struggled for the right words to say, Alan silently brought down protecting energies. He saw Jason relax a bit and then look directly into his eyes.

"Alan, I don't have the right words to tell you the story of my life. I have been your brother and I have never felt the need to hurt or deceive you."

Alan started to speak, but Jason moved his hand and shook his head. "No, you must let me continue. I have deliberately deceived others. For years I have lived two lives and availed myself of an evil power. In this day and age, it sounds peculiar, I know, to talk about good and evil, but it does exist, as I'm sure you know. Much of what I have done has been harmless, but these last few months it has become worse. Much worse. Alan, I now believe I am possessed. Before I completely lose my sanity, I want to tell you as much as I can."

Alan leaned over. "Jason, believe me, I know more than you think I do."

Jason's expression was painful. Alan told him that he was gifted with higher powers and had wanted to approach him before now, but was afraid of what might happen. In the short time they had been speaking, Jason's strength was slowly draining away, and Alan tried to give him all the love a brother could. "I have no more time for shame or humiliation," Jason said. "What I have to tell you is of the utmost importance to many people. Please write this down."

Alan grabbed his pen and note pad.

Jason continued, "In my briefcase there are legal documents already prepared and signed. Please see that my wishes are carried out, won't you?"

Alan nodded and Jason talked quietly, relating every detail of procedure and revealing many things to his brother. Finishing, he said, "On the eve of Blodwin, do these things for me and love him who has more love than I to give. I know that I will remain in your memory always and shall thrive and progress on your prayers. Your happiness will be my salvation." He stopped, his body sagged with exhaustion and he fell asleep.

Looking at his watch, Alan began to prepare the room.

"Hello, Alan." It was Jonathan.

After greeting each other warmly, they put Jason back to bed and continued to prepare for the full moon.

"How is he?" asked Jonathan.

Alan looked sad. "Not good. I wish it was all over." Then, fixing them both a bowl of soup, he sat on the couch and said, "You know, Jonathan, I don't think he can physically or mentally take much more."

A determined look came over Jonathan's face. "He can and he

will.''

Shrugging his shoulders, Alan dipped his bread into his soup. The room was getting dark. The mantelpiece clock chimed the half-hour.

Jonathan checked his own watch and looking steadily at Alan, said, ''It's time.''

Jason was asleep. They lifted him gently and brought him into the living room. Placing him on the couch, Alan lifted his head and placed a pillow underneath. The moon was full and brilliant. The evening had been still and warm; now the room was slowly becoming damp and chilly. Alan and Jonathan were deep in prayer.

Suddenly the candles flickered and the rushing evil energy of Kradeno was among them. Unseen hands seemed to pummel Jason's body. He awoke, shocked by the disturbance. Seeing Alan and Jonathan, he reached out to touch them and immediately his hand was enveloped in flame. Drawing it back quickly, he lay still, wondering what would happen next. Dreading the voice of Kradeno, Jason closed his eyes and was astounded by the peace surrounding him. He saw himself in the future: he was successful, handsome and had everything a man could wish for. He was in a beautiful home and through the window he could see the ocean. A woman walked beside him. It was Catherine! She beckoned him to follow. Walking behind her, he couldn't help admiring the exquisite paintings on the wall. She looked lovely. As she went to open a door, she turned around and kissed him. They tiptoed into a nursery: asleep were two babies who were obviously twins. He knew they were his children, and that in one of the sleeping cherubs lay the evil seed. He now heard the voice of Kradeno:

''See how easy it is? I promised I would take the power from thee, for I would have another son.''

Jason looked around and felt the love of Catherine and his two children. The temptation was overwhelming. If he accepted Kradeno's offer, he could transfer his energies to the growing child and would no longer be a part of the demon's evil scheme. Once again Catherine kissed him on the cheek. He followed her to another room, which was theirs. She started to undress, and all he had ever wanted through the centuries was his to take. As he stepped forward, he was confronted with three bright lights. He raised his hands to his eyes and heard the voice of Cimraknus:

''Art thou willing to pass this evil seed to an innocent babe?''

Realizing that he had almost succumbed to Kradeno's evil temptation, he cried out, ''No, no, but what must I do? For God's sake, what must I do to rid myself of him?''

The light shone more brightly and an arc of royal purple surrounded the image of the Master Cimraknus. As Jason was suspended in total light, he saw instantly all that he had done

thoughout the centuries and that the only way to break the evil
bond was to allow the soul of his twin to re-enter his physical body
for the remainder of his earthly years. Fear surged over him as he
asked the Master, "What will become of me?" The Master's light
grew brighter, but he could hear the distant laughter of Kradeno.
Then he heard his brother:

"Hold on, old boy, don't let go. I'm here."

With this extra spurt of strength, Jason gazed more deeply into
the light of the Master, whose voice was soft and beautiful.

"Thou shalt remain earthbound till thy brother cometh into
transition. Thou shalt guide and influence him. Much wrong thou
hast done unto this soul, but now thou mayst pay thy karmic debt.
Think upon this and when thy decision is made, thou shalt find
peace at last."

As the vision began to fade, the voice added, "Look not backward or thou shalt be damned forever."

Behind him, Jason could sense the world he knew. Music,
people's voices, fresh flowers....

Kradeno spoke. "Art thou willing to leave all these things behind
thee, fool?"

His mother's voice was calling him: "Jason, Jason!"

Footsteps of children, and a pulling on his coat.

"Daddy, please come and play, please, Daddy."

Then the voice of Catherine: "Darling, I will always love you."

In his torment, Jason screamed for mercy and felt the warmth of
Alan facing him. His smile was beautiful and his arms were outstretched.

"It isn't difficult, old boy... come on, now."

He was immediately transported to the stream outside Cardiff
House. He was kneeling down on a rock and his big brother Alan
was holding out his hand.

"Come on, Jason, you'll be all right, I promise. Come on,
now."

As brother encouraged brother, the boy Jason left the man, and
for the first time, he was free, totally free. He knew love as he had
never before known it: the heavenly energies wrapped around his
newborn body. Now in a world above all the misery and pain he
had learned to live with, he cried for Rhaydhonasie and the voice of
his brother answered, "You may look around now, Jason."

Hesitating for fear of Kradeno, his last and final memory of his
evil companion for centuries left him instantly. The Master
Cimraknus spoke:

"There is much to do, and thy physical body needeth nourish-
ment and rest. For the first time, thou shalt face the brother who
hath dwelt with thee throughout thy miserable life. Thou hast
deprived him of his birthright and thou shalt now relinquish thy
earthly rights to him."

Before him was the sweetest smile and the deepest love emanating from this radiant being. His embrace made them one, and in this new strength, Jason knew he was forgiven. As he waited for the transition, he found that he no longer craved an earthly existence. He was filled with joy and the desire to help his brother fulfill his earthly destiny.

Outside the cottage, all hell broke loose. Torn branches ripped from the trees, windows broke with the rush of evil energies and Kradeno's screaming curses sounded fainter and fainter, until the room became still again.

Jonathan and Alan embraced in spirit the departing soul of Jason. His twin now slept in Jason's tired body.

Waking, he became aware of thought restriction. He had dreamed this terrible dream in which he had been killed and cast out of his mother's womb by his evil brother. Seeing the two men, he smiled and apologized for having fallen asleep. His furrowed brows were now smooth. His smile reached his eyes as nervous tension was replaced with ease and quiet confidence.

"How long have I been ill?" he asked Alan.

"Just a few days, old boy. It's good to see you back."

"I think the worst is over," said Jason. "Now I think I'll get along to bed...."

As he moved toward the door, both Jonathan and Alan could see the radiant aura of the redeemed Jason they had known—the twin brother who would always be there to guide and direct the new Jason.

Chapter Twenty-seven

Jason stayed several days at the cottage to recuperate. When Lady Margaret called, he was anxious to go and visit her. She heard a joy in her son's voice that she had never heard before.

Alan felt very close to his new brother, but the love he felt for the old Jason was immeasurable. Often he was aware of his hovering presence and would acknowledge him inwardly. He was out of Kradeno's reach now and the only thing that concerned him was the Eve of Blodwin.

Riding to Cardiff House, Alan wondered how the new Jason would accept the return of Blodwin on New Year's Eve.

As though he had picked up his thoughts, Jason, now looking fit and well, told Alan he had something to tell him.

"Go ahead, old man, I'm listening," said Alan kindly.

"I want you to know that I know what has happened."

Alan eased his foot off the accelerator. Jason suggested they stop for a moment. The shock of Jason's remark made Alan nervous. Parking the car outside the Black Bull, he said, "Now what is it, Jason?"

"I know exactly what has happened. I know who I am and what happened to the first Jason."

"You do?"

"Yes," said Jason. "And I can deal with it, so don't worry. I want to thank you and Jonathan for your help and I know for sure that my brother thanks you," he said, looking over his shoulder.

"You do know what this means when we meet on New Year's Eve?"

"Yes, I do, and I can assure you that I will be perfectly all right."

Embracing each other, the two brothers decided they would get a pint at the Black Bull before going home.

"I feel very strongly that there are three of us," said Alan as they went into the bar.

"There are," said Jason, smiling. "So let's order three pints."

Lady Margaret greeted them warmly. Holding Jason at arm's length, she said, "Let me take a good look at you, son."

For the first time, Alan realized that Lady Margaret knew more than she had ever allowed them to believe.

"Before we do anything, Mother, may we all go into Father's old study?"

Smiling and not in the least surprised, she nodded, and putting an arm in each of her sons', she walked them down the corridor.

After sitting down in the old leather chair, Alan said to his mother, "You know, darling, don't you?"

Laying her hands on theirs, she said, "Yes, I do, Alan. I've known all along. When I was carrying my twins, my life was in jeopardy and the higher entity, Cimraknus, came to me in a vision and told me what was happening. The shock nearly killed me, but I was determined to see the whole thing through."

"Did Father know?" asked Alan.

"Yes, he did, and during my last weeks of pregnancy, he and the Higher Order kept a constant vigil. I had thought of aborting, but then I would have passed the karmic debt on for another generation, and the evil of Kradeno could have destroyed many innocent people. I was assured that if I could bear the pain and trauma, I would eventually see the son I grew to love find his peace...and then find my second boy." Hugging Jason tightly, she told him that he must continue to pray for his released twin.

"He's fine, Mother. I'm in constant communication with him. This is the gift he was given for releasing the physical body. We all love him and admire his courage."

"We certainly do," said Alan. "And the courage of this lovely lady, our mother."

Alan helped Jason sort out their brother's papers and requests. The new Jason was happy to be a part of the family and decided, with the approval of Lady Margaret, to take over his father's study and look after the estate.

Meanwhile, Mike Wilcox had received a mysterious call. He listened carefully to the woman's voice.

"I have read your articles and I think you are the kind of person I want," she said.

"I don't understand," said Mike, trying to light a cigarette. "What are you offering me?"

As soon as Hilary heard this, she was beside the phone trying to listen. The voice was cultured and obviously English. The woman now sounded rather impatient. Sighing deeply over the phone, she said, "I would like you to consider running a newspaper, a small country edition. If you are satisfactory, I will then let you buy the business from your income."

There was silence.

"Are you there?" asked the woman irritably.

"Oh, yes...sorry, I'm here. Err, I don't know what to say, quite frankly."

The woman replied curtly, "Well, why don't you just say 'yes' and then meet me in the morning at nine sharp and we'll settle the details?"

"Where?"

"The Dorchester. Goodbye." She was gone.

Mike was speechless. Standing with the phone still in his hand. Hilary took it from him carefully and almost whispering, asked, "What is it, darling? What's happened?"

He sat down and went over the conversation in his mind. "I don't even know the woman's name."

"What woman?" asked Hilary.

"How the hell do I know?"

She poured him a drink, which he ignored, then, snapping out of his mood, he took hold of Hilary's arms and told her what had happened.

"I'll never sleep, I know I won't! I can't. Oh, Mike, I can't believe it! Do you really think it's true?"

"I have a strange feeling it is, Hilary. I feel it in my bones."

Sharply at nine, Hilary and Mike were waiting in the lobby of the Dorchester Hotel in London.

"Are you Michael Wilcox?" asked that same voice.

"Yes," replied Mike, turning around to see a well-dressed woman in her fifties holding onto a poodle.

"My name is Genevieve Pickering, a friend of Jason Griffiths. Let's go to my suite and talk business."

Mrs. Pickering was a wealthy woman and was now ready to live abroad. Jason had told her of Mike's dream to own a country newspaper. She then took it upon herself to investigate his background and writing ability and found it satisfactory. Hilary was so excited, she couldn't speak. Mrs. Pickering asked if she was always so quiet.

"No," said Mike, laughing. "You have to understand, Mrs. Pickering. You are the answer to a dream. It's difficult for my wife and me to comprehend all this."

"I would consider it the answer to a prayer," she said, smiling. "My lawyer will contact you within the next few days to get the papers out of the way. After all, I'm sure you'll want to be getting on with it. Incidentally, there's a small brick two-story house at the end of High Street in Manningstile Henlock that goes with the business. Would you like to take residence there?''

Not able to contain herself any longer, Hilary burst into tears and threw herself into Mike's arms. He was also close to tears. Genevieve Pickering thought it a good time to leave.

"Don't you feel in a hurry to go," she told them. "Lunch will be brought up soon and I do have to take Henrietta to the Doggie Parlour, so why don't you stay and have lunch and I hope to see you before I leave for Africa." With that, she left, and Mike swept Hilary off her feet.

They fell on the rug, laughing. A few minutes later, they were disturbed by a cough. "Lunch is ready, sir...."

"I do miss Catherine," said Lady Margaret to Alan and Jason.

"Me, too, Mother," Alan said. "I expect to hear from her any day now."

They were still feeling warm and content from the Christmas lunch; it had been wonderful. Many friends had visited Cardiff House and they had all enjoyed Christmas Eve at the Blue Feathers.

Thinking about all the friends they had made this year, Alan said, "We are well blessed, Mother."

"When am I to plan a wedding, then?" Lady Margaret asked.

"That's a good question, Mother," said Jason. "If I'm to be best man, I must know in plenty of time."

Not feeling in the mood for light conversation, Alan lit his pipe. Jason and his mother continued to laugh and talk about his future wedding. The more they talked, the more he missed Catherine.

"Please change the subject," he asked finally, feeling sorry for himself.

"But why? I think we *should* know when the wedding is."

Startled, not believing his ears, Alan jumped out of his chair. Catherine was standing there, smiling broadly. He ran to her and holding her tightly, murmured her name over and over. Alan had never felt happier. Holding his Megan, he knew he could never let her leave him again.

"Where's Nickie?" he asked after a few minutes.

"She stopped off at the Blue Feathers to see Frances and Tom. She'll be here later."

"Why didn't you let me know, darling?" he asked, smoothing her silky hair away from her face.

"It was your mother's idea. She thought you'd like me for a surprise Christmas gift," said Catherine, laughing. Taking off her coat, hat and boots, she couldn't help but notice Jason. There was something different about him. She couldn't put her finger on it, but he had changed—and she liked the change.

"This is the kind of Christmas I've always dreamed of," said

Catherine. "A roaring fire, someone you love, and lots of real friends."

Lady Margaret brought in a tray of hot toddies. Christmas carols were being sung outside the window.

"This is just perfect," said Catherine, tears of happiness streaming down her face.

Jason opened the heavy oak door to invite the carolers in.

"Hi, everyone! Merry Christmas!" shouted Nickie.

The carolers were Jonathan, George, Nickie, Frances, Tom, Hilary and Mike. The spirit of Christmas lit up everyone's heart as Martha helped Lady Margaret keep all her guests happy. The party continued till the early hours of the morning. No one wanted to leave, so Lady Margaret encouraged them to stay and get a good night's sleep.

"I can't leave you," said Alan urgently to Catherine.

"Yes, you can, lover boy." His seriousness prompted her to jump up and ask Nickie if she was ready for bed.

"I suppose so," said Nickie, reluctantly.

"Come on, everybody," said Jason. "We have a big day tomorrow. Nothing but fun and relaxation. How does that sound?"

"Great," said Mike. "See you in the morning."

Alan lay in bed for a long time, unable to believe that Catherine was here in Cardiff House at last. "She asked for the wedding date," he thought, smiling. "In the morning, I'll suggest January 1st...."

As soon as Catherine opened her eyes the next morning she had to blink to believe that she was back at Cardiff House. It had been wonderful to hear from Lady Margaret and she had loved the idea of surprising Alan. It had worked out perfectly. Not wanting to waste a single minute now, she jumped out of bed and into the shower. When she came back into the bedroom, Nickie was sitting up in bed, smoking.

"My, you're up early," she said.

"Can't wait to see him, Nickie, honestly I can't."

Thinking about George, Nickie stubbed out her cigarette and went into the shower.

The days between Christmas and New Year's were very happy ones for the guests at Cardiff House. Frances and Tom came over frequently, and every minute was packed with the joy of Christmas. Nickie was the first to start joking about Blodwin's Eve, yet the tension grew. Jonathan talked to Jason and Lady Margaret for a while and told everyone there was nothing to fear.

After dinner on New Year's Eve, questions began to spill out. Catherine was afraid because she realized that her marriage to Alan depended largely upon what happened when they met with Blodwin. Jason sensed the tense atmosphere and suggested that everyone think about the last meeting with Blodwin and what they had learned.

They left the dining room and made their way to the huge hall. Lady Margaret, with Martha's help, organized the drawing room for Blodwin's Eve.

"What time do you think we ought to start?" asked Nickie nervously.

"I think we should go in now," said Alan, "and settle down."

"It's only ten o'clock," said Catherine. "I need another cigarette.

"Me, too," said Nickie.

Lady Margaret was playing Chopin, and the drawing room was peaceful and beautiful. The reflection of the fire in Catherine's hair reminded Alan of Megan, with her flaming red curls.

"I think about ten minutes before the hour, we should begin to relax and turn off the lights," said Martha.

As the clock slowly ticked toward midnight, all that could be heard was Chopin and quiet breathing.

"Wouldn't it be strange if nothing happened?" asked Nickie.

"Maybe nothing will," said Martha as she sipped her wine.

Suddenly the glasses on the tray by the door started tinkling and vibrating gently. The red flames began to billow out in pink and yellow puffs. The crystal chandelier began to move and tinkle, and a high-pitched voice from a long, long way off began to call.

Lady Margaret had lit a tall white candle and placed it in the center of the table. As its flame started to rise, everyone's eyes were focused on the phenomenon. From the high paneled oak ceiling descended circles of silver and gold. As the circles reached the carpet, they could see a form building within them. As before, the entity began to sway as it took shape. As though to boost this esoteric energy, ancient chanting began.

From the door thirteen hooded Masters walked in slowly, each with his head bent. The chanting grew louder. The room temperature was very cold now as Blodwin materialized. Everyone felt locked in time. They felt the sanctity of the ancient Celts permeate every fiber of their beings. They reached out to hold hands, forming a circle of energy around the old ones.

Blodwin spoke and every ear listened. "On this eve shall be completed the karma of all here present. Thou shalt be released from all deeds past to create naught but beauty in thy future paths. Evil now is banished; so long as thou livest on this earth wilt thou be free of Kradeno."

At the sound of his name, Kradeno and his demons swooped down behind the sitters. Fear froze them all as flames leapt up from behind them, reaching out toward the glowing form of Blodwin.

As Nickie attempted to turn, her head was instantly gripped by the hands of a hooded Master.

With great urgency, Blodwin said, "Do not turn thy heads or Kradeno will possess thee."

Terror was rising in their hearts as the evil laugh of Kradeno thundered through the room. A feeling of pressure gripped their heads, causing pain. The glasses by the door were hurled into the center of the room, smashing into a thousand slivers.

Then Blodwin raised her arms, and from above came pillars of white light which surrounded the sitters like a Grecian temple. Slowly the demons faded away with the voice of Kradeno screaming obscenities and curses. Heads bowed in prayer, the hooded figures slowly approached everyone sitting in the circle.

"Each of thee shall receive the protection of thy Master," said Blodwin.

Hilary was trembling as two figures stood beside her.

"Come into the circle, child," Blodwin said to her.

Afraid to move, Hilary just stared. Gently, the hooded figures picked her up and laid her down beside Blodwin like a sacrificial beast.

"Have no fear, child," said Blodwin. "This is to protect thee and the unborn soul from Kradeno. He is here and will make every effort to direct his evil into thy womb, even into the body of thy unborn child."

Hilary lay still as the two hooded figures knelt beside her.

Blodwin spoke again: "The one thou knowest as Jason is no longer with thee. The soul of Jason was tainted with centuries of evil and at the end he paid the price by offering his earthly existence to his soul-twin, whom he destroyed in his mother's womb. Thou shalt now witness his wickedness down through the centuries."

A purple light formed over Jason and he was brought forward to kneel beside Hilary with the two ancient Masters. The purple light of the Masters enveloped the mother and her unborn child.

Mike had never known such fear, but he was unable to move and break the circle.

"Raise thy heads," commanded Blodwin.

They did and were immediately confronted by the piercing eyes of their Masters. Slowly, they felt themselves being absorbed within the depths of space and time. Then they felt the sensation of moving rapidly through centuries. Years flew by and they were spectators of all that had taken place in their relationships with one another.

First they witnessed the virgin Megan, who in her innocence loved Gareth of Abergavennie. Secretly, the maid would meet with Gareth in the dark, damp cellar of Lord David's house. He knew of her meetings and would listen to their childish plans. It was Dylan, the brother of Gareth and their faithful friend, who would give signs to Megan when she was to meet Gareth. From his servants Lord David learned of the signs and arranged for his servant to deceive Megan as he made his plans to be there, waiting in the dark.

"Gareth, is that you, Gareth? Please speak to me. I am afraid," said Megan. As she reached the bottom of the stairs, she felt hands around her legs. Knowing this could not be Gareth, she cried out. She was dragged down on the cold, damp floor, terrified and screaming. Lord David did not speak to reveal his identity, but began to whip her mercilessly. She writhed in awful pain, tormented with fear and void of strength. He brutally tore her dress and undergarments and as Kradeno fully possessed him, mounted her body. Surrounded by evil rays of hellish light, Megan saw coming from his forehead a serpent, ready to strike if she uttered a word or dared resist. He delivered into her body his evil seed, which immediately took root in her womb. Having beaten and raped his future wife, Lord David left her weeping in the cellar. She remained there for three days after her attack. When her pregnancy began to show, Lord David accused her of adultery with Gareth of Abergavennie, who lived in fear of his life from then on.

"Throughout the centuries, this evil seed hath caused misery and many have been affected. The evil sign hath now been made known unto thee. The marriage of Megan and Gareth was not consummated, but still she committed bigamy and broke the laws of her faith and the Church. It is now done, and it is written in the book that Megan shall know her Gareth. When they finally meet again on their karmic path, they shall fulfill their true destinies and become man and wife."

Once again, their past lives were shown to all. Megan was brought to the doors of hell as she met the evil one in Lord David...Emmanuel...and Tobias. As her consciousness was raised and the chanting hooded figures stepped back into eternity, she felt Blodwin reach out and touch her. The room was full of vibrating colors, and as each of the companions returned to their normal level of consciousness, they saw the two hooded figures returning Hilary to her place next to Mike.

Blodwin's form grew larger and lifted high into the air. Then, smiling beatifically upon them all, she faded from sight.

Alan was standing in the center of the room, surrounded by white light, but all of them were watching Catherine. She knelt on the floor, her face lifted high. All could see the agonies of Megan of Manningstile Henlock pass from her and peace return to her. As she opened her eyes, she looked at her friends and asked in a hushed voice, "Who is Gareth of Abergavennie?"

Alan moved forward and gently lifted her to her feet. As he took her in his arms, he whispered, "I AM."